Shadows in the Caribbean

Shadows in the Caribbean

James Wollrab

Writer's Showcase presented by *Writer's Digest*
San Jose New York Lincoln Shanghai

Shadows in the Caribbean

Published by Writer's Showcase presented by *Writer's Digest*
an imprint of iUniverse.com, Inc.

For information address:
iUniverse.com, Inc.
620 North 48th Street
Suite 201
Lincoln, NE 68504-3467
www.iuniverse.com

ISBN: 0-595-09026-5

Printed in the United States of America

Foreword

To my Cuban-American friends who may have temporarily lost the country of their birth, but not their courage or humanity.

Introduction
Pre-Revolutionary Cuba

From the day in October of 1492 when Christopher Columbus first stepped ashore until the complex aftermath of the destruction of the battleship Maine in 1898, Cuba found itself under the control and influence of European colonial power Spain. The chronicle of Cuba during these four centuries is marked with human repression and misery, despite the island's dominant geography and rich Spanish culture.

In only three-quarters of a century the Spanish colonialists manage to wipe out most of the indigenous population on the island by introducing forced labor in return for Christian conversion. They are undoubtedly encouraged by the repugnant techniques of the Inquisition. As the native population dies off, the Spanish begin to import slaves from Africa.

During the late eighteenth and early nineteenth centuries, while the thirteen colonies are breaking British dominance in North America, a slave revolt is freeing Haiti, and Simon Bolivar is leading the quest for independence in Latin American, the Spanish are tightening their grip on Cuba. Slavery-centric political dissention in the United States defeats American attempts to purchase the island. By the mid-1800's, the labor-intensive nature of Cuba's economy results in a massive influx of slaves from Africa. Ultimately, these slaves account for more than fifty percent of the total population.

In 1843, a slave called Black Carlota leads an unsuccessful slave rebellion, and then in 1868 plantation owner Carlos Manuel de Cespedes begins the first war of independence. This conflict is often referred to as the Ten Year's War. A year later, the famed Jose Marti, a passionate anti-American revolutionary, emerges at age sixteen and publishes his support for the independence of Cuba and the prevention of American influence and control in Central and South America.

In late 1898, under the Treaty of Paris, which ends the Spanish-American War, Spain cedes control of Cuba to the United States, which installs a military government to pacify the country. The American flag flies over Havana until 1901, when Tomas Estrada Palma becomes president, and the U.S. military occupation is terminated.

Corruption in the government and substantial debt dependency to interests in the United States open the way for military juntas by 1925, permitting General Gerardo Machado Morales and Sergeant Fulgencio Batista y Zaldivar, among others, to take control of the country. Batista rises to power in the famed Sergeant's Revolt and is often referred to as The Sergeant despite his promotion to the rank of General. Subsequent to years of dictatorship and the devastating effects of a worldwide depression, a new Constitution is adopted in 1940.

During World War II, the Cuban government supports the United States by furnishing bases to the American Navy and Army Air Force. Batista even recognizes the Communist Party in 1943 and establishes relations with the Soviet Union, an ally of the United States.

Dictator Batista, facing certain defeat in the 1952 elections, in which recent law school graduate Fidel Castro is a congressional candidate, leads a coup and suspends the elections and the Constitution. Despite American recognition of the military takeover and foreign aid to the dictatorship, serious organized resistance begins to take shape in the country.

On July 26th of 1953, Castro, accompanied by his brother, Raul, and other revolutionaries, attacks the Moncada Army Barracks located at Santiago de Cuba. This skirmish marks the beginning engagement in the next Cuban war of revolution.

1

The First Shot

I heard all things in the heaven and
in the earth. I heard many things in
hell. How, then, am I mad? Hearken!
And observe how healthily-How calmly
I can tell you the whole story.

—Edgar Allan Poe, The Tell-Tale Heart

Santiago de Cuba, July, 1953

The dusty Cuban government limousine slowly rolled to a halt at the military checkpoint. Four heavily armed members of the Cuban military stood behind the rusted metal gate that barred the way to all traffic on the one-lane dirt road. The indifferent but fatigued expressions on their faces indicated that the soldiers had been on duty for an extended period of time.

The limousine driver was an elderly Cuban man. Despite his age, he appeared to be a strong individual with an exceptionally muscular frame. He wore a neatly groomed beard that reflected a grayish hue in the afternoon sunlight. His chauffeur's uniform was worn, but clean and neat, and his demeanor projected an expression of protective confidence. He seemed to understand that any sign of weakness in these times was a certain invitation to trouble for him and those he sought to protect.

The back seat of the vehicle held a distinguished-looking Cuban man about thirty-five years of age. Seated to his left and directly behind the driver was a small boy. The child was dressed in his finest clothes, and it was easy to see that although he was not comfortable, the distraction offered by the soldiers had piqued his interest.

The boy watched eagerly through the side window as he observed two soldiers approaching the vehicle with their weapons at the ready. The older man in the rear seat appeared disinterested and continued to look straight ahead.

Slowly, the driver rolled down his window and handed a bundle of identification papers to the lead guard. After reviewing the documents with some care, the guard stooped over and squinted as he assessed the identities of the two passengers in the back seat. Suddenly and with a great flourish, he snapped to attention.

"Good afternoon, Ambassador Chacon!"

The man in the back seat slowly nodded his head and then turned and smiled at the guard, but he did not speak.

"Please, gentlemen! Forgive the delay. And, please accept our escort to the barracks," continued the guard as he returned his attention to the driver. "We have been alerted to the possibility of rebel activity. Corporal Sanchez will lead you to the officer's quarters. The Commandant is anxious to receive you. He will personally escort you to the location of the ceremonies."

The soldier remained rigidly at attention as he awaited a reply. From the rear seat, the boy continued to watch the proceedings with a look of wonder and excitement painted across his face.

"Thank you for your concern, Sergeant," responded the driver. "We will be pleased to have your protection. The Ambassador appreciates your concern for our safety."

After a few moments, the metal gate was raised and one of the guards pulled up in front of the limousine riding on a small motorcycle. He motioned for the visitors to proceed through the checkpoint and into the military reservation. Once past the checkpoint, the vehicle and its escort made their way through the heavily barricaded main gate and under a sign that identified the facility as the Moncada Army Barracks.

As they proceeded through the outskirts of the military base, the boy studied the array of military buildings and structures nestled in the surrounding terrain. After several minutes, he turned to his father and began the usual barrage of questions typical of a boy his age.

"Where is Uncle Raymond?" the child asked with an unusual look of concern written on his young face.

"He will meet us at his barracks building, Son. Do not worry about your uncle. Some day he will be commanding the entire army!"

"Will Uncle Raymond always be in the army, Papa?"

"I do not know, Pablo. Today, he becomes an officer. And, as much as I would like him to go back to the University and study to be a doctor, I am beginning to believe that he really wants to be a soldier."

"Will he get to drive a tank or fly an airplane?" said the boy with a wistful look on his face.

The boy's question was seriously stated and his father studied his face for a few moments before replying.

"My son, being a soldier is very dangerous. A soldier may take lives, and he may have his life taken. A smart young lad like you should consider becoming a doctor. Doctor's may save lives and do many good things. It is an exciting life, just like that of a soldier. But not nearly as dangerous! And, I know that your mother would have wanted you to be a doctor."

The ambassador slowly looked away from the boy as his thoughts focussed on his wife. Her death had taken a great toll on his life. It was his love for his son that kept him going forward each day. Yet, every time he thought of her, a look of sadness settled over his face.

"He is my favorite uncle!" uttered the boy with the shrill voice of a five-year old.

The ambassador was snapped back out of his reverie by the sincerity in the child's voice.

"He is your only uncle, Pablo! He is my only brother," replied the Ambassador as he noticed that their escort had raised his hand and pulled to a stop on the side of the road.

Suddenly, there was a shrill whining noise from above and then a dull thud and concussion that shook the limousine. The force of the explosion threw the driver forward against the steering wheel as he instinctively slammed on the brakes.

The two passengers were thrown forward against the soft padding of a rear seat console. The boy tumbled to the floor where he lay stunned by the unexpected stop. As Ambassador Chacon reached for his son, another blast shook the limousine, blowing out the front and rear windows, and knocking the Ambassador unconscious.

The driver shook his head as he tried to recover from his impact with the steering wheel and then tried in vain to restart the engine and pull the limousine off the road. As he looked through the open windshield area, he could see the battered body of the military escort lying motionless near his heavily damaged motorcycle.

Quickly, the driver turned to check on his passengers. The boy was clinging to his father and sobbing. Blood was trickling from a deep cut on the boy's forehead.

"Papa! Papa! Wake up, Papa!"

The driver freed himself from the front seat and after several attempts he opened the rear door. He reached into the back seat and tried to pull the child out of the car.

"Pablo! Come! We must get off the road!" commanded the driver in a firm but raspy voice. "I'll come back for Papa Oscar as soon as you are safe! He'll be okay here until I come back for him."

The boy reluctantly released his hold on his father's arm as the driver pulled him out of the limousine. Pain shot through the driver's left leg as he tried to carry the boy to safety around the rear of the vehicle. As he glanced at his left knee, he could feel the flow of blood trickling down the outside of his leg. He put the boy down on the ground and firmly grabbed his hand.

"Pablo, we must climb up the hill to those trees! Keep your eyes on the top of the hill and don't look back!" The driver was hoping that the boy had not seen the dead soldier lying on the roadway. Straining every muscle, the driver pulled the boy up the hill toward the waiting tree line.

As they ran for the summit, both slipped several times on the wet grass only to struggle back to their feet and continue up the hill. Then, just as they were about to reach the cover they sought, a sudden flash of light and the accompanying blast brought a deadly silence.

2

The Bunker

If Batista's not aboard,
I'll eat your sombrero.

—**David A. Phillips, CIA**

Cuba, 31 December 1958

As the winter sun was setting over the warm waters of the Caribbean, four camouflaged military vehicles carefully crawled up and down the rolling hills of the south coast of Cuba. Three of the vehicles were heavy trucks, each carrying a driver and a guard. The heavily armed men wore camouflaged fatigues and possessed M1 rifles and carbines. Grenades could be seen hanging from their belts. The fourth and lead vehicle was an old World War II vintage Jeep.

The Jeep guided the caravan over the muddy dirt road that ran along the seacoast. The area had been hit with several rain showers just before sundown, and now, with the darkness of evening well established, the pace had slowed considerably.

The last truck in the group carried a .50 caliber machine gun mounted in the cargo area. The men in this vehicle had been previously instructed to act as a rear guard and pay special attention to anyone who might be tracking the convoy.

With a series of hand signals, the passenger in the lead vehicle called the column to a halt near an overgrown crossroads. He was a young man who wore the uniform of an officer in the Cuban Armed Forces. Then, the officer jumped out of the Jeep and waited silently for his cadre to assemble.

His whispered instructions were concise and conformed precisely to the orders issued by the Military Command in Havana.

"Gentlemen, we are close to our objective. We will be able to reach the site without using our headlights. Maintain radio silence. Keep the formation tight. I would estimate half an hour to the unloading point. Any questions?"

The men obviously understood their orders and they remained silent waiting for their leader to continue.

"Excellent! Mount up."

The leader returned to his vehicle as his convoy once again began to roll through the wooded terrain. The Jeep maintained a speed of ten kilometers per hour, and the trucks fell in line. As the patrol moved along the bumpy roadway, the driver of the Jeep made a request.

"Captain Ray! Light one for me, please. This is for 1958! I celebrate the passing of one hell of a year. And I toast my last day in mother Cuba."

The driver glanced at the passenger with a sly smile on his face as he continued.

"When we get our hands on some rum in Miami, we will drink to our eventual return. To better days!"

Without speaking, the passenger lit a cigarette and passed it slowly to the driver. It was apparent that, despite their difference in rank, the two men had been friends for a long time.

The vehicles continued down the dirt road until they came upon an old water tower. The passenger checked his watch and smiled.

"There's the old water system, Rene. About two clicks to go. If nothing unexpected occurs and our luck holds, we should be able to unload by midnight and be out of here by 0300. We must get out tonight. After tonight, Oscar won't be able to help us."

The driver delayed his response as he slowed the Jeep to a crawl and maneuvered around several fallen trees.

"I never would have imagined that we would be riding down the same dirt road carrying real weapons, using live ammunition. Our youth goes by too fast, my friend!"

The driver's voice became very melancholy. The passenger stared at his friend as he replied.

"You are far too romantic, Rene. I fear that you will miss our country and our friends even more than I will."

The driver nodded in agreement as he puffed slowly on the cigarette. That glass of rum seemed so very far away.

"With all this confusion, what's going on up north, in Havana?" asked Rene. "Isn't Batista going to counterattack?"

"No chance!" commented the officer as he began checking his weapons. "A junta is being installed. General Cantillo is in charge. The General specifically ordered me to bring the patrol back to Havana after concluding this mission. From what we've seen in the countryside this afternoon, that would be a bad idea. Oscar is correct, as usual. We must get out of here, and now!"

"Raymond, the ambassador is a very wise man. And, we all appreciate his concern for our safety. If I don't get to see him, please tell him that we are all thankful."

"We will all make it to Miami!" replied the officer in a firm tone. "And that's an order!"

The sureness and confidence of his leader gave Rene the reassurance he had been looking for. He listened attentively as the Captain continued his analysis of the situation.

"Batista plans to leave tonight with most of his supporters. If we go back to Havana, there are only two possibilities. In the first, we die fighting the rebels and, in the second, we spend the rest of our lives in jail on the island. Oscar believes that only a fool dies for his country. And, I have rarely known him to be wrong. My job is to make sure that all of us live to fight another day."

The driver heartily agreed as the convoy negotiated a series of steep switchbacks. Their speed had dropped below five kilometers an hour as an intermittent mist of rain began falling.

"I know I shouldn't ask this," whispered the driver hesitantly. But, before he could pose his question, the officer interrupted.

"You want to know what our cargo is? What's in the containers?"

Raymond cracked a brief smile as he glanced in the side mirror at the images of the following vehicles.

"I just..." Raymond again interrupted the driver's attempted explanation.

"Rene, only my imagination has seen inside those containers."

"Okay, what does your imagination see? Good or evil?"

The Captain hesitated as he composed his thoughts, but he saw no harm in speculating.

"It envisions military intelligence, weapons and ammunition, and most of all, anything of value which Batista could not carry with him during his escape! I do know that those containers are heavy! I might even smell some of our country's gold reserves. My imagination suggests that the balance of the reserves are probably now resting safely in the Dominican Republic or the United States."

The Captain turned toward Rene with a question.

"What does your imagination say?"

The driver placed his right hand on his forehead in mock disbelief.

"Wow! I guess my imagination must have been asleep. I never thought of it that way. I can see the files and the intelligence. Even the weapons! But, the gold reserves? Brilliant!"

"You've seen all those casinos in Havana, all those whorehouses, all those tourists. Where does all that money flow? All the sugar cane plantations the Americans bought when the price of sugar went through the floor created a lot of cash flow, too. Where did it all go?"

Raymond hesitated to allow Rene to ponder his question. When Rene did not respond, he continued his analysis.

"Follow the flow of the water, and you will find the fish! Meanwhile, the people of Cuba are sitting here, poor and getting poorer!"

"I guess I always knew that was true," uttered Rene. "And, we are just as much to blame as Batista. We took his orders and executed his plans."

"I've been thinking about that very fact, Rene. Here we are, doing it again!"

"Don't be too hard on yourself, Raymond. I have a feeling that our new rulers aren't going to be a bargain for Cuba, either! No matter what happens. If your guess about the contents is correct, these containers are best hidden away. But, I'm sure that Castro will be pissed when he finds no cash waiting for him in Havana!"

Suddenly, the officer raised his hand and the patrol came to a halt at a fork in the road. After carefully surveying the features of the roadside, he signaled for the patrol to continue down the left side of the fork.

"Yes, indeed! He is certainly going to be pissed!" Rene muttered with a grin.

The officer lit another cigarette for his companion and passed it over to him. The rain had become heavier, and the driver reached over and grabbed his fatigue hat. He placed it on his head knowing even as he did it, that it would be of little use against the downpour.

"My current concern isn't Castro or Guevara. They're heading for Havana. It's these newly born revolutionary patrols. Once these people realize that Batista is in flight, they will take their revenge out on anything associated with him. And, that certainly could be us! I think I'll have one of those cigarettes myself."

As Raymond reached for the pack of cigarettes, he realized that the patrol had reached its initial destination. He placed his hand on Rene's shoulder and the driver brought the Jeep to a halt. The other vehicles stopped in response. Raymond then turned to Rene with his instructions.

"We have to check out the compound before we approach it with the trucks. You and I will take the Jeep ahead and scout the site. Tell the men to pull over there." He pointed to a flat, relatively clear area just off the dirt road.

After the trucks were positioned, the two men returned to the Jeep and moved forward along the road, which was now running much closer to the coastline. After several minutes of slow progress they stopped their vehicle below the crest of a hill. They made their way on foot to a position on the ridge, a viewpoint that allowed them to observe the coastline and the relatively flat expanse of land separating them from the next ridge. An irregular concrete seawall ran along the shore, interrupted only by the entrances to two short canals.

Below them, running parallel to the water, the men could see the outline of a series of buildings. These were strung out like a necklace, each connected to the nearest neighbor by a dirt road. The roads, buildings, and docks were overgrown after years of obvious neglect. Viewing the compound below, numerous questions now raced through Rene's mind.

"Why did Batista pick this particular place? It's isolated all right, but other than that, I don't see any advantages. And, what were those tanks used for?" The driver pointed toward a group of storage tanks located near the far end of the compound.

"This is the Girard Chemical Complex," Raymond whispered. "It was used for the manufacture and testing of chemical warfare protective devices and clothing. Specialized protection gear for chemical warfare situations was one of Batista's pet export projects. This facility was developed in cooperation with the Americans and the French.

"There was an accident here over ten years ago, and the place has been off limits to civilians ever since. The facility is probably still somewhat contaminated. Batista moved to take advantage of a bad situation and had a secret shelter built here. At the mission briefing I was told that it is stocked with food and weapons and shielded from the contamination. Our orders are to put the sealed containers in the shelter, unopened!"

Rene listened intently as he and Raymond scanned the compound. Neither of them could detect any signs of human activity. Raymond continued his answer to Rene's question.

"The accident killed over twenty people. Several were supposedly American and French scientists and engineers. Do you see those fences running along the perimeter of the compound? They were put in place the day after the accident, but, with time and the elements, the fences should have rusted severely. We should be able to get inside with relative ease."

"Is there still any danger for us, Raymond? I couldn't help but notice the chemical suits back there in the last truck!" Rene spoke with a look of concern.

"The command was careful not to give me any information on the contaminants, but the word is that the place was loaded with phosgene and several types of nerve gas. That should have dissipated, but I'm not exactly sure what else we might be facing here, Rene. But the rumors around the base indicate that the contamination was extensive. I was told that the government paid a fortune for cleanup afterwards and then again to have the bunker built. Imagine building an underground shelter while you're wearing a contamination suit. That's not my kind of job!"

Raymond couldn't help but notice the continued look of concern on Rene's face.

"But, don't worry, the suits will protect us until we enter the bunker." Raymond's voice was reassuring.

"How come I have never heard of the accident?" asked Rene as he scanned the perimeter fence with his binoculars. "I wasn't living that far away from here when it must have happened. I didn't even know this research facility was here."

"You've heard of it, but the news was all about the fish kill off the coast. Remember the oil tanker spill ten or so years ago and all of the dead fish that washed up on the beach? Do you remember seeing any of the oil along the beach?"

Rene slowly shook his head as he thought back to the incident.

"Come to think of it, I saw the dead fish, but I don't remember seeing any oil. Was that fish kill caused by this accident?"

"You guessed it! It goes to show you how the news can be twisted to suit the will of the government. We're told of an oil spill, and we curse the irresponsibility of the oil companies. But, when we get into our boats or walk along the shore and look at the sea, it seems clear and normal. We assume that the oil has dispersed or been cleaned up. So, if the fish you catch looks clean, you will eat it for dinner, especially if you are very hungry. But think back, Rene. Don't you remember that many people in this area got sick or died shortly after the accident? It was the flu, the government said. I'll bet it was really caused by the contamination of the fish by whatever chemicals were unleashed into the water. But we may never know the truth!"

As the men returned to the Jeep, Raymond turned to glance back at the abandoned chemical facility one last time. To his surprise he thought he saw a set of lights darting up and down on the far side of the complex. He stopped and watched carefully as tiny points of light bounced here and there in the distance. They looked like a lively bunch of fireflies moving toward one of the main buildings.

Raymond grabbed Rene's shoulder, indicating the need for silence. Keeping low, both men returned to the ridge from which they had been viewing the site. The rain continued to fall. Raymond grabbed his binoculars and carefully scanned the scene. To his surprise he counted about twenty armed men, and they were not members of the regular armed forces. They seemed to be searching the buildings one by one.

"Where did they come from?" whispered Rene. "I didn't see them before. They're inside the fences and they're not wearing any protective clothing. There's nowhere to land a plane or a helicopter safely, and I sure didn't see any other vehicles on the road!"

"Rene, look at the shoreline near the far canal. Boats! We couldn't see them before. They must have been hidden in the brush. And they're not ours. They must be fidelistas!"

Raymond pondered the possibilities of what they were observing.

"One of Che's patrols? They must not be aware of the history of the complex otherwise they would be wearing safety suits. They do seem intent on searching each building, as if they are looking for something. But I guess there's always a chance that they've just stumbled upon the site while on coastal patrol."

"Whatever they're doing here, it doesn't look good for our mission. We're outnumbered at least two to one," whispered Rene as he inserted a clip and removed the safety on his carbine.

"We have to assume the worst case, whatever that is, Rene. We have no choice! We have to scrub this location!"

Rene looked over at the Captain.

"Okay, what are our options if we can't put the containers in the bunker?"

Raymond looked once again through his binoculars carefully counting the shadowy figures moving across the facility below.

"No matter what, we can't take a chance on these containers falling into enemy hands. Listen, we grew up in this area! Remember that old country church? It's just off the road near where the trucks are parked."

"It's been abandoned for thirty years, Ray. Even the trail up to it has been overgrown for years."

"Yes, I know! My brother Oscar and I used to go there to smoke cigarettes when we were kids. It's well off the beaten track. We can put the containers in the basement. If we blow the building, no one will wander in and accidentally find anything."

"What about those guys?" asked Rene as he pointed toward the chemical complex.

"The intervening ridges will muffle the concussion. Even if they find the building, they'll never think to look under the rubble. Especially with all the crazies running around tonight shooting up the place! I think we can do it!"

Rene smiled. "Now I know why the Man put you in charge of this mission. You always have a backup. Always have a plan of attack!"

Both men continued to watch the activity below. Raymond kept considering the possibilities, knowing that the safety of his men and his cargo were in the balance.

"If they don't know exactly where the bunker is, they'll never find it. You can walk right over it and never realize it's there."

"Maybe they're looking for Batista?" Rene's mind was also racing through the possibilities.

Finally, Raymond reached his decision. There was no point even speculating about the enemy's intentions. His men and his mission took priority.

"It doesn't matter, Rene. We don't have enough time to wait for them to leave. We go with plan B. Let's roll this Jeep back down the hill before we start it up. And, let's hope that the church is still there!"

Ray and Rene carefully made their way down the hill and turned the Jeep around. Then they slowly rolled it down the long incline and into a ravine. Satisfied that the patrol at the chemical plant could not hear them, they started the Jeep's engine and headed back for the trucks. Raymond realized that but for a matter of seconds, they could have walked into a trap. Luck was playing a bigger part in this mission than Ray would have liked.

In five minutes they were back near the point in the road where the trucks were parked. Suddenly, Rene stopped the Jeep and shut off the engine. A look of concern crossed over the Captain's face. He could hear gunfire up ahead!

"Rene, we've been discovered! Let's get up to the crest of that hill. We need to survey the situation. Quickly!"

Rene pulled the Jeep to a position about a fifty meters from their deserted trucks, and the two soldiers scrambled up the hill weapons at the ready. From this position, they could observe the ongoing firefight below them.

A ragtag rebel patrol of seven men on foot had approached the parked convoy with the intention of searching each vehicle. Raymond's men had forced the group off the road with their superior weaponry, killing three of the men in the process. The remaining four fled into the woods below. Raymond's men quickly pinned the rebels down with a sustained barrage of gunfire that lasted for about thirty seconds. Several grenades exploded down in the ravine where the remaining rebels had chosen to make their stand. The gunfire ceased and a cold silence settled over the area. The last of the rebels were dead!

Raymond and Rene had arrived just in time to witness the final moments of the battle. By the time Raymond joined the group, his men had secured the area, hiding any evidence of the battle that had just taken place. It was time for the leader to explain the change in plans.

"There are rebels at the original destination," Raymond informed the gathered men. "We'll have to turn around and go down that side road we passed about a kilometer back. Then, it may get a little rough. We'll have to drive through the underbrush for several hundred meters. Rene and I will lead the way. At that point we should find an old abandoned church. We will place the containers in the basement. Next, we'll set charges on the ground level. The debris from the superstructure should cover the basement.

"We'll keep one truck out at the road. Use the one with the .50 caliber to cover our movements. From there it's about two hours to the airfield. We have a DC-3 waiting for us. We must get to it before the sun rises. Any questions!"

When none came, the Captain gave the order.

"Let's go and quickly!"

In a matter of seconds the convoy was on its way again.

3

Strange Bedfellows

*When the people know
what the exact laws are,
they do not stand in awe
of their superiors.*

—A Confucian scholar

Havana, Cuba

The two men sat alone in a small anteroom on the second floor of the Czechoslovak embassy. One wore the uniform of the newly formed Revolutionary Militia while the other was a high ranking civilian member of the Revolutionary Council.

"General, I am still having difficulty with this…this operation. From where I sit, I see the revolution aiding one of its enemies. This is not a good precedent for the council or for the militia."

The General was clearly uncomfortable about discussing the situation. But, he realized that it was important to have the support of the Revolutionary Council members who were aware of what was about to occur. He decided that his best course of action was to tell the truth.

"This is not a matter of major concern to the revolution, Julio. The revolution owes this man a debt of gratitude and of shame that it will never be able to repay!"

"General, I know he was an ambassador and that he served the country fairly and honestly. But, now he is in America, and I have heard that he is not coming back to serve the revolution. How can we owe such a man any debt?"

"Julio, does the date July 26, 1953 ring any bells in that head of yours?"

"Please, General! Do not mock me. It was the beginning of our independence."

"Well, Julio, it was also the date of the death of the Ambassador's only son! And, you were the ones who killed him during the attack. It was accidental, yes, but it happened."

"So, we are paying him back by sending his nephew to Brazil?"

"There is more," whispered the General. "Much more! The Ambassador was the one who convinced Batista to release Raul and Fidel Castro, among others, in 1955. You do remember that our leaders were in the hands of the government, do you not?

Julio nodded but looked away from the General as he spoke.

"Without his support, none of this could have happened. So you see, the Ambassador acted to free the very people who caused him to lose his son. It is an act that Raul Castro has not forgotten. And, he has personally charged me with the completion of this mission. So, you see, I am committed to its success, as you should be."

Julio still did not agree with what was about to happen, but he could see that his resistance would be futile.

"I can understand the situation better now, Sir. It would have been better to give the council this information from the beginning. We would stand a better chance of avoiding misunderstandings that way. Do you not agree?"

"Julio, you are the only council member aware of this action. It will be your secret. No one must know of our plans and intentions. But, if the information should leak out, then the council might learn that you were apprised of the situation in advance. I believe that it is in your best interests to maintain our secret. Don't you agree?"

The civilian shook his head affirmatively, but did not speak. Once again, it was obvious that he was being out-maneuvered by the General. Just as he turned to express his displeasure, the door to the anteroom opened, and a well-dressed man stepped through the door and announced his arrival.

"Gentlemen, please allow me to introduce myself. My name is Svoboda. Stefan Svoboda. I am the first assistant to the Czechoslovakian ambassador. The woman and the boy are in the next room. I have been briefed on certain aspects of the mission. Do you have the balance of my instructions?"

The General stood and handed Svoboda a plain manila envelope.

"Mr. Svoboda, inside you will find Cuban passports for yourself and the boy. His name is Carlos Chacon. You will also find the details of his medical status."

"General, I have been told that he has an incurable disease, and that his destination is a medical research facility in Rio. Is that correct?"

"No. But if you are asked about the boy, that is the explanation you will use. When you arrive in Rio, put the baseball cap you will find in the envelope on the child. Make sure that he is wearing it when you leave the aircraft."

Svoboda reached inside the envelope and withdrew a New York Yankees baseball cap. He placed it on his head but it was too small to fit properly.

"Take the boy directly to the information booth located just inside the gate. There you will see another man wearing this same type of cap. He is your contact. Ask him the three questions you will find on a sheet of paper inside your passport. If he answers correctly, give him the child and return to Havana."

"If he doesn't answer correctly?" asked Svoboda glancing at the questions on a small piece of paper.

"Then, you are on your own. Under no circumstances are you to bring the boy back to Cuba. Take him to your embassy in Rio and contact his father in Miami. All of the necessary information is in inside the envelope. After your mission is complete, destroy all of the documents and return to Havana."

"What's in this sealed packet? Is it another passport?"

"Open that at your own risk, Mr. Svoboda! Just make sure you give that to the contact in Rio."

"So, he's going somewhere else after he leaves me, is he! Why do I get the feeling that that place is called Miami? Wouldn't it be easier to just fly directly to Miami from here?" Svoboda grinned at the two men facing him.

The General did not laugh. Neither did the civilian, who had remained silent.

"Please forgive me, gentlemen. I can see that my attempts at humor are not appreciated. I will conduct this mission efficiently and with total secrecy. Should I report back to you once I return?"

"Absolutely not!" the General responded. "With any kind of luck, we will never see each other again!"

4

Trial by Fire

Virtue and vice,
moral good and moral evil,
Are then in every country,
Whatever is useful or
harmful to society.

—Voltaire, *Treatise on Metaphysics*

Miami, Florida

A single bare light bulb swung slowly from the ceiling of the darkened garage. The young Cuban man sat rigidly below the light in an old wooden chair, restrained by wire, rope, and tape.

"This is the last time I will ask you politely, Luis!"

To disguise his face the speaker wore a hood that resembled a crudely fashioned ski mask. His voice was stern and his English was polished, but Luis knew that his captor was definitely Cuban. He could see the flashing eyes of his adversary through the small round holes in the mask.

After a moment of silence, Luis queried his captor with a defiant tone, but he spoke slowly enough to conceal his fear.

"You have me at a disadvantage, Sir. Who the fuck are you, anyway?

His response was met with a damaging blow to the head, but one that Luis knew only represented a warning. In spite of the pain, Luis continued.

"Are you working for Batista or Castro? Or maybe the Americans have put you up to this? Which is it?"

"Luis! Goddammit! Never answer my questions with a question," roared the interrogator as he stooped over and brought his face close to that of his captive.

"It is very, very impolite! I do not want to hurt you, but your insolence cannot be tolerated. Besides, my identity and that of my colleagues is irrelevant to you. Your associate, I believe his name was Fernando, asked the same questions. And, in the same insolent manner I might add. Don't make the same mistake, Luis! As they say in polite circles, he now sleeps with the fishes!"

A bolt of fear shot through the hostage. As he looked cautiously around the garage, he counted seven motionless and hooded men, all armed. The eighth man, his interrogator, was the only one to speak.

"Luis, give me the answer, and you will walk away from this experience. You do not know our identities and that is the secret to saving your life. You are too late to save Fernando's life, but you can still save Captain Chacon. Just tell us what we need to know, and I will loosen your bonds and leave you here. Alive! In a matter of minutes you will be able to free yourself and return to your family."

Luis looked up into the eyes of the hooded man and nodded his head deliberately, as if to signal his capitulation.

"I will tell you! I will tell you everything I know."

Under his hood, the interrogator felt a smile sweeping across his face. The months of work and searching would not be in vain.

"Luis, I have a tape recorder here. Speak slowly and clearly. I will keep this tape as insurance that you will not tell the Captain of our conversation. Am I clear?"

"You have my silence!" responded the hostage in a firm voice. "I will not speak of this matter to anyone, not my friends and not the police and not Raymond. I know that my life and his life depend upon it."

The hooded man reached into his shirt pocket and removed a map. He motioned to one of the other men to drag a small card table over to where the hostage was seated. Once the table was in position, he spread the map in front of Luis and placed a crayon on the table. He then circled around in back of his prey and loosened the bonds that were restraining Luis' right arm.

"You see, Luis, we can be very reasonable men. Here is a map of the south of Cuba. You are certainly as familiar with it as Fernando was. All you have to do is tell us where you hid the…"

The speaker's voice trailed off as he searched for the proper word to finish his request. When it didn't come, he just started over again.

"Just show us were it is!"

Luis slowly pulled his arm up onto the table as he studied the map. The hooded man snapped a microphone to the hostage's shirt, as he watched from over his shoulder.

"Here is where we picked up the cargo!" Luis marked the map and began drawing a line, which ran along the southern coast in a westerly direction. He described the road and villages along the route in great detail as the tape recorder ran on.

The interrogator patted Luis lightly on the shoulder as if to reassure him. Unlike Fernando, Luis appeared to have reached a state of full cooperation with his captors.

"Please continue, Luis."

The captive carried the line to a position considerably west of Cienfuegos. He drew a series of lines to indicate roads, which were not shown on the map, and then he drew a circle near the shoreline.

"Here! We buried the cargo here! It is an old chemical test area with access to the sea. It was contaminated years ago. Batista built a bunker on the site several months before the revolution."

The interrogator placed his hands firmly around the hostage's neck and applied some pressure.

"Luis! I have been to this very place within the last three months. There is nothing there! Do not lie to me!"

Luis choked as he tried to respond. Slowly, the hooded man released his grip and waited for the answer.

"It is a bunker! A hidden bunker! It is hidden below one of the buildings near the center of the complex. If you do not know where the entrance is, you will never find it."

The interrogator slowly removed his hands from around Luis' neck and reached up to rub his own forehead, which was becoming irritated by the burlap material of his hood. He then softly placed his hands on Luis' shoulders in a manner that was almost comforting to his captive.

"Luis, can you lead us to this entrance? Can you show us the building under which it is built?"

Luis slowly shook his head negatively as he pondered his reply.

"Fernando and I were left to perimeter defense. The Captain took only two other men with him. We were over the ridgeline when they entered the complex. None of the other men could see where the cargo was unloaded."

"What about these other two men?" yelled the interrogator as he circled in front of Luis and pounded his fist on the table. His renewed anger caused Luis to brace for another blow that did not come.

"They were both Batista's personal guards, and I did not get a good look at them. General Cantillo personally placed them in our patrol. We rode in separate vehicles, and we never spoke to them. The Captain kept us separated! He was ordered to do so. Fernando was telling the truth when he told you that he didn't know who the men were."

"And, where are they today, Luis?"

"They were to return to Havana while we escaped. The Captain convinced them to tell General Cantillo that the rest of the patrol was lost in the engagement. They encountered an ambush just outside the chemical facility after we separated. By the time we reached them, they were dead. I never knew their names!"

The interrogator took his hands off of Luis' shoulders and patted him lightly on the back as if to indicate his satisfaction with the answer. Then, he stepped back from the table into the shadows before speaking again.

"Luis, we appreciate your candor and honesty. And, we trust that your silence in this matter is certain."

Luis nodded his head affirmatively.

The interrogator motioned to one of his men to retrieve the map and the tape recorder. He then turned and walked toward the side door of the garage. As he passed the two men who were on guard there, he issued a final order.

"Kill him!"

5

Moon over Miami

There is no political solution,
To our troubled evolution,
Have no faith in constitution,
There is no bloody revolution.

—The Police, *Spirits in a Material World*

Hialeah, Florida, December 1960

The white Chevrolet moved northwest up Okeechobee Road at a quick pace. It turned into a clean, well-lit gas station on the corner of 14th Avenue. As the vehicle came to a stop, a young Cuban boy hustled out of the garage section of the station.

When he arrived at the car, the driver's side window came down, and a Hispanic male in his thirties turned his head, smiled, and signaled for the lad to fill the tank with premium gas.

The lad nodded politely and began his work. Meanwhile, the driver and the second man in the car began a short conversation in hushed tones.

"Don't forget!" whispered the passenger. "Try to avoid the subject of his son. I know that deep inside his soul, the Ambassador hates the revolution and the faceless men who control it. But, we will be able to harness that hatred only by letting him release it of his own accord!"

The serious expression on the driver's face indicated his understanding of the situation.

"Amigo. I have never met the ambassador, but none of us can forget Moncada Barracks."

After a few moments of silence, the men stepped from the car into the warm southern air. They were both well-dressed in light summer suits and colorful ties.

The driver was a powerfully built man whose features identified him as Cuban in heritage. His forehead wore several small scars, but he possessed a full head of short dark hair and a handsome face with bright flashing eyes. He could easily have been mistaken for a prizefighter. As the boy watched him step out of the car, the man seemed to move like a sleek cat, smoothly and effortlessly.

The passenger also appeared to be Cuban. He was definitely older, easily in his forties, and he presented a very distinguished profile. His dark hair was highlighted by streaks of gray at the temples. He nodded to the boy when their eyes met, but he did not speak. It was the driver who approached the boy and addressed him in Spanish.

"Donde esta Oscar?"

The boy stopped pumping gas and turned toward the station. He pointed to a side door near the garage as he responded in English.

"Mr. Oscar is in the back office, I believe. Would you like me to go for him?"

The driver turned toward the station, smiled and this time he spoke in English.

"No, I'll surprise him. The ambassador was always one for surprising me. Do you know that his birthday is sometime this week?"

The man did not wait for a response before redirecting his words to his older companion.

"I can see Oscar's influence here. He is trying very hard to be an American. And, I cannot blame him."

The boy hesitated, then spoke softly while continuing his work.

"We speak English to our customers if they understand. We try to help them if they are new to our country."

The boy directed his attention to the older man.

"I believe it is Thursday."

The man shook his head clearly indicating that he did not understand.

"Mr. Oscar's birthday is Thursday." replied the boy with conviction.

"Thank you, Son," responded the younger man. "You are a credit to your employer. Would you please pull our automobile to the side after filling the tank? We will be visiting the ambassador, and we should be in the office for quite a while." The driver lobbed the keys to the boy.

The two men walked into the front entrance of the garage and then back through the work area to a rear door. There they hesitated for a moment without speaking. As the older man knocked on the door, he called out in a friendly voice.

"Oscar! Oscar! You cannot hide from your birthday. Father Time must have his way with you! Let us in so that we may share your joy and your discomfort."

After what seemed like ten seconds, a smiling Oscar Chacon opened the door for his old acquaintance.

"Come in, Manuel, and view me in my pain!" Oscar responded as the two men embraced. "Another year has passed, and I am none the better for it. It has been a long time since we last talked."

The two men followed Oscar into the room that doubled as a rest area and an office. There was a large desk facing the door, a matching credenza in one corner and a small cot pushed up against one of the walls. The desk held a modern calculating machine and a lamp. Several filing cabinets and three folding chairs completed the furniture ensemble.

Manuel Arbenz turned to his companion and placed an arm on the younger man's shoulder.

"Oscar, I want you to meet my dear friend, Francisco. Francisco Campa. But all his friends call him Frank. He is a good man, a faithful son of Cuba."

"It is my pleasure, Mr. Campa. Any man with the courage to drive with Manuel Arbenz is a truly brave man."

Campa extended his hand to the ambassador.

"I had the pleasure of meeting you briefly in Havana in 1952, Mr. Ambassador. It was at a reception given by General Batista just after the coup. Those were much happier times. I have heard many good things about you from Manuel and many others. I would hope that we can become good friends."

Oscar smiled and pointed to the coffeepot, which simmered on the credenza.

"Gentlemen, would you like some refreshment? We have many young people here so I cannot offer you anything stronger."

Arbenz stepped to the coffeepot and poured a cup for himself.

"I am grateful for this courtesy, Oscar. My days have been busy lately. We are have been busy reorganizing the government in exile. Coffee and conversation with an old friend will provide some relief."

After sipping the drink, Arbenz turned and faced his host. He handed him a neatly wrapped box and smiled.

"I believe that you will enjoy them. Montecristo at that! As I recall, they are your favorite."

Oscar slowly unwrapped the box that contained an ample supply of his favorite Cuban cigars. Arbenz could almost see tears forming in the ambassador's eyes.

"Thank you so much, my friends. These beauties are difficult to come by these days. But, I am certain that my birthday is not the sole reason for your visit."

"I am impressed greatly with your operation," remarked Arbenz, clearly avoiding the ambassador's implied question. "One has only to observe the young lad who pumped our gas. He is businesslike and polite far beyond his years. I see a strong element of training in his behavior. You are to be commended!"

"Thank you, Manuel, although, I cannot take the credit for all of this. You have met my brother, Raymond. He is the disciplinarian here. His education and military training have been very valuable to us. Even as much as I disliked the Sergeant's methods, I must give him some credit. Batista trained my brother well."

Manuel nodded and confirmed the Ambassador's thoughts.

"Raymond's military background is certainly an asset. With your financial brainpower and his organizational discipline, it is no wonder you are successful. I would wish so much for the revolution."

Oscar agreed with some hesitation as he began to perceive the real reason for Arbenz's visit.

"It was fortunate for me that I was able to get Raymond and, later, his little son Carlos out of the tempest. When little Carlos arrived, Raymond's whole life turned around for the better."

Arbenz nodded, hesitating before asking what he knew to be a sensitive question.

"What about his other child and his wife? Is there any chance for them?" Arbenz knew that Raymond still had a daughter and wife in Cuba.

Oscar shook his head negatively and looked away from his guests toward the wall. He was staring at a large framed map of Cuba.

"I was able to get little Carlos to come. But, in doing so, I had to make certain promises to Raymond's wife and our parents. Our mother and father do not want to leave the land of their birth. Life is not easy for them, but they have their friends, and they tell me that they are too old to start a new life. I made them a promise that I would not work to get my niece out of Cuba. Raymond knows this."

Oscar turned back to face his guests. They could see that powerful emotional forces and memories had been set in motion within the ambassador. After a pause Oscar went on.

"He has accepted it, as much as a father can accept separation from his child. But, I do not believe that he will be truly happy until he is back together with all of them, including his wife. I think she now knows that their separation was a mistake. She was young and couldn't fathom the political situation. She didn't have enough faith in Raymond."

Frank glanced at Arbenz and then back to Oscar. He recognized the opportunity to disclose the real reason for the visit. And, he knew that the ambassador already sensed what was coming.

"The opportunity is finally at hand, Mr. Ambassador! We have waited with patience and resolve. And, now our chance to respond has presented itself."

Campa turned back to Arbenz.

"Manuel is working to bring us closer to our families and friends on the island. He is ready to lead the exiled sons and daughters of Cuba back to the land of their birth."

Oscar looked back at the map on the wall, as if he were trying to find guidance there.

"That would be a wonder, Mr. Campa. But, it is only a dream, a far away dream that may never come to pass. So many of us had hopes for the revolution, but now events have turned our dreams to nightmares. Once again our optimism and expectations have been replaced with futility and pessimism."

Oscar slowly shook his head. His guests respectfully remained silent, waiting for the Ambassador to complete his melancholy thoughts.

"I do not hold out much hope for the future, my friends. I realize that Raymond and I may never again see our mother and father. We are so close and yet, so far away. Even the most violent acts of nature cannot compare to the suffering we endure at the hands of our fellow man."

Manuel stood up from his chair and turned toward the window. He thought over his response with some care.

"That is why I am here, Oscar. It is why we both are here. To see you! To revive our hopes and our dreams! To take our homeland back!"

He paused and glanced at the map.

"And we must take it by force! It is the only way."

Arbenz paused and turned back to look at the ambassador.

"We feel that the opportunity has come. And, it may not come again. So, we must seize it, and go forward."

Then he added the final argument that Oscar had been listening for.

"And the Americans will help us!"

Oscar looked down at his desk. The expression on his face displayed no elements of optimism.

"I am aware of our situation, Manuel, and, unfortunately, I cannot agree. We should not even consider the use of force! We are greatly outnumbered, and many of our people, on both sides, will die no matter how this evolves. We have no weapons, no training, no army, no ships, no planes, and, most important, not enough support from the Cuban people."

"But Mr. Ambassador," replied Campa in an attempt to save the argument, "that is why we are here. We have all the pieces to this puzzle!"

Campa paused to let his words sink in.

"Mr. Ambassador, I am but a soldier. My men and I have trained for the last six months with the Americans. We have a cadre of over a hundred able-bodied men. And now, we have approval from the Americans! We are beginning to build and train a force of Cubans exiles. We will receive weapons and transport. We will have ships and aircraft and, if we can expand our number by a factor of ten or one hundred, we will have the men to sail and fly them. And, best of all, the people of Cuba will come to our aid once they see that we have landed and that liberation is at hand."

Oscar looked directly at Campa. "Frank, I can see that you are a very brave and resourceful man. But, you are here in Florida with roughly the same information as I have. How can you say that an invasion force will be received with enthusiasm? My sources tell me of suffering and political corruption, of captures and escapes and of seizures and assassinations, of arms caches being discovered in the mountains and of landings on the coasts. But they say nothing of popular support! They say nothing of organized resistance to Castro! The people are too weak and hungry and confused to rise up. They are resigned to their fate!"

Frank Campa stood firmly behind his proposal. He put both hands on the desk, but spoke in a hushed and respectful tone.

"I cannot tell you everything I know, Mr. Ambassador. But, I will give you some information to consider. I have been to Cuba four times in the last year. I have organized some support in the south. The potential is clearly there. I have seen it! The desire for freedom is alive. Now that we have the support of the Americans, we should not fail to act. The opportunity may not come again!"

"Do not take offense, Frank," replied Oscar in a hesitant tone, "but I must ask you about something that has been bothering me for some time. It is very personal. You must understand that I have suffered enough losses for one lifetime."

"I have no personal secrets, Mr. Ambassador. And, I will take no offense no matter how personal the question. I know how you have suffered at the hands of these criminals. It is out of sincere respect for you as the Ambassador and as a human being that I am here this evening. Please ask."

The Ambassador looked at Frank Campa for a moment while he pondered the exact words he would use. He elected to be blunt and take the risks inherent in that approach.

"Were you involved in the DC-3 hijacking in October?" Oscar offered no other information but listened intently for Frank's answer.

Frank seemed surprised and was taken back by the question, so he hesitated before answering. He looked down at the floor for a moment and then turned and walked over to the window and stared outside gathering his thoughts. Campa knew that the success or failure of this mission was riding on his answer.

"No!"

Campa kept his back turned as he proceeded with the explanation.

"That was a foolish thing! They were not our people. It was an act of despair and hatred. I would not harm innocent people especially if they were my countrymen. It was an act of terrorism spawned by the same group that bombed the department store in Havana a few months ago."

With renewed confidence and a mild sense of righteousness, Campa turned and looked directly into Oscar's waiting eyes.

"They believe that fear will win the day. I apologize for their actions, but I am not one of them. Neither is Manuel. We learned of this action just as you did, from the news media. I had no idea that they would stoop to such depths."

Campa turned and looked at Arbenz. The latter found it advisable not to speak at this crucial moment because he could see the growing confidence in Campa's eyes. Campa gazed back at Arbenz and continued his explanation as a slight smile began to cross his lips.

"That is not to say that the time will not come when internal commando activities will be necessary. When we proceed with an invasion, communications and supply arteries must be disrupted, and the defensive and offensive capabilities of the militia must be eliminated. These facts are unavoidable! They define my duty, my mission, my contribution!"

As a paralyzing silence settled over the three motionless men, Oscar slowly began nodding his head in apparent satisfaction with the answer. It was time for him to respond.

"How is it that I can help you? I am not a soldier. And, I do not intend to be a soldier. I have found a home here in America. It is much more of a home than I ever had in Cuba even though I was fortunate enough to be a government official. I was right to come to America when I did. There are hardships, and there are misunderstandings. The Americans from the north do not always trust us. I am a hardworking citizen, but they often treat me as an outright foreigner. It is probably the same way their parents were treated when they came here from Europe. But, still, I am an American!"

The ambassador walked to the window and gazed out at the traffic. His visitors waited for him to continue.

"We must prove ourselves to be worthy. We must prove ourselves not only to those who came here before us, but also to ourselves. When I look in the mirror, I want to see a brave man who is a survivor. I want to see a brave man who can be an icon for those who must travel the same weary path. I want to be that brave man! But I do not want to kill those former countrymen of mine who have opposing political philosophies. I want to argue with them. I want to set an example for them. I cannot kill them!"

"You are truly a brave man, Mr. Ambassador," whispered Arbenz. "But, we do not ask you to slay your countrymen."

Oscar continued as if he had not heard Arbenz.

"I have made a life for myself, and I have rescued some of my family. It is possible that I could provide you with some financial support. I am not rich, but these stations do provide a comfortable living. I can contribute, but it would not be much."

Frank took over the conversation. He could see the emotion flowing over Oscar Chacon's face, and he needed to move the focus to the main reason for their visit.

"Mr. Ambassador, we are not asking you to fight. And, we have considerable financial support. Any contribution would be received with gratitude, but is not necessary."

Oscar looked up and posed the obvious question.

"Then, what is it that you want?"

"What we need is military expertise and experience and leadership. We need a team of men to go ashore separate from the landing force. What is needed is a small, highly trained and experienced unit that would perform a specialized mission. It is a mission that needs expert leadership. And, your brother, Raymond, is the one who is uniquely qualified to be its leader!"

The Ambassador looked at the small, framed picture that sat on his desk. It depicted a much younger Oscar with his arm around a young lad to whom he was obviously related. He slowly picked up the photograph.

"I suppose I knew what you wanted all along. But my brother is a free man. It is he you should approach with this request, not me!"

Arbenz walked slowly up to Oscar and placed his hands on the ambassador's shoulders before speaking.

"We came to you first because we respect you. We came to you because you are one of the reasons we wish to fight, and possibly die, for our country. We came to you because you represent the future of a free Cuba."

6

Duty Calls

And Jacob called
unto his sons and said,
Gather yourselves together,
that I may tell you that
which shall befall you
in the last days…

—King James Bible, Genesis 49:1

Gallatin, Missouri

Early March can be very unpredictable in northwest Missouri. The occasional snowstorms hadn't stopped yet, and the spring rains were waiting to begin. On Mother Nature's calendar it was a time of turmoil. For the farmers who worked the land in this part of the country, it was time to repair their equipment and fixtures and prepare for the spring planting. It was also an opportunity to look back over the past year and measure the progress and setbacks in their battle with the land.

This is how it all seemed to the young blonde woman as she stared out of the expansive kitchen window. The lifeless, drab colors of the countryside were only weeks from giving way to the greens and yellows of spring.

The old farmhouse was small, but plenty of hard work and good lumber had made it strong and secure. There were even plans to expand the old living room into a much more casual recreation area and to add a three-car garage and fully functional workshop.

As she gazed across the harsh landscape, Lottie thought she understood why people would learn to love this environment. There was a certain beauty and strength lying just below the surface, a certain reassurance in the abrupt passage of the seasons, in the renewal of life. Soon, blades of grass would be pushing through the frozen ground, and little creatures would be hopping around in search of food. It could all be very reassuring, indeed.

Lottie was a city girl. She had grown up in Tulsa and worked for a while in Little Rock. After her parents moved to Florida, she migrated to Kansas City and then to St. Joseph. She enjoyed making these visits to the farm that her boy friend called home, that is, when Ron wasn't out fixing something or feeding something.

It was a cloudy day with temperatures in the mid-20s. A slight glaze of snow and frost was spread across the rolling hills and small creeks, and Ron was working on a fence near the back end of his property. He had managed to put together four hundred contiguous acres west of Gallatin with over half a mile of frontage on a paved county road. The land formed an area that was more or less rectangular and shared common boundaries with several other farms.

Farming was a new enterprise for him, but he had considerable organizational skills and lots of patience. He had managed to develop over two hundred and fifty tillable acres. To this he added some pigs and chickens as well as a narrow landing strip. The latter was useful for his promising crop dusting activities.

Between the pigs, the plow, and the plane, it was a good living. His spraying business alone generated enough cash flow to cover the basic operating costs of the farm. He also found that he was capable of performing minor tractor repairs and giving occasional flying lessons at the local airfield.

The last year had been especially good for him. So much so that he was in the process of planning those additions to the main house as well as a new barn for his equipment and the purchase of a few additional head of livestock and two horses.

Ron's neighbors were friendly enough. They helped each other considerably during the intense planting and harvest seasons. Raising a barn was always a neighborhood affair, and a good excuse for a weekend barbecue and beer party. His fellow farmers were quite sociable. It wasn't unusual for them to invite him into their homes at Thanksgiving and other major family holidays. He reciprocated with good engineering and investment advice that was always in demand.

Ron's brief encounter with domestic life hadn't worked out well at all. He was married at nineteen and divorced at twenty-two. Fortunately, he didn't get a quick start on a family. His military career delayed those thoughts so the usual financial penalties associated with the termination of a marriage were avoided. His ex-wife didn't want a piece of his future so he walked away ready for a new start.

Then he met Lottie by a twist of fate. His car broke down in St. Joseph and while he was waiting for repairs, he struck up a conversation with a young waitress at a restaurant near the garage. The attraction was mutual. The rest is history.

At about three o'clock on this Wednesday afternoon, Lottie paced in front of the kitchen window, looking north to see if Ron was in sight. She had a job in St. Joseph, and her departure time was approaching. Lottie knew that she would see Ron that weekend, but she did want to kiss him goodbye.

She wandered over to a mirror that was part of a large cabinet in one corner of the kitchen. As Lottie scanned her reflection, she realized that her time on the farm was beginning to change her habits and appearance. When she was here, her whole personal perspective changed. She noticed that she had forgotten to put on her makeup. As she began brushing her hair, she detected a slight grin on her face, a smile that started to come naturally for her. It was the beginning of a smile that she hadn't seen in a long time.

The smile widened after she stepped on the old bathroom scale that had found its way into the kitchen. The exercise and better diet inherent in this rural life meant that she began to feel and look better each time she came to the farm. Her job exposed her to a constant stream of fried foods that had taken their toll. Now, she was determined to change all of that. She would pass on the French fries and hit the baked potatoes. More fresh fruits and salads would do the trick. Her smile broadened even more.

Just as she was ticking off a list of groceries to be purchased for her refrigerator back in St. Joseph, the telephone rang, and Lottie stepped over to the counter to answer. The man on the other end of the line spoke slowly and quietly.

"Hi! Is Ron home?" The caller paused.

"He should be back soon," Lottie responded. "He's busy with some fencing."

"I'm glad to hear that he's working that farm. He's sure an energetic fellow. Say, would you tell him that his old friend, Jack Sheehan, called to see how he was doing? And, who do I have the pleasure of speaking with?"

"My name's Lottie. I can leave a message for Ron so that he gets it when he comes in."

"Thanks, Lottie. Just let Ron know that I haven't forgotten about him."

"I'll do that, Mr. Sheehan. Does he have your phone number?" Lottie reached for a pencil.

"I'm on the road right now. Tell him I'll call back. How soon will he be returning?"

Lottie looked out the window again and scanned the horizon without success.

"He's supposed to be here now. I have to go to work, but I'll leave him a note. If you can call in an hour or two, he should have returned by then."

"Thanks." The caller paused for a second and then continued. "Say, tell me, has he been flying much lately? I knew him when he was in the Air Force. He was very good at it."

"Flying is what he lives for, Mr. Sheehan. He has this little spray plane. I like to go up in small planes, but not that one. It's a rattletrap. I honestly don't know what holds it together. He scares me with it. Don't tell him I said that about his darling airplane. He might never forgive me."

"Oh, don't worry, Lottie. I know exactly how you feel. I've been in that situation myself, believe me! Well, tell him to be careful. Don't let him buzz your house. He used to scare us all the time with his maneuvers. Thanks again."

Lottie said goodbye and hung up the phone. She was surprised as she turned back toward the window. Ron was standing in the doorway smiling.

"I'll bet you thought I forgot about you!" he said as he entered the kitchen tracking in considerable mud with each step.

"Hey, you bum, I just cleaned up this dump so try not to mess it up before I leave for work!" Lottie reached for the broom and handed it to Ron.

"You can call in sick, honey. It's going around you know."

Ron smiled as he took off his jacket. Most of his six-foot frame was covered with mud and debris from the fields. He was wearing an old pair of cowboy boots that he had purchased the last time he was in Houston along with his standard field uniform of jeans and a flannel shirt under his jacket. His head was protected by an old St. Louis Cardinals' baseball cap, which was clamped with a sturdy set of earmuffs. Ron was always complaining that his hands were cold, so Lottie was proud to see him wearing a set of well-insulated field gloves that she had recently given him.

Lottie reached for her coat, then remembered the phone call.

"Some guy named…." She glanced at her notes. "Jack… Jack Sheehan, called."

Ron's eyes lit up instantly.

"Good old Jack! I wonder what mischief he's up to these days? He's a career military type. I always liked him because he could keep his mouth shut, especially when I was late or did something stupid. What did he want?"

"He just called to see how you were doing."

Ron shook his head vigorously and raised his hands into the air.

"Jack never calls to see how anyone is doing! He always wants something. He's a good guy, but he's not real sociable. He wants something from me!"

"He asked me if you were doing any flying," said Lottie with some apparent misgivings in her voice.

"Ah! That's it! He needs a pilot! What could he need a pilot for? What kind of sneaky plots are brewing among his pals at the CIA?"

"CIA! He's with the CIA?" Lottie's tone became much more apprehensive.

"Nope. Not Jack. He just works with The Company. More like a lion tamer with a whip and a chair. He keeps them at a distance. He feeds them information, but he's not one of them. I just think Jack enjoys the intrigue. He sees himself as something of an amateur secret agent. If the cold war ever ended, he wouldn't know what to do with himself."

"Well, while you're figuring it out, kiss me, and I'm out of here." Lottie relaxed again, and the worried look on her face was replaced with a radiant smile.

Ron walked Lottie to the front of the house while they talked about Friday night. After some hugs, Lottie jumped into her car and headed for St. Joe and her job. Ron returned to the kitchen and glanced at her note. *What did old Cracker Jack want?*

Ron was twenty-eight years of age when he left his flight engineer's job in Kansas City for the rural life. The airline was cutting back, and he wasn't really enjoying his civilian career. When one of his old Air Force friends told him about this acreage, he couldn't resist the chance to get closer to the land. Something new and challenging. Besides, there were plenty of aircraft related-enterprises he could dabble in if he got the urge. That was five years ago, and so far he had found plenty of distractions to keep him busy.

That friend had also done a stint in the Air Force. His M.O.S. was intelligence. Ron was continuously amazed by the amount of information Charlie Bill had on almost any subject worth talking about. They were the same age, but whereas Ron was born in Texas, Charlie was definitely a Missouri boy. If you needed something or wanted to find someone, Charlie was your man. He also knew how to run a farm.

Charlie knows Jack a damn sight better than I do. Ron's mind sped through the possibilities. *Maybe Charlie has an idea about what's afoot here!*

Ron's military reserve status provided several weeks of paid weekend warrior cash and diversion. His military record was exemplary. He never had trouble getting recommendations from his former commanders and military acquaintances. These came in handy when he purchased the farm, an act that required several government-backed loans. *Could Jack have a Reserve or National Guard project he need help with?*

No use guessing about it because Jack would eventually call back. After scanning the refrigerator Ron decided that it was time to replenish his supplies of food and beer so he jumped into his blue '58 Chevy and headed for town. He would call Charlie in the evening.

His trip took him past the airfield where his small spray plane was stored. He turned off the pavement and entered the airport by way of a gravel road. A recent snowstorm had deposited frozen drifts on each side of the road.

He stopped to check over his plane, which was always in need of some minor repairs. It was a converted Cessna with a good engine and great maneuverability. Ron didn't keep the plane on the farm during the winter because the weather had a way of doing nasty things to machinery left in the open. The hangar fees at this field were minimal, and it was a lot safer place to operate out of when the weather conditions were unpredictable.

After a stop at the hardware store and the post office, Ron headed for home. The sun was heading down, and the north wind was picking up in velocity. It was going to be a night of television…after he called Charlie. The last turn finally brought his farm and the house into view.

Surprise! I've got visitors!

His driveway was wide enough to hold several cars, and now, there was a dark colored, new Oldsmobile parked near the house. He scanned the car, but there were no occupants. *It wasn't one of his neighbors. And, it's got government plates.*

After parking his car, Ron removed several bags of groceries from the trunk and turned toward the house. As he did, Ron noticed that the vehicle displayed a familiar U. S. Air Force security sticker on the rear bumper. It was now very clear who his mysterious visitor was.

Once Ron rounded the corner of his home, he noticed two men standing on the back porch engaged in an animated conversation. One was Charlie Bill and the other was wearing a long coat over the uniform of an Air Force officer.

It's Jack, all right! And he does want something.

At the sound of Ron's approach, both men turned. Jack stepped forward with a genuine smile spread across his face. A clandestine project was certainly in the wings.

7

A Parting of Ways

We are and will
remain one nation.
And we belong together.

—Helmut Kohl, West German Chancellor

Hialeah, Florida

The two men sat in the evening darkness on the spacious porch of Oscar Chacon's home in Hialeah, Florida. Two large ceiling fans turned slowly overhead.

The men had just completed a Sunday dinner with family members and several visiting friends, but now they were alone toasting their good fortune with glasses of California wine as their thoughts drifted back toward Cuba and the ones they had to leave behind.

"I know how you feel about your daughter, Raymond. After all, she is also my niece, and I miss her very much. She was just like a daughter to me when she was growing up on the island."

Oscar paused to allow his brother to comment, but Raymond remained quiet and thoughtful. Oscar poured himself a second glass of wine, and he stared up at the stars as if they were listening to his thoughts.

"And we all miss Ana terribly. She is a very brave person, much braver than I could ever be. I could have arranged for her passage, but she also declined. She did not want to leave anyone behind. Ana has her family, and there was no way she was going to leave them, even for you, my brother. As you already know too well, she has no strong political preferences, and I think that's why she can't understand us. To her, we both must look like traitors, both to our country and to our families."

Oscar looked back at his brother and noticed that he had his eyes closed even as he spoke.

"You're right, Oscar. She just couldn't see the dangers. She couldn't understand why I wouldn't work for the revolution.

"Yet, as evil and corrupt as Batista and his government were, I can't just turn my back and ignore the incantations of yet another dictator in our homeland. Even if I could have joined the revolution, I couldn't have remained in Cuba for long because I would have objected to the way the people are still treated. And, those objections would have cost me and my family our lives!"

Oscar sympathized with his brother's feelings. He could remember the zeal with which Raymond worked for Batista's government. That energy combined with his native intelligence and skill quickly pushed Raymond to the top of the list of those trusted by the leadership.

But, then Oscar began to notice a change in his brother's phone calls and letters. Slow at first, but, then more rapidly, as Raymond began to see the poverty and greed at work on the island.

But now, two years after the revolution, both of them had seen the results of the change in leadership, and it spelled no improvement for the average citizens of the country. New laws, new slogans, new leaders, and new allies served as distractions. And the only reward for the citizens was an ever-escalating list of sacrifices.

"Raymond, I know you see this new circumstance as an opportunity to rescue your loved ones. At the same time, this appears to be an opportunity to prove that you have not turned away from them. But, go slowly! Things are not always as they seem."

"Oscar, you were the one who rescued me from Cuba at the moment I was in the greatest danger. You rescued me and my friends and each of us, to a man, will forever be grateful. We owe you our lives and nothing less! Without your help, I would have been taken by the revolutionaries and tried as a Batista supporter even though I really had no political allegiance to him.

"I owe my freedom and the prosperity of my life to you, my brother! And you have helped many others of our countrymen over the past few years. You have taken in people who needed jobs and helped children whose parents are still on the island. And, when we get to the point where the people on the island and the people who have left can talk with each other in peace, you will be one of those called upon for your advice and counsel. Even though I know that you don't want to be involved in this invasion, I know your assistance afterward will be essential to its success."

Oscar was embarrassed by the compliments, even from his brother. He was not the kind of person who enjoyed outright praise for his efforts and accomplishments. Oscar felt that the deed and its effects were sufficient recognition.

"Raymond, I can only hope and pray for the day when an opportunity to help rebuild and reshape our old homeland will come to me. As you well know, I still have many friends on the other side of the political and philosophical fence. And I have some hope that they will sit down with us and rationally discuss the solutions to our problems when the time is right.

"But, I still strongly believe that we should leave things as they are, until that moment of conciliation comes to us peacefully and naturally. Compromises like the ones we need cannot be forced upon two relatively equal protagonists and combatants even when they claim the same heritage and the same history."

Raymond reached for the bottle of wine, which sat on the small table in front of him, and poured another glass. Somehow, he knew

that this night would come and that he would have to make the difficult choice that had presented itself. He looked at his brother and
smiled as he raised his glass in appreciation for his hospitality and his
considered advice.

"I have been trained as a soldier. So, my contribution to my country
must come in that form. I certainly do not want to kill anyone. That's
why I would not go with the invasion force. As you can see, my brother,
we actually agree on that point.

"But it is clear to me, and I'm sure that it is clear to you, that this proposed invasion will go forward whether we agree with it or not. These
plans have been set in motion by forces much more powerful than you
or I. There is no way either of us can stop them. Under these circumstances, it appears that I have two choices. I can stay here and watch and
wait for another opportunity, or I can join this special op which has
been offered to me."

"Raymond, I'm particularly curious about the extent of knowledge
Frank Campa has of your mission for Batista. If he has the knowledge
he professes, why does he need you?"

"That's easy! He's looked for the bunker and couldn't locate it. It's as
simple as that. Cantillo had no first hand information on its exact position. And, it is very well hidden. I guess that I'm the only one left who
has the positioning coordinates within the complex."

"What about the members of your patrol?"

"Oscar, I told Arbenz that I would not go unless I picked my men. He
only insisted that I take Frank. I agreed. We will keep him contained.
There will be seven of us and only one of him. I like those odds."

"So do I, my brother. But, humor me and let me list the concerns that
bother me."

Raymond nodded and waited for his brother's objections.

"First, you are too well known near Cienfuegos. You will not know
whom you can trust.

"The second problem is the invasion itself. From what I gather from Arbenz's comments, the entire plan is flawed. The chances of success for a collateral mission are minimal. And, knowing the machismo attitude on the island, punishment would almost certainly be death! No revolution or country or treasure is worth your life!"

"And third, you are going with Frank Campa. His reputation is that of an opportunist and mercenary, not a patriot. My contacts tell me that he would waste no time sacrificing those around him to save himself. The fact that he has been selected to organize the mission by the Revolutionary Council in Miami is an indication of the influence he wields among the expatriates. And, his contention that he learned of the bunker and its supposed contents from General Cantillo is suspect. My understanding is that Frank Campa was not in Havana when the mission was planned and executed. He was not one of Cantillo's confidants. You were there! You must agree!"

Raymond knew that his brother's arguments were well based in fact. But, he countered the argument anyway.

"We do have several advantages. Frank Campa has limited knowledge and some of it may be faulty. And, my men are loyal, and as far as I can tell, he has no reason to suspect our suspicions."

Oscar sat back in his chair as he realized that he had failed in his attempt to dissuade his brother. But he also remembered that his brother was a very competent military officer and a person very capable of taking care of himself.

"Well, Raymond, I wish you good luck and health, and I hope and pray for your safe return to us. I realize that if there is anyone who can conduct this mission successfully, it is you. Keep us in your heart and remember that we love you. And, if anything should go wrong, rest assured that we will not rest until the day when all of us are together again."

Oscar paused and then added a final caution.

"Just remember! Watch your back!"

8

If All Else Fails

I saw her standin' on her front lawn
Just a twirling her baton,
Me and her went for a ride, Sir
And, ten innocent people died.

—*Bruce Springsteen,* **Nebraska**

Somewhere in the Dominican Republic

The man who stepped through the front door of the single story beach house at midnight wore sunglasses and a military fatigue hat pulled tightly over his forehead. When he saw the prisoner and his interrogator, he issued his commands.

"Don't kill him, Hernando! You should have waited. I wanted one last chance to talk with him. He's the last member of Batista's personal guard who might have seen the orders. Now, I'm left with the members of Chacon's patrol. And, that's not going to be easy!"

The interrogator stepped away from the motionless prisoner.

"Sir, before he lost consciousness, he spoke of the chemical complex. He said he was there just a month ago."

"Interesting! These men are loyal to a fault. Can you revive him?"

Hernando shrugged his shoulders as he turned back to the bed on which the prisoner was lying.

"He was in much pain near the end, Sir! And, he gave us much detail. I believe he was telling the truth."

"What else did he tell you, Hernando. Give me all of it!"

"Yes, Sir! I recorded the interrogation as you instructed. It's on the machine over there. As you indicated, he admitted to being one of Batista's personal guards. He came to the Dominican three days before the Sergeant. He was charged with storing and protecting a significant amount of gold and currency. He attended Batista's farewell party here in the Dominican Republic. He said that he did not go to Spain with the rest of his countrymen because his wife is Dominican."

"And, he knows nothing of the items Batista left behind?"

"Sir! Several of the men under his command helped pack the containers. They spoke of gold and weapons and military intelligence."

"Did he indicate where these men are now?"

"In Spain, Sir. The entire cadre left for Spain with the Sergeant. He was the only one to remain here, or so he said."

"What about their sortie in November 1959? The bunker had to be their main objective! What did they accomplish?"

"Sir! The prisoner said that his patrol searched the entire complex with a cadre of twelve men. He claims that the landing, at night, cost the loss of four others, including the two men who knew of the exact location of the bunker."

"Cuban patrols?"

"No, Sir. There is a small reef out there of the coast. One boat became grounded and in the process of freeing the craft, one man was knocked unconscious and swept back out to sea. Another was lost in the rescue operation. He didn't say anything about the other two. That's all he said."

"What are the odds of something like that happening, Hernando? Seventeen men in all! Am I correct?"

Hernando nodded affirmatively.

"Seventeen men attempt a night landing on the south coast of Cuba. The seas are calm and the men are experienced in landings and are knowledgeable of the area. Two of those men are entrusted with the vital information, the bunker location. Seventeen men attempt a night landing and four are lost! And of the four who are lost, two of them are the men with the essential information!"

Frank Campa slammed his fist down on a nearby table as his anger ran rampant.

"Hernando, I have a strong belief in the power of statistics and the power of experience. A very strong belief! This man is lying. I will bet you that he is one of the two men who knew where the bunker was located."

"Yes, Sir!" replied Hernando, mostly out of fear of his leader. "I will do my best to revive the man. But, his pulse is very weak. We might have overdone the interrogation, Sir."

"What did he say about the search and the withdrawal?"

"Sir! He indicated that the search covered two full nights. He said that they did not search in the daylight for fear of being discovered."

"What else did he say?" Campa bellowed as he turned his back on Hernando.

"Sir! He spoke of construction materials from the bunker, debris that was supposed to be removed from the site. He said that their search was that thorough. His party observed a significant number of dead fish near the site, an indication that the level of toxicity is still critical."

"And, what about the return trip?"

"Sir, that was uneventful. He indicated that they left the site during a squall and made contact with their mother ship in less than three hours. No government patrols were sited, in the water or in the air."

"Anything else, Hernando? Anything that might help."

"Well, he did mention that Batista was furious. Absolutely furious! But, eventually he took the blame himself. Batista ordered the prisoner to organize another attempt, but the Sergeant left for Spain before anything else was accomplished. And, he never told the prisoner of the exact location. That is his story, anyway."

"Thank you, Hernando. I will listen to the tape now."

9

Volunteers

Power is not a means, it is an end.
One does not establish a dictatorship
in order to safeguard a revolution;
One makes the revolution in order
to establish the dictatorship.

—George Orwell, *Nineteen Eighty-Four*

Kansas City, Missouri

The municipal airport was nestled near the winding Missouri River in downtown Kansas City. There was talk of a new facility to be built to the north, but for the time being this was the main airport for eastern Kansas and western Missouri. Ron had spent quite a bit of time here when he worked for the airlines, and he still had friends at the terminals and in the repair depots.

After the luggage was unloaded and the car was parked, Ron and his companions made their way to the terminal for check-in. Lottie and Charlene waited while Ron and Charlie took their bags to the counter and displayed their passports for the flight to Guatemala City.

After receiving their seat assignments and boarding passes, the group moved to a small restaurant near the entrance to the international concourse. The flight wasn't scheduled to leave for three hours so the four of them sat down in the restaurant. Once again Ron and Charlie tried to explain, to themselves and to their companions, the reasons for accepting the dangers of their mission. It was a tense moment of parting for everyone involved.

The quickness of the decision had cut through Lottie like a knife. She had always wanted to be with someone like Ron, and now he was heading to war. In such a peaceful town with such friendly people, how could anyone even think of war? War was something you read about in history books or saw in movies on television. What kind of madmen would start a war on purpose? And, it wasn't even an American war. It was going to be Cubans against Cubans. The more Lottie thought about the situation, the more upset she became. As the terrifying possibilities flashed through her mind, she tried hard to listen to Ron's explanation.

"Honey, I must have mentioned my grandfather to you, the one from Cuba? He's gone now, but his memory has had a lasting impact on me. He was very active in the fight for Cuban independence. He was wounded twice in the Spanish-American War. In Cuba, they call it the American intervention in Cuba's War of Independence!

"I used to sit in the backyard on a swing and listen to my grandfather's stories about the actions leading up to the Battle of San Juan Hill. He told me of the Americans he met and fought with against the Spanish. He also taught me all of the Spanish I know. His memory tells me that I'm doing the right thing."

A tear ran down Lottie's face.

"And he was just a good, hard working man. Once Cuba became independent, he established his business and he helped raise his family and the families of his children. His only mistake was marrying an American.

"When Castro took over two years ago, he decided that Gramps was too influential and too American. So instead of utilizing his experience and knowledge, he was executed as an American spy! He was eighty years old!

"So, you can see why I can't pass up this opportunity for some pay-back. He never liked bullies like the ones who killed him. I know that he would want me to do this for him."

Lottie saw the anger on Ron's face, and she knew that his reaction was normal for a man under these circumstances. But she didn't believe that revenge was a good enough reason for risking his life.

"I'm all in favor of freedom and bravery and all those things that are important to strong men, to men like you. But even though I never met your grandfather, I can't believe that he would want you to risk your life and your future. No matter how successful you are, you will not be able to bring him back! And if things go badly, you could also become a vic-tim. If that were to happen, you know he would suffer with the knowl-edge that you were captured or killed trying to revenge his death."

Ron looked at Lottie as she spoke and listened to her words, but he did not respond.

"And I don't want to lose you, honey, not even for the freedom of a million people. There must be another way! You must be patient and wait for a better opportunity. Why do we even care about these people in Cuba? My parents are from Poland, but I wouldn't go back there to bomb the Russians or the Germans or anyone. I'm an American and so are you! If I fight, I fight for America! If you fight, it should only be for America!" Fresh tears began to flow down her cheeks.

Charlene had come to accept the inevitable. She realized that Charlie's friendship for Ron transcended any danger or logic she could construct. Charlene saw that this was an opportune moment to ask a question that might ease the tension.

"Ronnie, tell us more about the plane you will be flying. Is it a jet or a propeller plane? Have I seen one of them at the airport?"

"It's a B-26, Charlene. The aircraft has two large engines and was used as a bomber in World War II. I don't know exactly which model we will be flying, but they probably have been upgraded to increase their range. They cruise at about 280 miles an hour and should have a range of about 1500 miles. I could be off some, but that should be close.

"You probably saw one in a Jimmy Stewart war movie. When we get back, we can go to one of those flicks so that you can see what Charlie was in for. Anyway, it goes far enough so that Charlie shouldn't have to swim for shore. By the way, Charlie, did you bring your water wings just in case we run out of fuel?"

A warm smile spread across Ron's face as he noticed that Lottie had relaxed somewhat.

"As if water wings would help me!" laughed Charlie as he reached over and slapped Ron on the back. "I'd sink like a rock. Whenever I'd go to the quarry to swim, I'd have to bring an inner tube with me to keep afloat. Maybe I should go back to the garage and get one for this trip."

"No, you won't need your floating giraffe on this trip, Charlie. Jack assured me that we would have full open-water survival gear, which means a sturdy raft with food and clothing and a radio with flares and shark repellant, too. You won't have to swim even if we ditch in the Gulf of Mexico, if that's where we're going!"

Charlie moved closer to Charlene and put his arm around her. "Hey, honey, I wouldn't go if I thought we wouldn't come back in one piece. I've got the best pilot in the Air Force and a real good plane."

Then Charlie turned to Lottie.

"I wouldn't let Ron go on this thing if I thought the risk was too high. This plane is heavy and slow, but Castro has only limited air defenses and no modern aircraft. And, remember this, we're just backup for the expatriate pilots who will be doing the real work. By the time we get into Cuban airspace, the Cuban air force will have been destroyed."

"Besides, the plane is slow for a reason," added Ron when he saw that Lottie's mood was improving, even if only slightly. "It's built like a flying tank. The actual loss rate in combat was about one in a thousand in World War II, and the enemy had some real anti-aircraft capabilities. That's better odds than driving from here to the farm safely!"

Lottie had a question for Charlie Bill.

"Charlie, where in Guatemala are you going?"

"The field we will fly out of is probably somewhere near the Gulf of Honduras. We won't know until we get there. Too much security."

Charlene looked puzzled.

"What do the Guatemalans have to say about this?"

"You'll have to ask the CIA. They have plenty of small, hidden airfields over there. The average Guatemalan probably isn't even aware that they exist. From there, a force could reach anything in the Caribbean and Central America. The CIA is like an octopus with tentacles stretching all over the region. Now we get to see it first hand and get paid big bucks at the same time!"

Lottie moved over closer to Ron and whispered in his ear.

"I'll be here waiting for you, honey. Just complete one good and safe flight, and then bring yourself and Charlie back to us. We'll be here waiting for you!"

10

Comrades in Arms

Let us hasten, friends,
to terminate the Revolution.
He who makes it last too long
Will not gather the fruits.

—John Reed, *Ten Days that shook the World*

The Florida Everglades

The Florida sun beat down on the five men as they made their way through the tall grasses of the central Everglades. Raymond Chacon was not the oldest, but he was the leader. The members of the patrol were dressed in military fatigues and armed with M1 rifles and .45 caliber handguns.

Alberto, Edgar and Tomas wielded machetes as the thin line flowed silently through the swampy underbrush. As they moved, hand signals were exchanged to execute course changes. Alberto and Tomas each carried sections of two collapsible rafts, which the patrol used to cross the watery barriers they encountered.

As Raymond signaled a halt to give his men a rest, he looked back at Rene who was searching the horizon with his binoculars.

"How far back were Levon and Rico when we crossed the swamp?" There was a definite trace of concern in the Captain's voice.

"I'd estimate ten minutes," Rene replied as he kept up his vigil, "but, those boys can travel faster than the rest of us. I would have expected them by now."

"It's another thirty minutes to the base camp, Rene. I have a meeting with Frank Campa and one of the officers of the ship that will deploy us. After that, don't forget, we have a dinner appointment with Oscar. He wants to see all of you before we disembark. Make sure that the men get to Hialeah after they clean up."

Raymond looked at his charges with a feeling of pride. These men were not only well trained, but they were his friends.

"Rene, I only wish that Fernando and Luis were here with us. Oscar and I have tried everything we know to locate them."

"Sir, Tomas and I tried our best to find Fernando. For the last two years Tomas has talked to him about once a week on the telephone. He lives in Houston. Then, without a word, he lost contact. Fernando's family and friends in Texas have no idea where he is. I'm worried about him."

"We will have to try again, Rene. Luis has also vanished. It's just not like him!"

All of a sudden, Rene's frame stiffened, as he strained to see through the waving grasses of the Everglades.

"It's Rico! He's double-timing toward us. But, he's alone! I don't see Levon! Something must be wrong!"

Raymond jumped up and studied the distant figure as he made maximum speed toward their position.

Raymond turned and looked back through the tall brush toward the place where the rest of his men were waiting some twenty yards away. They were busily cleaning their weapons and celebrating the successful conclusion of this final training mission.

"Here he comes, Captain! He's exhausted!"

Rico stumbled into the small clearing where Rene and Raymond were standing. He dropped his rifle to the ground and fell to his knees, his hands trembling as he looked up."

"Are you okay, Rico? What is it? Where's Levon?" Raymond asked his questions as he knelt down next to the shaken soldier.

"Levon is dead! Dead! They killed him! They shot at me and chased me, but…"

Rene jumped back up and surveyed the horizon through the binoculars as Raymond tried to determine what had happened.

"Tell me, Rico! Where is Levon?"

The soldier caught his breath and attempted to stand with Raymond's help. He then pointed into the grasses to the west.

"We completed our crossing of the swamp and removed our trail markings. Levon went back to retrieve the raft when I heard several incoming rounds and Levon's cries for help. I dropped my gear and ran back to his position. He was sprawled on the ground. He had taken several hits in the back."

Rico paused to catch his breath as he removed his canteen. He pointed to a sharp indentation on the side.

"They fired three rounds at me while I was on the ground with Levon! One grazed my canteen. When I felt the round, I just ran! There was no cover!"

"Did you see who was engaging you? Could you see anyone?"

"No, Sir! I remembered your advice. If you're outnumbered and out-gunned, get out! That probably saved my life!"

Rico was beginning to cry now that the gravity of the situation had set in. He pounded his fist into the ground several times.

"Who would do such a thing. This is a training exercise! Levon's dead!"

Raymond consoled the heartbroken soldier as he helped him to his feet. Then he turned to Rene.

"Alert the men! We're going back for Levon!"

Then he turned back to Rico.

"You'll have to lead us back to Levon's position. I have a bad feeling that someone knows about our mission and doesn't want us to complete it!"

11

A Gathering of Eagles

Tyranny, like hell,
is not easily conquered;
yet, we have this
consolation with us,
that the harder the conflict,
the more glorious the triumph.

—**Thomas Paine,** *American Crisis*

Eastern Guatemala

The old station wagon roared up the one lane trail to the crest of a hill that commanded an excellent view of the surrounding tropical vegetation. The driver was a young boy of sixteen who was familiar with the local geography. He brushed his long damp hair out of his face as he stopped the vehicle at an overgrown crossroad. There he carefully checked for other traffic.

Two passengers were riding in the back seat. The boy held the station wagon back as if he were waiting for something to happen. Finally, the driver saw what he was looking for; two armed men emerged from the brush and approached the vehicle. They were dressed in military fatigues, but their general appearance told the passengers that they were not regular army.

The boy leaped from the station wagon and ran quickly toward the men. After a short conversation in Spanish, they waived the driver on as they resumed their positions in the jungle. Quickly, the driver jumped into the wagon and sped down the backside of the hill.

Five minutes of twists and turns brought the vehicle to the bottom of a broad valley, next to what appeared to be an old aircraft hangar. With little hesitation the driver exited the front seat and opened the rear door to unload the luggage. The passengers stepped out of the vehicle with some hesitation as they attempted to remove the mud that had covered them during their bumpy ride through the rain soaked jungle.

"Gentlemen, please wait in this building," stated the boy in excellent English. "Someone will be along shortly to guide you to the command center. It has been a pleasure, but I must leave immediately. May the rest of your journey be a safe and pleasant one."

The passengers expressed their thanks and as the vehicle returned to the trail, they picked up their suitcases and walked into the hangar. It was still dark, but they could see the outline of a large aircraft directly ahead of them.

In a few steps Ron found himself walking around the fuselage of a B-26 bomber. It had been quite a while since he had touched a military aircraft of this size with his own two hands. And, he was betting that his partner probably had never even seen one of these monsters close up.

"She's in good shape, Charlie. Actually, she's in great shape for being so old," offered Ron as he inspected the exterior of the plane. "Someone's been taking care of her. Someone's been taking real nice care of her! I've got to meet the mechanics assigned to this one. You can tell it's been a labor of love."

The view of the jungle became surreal as the rays of the rising sun reflected off of the metallic surfaces of the aircraft, which almost seemed to be coming alive, breathing in the warm equatorial air and stretching her wings. It was the realization of a fantasy for Ron Hernandez. This war bird was ready to go wherever he might lead her.

The B-26 was not as sleek as modern jet warplanes, but it did look nasty from any angle. Slow, but nasty! The meanness, which emanated and radiated from the plane, was somehow reassuring to two men who had never flown a combat mission.

"Looks like this hangar and these storage and repair areas have been here for a quite a while, doesn't it?" Ron remarked. "And, most of these signs are in English. That's very interesting! English here in the middle of Central American. Is this an old U.S. airbase?"

"Not exactly. This was one of the first places outside the States that the CIA began to operate. The kid who drove us wouldn't talk about it, but he didn't have to. He was definitely a Company man. I did notice that the entrance had no identifying signs other than the usual trespass warnings. And no flags, no military markings anywhere. I'm not even sure which country we're in, Honduras or Guatemala."

Ron turned toward the plane and pointed to the near side.

"And look at this! Cuban markings! This isn't an F.A.R. plane. You know what I mean, Charlie, *Revolutionary Air Force*. These have been refitted in the States, and these markings have been added more recently. It sure looks like a fresh paint job. No, our employers have been here long enough to provoke some of their hosts."

"I'm sure that the Guatemalans don't like this arrangement any more than Castro does, but sometimes help comes from the most unpredictable sources."

Ron was curious about the relationships involved here, and he knew that Charlie could provide some of the answers.

"Charlie, what do you know about all this? And don't give me that classified or need to know crap!"

"Most of my work has been in Europe. But I do know that the Cuban expatriate pilots based in this area helped the Guatemalans suppress an attempted coup fairly recently. I wouldn't be surprised if this baby was used to put that rebellion down. The winners are glad that we're here. It's Castro's and Guevara's pals who might object to us."

Ron nodded. "I see what you mean. Today is a perfect example of why he might not like us being here, wherever *here* is!"

Charlie continued. "If we can locate the flight logs, they will tell us a lot. I'll bet this plane has had plenty of training flights in the last year although it doesn't look like she's been over Cuba yet. No bullet holes that I can see! Your friend Jack has probably been saving this baby for you."

"Nothing like planning ahead," countered Ron as he walked toward the hangar door. Charlie quickly followed him.

"Let's see if anyone else is around, Charlie."

Charlie squinted as he scanned the rest of the field. At first he couldn't see any obvious signs of human activity. But, he soon came to understand why. The jungle had covered and embraced the fuel facilities, the hangars, the control towers and the other artifacts that typified an airfield.

"They must have anticipated launching operations like this a long time ago. It certainly couldn't be located in a better place, and the cover is incredible. The Cubans don't have anything with sufficient range to attack a place like this. And reconnaissance is almost impossible."

"Everyone knows the Cubans have B-26's," added Ron, "but those old birds probably haven't been upgraded since the war, and they might make it here, but they probably would have serious trouble getting back. Even if Castro could find this operation, he probably is incapable of attacking it by air."

Ron turned back to take another look at the plane. It was like a dream for him. In all of his years in the Air Force and as a commercial pilot, he never felt more like flying a plane than at this moment. And, he hoped that this particular one would be the one he would fly into combat. His instant love for this B-26 was difficult to hide, especially from his friend Charlie Bill.

"This one should be in a museum, Charlie. It's a perfect specimen! Enemy guns haven't laid a scratch on this baby. Let's hope it stays that way! Let's hope that Jack lets us fly this one today."

Charlie's eyes swept across the underbelly of the B-26 as he concurred with an enthusiastic nod. After a complete visual inspection of the exterior of the plane, Charlie turned and pointed across the field.

A small two-story structure was buried in the far edge of the jungle. A narrow stream ran along the north side with small bushes and irregularly spaced trees spread around the perimeter. These features were supplemented by a large clump of vegetation directly in the center of the field. From the air this field looked more like a racetrack than a landing field. The jungle's secret was also protected by the almost continuous cloud cover characteristic of this part of Central America.

"Hey!" yelled Charlie. "Look at those three over there. I couldn't see them when we first got here. But, now they look like a covey of hawks hiding under a hedge."

Ron confirmed the presence of several similar B-26 models poised and ready for action in camouflaged hangers far across the field. The two men also noticed eight other hangars that seemed empty. Ron pointed across the field toward the unoccupied hangars.

"I'll bet those birds are over Cuba right now! I wonder if they're coming back here or going to the Keys or Dominican Republic on their return trip? It isn't absolutely essential, but I would like to get some firsthand intelligence from the pilots. They've been over the target a few times and must have a pretty good idea of the defenses we'll be encountering."

"Do you think that they've started the air campaign already?" asked Charlie.

"I'm almost certain of it," answered Ron in a confident tone. "Otherwise, those hangars wouldn't be empty."

Ron's thoughts drifted back to the aircraft standing behind him. He felt privileged to have had some flight experience in this model. Little wonder that the boys at the Company had contacted him for this mission. The Cuban expatriates had too few pilots in any case and almost none who were really comfortable with this plane. Officially nicknamed the *Marauder* in World War II, it was also known to the members of the U.S. Air Force as the *Widow Maker*. The old B-26 wasn't very forgiving of pilot error.

It had been a quirk of fate that gave Ron his experience in the B-26. While stationed in Florida and then again when he was in Mississippi, hurricanes had threatened several nearby bases. These storms posed a major threat to aircraft on the ground, and a quick turn in the storm could put many aircraft in jeopardy in a short period of time. When he volunteered to help transport some of the older planes to safety, the Air Force quickly took advantage of his interest.

He picked up the necessary skills rather easily. So after the first set of storms had passed, he got plenty of hours in the old birds, many with combat pilots experienced from World War II. It was almost a religion to them. Ron enjoyed their war stories, and he found that the more he appreciated the old aircraft, the more the veterans would confide in him. When they began to show confidence and trust him with the older planes, he knew that he had been admitted to a very special club.

So now I get my reward! he thought. *I still remember the good news about these planes; they can take a hit or two and keep going. That may be a serious advantage on this mission.*

Suddenly, Ron and Charlie detected someone coming up quietly behind them.

"She's a beauty, isn't she! Jack said you would like her. She's the best of the group. You can't even tell that she's taken a few rounds in the belly."

The voice was that of their military contact, a warrant officer with a grizzly beard and worn uniform. Ron smiled and enthusiastically shook hands with the new arrival. It was someone he had met before.

"Paul Simpson! Great to see you! What are you doing in the fucking jungle? Hey, this is my good friend, Charlie Bill. He's an Air Force type, too."

Paul and Charlie shook hands. Unfortunately, Paul had some bad news for his old friend.

"The current situation doesn't look too promising, boys. There are heavy clouds over Havana, and we have no other reliable info from anywhere except Guanta'namo Naval Base. It's raining there, but they say it should clear in a few hours. We're just not sure about the local weather in the individual target areas."

"Is it just the two of us, Paul, or do we get some help? You know that we really need a crew of five or six."

"I'm not sure. We're pretty shorthanded. This thing came up faster than we anticipated and the lid is real tight. The Cuban pilots have been working eighteen hours on and we've lost a few. Your names were pretty high on a short list so I know the powers that be are glad you're here. The Company boys will be around in an hour or so. They've had a long shift, too. We had a lull after midnight so they took off to get some sleep a couple miles down the road. We've got some air conditioning down there."

Paul paused while he observed several locals carrying boxes on their shoulders hustling across the entrance to the hangar.

"You're scheduled to check out at 1400 hours and go between 1600 and 1800. I know that they were looking for ten volunteer aircrews. Several crews from Texas arrived yesterday. You're the only ones I've seen so far this morning. How about some…"

Before Paul could finish, the blast of a warning alarm filled the air and the airfield sprang to life in front of them. Several small trucks sped out of the vegetation and began racing along the perimeter. The activity was centered at the far end of the field. Paul squinted as he looked into the rising sun.

"There she is! It's a 26, and she's in trouble! Quick, let's get up on the roof. It's best if we stay out of the way. The rescue crews are already on it."

Paul led the way straight to a metal stairway that reached to the top of the building. It was old and rusty, but appeared capable of holding the weight of the three men. The roof was constructed of several large sheets of aluminum siding topped with layers of debris from the forest. It was a natural form of camouflage.

Paul was the first to step onto the structure. He turned back and offered some assurances.

"It's okay, boys. We play tennis up here when things are slow. This thing can easily hold twenty of us. Okay, maybe only ten, but it's sturdier than it looks!"

He motioned for his companions to follow him as Charlie and Ron stepped gingerly across the top of the building. After a few steps came confidence, and they were able to focus on the events unfolding on the field below.

"There it is!" yelled Charlie. "Smoke! Isn't she coming in a little low?"

"She'll make it, Charlie," offered Ron with some optimism. "At least she's level. Just another few seconds, and she'll be over the field."

As it cleared the edge of the field, the plane wobbled slightly and then began its final descent from about two hundred feet. Smoke continued to pour out of the starboard engine. The pilot dropped the plane onto the dirt and held on as the ship bounced several times before rolling steadily down the runway. Two emergency trucks were in close pursuit. The men could now see flames issuing from the smoking engine.

"Look at the vertical stabilizer," said Charlie as he followed the path of the plane with his binoculars. "It's full of holes big enough for cannon balls! What kind of ordinance are they using against us?" Charlie was clearly excited and a little unnerved by the sight.

"No problem, Charlie. She's holding together like a champ! Four hundred miles with those gigantic holes in her! These old airframes can sure take a pounding and come back for more!"

Once the ship rolled to a halt, the two emergency vehicles sprang into action. Two men in fire safety gear began working to control the fire in the engine. This B-26 was fitted with four, one hundred-gallon fuel cells in each wing, one outside and three in-board the engine nacelle. The cells were of the Mareng type, which meant they were self-sealing, but the ground crew was taking no chances.

The first crewmember to emerge was the tail gunner. He jumped from a small hatch underneath the port tail-plane. All eyes were fixed on the nose-wheel bay. In seconds, members of the ground crew raced to a position under the bay, out of view of the observers on the roof of the hangar.

The intervening seconds seemed like minutes to Ron and his companions. Finally, the three remaining crewmembers emerged from the bay with help from their rescuers.

The flaming engine was sprayed with gray-colored foam as black oily smoke curled up into the sky. A makeshift ambulance and three additional emergency vehicles arrived on the scene. One of the crewmembers was placed on a stretcher, but he seemed to be in reasonably good shape.

The ground crews had acted with incredible speed. The engine fire was already under control, and a bulldozer was beginning to spread gravel across the damaged portions of the runway.

Ron turned to Charlie as the excitement subsided.

"Let's hope we have better luck!"

12

Darkest Before the Dawn

*A constant naval superiority
upon these coasts is the
subject most interesting.
This would instantly
reduce the enemy to a
difficult defensive.*

—General George Washington

South of the Zapata Peninsula

It was just before midnight as the shadows slid silently through the warm Caribbean waters south of Central Cuba. The first vessel turned to the north and was followed like a ghost by a second, somewhat larger silhouette and then by a third. Some randomly spaced clouds provided precious little cover as the vessels glided over the nighttime waters. The *Marsopa*, the *Houston* and the *Rio Escondido* wore no national markings or identifications as they made their way to their uncertain meeting with destiny.

As the motley armada came within sight of mainland Cuba, the ships took up flanking positions and waited for a timetable of events to unfold. They arrived at their destination about forty-five minutes ahead of schedule. The overall plan had allowed for up to a two-hour weather delay so the promptness of their appearance gave the men ample time to check their equipment and break up into landing teams for last minute briefings.

Aboard the command ship *Marsopa*, preparations were under way for the initial phase of the invasion. Weapons were readied for combat while food and medical supplies were being distributed. Aboard the *Houston*, communications gear was positioned for loading into small boats strapped to the side of the ship. Everything was proceeding according to plan.

The invasion force, *Brigade 2506*, was mostly a ragtag band of Cuban expatriates led directly by Cubans and indirectly by Americans. The uniforms of the invaders were irregular and, in most cases, incomplete, but the troops were relatively well armed and very eager to proceed. All told, these ships, along with several smaller vessels, carried a complement of approximately twelve hundred troops and a smaller number of support personnel whose morale was high.

As the main force waited to commence the landing phase, eight men began executing the first elements of their secret mission. Quietly, in the darkness of this April night, they carefully made their way down heavy rope ladders which hung over the side of the Marsopa like a spider's web. Below in the calm Caribbean waters, a large patrol boat listed against the waves. It held two smaller rafts equipped with food, communications gear and ammunition.

Once the squad was aboard, the craft moved away from the *Marsopa* to the east on a course roughly parallel with the shoreline. The minutes passed slowly as the boat hummed quietly through the water until it reached a point some fifty kilometers from the invasion force. No other vessels were encountered during the journey. The coastline was dark, and the gathering clouds kept the mission undetected.

The eight men dispersed into the rafts with a silent efficiency. The patrol boat held its position in the darkness until the two rafts quietly slipped out of sight.

Raymond Chacon was very familiar with these waters. After all, he had lived most of his life just a few kilometers to the east. As a boy, he had grown up in a small coastal village near Cienfuegos where his grandfather had been a fisherman, and Raymond spent much of his youth in the Caribbean searching for the schools of fish, which would provide his family with a steady stream of income and food.

Whenever he touched these waters, he thought of his youth and of the stories passed down to him by his grandfather. Some were just myths or fables that had survived the generations. Others were genuine history in the making. He was particularly moved by the stories that described the battles for Cuban independence. He had first captured his sense of history and his dislike of President Ulysses Grant from the legends of the Ten Years' War and the struggles of the late 1800's.

Raymond knew that Grant was the American president who was presented with the perfect opportunity to bring North and South America together in a common cause to eliminate slavery from Cuba and free it from the shackles of Spanish rule. The proposed compromise would have reimbursed Spain, and no lives would have been lost. But Grant vetoed the plan and planted the seeds of distrust of America among the modern generations of Cubans. Raymond wondered whether this invasion would just add more turmoil and confusion to the island's already treacherous history.

Raymond had placed Alberto in command of the lead raft mainly because he was the most experienced sailor in the group and also because Alberto was very familiar with the shoreline in this region. His passengers were Frank Campa and Carlos Rumbart along with Raymond's longtime friend, Edgar Hernandez. Campa had handpicked Rumbart for this mission as the replacement for Levon Valdez. Valdez had been killed in the Everglades training exercise, and his killer remained unidentified.

Raymond took his place in the rear of the second raft. He put Rene in command of this craft, which also carried Hector and Tomas. From this trailing vantage point, Raymond could easily keep an eye on both rafts.

As he reviewed the plan for his mission, Raymond's mind sped eastward to Cienfuegos. It was a bigger town now, set back into the mainland by a large bay. Most of Raymond's family had lived in or near this town, and he was a frequent visitor to his cousins' homes on the eastside of the bay. He had played on the southern beaches and hiked through the nearby hills. He wondered what two years of revolutionary government had done to his hometown.

Suddenly, the Captain's thoughts were interrupted when he felt Tomas tapping him on the shoulder.

"Raymond, I think we're being followed," Tomas whispered as he pointed back over his leader's shoulder. "I see the glint of a torch or flashlight every few seconds. We should check it out before we proceed."

"I see it, Tomas!" Raymond confirmed. "Rene, signal Alberto to come about. We appear to have company! Tell him to hold his position while we investigate."

Rene nodded and signaled the lead raft. Rene then brought the trailing raft about and waited for Raymond's signal. Tomas and Hector readied their weapons. Cautiously, the Captain directed Rene to advance toward the craft that was steadily approaching.

Raymond carefully studied the vessel through his binoculars. It appeared to hold two fishermen who seemed to be unarmed. An old man in foul weather gear was standing forward in the stout fishing boat, which appeared to measure some twelve meters in length. He was holding a lantern, which he was swinging back and forth.

"Militia! Militia!" he shouted over the groan of his engine and the wash of the sea. "I have a report for the Militia!"

"It's Felix Gonzales and his grandson," whispered Rene. "We can't let them recognize us!"

"What is your business?" yelled Raymond with some authority as he tried to muffle his voice.

"Commander! I have seen several large vessels heading for the shoreline and running without lights! And, they are not flying the revolutionary colors! I believe that a foreign force is attacking! I have counted at least five large ships with many troops!"

"Calm yourself, Citizen!" yelled Raymond with authority. "There is no reason for alarm. This is a training exercise!"

"What do you mean, Sir? Were those our ships we saw to the west?"

"Yes, Citizen! We are training for a possible invasion. Haven't you heard of the bombings near Santiago?"

"Sir, I have heard many things this day. Bombings, invasions, and all the rest that goes with such stories! One man even told me that Havana has been occupied by the Americans! I did not put much stock in such rumors until I saw the ships!"

"You have not seen an enemy invasion, Citizen. Tonight we have a secret exercise. Many thousands of militia are involved. The landing is occurring on The Zapata. Our patrol is conducting an infiltration of Cienfuegos and Camp Columbia. The militia members who are defending are trying to find our location. So, we would appreciate your cooperation. It is their task to find us by their own wit and reckoning."

"Oh, I am so sorry that I have delayed you, Sir. My son and I will not speak of our meeting. Allow me to douse this light so that I am not the cause of your detection."

"We thank you, Citizen! We must now leave you for our objective."

"Have we met before, Commander? Your voice is very familiar to me."

"I am from Havana. It is unlikely that we have met. However, it is a pleasure to meet you. Have a good catch and a safe return!"

With a wave, Raymond ordered the raft to come about and resume its easterly voyage. After a few minutes Raymond scanned the western horizon and breathed a sign of relief.

"My God, that was close!" whispered Raymond to Tomas. "Luckily, Felix does not have the eagle eyes he once possessed when you and I were children, or he would have recognized us. You did well spotting them when you did. I don't know how we would have dealt with them had they identified us. Let's get to our landing point before we encounter any more helpful fishermen or real militia!"

The team continued to move swiftly, but carefully, along the shoreline. Several other small fishing boats were detected slowly plying in and out of the harbors that dotted the coast. Although no armed Cuban naval vessels were encountered, several groups of Cuban Militia were sited manning seacoast positions. The lack of activity at these positions led Raymond to believe that the main invasion force still possessed the element of surprise.

As the patrol reached a particularly dark section of shoreline, Alberto executed a turn toward the beach. Quietly, the two rafts landed on the marshy coastline near the mouth of a creek that trickled into the Caribbean Sea. The creek marked a point about seven kilometers west of the Girard Chemical Complex. The location was particularly suitable for hiding the landing craft and any cargo the patrol might acquire. The shoreline along the creek held dense vegetation and was backed by rock formations and rolling hills. It was a perfect base camp location.

The group brought the rafts ashore and hid their supplies in the brush about twenty meters inland. There was still no sign of hostile forces, and the thickening clouds provided much needed cover from the air. Once the equipment was secure, Frank Campa approached Raymond and Rene. The look on his face telegraphed his approval.

"A job well done, Captain! Your men are a credit to you. And Rene! This cove was an excellent choice. We should be quite secure here. As you can see, Carlos and I are anxious to observe the complex and find the bunker."

"As soon as the perimeter is secured, we will send a reconnaissance patrol to the complex and set up a communications link with the command ship. We need firsthand information on the main landing. As far as the chemical complex goes, I would hope that the reputation of the place has been enough to keep the locals and militia out while we've been gone."

"I'd like to go with the recon patrol if you don't mind, Captain," said Campa.

"I'll send two men with you, Frank. Observe the site for half an hour, then get back here. The sun is coming up, so we'll have to be careful. Cuban aircraft will be over this area once they discover the landing. We will lay low until sundown, then go to the bunker. At the same time, two men will infiltrate Cienfuegos. We need to know how much support the main force can expect."

"It's a good plan, Raymond. Let's make it work and hope that our brothers up the beach are having some success."

13

The Moment of Truth

Who sees these dismal heaps,
but would demand,
what barbarous invader
sack'd the land?

—Sir John Denham

Langley Field, Virginia

It was a dreary and overcast spring day as Colonel Jack Sheehan and his aide, Captain Robert Ross sat inside a second floor conference room with several other Air Force officers waiting for the meeting to begin. They had arrived at the building near the center of Langley Field over an hour earlier.

"If we sit around here long enough, Colonel, the fucking war will be over before we can do anything useful!"

The two men had worked together for most of their Air Force careers and each had developed a distinct dislike for certain other governmental agencies.

"I wouldn't worry about it, Rob. I was in this building about two weeks ago getting clearance for this meeting, and it still took me fifteen minutes and three security badges to get in here this morning."

"Sir, I never did ask you whether you ran into any of my old friends on your recruiting mission."

"Why, I believe I did!" replied the Colonel. "In Missouri I ran into Charlie Bill. I can never remember that boy's last name. He's teaming up with Ron Hernandez."

"Ah, good old Charlie. He's a piece of work! Never met anyone who knew so much about so many people. And, geography! He can sit down and draw a map of the United States, to scale, with all the major cities and State capitols."

Rob looked around the room and spotted what he had been looking for. The attendant had arrived with more food for the refreshment table. The group of CIA agents was busily conducting its own private meeting at the far end of the room.

"Say, Colonel, I'm getting another donut before the action begins. A sugar high is always good when you're in company territory, and it makes you look and feel normal, too. Do you want one?"

"Sure, why not?" replied the colonel with a smile. "My diet isn't working anyway. But, hurry up, the general should be here soon!"

As Rob returned to the table with the coffee and donuts, an Air Force General entered the room with several civilians and his presence brought everyone to attention. After some informal introductions, the committee members took seats at the table, and the door was secured. The General, seated at the head of the table, reached into a folder he was carrying and passed copies of a condensed intelligence report around the room.

"Well, he's finally come out of the closet. We were right all the time about the bastard!"

The speaker was one of the CIA agents, and he directed his comments to no one in particular. The puzzled look on Rob's face begged for a more detailed explanation.

"It's Castro, Captain Ross. He's defined his revolution as socialist. All that time in college and in jail and in the woods must have affected his mind adversely. The Yankees wouldn't let him pitch at the Stadium so he wants to take on Uncle Sam just to prove himself. He's just begging us to invade his little sugar and cigar kingdom."

The speaker scanned several reports he was holding in search of a particular phrase. When he found it, he stared right at Captain Ross and continued.

"Here's the quote. '...*right here under their very noses or to see how we have made a revolution, a socialist revolution, right here under the very nose of the United States.*'"

"He's big on noses!" muttered one of the CIA agents. "With that beard he's wearing, it's hard to see his nose."

Some laughter spread through the room until the General waived his hand in a manner that brought the meeting back into a serious vein.

"Comments?" The general looked down the length of the table.

"He is asking for it, you know," replied one of the other CIA officials. "It will take some courage for the President to back off of this one. But a war with Cuba at this late stage could be a lose-lose situation. All of Latin America is watching and waiting to judge us by our actions."

"And especially after President Quadros of Brazil sticks his two cents in and offers to arbitrate our differences," countered one of the military commanders.

"Talk about a dumb politician! Here's a guy who can't balance his checkbook, and he's going to broker world peace. Someone should tell him that this is no game for amateurs!"

One of the other CIA agents shook his head slowly in mild disagreement.

"Brazil is not the problem for us. Quadros has just taken office there, and he wants to make an impact. Those people in South America don't pay attention to their elected leaders, anyway. Our problem is the Big Red Machine. The Russians!"

The officer listened intently and then offered a rebuttal.

"I can't disagree, Fred, but I'm not sure the Russians are as dangerous as we make them out to be. With the history they've had, it's no wonder they are paranoid. They would put a buffer state on the moon if they could get there. And I'm not sure I'd blame them.

"And remember this important fact," the officer continued, "they may have bombs, but their economy is not built for world domination. They don't have the means to supply a fighting force operating half way around the world."

At this point another civilian entered the room and listened to the tail end of the conversation. After he took a seat next to the general, he glanced at the agenda and then proceeded to address the group.

"Okay, let's get down to business," he said quietly. "We can analyze and speculate on international relations later. What do we have on the air campaign, if anything?"

Rob thought it was a good time to get some answers he needed to complete his assignments. He directed his question to his commanding officer.

"General, I've seen another report concerning the bombings near Santiago. Was that one of ours or one of theirs?"

Rob looked directly at the general as he spoke, but his tone was soft and not aggressive. No one answered immediately, and the question seemed to hang in the air.

The general turned toward the civilians.

"Mr. Hull, do you have any additional information on the D-2 raids?"

"No sir. You have as much information as we do. The plan was to begin some strategic bombing on the fifteenth and again on the sixteenth. This was to be coordinated with leaflet dropping over the major cities and then by the invasion on the seventeenth."

"Are you referring to raids using aircraft like the one shown in this photo on the front page of our favorite newspaper?" The respondent was an older man who had obviously been with the Company for quite a while.

"I wouldn't be surprised if Castro has a subscription to this rag. Where else could he get such good intelligence."

He paused as he scanned the paper.

"They would have to show the front of the ship!" the man continued as he looked at the photograph. "And I hate to see us shooting holes in a perfectly good B-26. And look, the guns are clean as a whistle. No reason to get them dirty in combat! As a taxpayer, I'm mortified! Shooting holes in our own planes!"

The man slid the paper to the middle of the table so that the other members could see the photograph. Despite his feelings that this was not the time for humor, Hull continued his answer to the original question.

"She has F.A.R. markings. She sure looks like one of Castro's B-26s. He does have B-26s, doesn't he?" The sarcasm in his voice was clear to all.

Jack Sheehan had already known the answer to the question. He was one of the Air Force officers assigned as a consultant to Operation Zapata. In spite of this, Jack did not have privy to all of the details of the operation, and he was especially blind on those aspects of the invasion that were planned and executed by the CIA.

He felt it advisable not to make his personal feelings known in the atmosphere that prevailed at the meeting and before people he didn't know or trust. And not to his fellow officers either. His many years of political experience with these agencies told him that this was no time to make new enemies or confuse his friends. But, it made him uneasy about the whole situation when he learned of the D-2 bombing raids in Cuba. This was an action that, as far as he knew, had not been recommended by the Air Force or endorsed by the President or Congress.

He glanced at the picture again to confirm his suspicions. *There was so much damaging information in that photograph!*

"Who was the pilot? Do you know him, Jack?" The voice was that of the civilian sitting at the head of the table.

"No, Sir!" Jack replied. "Let me see if he's identified in the article."

Jack Sheehan read a few sentences on the front page article and then held up the New York Times to display the man's silhouette.

"Mario Zuniga, Sir. He says he's a defector. A defector from the Cuban Revolutionary Air Force"

"Yeah! And he probably defected from Guatemala or Nicaragua, not Cuba," commented one of the other CIA members. "That's not the only problem. Now Castro has all of the information he needs. He can tell the population that General Batista is attempting a comeback."

Jack thought about the situation from a economic point of view. *Why should we care if Cuba is socialist or communist? As long as they weren't arming for an attack, it wouldn't matter!*

"General, I'd like to repeat something I put in my summary report for Operation Zapata."

"Go right ahead, Jack. We need all of the information we can get."

"It involves economics, Sir. As long as Cuba is not a military threat to us, why should it matter whether they are socialist or communist?"

"It's too late for that, Jack," the general replied. "We've launched an invasion, and we have to see it through. Let's get back to this defector."

Jack looked at the photo again. There was something about the nose of the plane. *That's what they meant by the front of the plane! It's opaque.*

Jack searched his memory. He remembered the old B-26's which were placed in Cuba after World War II. They all had clear nose sections. It was highly probable that only the American B-26s had been upgraded. The retrofitted nose capsules on U.S. planes of this type were all opaque. The plane flown by the supposed Cuban defector was clearly American! So much for the argument of plausible deniability!

Jack figured that it was no time be a hero, so he quietly continued to scan the intelligence report as the subject of the discussion shifted. The meeting progressed for about thirty minutes with the conversation centering on whether or not additional air support, covert, American or both, should be recommended to the President.

Mr. Hull continued.

"We have an additional group of B-26's in Nicaragua, Honduras and Guatemala. They are ready to go. The pilots are mostly Cuban, but there are a few Americans down there as backup. I suggest that we authorize them to go if the local command deems that the conditions are appropriate."

Jack thought back to the expatriate forces waiting in Central America. He wondered exactly how many Americans were now in the pilot pool down there. Most of the men he had recruited had combat training, but no real combat experience.

Jack turned to Hull.

"Sir, do you know how many of our crews are in Nicaragua and Honduras?"

Hull turned to look at Jack and noticed the worried expression on his face.

"Last report gave us ten full crews, about half American."

Jack thought of the men he had recruited. How would they come out of this? His conscience would be difficult to live with if they didn't make it back!

14

To Be or Not To Be

Had we a place to stand upon,
we might raise the world.

—Archimedes

The Caribbean Sea off of the Zapata Peninsula

It was 0430 hours and the command ship *Mariposa* slowly bobbed up and down in the waters just south of Cuba's coastline. There had been considerable activity aboard her and her sister ships. The fuzzy outline of the Zapata Peninsula was visible in the distance through a light fog. Small landing craft had been loaded and were softly buzzing toward the beaches. A general sense of optimism pervaded most of the officers and men of *2506 Brigade*.

On the makeshift bridge of the *Marsopa*, three expatriate commanders braced themselves against the choppy movements of the shallow water. It was a moment they had planned and waited for. But for Pepe San Roman, Jose Antonio Fernandez and Gustavo Villoldo, it would be a fateful night. They did not share the outright optimism of their troops.

Gustavo was the first to express his misgivings.

"That fucking beacon from the lighthouse should have been knocked out days ago! The militia must have observers up there. And, I could swear that I see flashes coming from the beach. It's small arms fire for sure! The goddamn militia is probably sitting there, waiting for us!"

San Roman was the leader of the task force, and he had just received alarming information from a courier.

"Gentlemen! The landing force at Red Beach is reporting problems with the outboard motors. Equipment failures, no nighttime air support, a fucked up landing site! I should have never agreed to cooperate with the Americans. Never let civilians run a war!"

"Pepe, we were promised air cover at dawn. Right? Do you know how many planes we will have in the air?" The question was posed by Gustavo. "That's the key. If we get the air strikes on time, we might be okay."

"With the boats out, I haven't been able to send any troops to Green Beach," said San Roman, completely ignoring the question of air support. "And this report from Red Beach is not good. They think that one battalion made it ashore but lost most of its supplies. But they're not sure. Most of the communications gear was submerged when the boats quit, so we have no confirmation of their status.

"I can't count on Red, and we've abandoned Green. That leaves us with one hope. If Blue Beach doesn't work, we're dead! We've got to get Red Beach some help after dawn. What the hell else can go wrong?

"I understand," said Gustavo softly, "but, air cover would solve a lot of problems."

"Look, Gustavo, we just couldn't think of an instant solution for every contingency, but, rest assured, the goddamn air attacks will begin at dawn. Right now, I don't give a rat's ass about the lighthouse or the air strikes. We have a major problem with the landing craft. Most of our men are wading ashore! And, their communications equipment isn't worth a shit!"

"Sorry, Pepe, I guess I'm just nervous," replied Villoldo to San Roman in a contrite voice. "When we get the main communications site set up on shore, that should solve the intelligence problem. Jose and I are ready to go. We will make sure that you have as much information as we can gather up there."

Fernandez finally broke his silence.

"Since we're going through all the dirty laundry now, Pepe, tell me again about the popular support that is going to help us once we're established on the beachhead. The CIA seemed absolutely sure it would materialize."

San Roman spoke but was motionless. He had just reviewed another intelligence report that was not to his liking.

"You ask too many questions, my friends. How the hell am I supposed to know? Our job is to support these poor bastards up there on the beach. Fourteen hundred men, that's all we can count on! I'll bet Castro has twenty thousand facing us in two days. This popular uprising I've been hearing about better have happened yesterday, or we're fucked."

"Swan Radio is supposed to jump on the air later this morning," said Fernandez as he strained to watch the action on the beach. "What if no one's listening? They'll be too busy smoking grass and shooting at us to listen to the damn radio.

"And, then there's the beach! There is no beach here! I've told the Americans a hundred times, but they wouldn't listen. That's coral up there, not sand! And, now that the motors of the landing craft have rusted in the salt water, our men are wading to shore over that shit. It will cut them to pieces even before the militia get to them."

San Roman looked away from his companions with a look of hopelessness painted on his face.

"As you know, I would have preferred that we put ashore in Havana," he said despondently. "We'd be closer to the States, and at least we'd have some friends."

Just then another soldier ran onto the bridge with an intelligence report for the commander. He read it and shook his head in disbelief. But, he didn't share the bad news with his companions.

"Look, Castro has a long shoreline to defend!" Fernandez was trying to put a brave face on the situation. "And, even when he discovers us, he won't be sure whether or not this is just a feint designed to draw his forces away from Havana. If I were commanding his defenses, I certainly wouldn't commit my main troops against a landing of only fourteen hundred men. It would look like a fake to me. I'd probably believe that the North Americans were going to hit us somewhere else with a much bigger force."

San Roman was not impressed.

"The militia has more options. We have the element of surprise, but that will vanish very soon. We need to exploit it quickly."

Fernandez pointed toward the peninsula.

"This is a perfect spot to draw the defenders into the open. If Fidel commits his main force here, I'd hit him with everything I had in the air during the day. Then I'd land my main force near Havana. I'd have him in the bag in two days."

"Unfortunately, this is our whole force," muttered San Roman. "And, it's a crime! The Americans are missing their chance here. After we draw Castro's defense forces out, a division of marines in Havana would end it, and with few casualties and a lot of happy Cubans. All we would have to do here is engage them and make them believe that this is the main thrust.

"But, Lynch and Robertson think that this is Guatemala and that we can fake our way in! And they forgot that Arbenz was a civilian, a civilian they could remove with a hundred and fifty men. They also forgot that Castro is not a civilian!"

"I wouldn't worry about it," laughed Gustavo. "Fidel can't hit shit! He was supposed to be a big time ballplayer and look what it got him. Years in the trees and now, if he holds out, years of ducking CIA bullets and bombs. And, besides, he's dug-in over in Havana about now. I'll bet that he hit the dirt the minute he heard about those bombing runs on Saturday. If he's smart, he'll stay under his rock!"

As they talked, the landing proceeded. They could see the beach area that had been illuminated by some of the landing teams. *At least some of the Blue Beach teams seem to have made it,* Pepe thought to himself. No Cuban ships had been sited, and the air was relatively clear of aircraft. The need for ship to shore communication was critical, but with the coming of day the air attacks might cover for the mistakes made in the landing.

Jose Fernandez grabbed some equipment from the deck and slapped Villoldo on the shoulder.

"Come on, Gus. It's time to hit the beach. We've got to get that signal site running. Let's find out what kind of hold Fidel has on our people."

The two men headed for the rear of the ship. From there they watched as the remaining supplies were loaded into a small boat. San Roman followed their progress from the bridge and as they disappeared into the fog, he wondered whether he would ever see his two comrades again.

15

The Patrol

When the people contend
for their liberty,
they seldom get anything
by their victory
but new masters.

—George Savile, Marquis of Halifax

17 April 1961 near Cienfuegos, Cuba

Frank Campa anxiously checked his watch as he listened to the sounds of muffled artillery fire in the distance. It was 0950 hours, and heavy enemy air traffic along the coast had delayed his patrol to the chemical complex. Several groups of militia had been spotted on the dirt road that snaked its way along the summit, but they moved swiftly along its path, and there was no indication that the landing had been detected.

At sea, several Cuban military craft were sited moving toward the Bay of Pigs, but they were small converted fishing boats with little speed or firepower. They were also running surprisingly far from shore considering the potential of air attack by the expatriates or the U. S. Air Force.

Campa reviewed a hand-drawn map of the chemical complex. For security reasons the actual location of the bunker was not indicated. Raymond had placed several marks on the chart well away from the bunker location to divert attention away from the bunker should the map be captured. Campa had committed the actual location to memory.

At 1100 hours the patrol finally set out along the coastline toward the chemical complex. They moved slowly through the cover provided along the shoreline. Although the dirt road at the summit was not visible, they could occasionally hear groups of vehicles moving west toward the Zapata.

By 1145 hours, the group had worked its way onto the semi-circular ridge that encompassed the complex. The men now began an extended surveillance of the facility. A steady rain shower spread across the area. Birds were chattering and singing, but no human activity was observed in the complex.

As a final precaution, Edgar lobbed a large stone toward the old, rusted water tower. The projectile slammed into several sheets of aluminum siding which were lying on the ground producing enough noise to be heard across the entire complex. The four men waited for a reaction. When no movement was observed, the patrol made its way into the complex to locate the bunker.

Campa and Edgar moved down the incline to an area where they could easily pass through the old set of rusted chain-link fences that hadn't been maintained since their installation over a decade ago. Hector and Carlos Rumbart took up hidden positions on the ridge to provide cover.

Frank Campa and Edgar Hernandez moved carefully toward the base of a nearby water tower and held their position for several minutes. Next, Campa began pacing off a measured distance to the north across an old interior road and into a dilapidated chemical storage area. The roof of this building had been blown off by the coastal winds, and benches and shelving could be seen scattered inside the structure.

Campa knelt down and began digging in the soft, damp earth with a trenching tool. After about a foot of loose dirt had been removed, he hit a metallic object. In another ten minutes Campa was able to access a small porthole which provided access to a combination lock. After several attempts with the combination Raymond had supplied, the lock submitted, and Campa slowly rotated the porthole cover to the side. A mild blast of stale air rose through the opening. Campa retrieved a small flashlight from his jacket and signaled to Edgar, who carefully made his way over to the storage shed.

The volume of the structure was much larger than either had imagined. The porthole was sufficiently wide to permit Campa to enter the enclosure. He crawled down into the bunker with the aid of a steel ladder that was mounted into the concrete.

Campa was surprised by the detail and physical integrity of the bunker. Edgar looked down through the porthole and was equally impressed by the expanse of the structure.

"Batista really outdid himself with this thing," whispered Campa. Can you tell where the canisters are stored?"

"This main enclosure contains the control systems. There are several smaller rooms off to the side. That's where Raymond said the containers were stored."

Campa made his way to the southern end of the bunker and found a food storage locker, which contained dried foodstuffs and bottled drinking water. Next to that there was a climate control system while the third door opened into a complete restroom facility with showers and toilets. He returned to the central room and went to a rather large double door on the east wall.

This must be it! Campa thought. *Batista didn't build this hideout unless he had something to hide.*

As he opened the doors, he saw what he had been searching for.

"Here's part of it! I count twelve rather large storage containers and about twenty smaller ones. They do appear to be waterproof, at least enough to survive a trip to the boats."

Campa pulled one of the smaller containers along the floor but only with great difficulty.

Heavy! Very heavy! It must be gold or weapons. These containers were specially built. Couldn't have been here in Cuba.

Campa searched the outside of the plastic container for markings, which might identify the manufacturer.

Definitely European design! He concluded. *The bastard had friends everywhere.*

"Edgar! I can't open any of these. If I do, they will not be watertight. We have no way to reseal them. I'm coming back up."

After surveying several other storage rooms, Campa crawled back up the ladder and looked at Edgar.

"This is it, no question. There's not much we can do now. We'll have to come back this evening and unload it. They must have placed the larger containers inside before they completed the construction. They are much too large to get through this porthole!"

Edgar nodded. "Can you tell what's in those containers?"

"It would take us too long to find out. We'd have to unload the contents before we could do an inventory. I'd rather not stay in here too long in the daylight. If the wrong people come along, we could be trapped. Let's get back to the base camp."

Campa resealed and covered the entry hatch, and the two men made their way back out of the complex to the spot where Hector and Carlos were waiting. Campa turned to Edgar with a question that was bothering him.

"You know, Edgar, there was a lot of unused storage space in that bunker. Just glancing around, I'd say Batista had planned for about twice as much material. There were at least a dozen empty storage containers on the western end of the bunker, and they were the large ones, which were probably put there during construction. It looked like he was planning to use them for something. Do you have any ideas?"

"Sorry, Frank. All I know is that Batista played his cards close to the vest. He didn't tell any of us what he had in those containers or how many there were. It's possible that he wasn't able to get everything here in time. And, besides, it doesn't appear as though anyone found the bunker and removed anything. If someone had stumbled on the structure, they surely would have opened all of the containers."

"I guess you're right. It just seems unusual. I'll have to see if Captain Chacon has any ideas. Anyway, let's get going."

16

Changes in Latitude

Come on my sweet little thing,
What new things can you show me today?
I got one question,
I believe it's subjective,
What is a wasp without her sting?

—The Black Crowes

Eastern Guatemala

Charlie could hear footsteps coming down the hallway. As he looked around the darkened room, all he could see was the outline of his partner engaged in a deep sleep. Charlie jumped up out of his swinging bunk and began getting dressed as the footsteps entered the room. After nodding to the man in the doorway, Charlie quickly made his way out into the hallway in search of food.

"Wake up, Ron, it's almost 1900! We should know pretty soon." The warrant officer gently nudged the sleeping pilot to get his attention.

Ron was somewhat groggy and a little disoriented as he turned over and rubbed his eyes.

"Thanks. I guess I didn't think I'd be able to sleep very long in this hammock, but it's pretty darn comfortable. I'll have to get one for the farm and put it out back between those two oak trees."

As he tried to wake up, Ron realized that it was getting dark outside.

"Hey, I thought we were set to go a little after noon?"

The warrant officer took a seat on a bunk near Ron's hammock.

"Things change and so does the weather. It turned on us so we saved half the squadron for tonight. Besides, you two were sleeping so soundly, I didn't have the heart to wake you. As it stands now, you can take your time and lift off whenever you're ready, but my suggestion is that you wait until 0100 or so, then you could catch the bad guys right at dawn. It's your call."

Ron rubbed his eyes again and scanned the room for Charlie.

"Hey, where's C.B.? I could swear I dreamt that he was snoring away right over there."

"He probably was. You'll have to teach him to sleep with his mouth shut. Imagine being out in the field with him. As I remember, they used duct tape on me to keep me quiet. I learned to breathe through my nose pretty quickly!"

Paul was smiling as he remembered his training missions.

"Just put the pillow over Charlie's mouth if he's sawing logs, and he'll be up like a jack rabbit. He was here just a second ago. The boy must have been hungry, or he had too much to drink last night. My guess is he's headed for the chow line again."

"What did you make of the debriefing?" Ron said as he stood up and stretched.

"I'm not a combat veteran," said Paul as he shook his head. "But I guess if it were my country, I'd go back for a second and a third helping. It seems like you would be well advised to make only one pass over the targets. Those 26's are too slow. Surprise is your only advantage and that doesn't last very long these days."

"How true!" Ron replied in agreement. "Even a lousy shot could hit something that big and slow. And C.B. will be learning as he goes on the bombardier routine. I think he likes the prospects of the bombardier role so I told him he would do B/N on this run. I've spent some time studying the southeast coast so I think I can find the targets on the first pass. Then, with any luck we can make a run straight north to the Keys."

Ron reached for his shirt as he remembered part of the dream he had just finished.

"Do we have the water survival gear I requested? I dreamed that we were floating in the Caribbean and listening to Buddy Holly. What a gas!"

"That's the first thing I checked," answered Paul. "You can go shark hunting with impunity. If you go down, just get out into the Gulf Stream. The boys will pick you up from the beacon. There's enough food and water for a full crew for almost two weeks. If you reach Greenland, you're in trouble."

"I'm glad to hear you say something about a full crew! That must mean we'll be getting some help."

Paul shook his head positively. "We wouldn't let you get out of here without a gunner. This guy's good. He can help Charlie deliver the pay-load, and he can get you out of there if you get lost."

"So he's been over the target area before. That's a big help, especially if we go in at night. What about the other flights?"

Paul pointed toward the field.

"The first six are ready to go in the next two hours. You're last in line. Fortunately or unfortunately, the sky is clouding up again over most of the island."

Paul got up from the bunk and walked toward the door. "Let's get some dinner."

He watched as Ron slowly buttoned his shirt and reached under his swinging bunk to retrieve his boots.

"How's the landing coming along?" was Ron's next question.

"Don't ask! It doesn't look good at all. But then these things proba-bly never look good until they're over. They've lost the command ship and a support ship, and they've lost a whole bunch of backup troops at sea. Communications are tough, and the landing craft engines failed in the salt water. I guess the main problem is that there isn't any good news to report."

"Ah, Paul, you are too much of a pessimist. Charlie and I will give you some good news to give the brass."

"You can still scrub the mission, you know. It's not your country, Ron. You don't have to be a hero."

"I didn't crawl all the way down here to turn back now. And I always wanted to practice my Spanish. What better opportunity could I ever get? Let's go for it. Besides, my blood runs about one-sixth Cuban. My grandfather wouldn't like to hear that I chickened out even if he is dead. His ghost would haunt me as long as I lived."

Paul indicated his acceptance of Ron's reasoning by nodding.

"I ran over to control while you were asleep and had a little talk with several of the field agents from the Company. Those boys still think this is going to be as easy as Guatemala. From what I'm hearing that might be wishful thinking."

"Do they have all of the latest information on the landing? Maybe the invasion is getting some support from the population?"

"I seriously doubt it, Ron. Ever since the 26th of July Movement started, Fidel, Che and their boys have been nothing but trouble. Personally, I would just leave them alone because they can't be any worse than Batista."

"Yeah, but at least Havana was a fun place to go when Batista was running the place!"

"I've been in this area for quite a while, Ron, and I have my own theories on governments and political systems. In my humble opinion, to have a real democracy, you need a strong constitution…a strong set of rules that are enforceable. And the military must be under the complete control of the civilian government. Otherwise, every other military commander, or even a Sergeant like Batista, will dream of taking control of the country and establishing himself as supreme leader.

"Unless wealth and power are distributed over the various political sectors of the country, it's ripe for dictatorship. I guess that I would have to side with Socrates in a situation like this. What's needed in Cuba is a government run by a small group of very smart people. A republic without all the elections and meaningless committees. Otherwise, the turmoil will continue, and they'll never get anywhere."

As they walked toward the mess hall, Ron looked out at the fading rays of sunlight. He was beginning to feel a little nervous about the mission.

"So you believe that Castro's revolution has just replaced one tyranny with another?"

"I'm afraid so. Even if the expatriates win this battle, we'll just get another dictator. The only difference is that this one might be friendly to the U.S. And we can open the casinos in Havana again. That's actually what I'm fighting for in this little war. I love to play craps!" Paul smiled as he simulated a roll of the dice to emphasize his point.

"At least I got you one of the best!" said Paul as he pointed out toward the location of the plane. "Jose is a good kid, and he knows the area. He's been up and down in one of these so you'll have some help if you get into trouble."

They turned around a corner and entered the mess hall. Most of the crews had already eaten and were in their aircraft. The familiar sound of piston engines in the distance made Ron feel good. He was ready for this experience. Ron immediately spotted Charlie at the table by the window. One glance told Ron that his partner was ready to go, too. Charlie was absentmindedly buttering a baked potato as he watched the activity outside.

After completing the meal and sitting in the lounge area for several hours discussing the details of the mission, the trio headed back to the hangar at the far end of the field. A young airman was checking the external armaments of the aircraft and waived as soon as he saw the men approaching. The B-26 was fueled and ready to go.

After introductions the three crewmembers shook hands with Paul and boarded the plane. Jose Cruz was a Cuban expatriate from Santiago. Ron remembered seeing Jose's name in the flight log. It was nice to know that he had been up in this plane before. As it turned out, Jose had been a Company man for several years. And he had flown one of the earlier missions with some success.

Jose handed Ron the clipboard containing the pre-flight checklist.

"Captain Hernandez, I have inspected the emergency survival gear as instructed. Also, I have packed three parachutes just in case we need them. I realize that we will be at low altitudes most of the time, but I thought we all might feel better with the extra protection."

"Jose. Please call me Ron. And that guy over there is Charlie Bill. You can call him C.B. if you're nice to him. Thanks for coming along. We can certainly use your experience and knowledge of the target areas. Charlie has our passports and some currency. I'm going to finish the pre-flight and take another look at the situation map they gave us back there. We should be ready to go in about thirty minutes. If you get some time, go over the ordnance with Charlie."

"Very good, Ron. Let's hope this is fun! Do you have a list of the targets for me to look at?"

Ron pulled a folded piece of paper from his back pocket. After opening it he handed it to Jose.

"Yes. The first is a military post and airfield near Santiago de Cuba. The second is a similar site just east of Trinidad and the alternate is the Columbia Camp near Cienfuegos. Let me know if you see any problems with these."

"Thanks, I'm familiar with all of them. If we can get there near dawn, we should be able to do some damage. I'll check the ordnance and give Charlie a tour of the turret."

As Charlie and Jose climbed into the aircraft, Ron gave the outside of the plane a final once over.

Finally, the go-signal came. They would be the last to lift off from the rainforest, and it was with some relief that Ron pushed the B-26 into its takeoff position.

Their final worry had been the weather over the target area. Meteorological speculations from Miami and Kingston both indicated a reasonable probability of low hanging scattered cumulus clouds near the shore. This was good for cover from ground fire or attack by the T-33s, but target acquisition might be tough.

The old aircraft's engines shook as they came up to speed, and Ron slowly moved the bomber down the runway. It was just after midnight, and there was a slight headwind, but otherwise the rain had ceased and the sky was clear. Ron could see Paul standing near the hangar so they exchanged thumbs up gestures and salutes.

This is what I've been waiting for. Let's get it going and hope for the best.

Ron guided the B-26 down the runway and up through its slow ascent. As the plane left the ground, the engines seemed to smooth out and hum more like a spinning top than the garbage disposal they had reminded him of when he first fired them up. In minutes the Caribbean appeared below them glittering like a black blanket covered with reflected starlight. Soon the sparse clouds moderated their view of the water, and the plane turned north toward Jamaica and the shores of Cuba.

17

Dog Fight

If the future's looking dark,
We're the ones who have to shine.
If there's no one in control,
We're the ones who draw the line.
Though we live in trying times,
We're the ones who have to try.
Though we know that time has wings,
We're the ones who have to fly.

—Rush, *Counterparts*

Southern Coast of Cuba

Two men huddled in the darkness near a large cypress tree. They had just completed a dangerous mission, which took them into the town of Cienfuegos and through the nearby hillsides. They had been undetected in spite of several close encounters with the local militia.

The clouds above dropped a fine mist of rain over the forest floor as a third man approached cautiously through the underbrush. The height and stride of the man reduced the probability that he was an intruder.

"Captain, we're over here!" whispered Alberto from his position behind the tree.

The lone man nodded his head and took a seat on the ground next to his friend.

"I couldn't find either of them! The house has been converted into a chicken coop, and the garage is full of trash. It's very disheartening. They haven't been in town for quite a while and most of their neighbors are also gone."

"Raymond, don't despair. We have some good news for you. Ana and Alicia were moved to Havana several months ago."

"Havana! How can you be sure?"

"Ana has a job there with the Cuban Electric Company. They are safe and far away from the fighting. Apparently, your parents still have some connections in Havana. I got the information directly from them although they seemed a little suspicious so I didn't get much more. I told them that you were looking for them. They don't want to leave, but they're safe."

Alberto smiled as he saw the impact of his words on his friend.

"It could be Oscar's doing, you know. He's always got something going over here. I'll bet he got her the job."

"How do my mother and father look? Are they well?"

"I know that you're always worrying about them, but they looked good. They were excited to know that you are here, but they were trying to be careful, too. I don't think that they trust all of their so-called friends. Everyone is afraid Batista is coming back, in force."

"What did you find out about my daughter?" Ray searched Alberto's face for reassurance.

Rene put his hand on Raymond's shoulder.

"Alicia is fine. My aunt helped them pack their belongings. They have a small apartment just south of Havana. Apparently, your wife's education in Europe is coming in handy. Fidel doesn't have a lot of skilled help for his revolution, and he has to try to keep the lights on.

"My Aunt Isabelle mentioned that Alicia has talked about you all the time. I didn't ask for that information so it's probably true. And believe me, my aunt is one person who's not accustomed to exaggeration. But, we'll worry about getting them out later. Now we have to get to the containers and then to the boats!"

"What did the church look like, Alberto?"

"Just like the day we left it, with a little more vegetation. I climbed down into the basement through the old sewer pipe. Everything is still there just as we left it. Are you going to tell Campa?"

"I should, but something tells me to wait for the last minute. First, we'll see what happened at the bunker. I can almost hear Oscar warning me."

"Raymond, we can always make a second trip to the church. He doesn't need to know until we are sure of his loyalty."

"What about the others, Alberto? Is anyone leaving with us?"

Alberto pointed to the west.

"We sent the civilians ahead. Just five have shown up so far. We had to be careful not to be noticed. We only approached people we trusted. I believe that seven or eight more have taken an inland route. We've seen more militia in the area, moving west. I don't know if that's good news or bad news."

Raymond got up from his crouched position. Even in the dark his friends could see the relief spread over his person. *His wife and daughter were safe. They might not know that he cared for them, but they were safe!*

"Alberto," whispered Raymond. "Did everyone get the news about the beachhead?"

"Yes. We found Campa and Rumbart and told them, too. We believe that the *Houston* and the *Mariposa* have both been sunk. The *Rio Escondido* may be gone, too. Apparently, *Caribe* and *Atlantico* have moved far off shore to avoid air attacks. Most of our aircraft are also lost. Let's hope that there's some good news somewhere to go along with all this gloom." Alberto momentarily closed his eyes.

"Rene, what about a relief force? How did we do? Were you able to organize any resistance?"

Rene looked back up at Raymond through the darkness.

"Morales organized a group of over a hundred ready to fight. You remember Morales, don't you?"

"Ah, yes. Morales would take the lead, wouldn't he! Did you talk with him?"

"Yes, we did. He was very nervous and excited. He almost cried when he saw us! Without knowing it, I believe that we renewed his courage."

"Did he have a plan?"

"Did he ever! He must have suspected that an invasion was coming. He was going to take the Columbia Barracks first, but then the bad news came. He was okay, but some of his cadre lost their courage. It's hard to blame them. Some can go back home, but most of them are known to the militia by now. They turned to the east. Morales said he was going to follow them and try to organize a guerilla force. Morales also mentioned that they had a cache of arms hidden in the hills. He asked us to go with him. I felt badly about turning him down. I told him that we had to complete our mission. The main force was depending on us. Unfortunately, the truth is that there isn't much we can do for them at this point."

"Morales is a fighter, Alberto. He'll do well. He doesn't need our help. We have our own problems. Campa should have completed his search of the bunker by now. If all went well, we'll find out what Batista hide there before he left the country. Let's get out of here!"

Cautiously, the three men moved along the coastline toward their base camp. Every few minutes they could hear traffic rumbling west on the coastal road toward the Zapata peninsula.

At a convenient spot on a hillside, Raymond called a halt, a brief rest before the final leg of the journey. Their position allowed a view of the shoreline as it stretched into the distance toward the cove where Frank Campa and the rest of their team should be waiting. Raymond closed his eyes as his thoughts drifted to his wife and daughter.

Dimly at first, and then more clearly, the men could detect the roar of engines and the rattling of gunfire. First one, then two and then three dark silhouettes could be seen hopping along the horizon. Raymond immediately recognized the two smaller jet planes as F.A.R. T-33s. They were pursuing a much larger but slower propeller-driven aircraft.

"It's a B-26!" whispered Rene excitedly. "Followed by two others!"

The larger plane was hugging the terrain and seemed to be executing calculated twists and turns, first to the left and then to the right, in an effort to evade its followers. The smaller jet planes, which were considerably faster, seemed to be having trouble locating the B-26. They would gain some altitude, hesitate as the pilot attempted to plot a trajectory toward the enemy, and then dive down into the darkness. As they approached the B-26, tracers could be seen issuing from the upper gun turret. But, for the most part, the weapons were missing their targets.

The cluster of aircraft made what seemed to be a complete circle around the observers on the ground. The B-26 had flown out to the edge of the coastline and then turned back to the north and the cover of the hilly terrain.

As the first of the T-33s made its pass over the B-26, it abruptly turned up into the sky and a stream of flames could be seen exiting from its fuselage. At several thousand feet, the plane turned back to the east disengaging itself from the battle. Smoke and flame were issuing from its fuselage as it disappeared over the horizon.

Gunfire was still being exchanged between the second T-33 and the larger aircraft. Both seemed to be suffering some degree of difficulty. Finally, after two slow turns through the sky, the second T-33 broke off its attack and turned north and then east. Its engine seemed to be operating intermittently as it twisted and turned to avoid gunfire coming from the larger plane.

Once it was apparent that the two T-33 aircraft had broken off contact, the larger plane again turned south toward the coastline. The men on the hillside could now see smoke and flames rolling out of one of its giant engines. The aircraft was losing altitude rapidly as it searched for a place to land. The speed and rate of descent of the plane dictated that it would not make it to the water. The men on the hillside watched in awe as the plane waffled and turned slightly. It was going to attempt a landing in the creek bed that wound lazily just below their position on the hillside.

Helplessly, the giant bird dropped from the sky. There were sounds of breaking tree limbs and the scraping of the fuselage on the rocky soil. The roar of the engines stopped with a gasp, and the plane came to an abrupt stop. The B-26 found itself wedged against some foliage near a point where the creek turned to the west.

It was a skillful touchdown given the circumstances and the terrain. By landing in the creek and sliding through the water, the pilot had managed to squelch the fire that had paralyzed one engine and had threatened to spread to the entire airframe. Nevertheless, it was questionable whether the occupants had survived the crash.

After the tumult of the last several minutes, it now seemed almost unreal as an ominous silence settled over the hillside. And, almost on queue, a gentle fog began to roll in off of the water as if the sea herself was attempting to cover the plane's hiding place.

"It must be one of ours," said Alberto, breaking the silence of the moment. "I've never seen anything like it. We couldn't have been in a better position to see the last part of their battle."

"Let's get down there and see if there are any survivors! But, be cautious. These people will think that we are militia."

Arriving at the crash site, they saw two men lying motionless on the ground near the fuselage as a third man attended to them. The third man jumped up when he saw the group approaching although he did not appear to be armed.

Nevertheless, Raymond signaled Rene and Alberto to drop back and take cover, realizing that these men had no way of knowing who he was or which side he was on. As he began to walk toward the plane, Raymond put his arms out, palms up, to signify that he was not holding a weapon.

Both men stared at each other for a few seconds. Raymond measured his response carefully. The crewman did not appear to be Hispanic, so Raymond began with his best English in hopes of calming the man's fears.

"Are you okay? We are not your enemies!"

The man nodded but did not speak.

"We are not Cuban Militia!"

Raymond turned slightly and pointed toward Rene and Alberto.

"My companions will stay back and secure the perimeter. Do you need medical assistance?"

Slowly the man steadied himself and slowly displayed a handgun he had hidden behind his back.

"I'm putting my weapon in my pocket," Charlie Bill said cautiously. "How about some help here. These guys are out cold, but I think they are alive!"

Just as he spoke, one of the survivors groaned, grabbed his head, and slowly lifted himself into a sitting position. The airman next to him moved, but made no sound.

"Charlie, are you okay? Where's Jose?"

Then the pilot slowly turned his head and noticed the stranger standing in the distance.

"Who is this, Charlie?"

"Friendly forces, Ron. We are in no position to resist if they aren't."

Charlie knelt down next to Ron and signaled with his hand for Raymond to approach.

With the signal, Raymond quickly moved in to help the downed crewmen. Once he was close enough to see the details of their faces, Raymond exclaimed, "You're Americans! What are you doing here? The markings on the plane are Cuban!"

"We're just dumb volunteers who dropped in to join your party," Charlie responded.

"You have fought very well. The Revolutionary Air Force has lost at least two aircraft tonight! Nevertheless, if they find you in the vicinity of this plane they will treat you as spies. Summary execution!"

Ron looked up as he wiped the blood and sweat from his forehead.

"I agree with you! But why are you helping us?"

Raymond knelt down on one knee and reached for his canteen. He handed it to the dazed pilot.

"I am Captain Raymond Chacon. My men and I were returning from Cienfuegos when we witnessed your battle with the T-33s. Our mission shouldn't concern you. But, the militia patrols crawling through these hills should!"

Charlie pointed to the aircraft.

"We have emergency supplies and a raft. We can make a run for the water. The coast is just over that hill. We should be able to get all of us in the raft."

Raymond was attending to Jose who had now regained consciousness.

"This man needs a doctor. Come, get your supplies and follow us to our departure point. It's only a few minutes away. Several members of our patrol are waiting for us there."

18

The Double-cross

It's not a matter of mercy,
It's not a matter of laws,
Plenty of people will kill you,
For some fanatical cause.

—Rush, ***Hold Your Fire***

Near Cienfuegos

The enveloping darkness of night provided much needed cover for the group of weary soldiers as they hurriedly began their escape from the crash site. After Alberto and Charlie had struggled for a few hundred yards with the stretcher, Jose groaned and waived at his bearers to request a stop.

"Amigos, I am feeling much better. I must have hit my head on something when we touched down back there. Just give me a second or two, and I can walk."

Jose paused to adjust the bandage that had been applied to his head. "Do we have any water?"

"Here, Jose, we have plenty," whispered Charlie. "Unfortunately, we're a little short of ice cubes. Take your time! We can carry you, don't worry about that."

"No, really, I'm fine. Just a drink, and I'm up."

Charlie handed his weary companion a canteen and after a few careful drinks, Jose smiled and pointed to his foot.

"I must have kicked the shit out of something real hard, too. It's okay, but it feels like I was playing football with a concrete block!"

Jose pulled himself up off the stretcher with some help from Alberto, and after a few attempts at flexing and stomping his left foot, he confirmed that he was able to walk. He steadied himself by using one of the rifles as a crutch. Then he waived to Raymond signaling that he was ready to go.

Rene had already moved ahead to the water's edge and after some time returned with good news.

"The cove where we hid the supplies is just ahead. I didn't see any traffic off shore, and the road above seems to be clear. We should be able to proceed immediately."

Just as they were about to continue, several jet aircraft streaked overhead. Raymond signaled for the group to take cover.

"Cuban T-33s!" exclaimed Rene as he hit the dirt.

Raymond turned toward Ron and Charlie and whispered, "They must be looking for you!"

Ron nodded. "I don't think they'll see the plane under the brush especially in the darkness. Those aircraft aren't equipped with infrared equipment for nighttime surveillance. They are just converted trainers. And they'll have no starting point for their search especially if they haven't found those two pilots we engaged."

"I hope you're right. They'll probably make the easy assumption that you made it out to sea, or that you're dead!"

"And we weren't alone!" as Ron pointed to the north. "Our wing mates are probably giving them something else to think about farther inland."

"What we have to worry about right now," added Raymond, "is a ground patrol. I'm sure they'll comb the area in the morning so we've got to make tracks!"

"I couldn't see either of them after we broke off," said Charlie, "but I had a close look at both of them near the end. They were both hit and smoking something fierce. It's possible that they crashed before we finally went down. You might have had a better view of the situation from the ground, Captain Chacon."

"We were on the hillside, but we couldn't follow the fighters very far," Rene responded. "The field at Cienfuegos isn't very distant, so they could have made it back in a short time. But that monster you were flying served you well. All three of you are alive and upright. And as we watched your landing under such dangerous conditions, we were amazed at your ability to put down so softly and with such limited damage. You should give yourself a lot of credit."

Charlie concurred. "There's something to be said for coming out standing up. This boy, Ron, can sure fly those old clunkers! And I don't think those two assholes who were chasing us made it very far. Jose was making Swiss cheese out of them."

Moving slowly for a few hundred yards through the underbrush the patrol reached the small inlet where their rafts and supplies were stashed. They were apprehensive for several very good reasons. If the Cuban forces had discovered their hiding place, an ambush was likely. On the other hand, some of the other members of their party could have been captured and forced to disclose the location. Raymond knew that care would have to be taken in their approach.

As they reached the edge of the heavily wooded point that defined the eastern end of the cove, Raymond signaled a stop. Their timing was almost perfect. Reasonably heavy cloud cover had just rolled in, and the wind was swirling over the water making their approach less detectable. As the men gathered under a clump of thick bushes, Raymond called for a strategy meeting.

"This raft from your plane is designed for six, am I right?"

Charlie nodded. "Six is standard, eight or nine in a pinch."

Raymond continued his instructions.

"This spot is sufficient for embarkation. If our original equipment is compromised, we will leave from here. We must stay to the east until we are well out to sea.

"One of us will have to survey the equipment in the cove while two others secure the perimeter. First, we get to the ridge, and once that's secure go on to the western bank. The sea looks clear of traffic.

"Ron, you and Charlie and Jose stay here. If we run into a firefight in the cove, get out immediately. Go straight south as fast as you can. Don't worry about us! We were going to have this problem before we found you."

"I don't think we want to leave you stranded," said Ron. "We're in this thing together, Captain! Without your help, we wouldn't have had much of a chance. If you get into a fight, we'll back you up. In the meantime, we'll get this rig ready to go. Check out your base camp, and let us know what you find. I'm sure that Charlie and Jose agree with me. We'll wait."

Rene glanced at Ron and Charlie and then at Raymond.

"What about Frank Campa and our mission?"

"Campa should be back already. If so, we'll contact the ship and send him out with three of our team and at least two or three civilians if any have arrived. Then, Rene will take this raft out with the three of you.

"If you think you can handle two or three more, we'll give you any children who might be in the group. Alberto and I and two others from our team will complete the rest of our mission. Campa can direct the ship to pick us up. We can get our cargo down here before dawn, but we'll have to wait until tomorrow to go to sea with it."

Ron looked surprised. "You have cargo? Waiting until tomorrow night is taking quite a risk isn't it?"

"We'll have to evaluate the situation once we see what lies up ahead. The cargo is valuable, but it's difficult to move. Let's see what happens before we decide."

Having settled on a general plan, Rene, Alberto, and Raymond started toward the interior of the cove keeping a separation of about twenty yards from each other. In a short time they arrived at a position where they could see the location of the rafts and supplies. In spite of the fact that their eyes had adjusted well to the darkness, the density of vegetation in the cove made the night almost impenetrable. At first, it was impossible to tell whether any of their compatriots had made it safely.

Raymond and Rene left Alberto while they checked the ridgeline and the far point of the cove.

Alberto proceeded slowly down the hillside to the place where the rafts had been stored. With his weapon at the ready he painstakingly worked his way toward the shoreline.

Suddenly, he detected motion ahead of him. He froze while he watched and waited. After several moments a tiny figure darted across his field of view. It was too small to be an enemy soldier, he thought. It must be an animal or a small child. *A child*!

Alberto continued to watch the motion in front of him for several minutes. Finally, knowing that he would have to make the first move, Alberto stepped out of the bushes with his rifle trained on the source of that movement. He was silent and waited for the situation to resolve itself.

To his surprise, he found a group of men, women and children huddled under the thick bushes and overhanging trees. They were covered with mud and almost invisible in the darkness. From the expressions on their faces, they had been hiding in this location for some time.

Alberto kept his weapon trained on the group.

"Edgar, where are you? Edgar Hernandez! Hector, are you here?"

At first no one responded. Then a young woman slowly stood up and faced Alberto. "We do not know Edgar Hernandez. There is no Hector here. When we arrived at this place, there was no one… no one alive!"

"What do you mean?" exclaimed Alberto. "Has someone died? Tell me, quickly!"

"We came to this place, and when we arrived we found those three people over there dead, on the ground by the raft. Then we found those two men, over there, dead in the water! We have not moved or touched anything. This raft was the only other thing here. And it has many holes in it!"

Alberto cautiously made his way over to the three bodies. A Cuban man and woman, both probably in their late thirties and a young girl about seven or eight lay face up on the ground. Sharp jagged wounds were scattered over the lengths of their bodies.

This was no grenade or mortar attack. The raft had been booby-trapped! What about Edgar and Hector?

Alberto turned to the survivors looking for answers to what he had found.

"Where are the other dead men? Show me!"

Alberto lowered his weapon and walked toward the huddled group.

"They are over there in the water!" cried a woman through the darkness, half in fear and half in pain.

The woman pointed toward the shoreline.

As Alberto approached the bodies his worst fears were realized. There were two bodies floating up against the shore. Their orientation made it likely that both had been thrown into the water after they were shot. Alberto scanned the area for their weapons but found none. He pulled the body of his friend Edgar out of the water and looked at his wounds. Edgar had been shot in the back. The other body held similar wounds.

They were executed! They never had a chance. Only a coward would do this!

Alberto knelt on the shore as a deep feeling of sorrow came over him. Edgar and Hector were good soldiers.

This couldn't have been the militia! They would have taken them prisoner and they wouldn't have executed the civilians. And wouldn't the mili-

tia have stayed here and set a trap in case others were coming! What were the other possibilities? Where were the supplies and the other raft? And there is no sign of Campa or Rumbart!

A man from the group appeared out of the shadows and tried to project a sympathetic smile at Alberto. It was one of the civilians who had gathered near the remaining raft. Alberto was upset so he yelled at the man as he approached.

"Where are Campa and Rumbart? Are there more bodies?"

The man shrugged his shoulders. "We found no one else, Sir. No one else was here when we arrived. But, I did see a craft in the water."

"A craft?" yelled Alberto. "What kind of craft?"

"One about the size of that one," the man said as he pointed back toward the shredded raft. "It was slowly heading that way, and it was low and long." The man pointed due south from where he stood.

"What do you mean by low and long? Did it have sails?"

"Oh, no! It was in several pieces. I could not see it well. There were two men aboard, but they did not respond to our calls. Then I heard the explosion over there."

Alberto tried to picture what the man had described. At that moment, Raymond and Rene appeared out of the darkness. Raymond was visibly disturbed.

"Rumbart and Campa are gone! They've removed the containers from the bunker at the complex, and made for the ship."

"I believe that this man saw them escaping," said Alberto. "Do you have more information?"

"Rene and I found this woman hiding up near the trail. She saw the whole thing. She led us to Tomas. He was shot twice in the back of the head and his body was left in the bushes near the road. Have you found Hector or Edgar? Maybe they were able to escape."

Alberto motioned toward the shore.

"I have more bad news! Edgar and Hector have been shot. Executed! They've been shot in the back! At first, I thought it was the militia. But, then…"

"No, Rene, it was our own people!"

"I will cut out their hearts for this, no matter how long it takes me to find them!" Rene began to cry with anger.

"Revenge must wait, my friend" muttered Raymond. "We must get these people to safety and quickly."

"Where does that leave us, Raymond?" asked Alberto as he searched for answers. "We needed the two rafts for our escape! Campa wanted to make sure we didn't follow him. That bomb was meant for us!"

Raymond pointed over his shoulder.

"That's not our only problem. There's a patrol of militia looking for the crew of the B-26 down the coast. Rene spotted them from the ridge. That gives us about fifteen minutes to get out of here!"

Raymond called Rene and Alberto over to the side away from the civilians.

"I'm going to put the two of you in command of the raft from the plane. Rene, you take the crewmembers and as many of these people as possible. We have enough supplies for all of them. Get over to the raft and get out of here. I'll try to contact the ship from here. Go straight south. If you can't find them by 0800, then turn east and make for the islands. We'll have to forget the containers at the church. There's no time."

Rene grabbed Raymond's hand and looked him in the eye.

"Be careful, my friend. I don't want to lose you, too. We have room for you on the raft. Don't be a hero."

Raymond shook his head. "I've got another way out. Don't worry about me. Get those people on the raft. We're going to make it. I'll meet you at Oscar's in a week."

Raymond then turned to Alberto with a warning.

"Keep your eyes open for Campa and Rumbart. If they know that you have escaped, they'll try to kill you. That goes for the Americans, too, if they find out that they are with us."

Rene and Alberto quickly gathered the civilians and led them along the coastline to the point where the three crewmen had readied the raft from the B-26. Alberto explained the situation to the crewmembers of the B-26 and began loading the boat for the escape. With some effort everyone managed to get aboard along with the food and water rations and the ammunition and weapons. The overcrowded raft struggled to make headway in the water.

As it reached a point about twenty yards off shore, three children could be seen jumping from the edge of the raft. Quickly, they swam for the shore. Raymond helped pull them from the water.

"Why did you leave the raft, boys? We have no other way of escape. Get back out there!"

The oldest spoke first.

"My name is Ernesto, and he is my brother, Chico. My friend Juan wanted to stay with us. The boat was too heavy, Sir. We can get along here until another opportunity comes for us."

"Where are your parents? Do they know you're here?"

"Our parents were killed by the explosion," replied the oldest child. "They were pulling it toward the water with our sister when it exploded. They are all dead!"

"What about you, Juan?" Raymond asked in a quiet voice.

"My parents are at home, Sir."

"I'm so sorry, boys. I know this isn't much help, but you're going to have to take care of each other now. Ernesto, were your parents going to America?"

"Yes, we were going to live with our friend, Mr. Oscar. Chico is eleven and I am thirteen. Juan is just eight. We can help you do whatever you need."

"Do you mean Oscar Chacon? Is he your friend?"

"Yes. My father was going to work for him in Florida. He said I could work there, too."

"Getting off the raft, that was a brave thing for all of you to do." Raymond patted Chico's head.

Ernesto put his hand on Raymond's arm. "May we go with you?"

"I'm afraid that you cannot go with me on my journey. It would put you in grave danger. I am going to Havana, and you are safer here. You must hide now and wait for morning. Then you should go to Juan's home. I will come back for you when I have another boat, and we can leave for America together.

"Now, I must try to contact the ship which should be waiting for the raft you were on. Where does Juan live? I will come for you once when I return from Havana."

"His house is on the old sugar mill road across from the storage building," Ernesto whispered. Do you know of it?"

"Yes, I have walked past that house many times. It has a well on the side and a small stream runs past it on the north."

"That is Juan's home, Sir. We must find our Uncle Milan so that he may come for our…parents."

Ernesto began crying, and Raymond put his arm around the boy.

"Boys, we are in danger as we stand here. Quickly! All of you, hide in these bushes until daylight. Stay awake, no talking and no moving around. Your lives depend on it!"

The boys moved hurriedly toward the bushes. As Raymond watched, they crawled into the vegetation. Raymond knelt down near their hiding place and whispered.

"If anyone comes this way, don't show yourselves. You'll be okay if you stay hidden like this. Wait until the sun is well up and go straight home. Don't tell anyone what has happened here or of the people on the raft. And tell your Uncle not to talk about this place."

Raymond whispered goodbye to the boys and headed for the transmitter. He had hidden it in the bushes just up the coast from the disabled raft; however, he was sure that Campa and Rumbart also were aware of the location. As he pulled the brush away from the equipment, he could see that the transmitter had been destroyed.

Rumbart and Campa have certainly betrayed us!

As Raymond was hiding the damaged communications equipment and other evidence of their presence in a rock enclosure which nature had created near the stream, he could hear activity up on the ridge road. It was the militia patrol! Quickly, he grabbed his rifle and refreshed his ammunition. Then he began heading east along the coastline in search of a new hiding place.

Captain Raymond Chacon was now alone and facing some difficult decisions. The journey to Havana to find his wife and child would be a dangerous one.

19

Narcoterrorism

*We use the tactics that
we learned from the CIA
because we…we were
trained to do everything.
We are trained to set off a bomb,
we are trained to kill…,
we are trained to do everything.*

**—Orlando Bosch,
Commando of United
Revolutionary Organizations**

Somewhere in the Dominican Republic, October 1976

"Francisco, how do you like our Dominican ranch?"

"Much nicer than the old place. As much as I like Mexico, this place beats our Vera Cruz facility all to hell. It's as nice as the one the Americans have in Costa Rica."

"Do you have the package? Guillermo has the courier ready to carry it to Barbados."

"Of course, Ricardo. We tested the prototype again this morning in the Bonao, and it worked perfectly."

"Excellent! The Americans have trained you well. I know I shouldn't even ask, but we're sure the materials aren't traceable back to us, correct?"

"No problem! Posada had everything we needed. The device is almost identical to the one he used on the Costa Rica-Cuba Cultural Center back in July. And it's certainly more reliable than the one we used in Panama. He has the capability of producing several more if we need them, but it would take some time."

"By Panama, do you mean the Cubana Airlines thing in Panama City? I thought that one worked okay."

"No, and Orlando Bosch was pissed. He doesn't want a screw up like the Kingston device. That one blew up before it was loaded on the plane. This flight will have plenty of Cubans and a few North Koreans as far as we know. We just have to be absolutely sure that there are no Americans aboard. And, I mean absolutely sure! No fuck ups on that score."

"Don't worry, Francisco! We will have two people in the terminal. If we see an American stepping through the gate, we phone in a bomb threat. You know as well as I do that those boardings can be a Chinese fire drill! We are doing everything we can on this end. By the way, just as a matter of curiosity, do the Americans know who's doing this or how we're financing it?"

"Some suspect it's CORU, but we have support in Washington. As long as we work with the agencies, they'll let us slide on the imports. They know we control the drug traffic in Miami, but we give them so much information and enough payoffs that they can't pull the trigger on us. Let's just keep it that way. The only problems I foresee in Miami are our dealings with the Colombians, particularly the Medellin cartel.

"But, Washington is another matter, Ricardo. The American election is coming up, and it looks like the Democrats will not support us. We have to cover our tracks up there so they don't decide to switch sides all of a sudden."

"That's the trouble with popular elections," said Ricardo. "You never know what you're going to get. This Jimmy Carter is a typical do-gooder. He'll try to mend fences with Castro, and that could be counter-productive. We have to get this project done on schedule."

"What is today, the fifth? Yes! October the fifth! There is less than a month to the election, too little time to set up another operation this complicated."

"When are you delivering the package to Guillermo?" asked Ricardo of his guest.

"As soon as he shows up. I've got the package in the car. There's no need to bring it in here. By the way, how is he going to get it aboard? A regular suitcase might not work. Cubana is definitely on alert."

"Francisco, we are in luck there. The boy I told you about is with the Cuban fencing team. Imagine that, a sports team! He'll check his equipment with the rest, but he won't board the plane. Guillermo will get him out of the airport and from there to Venezuela with us before anyone can determine what happened."

"You're putting the bomb in the fencing equipment?" Campa said in amazement. "Ricardo, you are getting good at this. The Cubana officials won't be expecting something as devious as that. Are Lugo and Lusano working on the inside?"

"Yes, everything is set to go. Just deliver the package, and you can leave. We are all going to Venezuela until things blow over. Remember, we've got room for another on the plane if you want to join us."

"No, thanks, my friend. I want to stay away from there. It's going to be hot everywhere down here but especially in Venezuela. You can contact me in the usual way in Mexico City if you need any help. Just don't tell Bosch that I opted out. He takes too many risks for my liking. I try to avoid the fellow whenever possible."

"As you wish, Francisco. My lips are sealed."

"Learn to call me Frank. The less I look and sound Cuban, the safer I'll be. I might suggest that you to do the same."

"I might heed your advice, Frank. Your longevity means you must be doing a lot things correctly. God knows how many Central and South Americans must be after your ass these days."

"Well, I'd rather be careful than have my countrymen think of Frank Campa as a fool! And, I especially don't want to be remembered as a dead fool!"

"Ah, here comes Guillermo now!"

20

Another Shadow

When paradise is no longer
fit for you to live in,
And your adolescent
dreams are gone,
Through the days you
feel a little used up,
And you don't know where
your energy's gone wrong.

—John Mellencamp, *Scarecrow*

Fort Lauderdale, Florida, 1983

The snowbirds were making their way back to the north. As usual, the winter in South Florida was warm and wonderful. The Gulf Stream flowed from the equator north past the East Coast of Florida, and its warm currents buffered the temperatures on the peninsula. No freezing, no shivering, just beautiful days and balmy nights.

One of the beneficiaries of this geographical advantage was Fort Lauderdale, a relatively small city located on the coastline just north of Miami. The mobs of spring-breaking college students had just left the beaches as the residents settled in for a warm but peaceful summer.

At the main airport, it was business as usual. On the busier and more developed eastern end of the field, the large passenger airlines were busy transporting their customers on both domestic and international flights. On the remote western edge of the field, a different aspect of the aircraft business was being conducted.

"Ted! This baby is about ready to go."

The voice was that of Bill Wallers. His friends often called him *Blind Bill*. He was an aircraft mechanic whose specialty was vintage propeller driven aircraft. At this particular moment, he was fueling a Beech 18 for Ted Michaels, the youngest son of Frank Michaels, owner of Michaels Air Company.

"Good! Let's get out of here by noon. If we're lucky, they'll still have the field lit when we get there. Landing on that strip at night is never much fun especially when it's pitch dark."

Ted reached the open cabin door of the Beech and slid the suitcases toward the back of the plane. He had already loaded several cameras along with business documents and small boxes that contained spare aircraft parts.

Michaels Air Company's location on the distant western end of Fort Lauderdale International Airport gave it a certain degree of anonymity. Only customers who operated relatively old propeller driven aircraft had much familiarity with this part of the field, and it was not unusual to see older planes like the Douglas DC-3 in the Michaels Air hangar.

Frank Michaels' main customers were intrastate mail delivery carriers, flying clubs that owned vintage aircraft, small cargo operations and Caribbean operators who ran facilities in Central and South America. Michaels owned one such facility in Honduras and although it provided him with a multiplicity of headaches, it was also the source of considerable offshore revenue.

Bill adjusted the ladder he was using and turned to reply to Ted.

"No problem. My wife is coming to get the truck. She's got my suitcase and cash so I'll be ready whenever you are."

Bill completed the fueling and was crawling down the ladder when he saw Kathy Michaels motion to him from the front door of the house trailer that served as an office for the company. Kathy was Ted's only sister.

"Hey, Ted. I'll be over in the trailer. Kathy wants me to take some shit down to the staff at SETCOMP. I hope it's in Spanish. I can never communicate with those bastards unless they're drunk and suddenly start understanding English."

"Go ahead," Ted replied. "I'm going over to Central Air with this manifest. We need a few things from them before we can depart. I'll be back in thirty. Do we have any beer?"

"Yeah! Lindy is bringing a cooler with Bud and Heiny. We've got chicken wings, salami sandwiches and a bunch of fruit salad. You know what a health nut she is. No salad, no beer! No fruit, no pretzels! We can always drop the salad to the fish, but she'd find out so be prepared to eat some of it."

"Bill, you are truly a lucky man. If my girlfriend could cook half as well as Lindy, I'd marry her!"

Ted laughed and thought again about what he had just said. "Well, probably not marry her, but I would at least like her a lot more. Lately, she's been totally useless. And *blah, blah, blah* is all I hear. This trip should help my state of mind if nothing else."

"That's not nice!" mumbled the mechanic as he crawled down the ladder. "You're too hard on the poor girl. Just because she doesn't know a rotary from a jet doesn't mean she's dumb. She certainly looks good all the time. And just because she can't pick horses, and is a consistent loser at jai alai doesn't make her useless. At least she tries. And she's a lot better fisherman than you are, and you know it!"

Ted knew that he was fighting a losing battle. All of his friends and family liked Amanda even though he couldn't figure out why.

"Okay, Bill. But she does fit the stereotype. She's a dumb blonde! She fits that class perfectly. Oh well, it could be worse. She could be dumb and ugly. But be careful, I might ask for a trade one of these days."

Ted waived his hand over his head as he climbed into the aircraft, and Bill headed for the old trailer that sat next to the hangar. Bill had often wondered why such a prosperous company had such a dumpy office. He had visited similar operations all over the Western Hemisphere with most of them not being anywhere near as profitable as Michaels Air. And yet, Michaels Air was on the bottom when it came to comfort and opulence. It was always easy for Bill to ignore this fact mainly because his paycheck was quite generous. Frank Michaels certainly wasted none of his cash flow on creature comforts.

After he walked up the stairs and entered the office, Bill received a cheery greeting from Kathy Michaels. She was holding an old battered company briefcase in her arms.

"Dad wants you to take this stuff to SETCOMP. It has all of the drawings and invoices you'll need on this trip. You should have plenty of room next to the cases of beer."

"What beer?" Bill had that shit-eating grin on his face.

"Ernesto should get this information. Don't give it to anyone else, or we'll never see this stuff again. If they have any questions about the invoices, tell them to call on Saturday between ten and twelve. Otherwise they should know what to do."

Bill looked through the documents with some care.

"What about the drawings? Can I push them on these repairs? I really don't want to stay down there for a month."

Kathy motioned toward her father's office.

"Before I forget, here are your return tickets. Apparently, Ted's flying back in the Beech in a day or two."

"Where am I staying, on the beach or in the jungle?"

"I've got you in the Holiday Inn for ten days. Oh, here's some money for food. Ernesto has a car for you, but they probably remember the last time you were down there and drove a car. I'll bet they'll chauffeur you this time!"

Kathy tried to take good care of Bill mainly because she liked his wife so much. *She'd do the same for me!* Kathy thought.

"Ah, Bill, don't forget to make your return reservations as soon as you know when you're coming back. Otherwise, you will be there for a month, and Lindy will be mad at me!"

Bill collected the items Kathy handed to him and turned toward the office. He knocked twice on the door and entered without waiting for a response. Frank Michaels was on the telephone, and he pointed to a chair for Bill to use as he was talking.

Frank finished his call and smiled at Bill as he hung up the phone.

"Bill, ready for a little Central America action I see."

Frank Michaels had his usual optimistic outlook on Caribbean travel that was spawned by the fact that it was someone else who was doing the travelling.

"We're ready to go, Frank. I'm just waiting for Ted to return from Central Air."

"Okay. Be careful and remember to give Ernesto my best."

"Don't worry, Frank, I will. Ernesto Diaz is the only guy down there at SETCOMP that gives you more than a day's work for a day's pay. And, the way things are going down in Honduras, it's good for an American to be with someone he can trust. People have a way of disappearing down there."

"I may own the place, Bill, but Ernesto is sure as hell in charge. And, that's the way I like it! Make sure he gets the drawings. I don't care that much about the invoices. We'll collect from those assholes sooner or later. Maybe I should say one way or another!"

"I'll hint that you're coming down. The last time that happened, your delinquent customers all paid up. Remember?"

"Actually, I wish I could go with the two of you. Harry has been driving me nuts."

"How's Harry doing? I haven't seen him much lately."

Bill really wasn't interested, but he asked to be polite.

"Up to his asshole in alligators. But before I forget, remember to watch Ted's back. He should be out of there in a day or two. Keep an eye on the plane. Don't let anyone screw with it. Lately, we've had a bit of a security problem down there. The place is crawling with government agents. I wish those fuckers would get real jobs instead of harassing me!"

Frank thought for a few seconds, then continued.

"In particular, watch for anyone asking stupid questions, especially when they involve Ted or Harry. Don't tell anyone who Ted is or why he's there. You know what I mean! Give them some story about Pittsburg. Give them anything but the truth. I would love to send those bastards off on a tangent."

"Do you suspect that someone's spotting for the feds?" Bill was a little uneasy.

"I know there is!" Frank pounded his fist lightly on the desk.

"Don't worry, Frank. I'll keep an eye on Ted's back and on the plane. He'll be okay. And I'll see you in about ten days or whenever Ernesto lets me go."

Bill got up from his chair and shook hands with his boss. Then, he returned to the front of the office where he retrieved the briefcase and waived goodbye to Kathy. As Bill walked out of the office and toward the Beech, he noticed that his wife had arrived with the supplies. He walked over to where she was standing and gave her a big hug.

"You've saved the day again, honey."

"Beer and Bill! Hey, it rhymes! They must just go together. You may drink the beer only if you eat the fruit and the salad. Don't pull any tricks on me! Ted promised me that he'd watch you. Can I trust him? All I really know is that I can't trust you when it comes to your diet."

Lindy smiled and gave Bill another kiss.

"I'm a changed man, honey bunch. You can trust me with this one. I've seen the light! *No salad, no beer,* is my motto."

Bill loaded the briefcase and cooler into the Beech. He turned back to his wife.

"Kiss the kids for me. I'll try to bring something weird back for them."

Moments after Bill's wife left, Ted reappeared, but he didn't seem too happy.

"Remind me to never, ever deal with those bastards again. They know when they've got me over a barrel. And we're gonna do the inventory ourselves when we get back! I'm tired of being held hostage over parts. We're not going to use those bastards ever again. I know that Dad's at the end of his rope, too."

The informal manifest listed numerous aircraft engine parts bound for SETCOMP in Honduras. Twelve small crates where strapped to the interior walls of the Beech along with four suitcases containing personal clothing and tools.

Once the plane was loaded, N503E obtained clearance from the tower and was on its way into the air toward the Atlantic Ocean and then south toward Central America.

"Well, here's to Honduras," said Ted as he toasted Bill with a beer. "Let's hope Ernesto is alive and well when we get there."

"Dad's worried about Harry, and I don't blame him. We're gonna have to be real careful down there. I didn't tell him that Harry had just visited SETCOMP. God only knows what he's up to."

21

The Cat and the Mouse

> *Which is more successful,*
> *the ant or the tiger?*
> *The individual ant subjugates*
> *his existence to the whole,*
> *while the tiger stalks his prey alone.*
> *If I am hunting, I want to be a tiger.*
> *If I am hiding, I want to be an ant.*
>
> —Carlos Lehder, *Medellin Cartel*

Everglades City, Florida

He loved to walk his beagle along the grassy shores of the Gulf of Mexico. Rey wasn't a particularly large dog, but he played the roles of man's best friend and watchdog extremely well. He was the perfect companion for a man who lived in the wild and undeveloped area bordering on the Everglades National Park.

No tall condominiums or attendant snowbirds are found in this wilderness on the western coast of Florida. Just plenty of mosquitoes and fish and an occasional trailer park. The nearest real town was Naples, Florida, about twenty miles to the north. This was a perfect isolation for a man who valued his privacy and coveted his love of nature and the outdoors.

Josef Gerona's modest mobile home backed up to a swamp and backwater providing direct access to the Gulf of Mexico. Heavy subtropical vegetation covered the shore and extended to the numerous little islands that inhabited the bay waters.

Although the mobile home was old, it was in good repair. The living room was inundated with amateur radio gear that kept Josef busy when he wasn't working. While Josef loved to talk with new contacts around the world on his low frequency equipment, most of his regular business connections were with Central and South America. Not much could happen in those areas of the world without Josef knowing about it.

The kitchen was small but neat and clean. Josef loved Italian food. He kept his cabinets and refrigerator stuffed with many different types of pasta and related sauces. He had a large freezer that was the holding area for many of the fish he caught during his numerous expeditions into the Gulf. He was a good fisherman and probably could have survived just on the fish he caught.

For his expeditions into the Gulf he used a refurbished fishing boat that was Rey's second home. When Josef wasn't out of town on the job, he and Rey could be found in that old boat exploring the endless fringes of the Everglades. With each trip came new knowledge of the multitude of animals that made this swamp their home. He especially loved the wild birds that frequented the area. In turn, some of them often gave him clues about the location of migrating schools of fish. Josef and Rey had learned to follow the gulls and herons with significant success.

But for all his love of nature, Josef was not a naturalist or anything close to it. He was a United States Government employee. He had worked for the Federal Drug Enforcement Agency for over five years now. His work ethic and dedication had created a solid reputation for him among his co-workers.

His language skills were impressive. He was fluent in Spanish, Portuguese, French and German as well as English. He could get by in Russian and Czech. During his high school and college years, he spent most of his summers in Europe and South America learning each language at its source.

When he completed his undergraduate education at Harvard, the DEA immediately spotted the potential value of his linguistic skills. But his main asset was his knowledge and use of local customs. He had the ability to adapt rapidly to the colloquial speech habits in most of the countries he visited. This gave him the ability to infiltrate minor governmental and criminal organizations in several Caribbean nations with the same confidence as if he were a local.

The information he gathered during these operations led to the interruption of several major drug connections. He quickly became the most important agent working the Caribbean.

Josef could easily pass as Cuban, Colombian, or Nicaraguan. His average height and weight, moderate build and simple features also kept him anonymous. After a brief encounter he was not an easy person to describe or identify because he didn't seem to have any unique physical features. Brown hair, brown eyes, light skin, and the ability to keep his mouth shut when necessary had all contributed to his success.

Josef was not noted for his sociability. After his training was completed he requested assignments that allowed him to work alone. Although this was not always possible, his successes brought him to the point where he could insist upon working undercover in the field. He had several DEA contacts in Florida, but usually those agents were left with the clerical tasks of writing reports and transporting evidence. Although Josef was quick to credit this support, rarely did his co-workers have a chance to see him in action.

As Josef and Rey walked along the crude trail that led back to his trailer, he wasn't surprised to hear his beeper announce the fact that someone wanted his attention. As a shield against his employer and his potential enemies, he kept a telephone answering service in Fort Myers. He received no calls or mail in his Everglades City home. This inconvenience was more than paid for by peace of mind and relative anonymity. He wouldn't have it any other way.

When he reached his trailer, it was already dark. He brought Rey inside, fed him some leftovers from the refrigerator and changed clothes. After a quick sandwich and a Coke, he jumped into his car and drove out to U.S. 41 and then northwest to Naples and a pay telephone at a roadside motel.

For local transportation he drove a '68 Mercedes 250 SE. The body wasn't in good shape and the interior had seen better days, but it was reliable. Long ago he had discovered a gifted Mercedes mechanic in Naples. The man was from Munich and treated the sedan like his own. The old Mercedes gave him another gift. It was anonymous. His beater wasn't the kind of car anyone noticed or remembered.

The number on the beeper was familiar…Washington D.C. He placed several coins into the telephone and dialed. After two rings the line was answered and a voice identified the location as the DEA.

"Phil Costello, please. This is Gerona."

The voice on the other end of the phone was courteous.

"Just one moment, agent Gerona. I'll have to page him. He was just here, but I believe he stepped out to the cafeteria to get something to eat. Hold on, please."

After about a minute it was Costello on the other end.

"Josef, my man, how the hell are you? As usual, we've been worried about you. Vacations can dull the senses and make you weak!"

Josef immediately identified the upbeat nature of his bosses' words.

"I'm in trouble already! I detect a good mood up there. Something's got to be wrong in Washington, and you want me to come up into the cold and fix it. Right?"

"Not so, Josef! Why do you suspect me of trying to extract you from paradise. I just wanted to alert you. Your little pal, Harry Michaels! Do you remember him by any chance?"

"How could I forget!" mumbled Josef sarcastically. "I wasted quite a bit of time and a few markers getting him to come home. And he's done nothing but play with us. If I were you, I'd just put him away or let me feed him to the alligators."

"You sell yourself short, Josef. Patience is the key here. Patience, my boy!"

Costello had a confident tone running through his voice, and Josef sensed that, for a change, something good must have happened.

"I must admit that I didn't think much of your idea when this first started," Costello said. "But, now our little bird dog has found the scent. And, he's pulling on our chain. Your insight in this situation was marvelous!"

Josef paused to reconsider the facts surrounding the case as he threw out an improbable answer.

"He's going to roll over on his brother and his father?"

"No shit, Josef! He's gonna do it! It might take a few days and a few threats, but he'll do it.

"Okay, Phil, you've got me baffled on this one. What are the details?"

"He's a lily-livered chicken-shit bastard, all right, but he may have come up with a live one this time. I didn't encourage him on this one, either. I know you're going to accuse me of encouraging him or badgering him in my spare time. But he has to feel cornered to respond. His type always do!"

"I forgive you in advance, Phil. All I know is that there is only one way he can help us, and if it isn't that particular angle, then I say we dump him in the slammer for as long as they'll keep him."

"Josef, did you know that his nickname is Harry, The Fox? That's really a joke! He's giving real foxes a bad name. When I got him alone, he couldn't roll over fast enough. I wouldn't put it past him, but I don't think he's smart enough to try to trick us."

"Tell me, Costello, does he even know that pilot?" Josef was getting tired of twenty questions and was sounding more serious.

"That's the best part of this whole thing. The pilot came to him. Can you believe it? Michaels was still trying to figure out how to get next to this guy and then, guess what, he walks right in the front door! Well, I should say flies right in the door. Right into SETCOMP. Now, I grant you that there aren't too many places to go down there in Honduras. And, SETCOMP has seen just about all of the regulars from Colombia. But the timing couldn't have been any better. Our eyes tell us that they hit it off almost immediately."

Costello knew what was coming next because Josef always questioned good news.

"Remember what they say about coincidences, especially coincidences which appear to help you. It may not have been a coincidence. What happens if this is a setup? What if Michaels is trying to set something up just so he gets credit. He can't be trusted any farther than you can throw him, Phil. You, of all people, should know that!"

"Please don't tell me what *they* say about coincidences. I've been having a great week, and you'll just ruin it for me. He didn't run up to Harry and kiss him! He just stopped for some repairs, and Harry slimed over to him. Being an American in that shit hole helped a lot."

"And what are we prepared to give Michaels in return besides what he's asked for already? That's if he actually has a deal."

"Hey, that's not your problem, Josef. Anyway, it looks like there will be two flights. They spotted his brother down there after Harry left. He was bringing in parts that looked okay on the surface. But, I can't believe that Ted would fly all the way to Honduras and not bring back some souvenirs. We don't have the resources to cover both. Anyway, we should catch the big fish first and then shut Michaels and his family down all the way. Besides, he's helped us a lot already, and doesn't even know it."

"Don't tell me! It's like fixing the car. You're going to get a little dirty in the process, right? Ah, never mind, Phil. What does it matter? Until we have a hold on the pilot, we'll have to keep playing with Harry and his pals.

"Josef, I thought you were chummy with all those big dealers in Colombia. Say, if you can't find Carlos, not much of a chance of us doing the same."

"Look, Costello, I've got a backup plan if this one fails. It's a long shot. But that's for later."

"You can tell me. What are friends for? I won't jump the gun on you. I made that mistake once but not again. You have my word on that! I apologized for that situation already so don't drag it past me again."

Josef paused before responding.

"It's not that important. It will just confuse things. Besides, until Michaels calls, I'm going fishing!"

"At night? Don't give me that crap. You've got a date with that girlfriend of yours. I know she's going to hate me for this, but just be ready. If it's a go, you'll hear from the office and from me on the Lear. We know it's near Sarasota so just drive your butt up there if I buzz you. This is serious, and we need your help! If we blow this one, the big rat will hide, and we'll never get a bead on him."

"Don't concern yourself about me. Even though you've screwed up my evening and probably my weekend, I'll be there. Maybe I shouldn't ask, but I guess I have to do it." Josef paused.

"Ask what? Go ahead. We have no secrets from you."

"You're leaving the locals out this time, I hope. That area is crawling with amateur detectives and amateur smugglers. We don't need either type on this one."

Costello cleared his throat before responding.

"You're damn right I am! I wouldn't include those bastards in a traffic stop. There's a leak down there big enough to run the Mississippi River through. I haven't forgotten. I'm going to find him or them if I have to put every local cop on the western coast of Florida through a polygraph. You have my word on that!"

"Okay. I just wanted to be sure. See you in Sarasota!"

22

Rollover

*…in my 30-year history in the Drug Enforcement
Administration and related agencies, the major
targets of my investigations almost invariably
turned out to be working for the CIA.*

—Dennis Dayle, DEA

Sarasota, Florida, April 1983

It was a typical Florida evening in the rainy season. A light drizzle was misting over the old Sarasota County Airport. The late spring rain showers seemed to follow one after another like the cars on a freight train coming from the east. They managed to delight only the multiplicity of palms growing near the roadway at the entrance to the airport and the blue jays who danced in the puddles nearby.

The airport was placed in a rather isolated part of the county. Undeveloped land and semi-tropical vegetation surrounded it. The economic expansion of the late sixties and early seventies had been stopped in its tracks by rising interest rates and an inflationary economy. The oil crisis didn't help things either. Even though interest rates had dropped appreciably, the building boom in this area of the county had failed to materialize leaving the airport with the status of a public white elephant.

The main terminal building was in a state of disrepair. It was cinder block and stucco construction that had been severely discolored by the minerals that poured out of the sprinkler system. There were several out-buildings, which served as hangars for the handful of small private aircraft calling this field home. Most of these planes belonged to flying clubs, not the elite business aircraft the county had envisioned when the field was expanded. Many of the planned support facilities that would have ringed the field were never started so the space under roof was minimal.

There were two main runways, which formed an 'X' when viewed from the sky. There was almost no field lighting and only relatively experienced pilots would use the strips at night. And then only in clear weather.

Then there was the obvious absence of a control tower. Sarasota County had come up short of cash when this facility was first constructed, and the planned tower was relegated to the second phase. The lack of conveniences and safety features caused local pilots to call it a *Land If You Can* strip.

Nevertheless, serious amateur pilots seemed to like the place in the daytime. Less traffic with no crossing patterns from Tampa and a lot of room for error during approach. There were no obstacles for landing or takeoff and the strips were much longer than normal although the years had taken their toll on the surface materials. The pilots and passengers could be certain of a bumpy landing regardless of the level of pilot skill.

A two-lane country road ran around most of the perimeter of the field. Because there was no landscaping to speak of, a lush growth of palms and indigent trees and underbrush had filled in most of the areas near the perimeter fences. This made it difficult to view the landing strip from the perimeter road. Without the signs, which directed people into the field, it would be quite easy to drive past it and never know that an airfield existed in the area.

The terminal was usually open until 10 P.M. on weekdays and midnight on the weekends. On this particular evening the parking lot across the street from the front entrance to the terminal building held several empty Sarasota County trucks. The county workers often parked its vehicles there rather than driving them all the way to their main facility, which was over ten miles away. A telephone company repair van was parked next to the single handicapped parking spot and four or five cars were scattered elsewhere across the well-shaded lot.

A security guard and maintenance man were the only ones standing near the front of the long, narrow building. The maintenance man kept his head down as he doggedly swept and then mopped an area near the entrance. The guard chuckled to himself as he tried to understand why anyone would need a mop on such a rainy evening.

The security guard was wearing casual civilian clothing with an arm patch identifying him as a representative of a local security company. The maintenance man was dressed in general aviation coveralls and an old baseball cap. The security guard leaned up against the wall near the door as a lone telephone repairman stepped out through the door. He was carrying his tools in an old toolbox.

"Thanks for not giving me a ticket, Chico", he whispered carefully, but sarcastically, to the security guard whom he obviously knew quite well. "Klaus is my name, and wire-tapping is my game! And, I'm out of here, pal!"

Chico Diaz smiled and gave the repairman a mock salute.

"Good job! Hey, don't forget to keep me up to date. I'm not planning on spending my life out here."

"I'll give you a call later. If it doesn't happen by midnight, just take off. I'll meet you at Crocks about 12:30 either way."

Klaus Schulz hustled back to his truck, hurriedly packed his tools, and jumped into the truck and drove off.

The maintenance man was starting to clean up some trash that had been spread across the sidewalk near the north end of the building, presumably aided by gusts of wind from the rainstorm. Several civilian pilots who had been flying in a club plane sat in the patio area around the corner. They were discussing their flight while downing cokes from the soda machine next to the building. The rain was just a mist that was turning on and off every few minutes. Meanwhile, the Sun was trying to peek through a break in the clouds. It wouldn't be long before it set and darkness would cover the field.

One of the front windows of the terminal building was distinguished by a worn and discolored Chicago White Sox poster touting the county as the spring training home of the American League team. The Sox were long gone, currently battling to stay above .500 in the early season race, but Al still cherished his visions of Richie Allen lofting a hanging curve ball far over the left-center field fence. After all, he had chased the ball down in the tall grass, and Allen had autographed it for him.

Chico walked over toward Al.

"Well, I'm just moonlighting. I'm a regular in Clearwater, but Killoran Security pays so well for these off-hour gigs that they're hard to resist. You should give this security guard routine a try!"

"The man has bigger plans for me, if you know what I mean." mumbled Al. "But why security all of a sudden. There's nothing here anyone would want to steal. What's the occasion?"

"Some of your typical basic telephone vandalism. Must be those teenagers who TP'ed the lighthouse last week. I would have thought that they'd be too wasted from graduation, but you never know. I should be able to leave by midnight. Then again, they may want me to stay all night. That last telephone guy fixed the problems so I imagine the phones are okay again".

"Sort of messes up your time-frame?" posed Al as he glanced at the new maintenance crew working near the South end of the building. "I wouldn't stay all night for those punks. They'll be on to bigger and better things tonight."

"I'll be out of here sooner than you think" responded Chico as he glanced down the road which approached the terminal. "I have the next two days off, and then I'm going to sleep straight through."

As Al walked away, Chico noticed the dark silhouette of an XKE as it rolled down the roadway under the limbs of old cypress trees and into the parking lot. The car came to a stop in the spot next to where the telephone truck had been parked. The occupant kept the engine running for several minutes as the drops of rain fell. Then he quietly shut it down and carefully surveyed the front of the building. He carefully watched the security guard standing near the door and the supervisor as he stood near the corner of the building. Several other people had settled in the patio area. After another minute or so the car door opened.

The man stepping from the Jaguar wore a light raincoat and carried a rather large, black umbrella. He crouched as if attempting to dodge the raindrops. Then, he began his walk slowly and hesitatingly around the puddles and across the pedestrian walkway toward the front door. Chico nodded to the visitor and watched him pass under the archway and through the narrow doors that led into the terminal building.

After the visitor had passed from view, Al returned and nodded his head.

"That doesn't look like a teenager to me. He looks more like one of those county government types. What do you think? Is he checking up on the phones or on us? Maybe both!"

Chico shook his head negatively as he walked away from the building and out to the curb. "You'd better get those boys of yours working just in case. I'm going to walk a simulated patrol out to the parking lot. See you later."

Inside the terminal the visitor carefully closed his umbrella and looked cautiously around the small central entryway. To the left stood a bank of telephones clustered in a small rectangle. Of the two rows of phones, the visitor selected a seat near the far wall and withdrew some change from his pants pocket. No one else was in view as he dialed a long distance number and dropped in a series of nickels, dimes and quarters.

A male voice answered.

"Drug Enforcement Agency, your party please".

The visitor mumbled something into the phone. He could hear the scuffling of feet and distant conversation on the other end. Then all was silent for what seemed like at least a minute. Presently, he was joined in conversation by a man with a deep, slowly resonating voice.

"Costello, who do I have the pleasure of speaking with?"

"If you don't know by now, you'd better get another job!" the visitor responded calmly.

It seemed as if the agent on the far end was measuring his words. "A little late in the evening, my friend." he said slowly and carefully.

"Don't expect overtime on this one!" whispered the visitor. "And when will you cheap bastards get an 800 number? I'm tired of search-ing for nickels and dimes every time I have to call you!"

The agent tried to respond but was interrupted.

"Don't talk, asshole! Just listen! It's tonight, or rather, tomorrow morning. Early, very early! And after this meeting, I want my stuff back, I want my friends out, and I want you to make me invisible or you can kiss your cases and your stupid career goodbye!"

"We already have a deal." the agent said with some confidence. "And we'll stand by our end of it.

"That's all I can tell you. A deal is a deal."

"So far, your record of standing by our deals is pretty miserable!" remarked the visitor.

"We never promised you every single thing you wanted, just our best efforts to get you off the hook and give you some cover, that's all."

Neither party spoke for a few seconds as they both realized that the conversation was drifting off on a tangent.

"I want to get out of here now. I've given you enough for two sen-tences!" the visitor said with some lack of confidence.

"Don't try to change the parameters now, or I will personally pull on your chain so hard you will be screaming for 30 years!" threatened the agent, raising the stakes.

"You can pull all you want, but you won't get him without me. And that's a fact."

"I told you we would take care of you! Just make sure you don't run off anywhere without telling us!"

There was silence at both ends of the line.

"What time is the arrival?" asked the agent in a very defensive voice. The visitor detected that he had instilled some fear into his target.

"Do I look like a travel agency to you? Tonight is my fee for invisibility!"

"You'll get it! How many times do I have to repeat myself?"

"I only promised you the pilot. You have to take it from there. I don't want them coming after me later. And you didn't hear any of this from me."

Again there was silence for a few seconds.

"You haven't given me any reason to trust you! So I want the money and the new identification before I deliver the goods! If you are bull-shitting me, tell me now because you're in this as deep as I am"!

"What's the time frame?" responded the agent. He was beginning to lose his patience, but he knew that he was in a delicate situation. *No time for a mistake*! His prey could be gone in the blink of an eye.
"Scheduled for 0400. That's 4 AM for you. If you miss them, it's your ass, not mine!"

A pause ensued as the agent carefully measured his response.

"Harry", he paused, then began again. "Do you know that these calls are monitored and recorded and that any threat issued to a Federal Officer might result in your incarceration for a very long period of time?"

Harry smirked, "Get off of it. Cut the power trip, Costello. Besides, it's my dime on this one."

"You'd better have your information correct this time. I don't feel like coming all the way down there for nothing."

"Hey, you need to get out once in a while", Harry laughed. "Oh, by the way, its Sarasota Municipal, just in case you weren't quick enough to track me. I'll meet you at the coffee shop near Highway 41. You can find the place, can't you? And make sure Josef shows up! He's the one who really owes me on this one."

"Don't attract any attention down there." Costello spoke in a much more official tone. "We don't want your buddies in FDLE screwing this thing up."

With Harry's silence, the agent seemed to have made his point. After a few seconds they confirmed their rendezvous point and time and the conversation ended.

The next sound was that of the visitor playfully slamming the phone into its cradle. The noise of the phone bouncing against the hollow wall was loud enough for the security guard to hear outside the building. Chico turned and slowly walked toward the door only to meet the visitor on the way out.

"Any problems?" Chico asked of the visitor as they passed.

"No, just a wasted trip, as usual. What's new?" Harry waived and turned toward his car.

"No problems with the phone, I hope. We've had some vandalism out here lately. They've just been repaired."

"The phone is about the only thing that did work." Harry turned back toward the guard. "Say, are you on duty all night?"

"No, just 'till midnight." Chico pointed to the doors. "After that, these doors are locked."

The visitor slowly put his coat back on and a confident smile slowly spread across his face. He began the short trek back to his car after once again scanning the terminal. As he walked, he was thinking to himself, almost speaking the thoughts as he considered them. *If Carlos shows up, will Gerona spot him? Heck, even if Carlos didn't make it, the pilot was the key to this whole thing.* All he could do now was wait for the trap to close.

23

Down on the Bayou

Harmlessly passing your time
in the grassland away,
Only dimly aware of a certain
unease in the air,
You better watch out,
There may be dogs about,
I've looked over Jordan, and I have seen,
Things are not what they seem

—Pink Floyd, *Animals*

Near Sarasota, Florida

"Alligators, bugs, and all the rest! I hate walking through this crap at night. Everything's feeding on me and all for a goddamn dog!"

"Chris, you look like a drowned rat. I told you to bring your rain gear, but no, not you. Next time you'll listen to me. Actually, you're covered with so much mud I can't see how you can get wet even if it keeps on raining."

"Okay, Josh, enough out of you. I'm going around that clump of cypress ahead and try and flush Rover out. Watch for him!"

"This has to be tick heaven!" Josh exclaimed with unusual enthusiasm. "One dog and two humans and all the blood they can suck in one evening. I'll sure be happy when we get back on days. This nighttime shit is a drag. Everyone I know, with the single, obvious exception of you, is out having a good time. And, they're probably dry at that! But not me, no sir! I had to work for the State of Florida and the Fish and Game Department, no less. It might have been more fun to go to jail for a few years than spend ten years up to my neck in shit. At least I could have gotten some sleep. What a great career idea this was. Adventure! Travel! See the world through a swamp! Be chased by alligators! What fun!"

Chris looked over toward his partner. "I must be crazy, but you sound the same as me. We must be the two biggest dummies on the planet. Maybe the biggest dummies in the solar system. Say, now that you mentioned it, when do we go back to days anyway?"

"Two weeks. Just two long, never ending weeks. Can you count to fourteen?"

Josh glanced at his fingers and started counting. "I can't even fit fourteen on both hands. I'll have to take off my boots and use my toes for this one."

Chris just grunted at the attempted humor.

"I'll just count the ticks on my left leg. That should do it. But I must admit, I finally found a good use for smoking. Just light one up and give it a good pull, then put the business end on the tick. Careful, not to burn yourself, son! Well, if ticks could scream, they would, because that baby is hot. They get off, no questions asked. Another pull on the cigarette, another tick gone bye-bye."

"You're definitely having too much fun on this job, Chris. I, for one, would just put the old leg in gasoline and light it off. It smarts for a while, but they all go to heaven at once."

"Maybe we should just arrest them!" shouted Chris as he sloshed his way through the swamp.

"Arrest who? It's been quite a few years, and you've never arrested anyone, and you know it. All of those fishing and hunting citations are just like parking tickets. We don't even have guns! How could we arrest whoever it is you're talking about?"

"Arrest the dog, who else! The ticks could crawl out between the bars."

The boys continued their search for the lost dog. They were both outdoor types, but each cut from a different mould. Josh was tall and thin. Chris had often wondered just how much blood Josh could spare to the ticks. Josh was always running and lifting weights and eating, but he never seemed to gain much over his standard one hundred and eighty pounds.

For his part Chris wore every pound of food he ate on his bulky frame. "Two hundred, thirty and arising!" he mumbled to himself.

Chris was stepping through the edge of a small pond with his flashlight scanning the terrain ahead. He'd thought he'd seen something moving up ahead.

"What's the dog's name anyway?"

"Harvey! The dog's named Harvey! What kind of a name is that for a dog? Maybe we're really looking for a rabbit. This dog's so dumb we should call him Fred! Yes, Fred sounds perfect." Josh was making reference to one of their supervisors.

"Here, Fred! Here, Fred! Come on in, Fred." Chris grunted his approval.

Just as the wayward dog came into view, Joshes' beeper whistled, and he waived Chris.

"Keep after Harvey while I get the truck. If you don't have him by the time I get back, he's on his own, another successful escape!"

As Chris was snapping a leash onto the lost hound, Josh reached their truck and drove to where Chris was petting the dog. He was a friendly hound and at least as glad to see the officers as they were to see him.

"Let's get to a phone so I can call the office. Then we can drop Harvey at the compound in the morning."

Harvey barked happily in the back of their truck as they made their way toward civilization. When they reached the phone at a nearby gas station, Josh made the call. Jenny answered the phone and after exchanging pleasantries with Josh, she turned the phone over to the duty officer.

Fred Cusack was also from Chicago, and he was ready to retire, but financial demands caused him to return to duty on the night shift. He had been a city cop during his younger days, but now he was saddled with a bunch of young fish and game people he had trouble understanding. Most of his charges on the night patrols were local boys and girls who had never seen State Street.

Fred still possessed his Chicago accent so Josh knew something was up when Fred immediately began speaking as if he were from Kentucky.

"Now, which one of you boys has a big time friend in Fort Myers?"

"What?" shouted Josh as Harvey began barking at just the wrong time.

"Are you armed?"

"With a shovel and leash and a ten foot ladder. What else would we need? Maybe a fork?" Joshes' replies equally sarcastic.

"Get your asses home and get your 12 gauge! I have a hot one for you. You've always wanted to slap the cuffs on someone, haven't you?"

Chris could hear only one side of the conversation, but he knew that something new and interesting was afoot. From Joshes' expression, he could tell that this conversation was not about a lost pooch.

"Does this mean we don't get any jelly donuts", yelled Chris, loud enough so that Fred would be sure to hear him.

Josh covered the phone with his hand and pointed it directly at Harvey. His face wore his most serious look of disapproval about the unwanted noise.

"Chris, do you want the eight to eight slice forever?"

Chris moved to quiet the dog as Josh finished the conversation in muffled tones.

"What's the problem, Fred? Fish robbing the river bank?"

Fred chuckled but quickly came back to the subject.

"No, it looks like we have some dumpers at Wild Acres. The last time we ran into this type, we got shot at. So be careful and take your gun. You know where Wild Acres is located, don't you?"

"Yeah, no problem. It's that abandoned subdivision west of here. Where did you pick this up, Fred?"

"We got a call from a construction worker. At least that's what he said he was. He said he knew his company was dumping trash over there regularly. He wouldn't give us a name, but sounded legit. He probably just got laid off, or he's pissed at the boss. He didn't want any publicity, but he insisted that tonight was the night.

"What about the sheriff's office?"

"You boys will have to cover this one. The sheriff seems to have something big going tonight. I called them first, but they couldn't spare anyone. Besides, this guy called us first. He must really be confused about the function of Fish and Game!" Josh could tell that Fred was getting a kick out of this assignment.

"Fred, sometimes I wonder about Fish and Game myself. How could I be so stupid?"

"Hey, don't worry about it Josh. Just be careful. Stake the place out until five or so and then come in. While you're there, look around and see if anyone's been dumping shit in the water. If so, we can send a crew out in the morning. I'll try to get the County to send someone over to look in on you before 0400. So don't shoot the cops, okay!"

"Okay. I think we can tell the difference, unless it's the Sarasota Sheriff's Department that's doing the dumping! In that case we'll shoot them. Thanks for the warning anyway, Fred. I'll call in later and summarize our big adventure for you." Josh hung up the phone and turned to Chris.

"Let's get over to your place, Chris. We need your twelve gauge and some shells, and we have to move fast. I really hate people who dump garbage in those canals. It would be nice to put a few of them in the slammer. We'll leave Harvey at your place until morning."

24

To the Rescue

Everybody wants all the world can give 'em,
Everybody wants to get all they can get,
Everybody's waiting on somethin' that hasn't
come yet.

—Tom Petty, *Hard Promises*

Washington, D.C.

"What a complete asshole! I wish I could snap his scrawny little neck!"

Agent Costello slowly lowered the phone. Dealing with informants was one part of his job he detested. Generally, they were unreliable and would say anything to get an advantage. This man was one of the worst. It was only because Harry Michaels provided the single, tenuous link to his prey that he dealt with him at all. That, and the fact that his Special Agent for the Caribbean was the only man with a chance to corner their adversary.

Josef Gerona had tracked and trapped Harry Michaels with the ease and grace of a exceptional bullfighter. He lured Michaels into a trap and made him feel in complete control the whole time. He even turned Michaels down on their first proposed venture, not something an undercover agent normally had the courage to try. That rejection made Michaels pursue Josef with a bigger and better deal that was converted into a bigger and better trap. Josef's patience and attention to detail had spilled over onto Costello. He listened to Michaels's insults and threats and recognized them as the cries of a weakened and desperate animal.

Costello turned toward the other man in the small conference room and pointed to the door.

"Get the Lear warmed up and ready to go! Tell Hank, non-stop to Sarasota Municipal. And while you're at it, get the Field Office in Tampa. We need at least ten agents on the ground. We'll need a helicopter, too, if they have access to one. And two chase planes or more if they have them. Tell them to check with Customs. No FDLE on this one! No contact with the State of Florida at all on this one! No exceptions!"

The younger man's badge read 'Arthur White'. He was a new agent who had been attached to Costello for training. Arthur moved toward the door with some hesitation, then turned to ask one of his many questions.

"If I might ask, what is the FDLE?"

"Where have you been all this time?" Costello seemed frustrated by the constant stream of questions coming from the young man.

"Wait! Call Orlando, too, and tell them to notify Customs in Ft. Lauderdale! They might have some support for us. Between the two offices you should be able to get everything we need. Here's a list with phone numbers so you won't forget anything. Give them our remote number in case they get confused."

"No problem. But the FDLE?"

If nothing else, Arthur was persistent. He had been warned about Costello's temper, but he also knew that his boss was mostly bark and very little bite, so he persisted.

"Florida Department of Law Enforcement! Just think of them as a bunch of peacocks! Always whining and crying like babies! They cannot be trusted! Remember that if you can remember anything."

"Sorry, but I might need to know some of these acronyms in the future."

"Arthur, just call Tampa and Orlando, and tell them that FDLE is blind on this one. I'll give you the whole picture on the way down. Now, hustle or you'll be watching this one on television from the unemployment office."

After Arthur collected himself and exited the room to complete his tasks, Costello picked up the phone and dialed a long distance number. His call was met by a familiar answering machine response. He waited while the machine clicked into operation and requested his message.

"Josef, this is Phil Costello. Tonight at Sarasota Municipal just like I predicted! And remember, I told you so! We'll be en route in the Lear within the hour so call me when you get this. I'm not sure who will attend, but we should be able to get the pilot on this one. No FDLE! Try to get there by midnight so we can set it up properly."

Costello paused then continued his message.

"Look, if this is a false alarm, I want you to jump all over Michaels. He's afraid of you! He knows enough to help us, but I'm not sure he's telling me everything. He should be there tonight so take it upon yourself to verbally abuse him a little. I'd appreciate it. We'll be at the restaurant on 41 near the airport. Be ready for some action. And please, don't bring your dog!"

Costello had been prepared for this trip for weeks, so it was only a matter of calling home, then checking on his men. Once he was sure he had everything he needed, Costello headed for the loading area in the rear of the building.

When he arrived at the dock, some hurried packing of equipment was still under way. Radio gear, night surveillance equipment, and weapons had all been loaded. The team leader was just checking the inventory. When he saw Costello, he indicated that the team was ready to go. Costello jumped into the lead vehicle, and the caravan headed for Andrews Air Force Base.

Traffic was light as they crossed into Maryland. In another forty minutes they were through security and ready to board the aircraft. Costello looked at his watch.

"Good work, Arthur. We're twenty minutes ahead of schedule. But don't insult me by asking for a raise!"

Arthur grinned sheepishly as he turned to Costello and offered him something to eat.

"I took the liberty to order up some donuts. I got a couple chocolate types for you. We'll have coffee on the plane. It's just like home."

The weather near Washington was clear, and the co-pilot indicated that it was mild all the way to Florida. Fortunately, none of the erratic weather that characterizes spring along the eastern seaboard was in the forecast. The only threat of rain loomed over Sarasota. The crew had made this flight several times in the last two months so no briefing was necessary.

With the plane barely in the air, the agents moved to a makeshift briefing area. There were six passengers in all. One of them was FBI. The rest were DEA. The group had worked together on similar operations so they seemed at ease with each other. Costello placed a large whiteboard on the front panel near the restroom door and prepared to update his men. Once everyone was seated, Costello began his review.

"This should be rather easy."

He turned and attached a map of the Sarasota area to the board. As was his habit, he was using an old eighteen-inch ruler as a pointer.

"We have an informant who has verified the intended landing of an aircraft carrying controlled substances at the Sarasota Municipal Airport. Arrival should be sometime around 0400.

"As you will see, this is a small, local civilian airport. It has almost no night traffic and does not have an operational control tower. The surrounding area is mostly undeveloped with the exception of the major North-South road here, about two miles to the East."

Costello enjoyed using maps in his presentations. It gave him the feeling of being in command during a battle. It reminded him of his days with the CIA as a control officer. He thought back to the many activities he had helped conduct in Central America. It was almost like being in a war, especially the operations in Guatemala, Nicaragua and Cuba.

"We should be there about three hours before the event. We'll set up on the ground near these hangars. Cover is important here. The target may make a pass over the field or have hidden observers in the area. Our contact is supposed to be in charge of ground operations, unloading, and distribution. But he cannot be trusted! So be very careful.

"Our plan is to let the aircraft land and commence unloading. Our contact will have the vehicles ready for us. The cargo is undefined, but we expect marijuana and Quaaludes. The payload itself is of secondary importance. The pilot is our primary target here. His picture is present in the handout I gave you. Make sure you are familiar with it. He's the main reason we're going down there!

"Now, as far as we know, these men are not armed, and no weapons have been reported by the informant; however, you never know what might happen in a panic situation. Keep your cover until the Sarasota task force has retained all of the ground crew members. Our job is to block the runway and take the plane. Just follow the plan. We'll go as the first product hits the pavement."

Costello paused for a sip of coffee. He had been through this speech before, but this was no time for slipups.

"Move the prisoners to the Federal Holdover in Clearwater. No radio traffic en route! We don't want the State boys in on this until we get to Clearwater. You all know that we believe they have a leak, and we have bigger fish to fry than just this ground crew. Take 41 all the way down, no stops! Arthur and I will take it from there. You should be back at Andrews by three tomorrow afternoon."

Costello stepped over to the service area and refilled his coffee.

"That's about it unless you have any questions. This is still a standard operation. Go by the book, and everything should be a piece of cake."

The meeting concluded with several minor questions as the agents settled down for the rest of the flight. Arthur came over to the table where Costello sat. His boss was busy preparing a report on the case.

"If you don't mind my asking, how did we get this informant, this guy Michaels?"

Costello realized that he had been in this position years ago. Things to do and no clue about what was happening. When he looked at Arthur, he saw enthusiasm and uncertainty. It was almost always the same with these new agents. *All except Josef Gerona!*

In Josef's eyes he had seen much more determination and dedication than he had seen in the others. Josef was a loner. He was single-minded about his job; there was no fooling around with him. Never an extended happy hour, and no flirting with the girls in the office. He was all business. Arthur held his stare on Costello waiting for some kind of answer.

"Harry Michaels is a Class I DEA Violator. That's right out of the book.

"But, first things first. You need to know about Josef. Without Josef there is no Michaels. And without Michaels there is no pilot. And without the pilot there is no Carlos. There is a hierarchy here. We have the first two pieces. Tonight we may get the third piece."

Costello took another sip of his coffee. He was now on his fourth cup and the effect of the caffeine were beginning to show.

"Josef is our special agent for the Caribbean. He's Cuban, but his English is flawless. So is his Spanish, Portuguese, and French. You can drop him anywhere in the Western Hemisphere, and he's at home. His main job right now is to bring in several major Colombian exporters. He knows how they think and how they act. It's like fighting fire with fire.

"Josef is always planning and asking smart questions. I've never come across a Cuban quite like him. He knows every move he's going to make before he makes it. And better yet, he knows his adversaries' moves before they make them. He is a dangerous man, very dangerous!

I sleep much better knowing that he's on our side, but something about him still scares me.

"He's the one who trapped Harry Michaels. As you know, Michaels is the guy who is leading this parade. He'd roll over on his mother if he thought it would help him. Michaels got himself into a deal with our target. We call him Carlos, and we have reason to believe that his full name is Carlos Chacon.

"This man Carlos is also a clever fellow just like most of the cartel leaders in Colombia. No one has any real, solid information on the man. No photos, no nothing. He's almost invisible. He's not as high a profile smuggler as most of his fellow cartel leaders. He operates out of Colombia for the most part, but we don't believe the other cartels work directly with him. We have leads on six or seven American pilots who we think have worked with Carlos. But none of them actually know him. That's what makes this pilot different.

"Well, before I get too far off the track let me finish your history lesson. Our boy Michaels got himself into a deal with Chacon. Michaels's father owns an air terminal down in Honduras or Guatemala, wherever. Josef has been watching him for quite a while. We've known that Frank Michaels has been dealing through Costa Rica and Nicaragua. But we want to use him to catch the bigger fish.

"So, as fate would have it, his son Harry gets cozy with Carlos' contact in Guatemala. One thing leads to another, and they set up a gig for Central Florida. Josef gets himself on the crew and nails them.

"Well, not all of them. I know for a fact that he let several of the ground crew escape. He must have taken promises from them. But as far as the report goes, the rest of the ground crew got away. And he walks away with Michaels.

"I've got to hand it to Josef for his style. He has some markers out there to be collected. He'll call them in when he needs them most."

"Hey, I can never promote the guy. He's too valuable out there where he is. And he seems to like it. Sure he operates a little outside of the book, but he makes my life a lot easier.

"Take a lesson from him! If you want promotions, stay in the office and drive that desk. It's the only way. The only way I got into this job was my injury. No more jumping from planes for me. Remember, flying a plane can get you killed, but flying a desk will get you promoted!"

"But you're out in the field now, aren't you?" said Arthur.

Costello laughed at the question.

"This isn't the field. When you get to the jungle or rainforest, that's the field! Or, when you find yourself floating around in the ocean while your plane is sinking, that's the field! Not these chump trips to Florida. This is more like retirement!"

Arthur wanted more. He loved to hear the experienced agents tell their war stories or just give their view on the present situation. He didn't care if this operation was supposed to be easy, it was his first, and he was excited.

"How is this operation going to help us get Carlos? From the briefings it sounds like we want the pilot instead. He seems to be the key."

"Josef has been after this fellow Carlos we've been talking about for a very long time. We may not get him tonight, but we should snag a pilot who is very close to Carlos. You're right, the pilot is our main goal tonight. Everyone or thing else is just gravy. I don't want to hear you mentioning any of these names out in the field. I know that you're smart enough to keep your mouth shut. Right?"

Arthur was nodding strongly in the affirmative when one of the other agents approached Costello with a message.

"Josef is coming. He doesn't think our man will be there, but the primary target will definitely be coming."

"Good."

Costello spoke softly and showed no emotion.

As the agent turned to return to his seat, Arthur carefully posed another question.

"Why is this pilot so important? How can he lead us to Carlos?"

"He may not lead us to Carlos, but Carlos may come to him. He could be the bait we need."

Art was still confused.

"Why him? He's an American, isn't he? Are they friends?"

"The word is…, and it's only a supposition, an assumption made by the department,…the word is that this man was saved by Carlos' father. It was at the Bay of Pigs invasion in 1961. You were throwing your rattle around your playpen in those days. Anyway, I knew Carlos' father. His name is Raymond Chacon. He led a reconnaissance team during the Bay of Pigs operation. They rescued about ten people, but Raymond Chacon stayed behind. We think he was trying to find his wife and daughter. After getting his team into the water, he headed for Havana. That's where he was captured."

"Castro's men got him? That's sad!"

"That's not the worst part. It could have been our fault! First, rumor has it that he was abandoned by two CIA operatives who were in his team. Then, when he reached the CIA contact we gave him in Havana, he was taken by the Cubans. Castro had turned her after the invasion failed and someone in his home town spotted him and told the militia. We believe our contact walked him right into militia headquarters, but we're not absolutely sure. In any case, he never had a chance."

"Did we punish those agents? The ones who abandoned him?"

"Arthur, this was war we are talking about, and what I'm telling you is more folklore based upon rumor and speculation than absolute fact, so be careful how you interpret it!

"Was Chacon executed? What about his family?" Art's interest was intense.

"He's alive, or at least, we believe he is still there! Fidel locked him up and threw the key away. I couldn't tell you much about his family, with one big exception, that is. Carlos is thought to be his son. Right now there are six open documented cases of missing CIA agents in Central America. When I left that agency, there was reason to believe that Carlos was behind at least five of the disappearances."

Arthur's eyes opened wide. "I get it! He's pissed. Real mad!"

Arthur paused to consider this new information.

"I guess I would be mad, too, if my father were hung out to dry by that agency. And yet, you say the people on this flight are probably not armed."

"As long as we're dealing with the transportation of drugs, we should be okay. Michaels tells us they are never armed. But if we get close to him, things might change."

Arthur thought of Josef's role in this drama.

"What about Josef. He knows of the danger, doesn't he?"

Costello nodded.

"That he does. He's our best and maybe our only chance to catch this guy. If anyone can do it, Josef is the one. And he has to do it by getting inside this guy's head. He has to think the way Carlos does so that he can predict his actions.

"You should learn a lot from this case, Arthur. Just watch Josef and see what he does and how he does it. But don't tell him I told you this. I don't want him blaming me if you start bugging him, understand!"

"Couldn't be clearer, Boss. Don't worry about me. I'll watch him like an hawk."

25

God Plays Dice

I'm waiting on the countdown
Sitting in the shade
Things about to turn around
How the madness fades

—Lindsey Buckingham…
Out of the Cradle

A house near Sarasota, Florida

"Where are the flashlights I put in here yesterday, goddamit? I thought we packed them in this suitcase this morning. This is so typical; every time I get the shit we need together, someone comes along and screws it up!"

As usual, Edward Gebinsky found himself disconcerted by the actions of his associates. No matter how carefully he planned and planned again, something always seemed to go wrong. And his frustration showed through clearly to his two companions who watched his body language and listened to his agitated voice. Gebinsky wanted everything to go perfectly, but it never seemed to happen that way.

Gebinsky wanted to be a ladies man, too, but his personal habits always worked against him as did his expanding waistline and receding hairline. To make things worse, he wasn't particularly tall and his imperfect diet caused him to be overweight by at least twenty pounds most of the time. To compensate for these perceived deficiencies, he always tried to place himself in command of every situation. The result was an insecure and unhappy man.

"I bought those things yesterday, batteries and all, and now they're gone already." Gebinsky scowled as he looked up from is work. He wasn't happy, again!

"Did one of you take this shit or what?"

Johnny and Juan looked back from the front of the van. This was a situation they had experienced before, and they were in no mood to incur the wrath of the person often referred to as *Little Napoleon*. They looked at one another, as if on queue, and each waited for the other to speak first. Neither wanted to be a hero.

When no response was forthcoming, Gebinsky began muttering to himself. "Why do I always get stuck with the goddamn children! I'm not a baby sitter! I didn't get divorced to have to go through this again! Forty years on the planet, and I'm still babysitting. Fuck it!"

Gebinsky slammed the suitcase cover closed and turned away.

Knowing that an answer was probably in order, Johnny glanced toward the garage door and then back at Gebinsky.

"Kathy might have them. She was going over the list this morning and could have picked them up when she was doing the inventory."

Gebinsky listened, but the answer was definitely not to his satisfaction. He motioned to Johnny for some immediate action.

"Well, go get her, and find out where the hell the flashlights are. I'm not going out there without them! If she lost them, she can go out to the subdivision and unload the product by herself. And you can tell her that I said so!"

The command caused Johnny to break from his frozen pose. He jumped out of the van and raced into the house. In a minute he returned with an excited look on his face.

"They're in the glove compartment," he whispered in a high pitched voice. "She put them in the glove compartment!"

Johnny pointed toward the front seat of the vehicle, and then sprinted around the van and opened the passenger side door. He quickly popped the latch on the glove compartment door and reached inside.

"Ah, here they are," he declared as a smile of satisfaction and relief spread across his face. "Right where she put them this morning. Do you want this stuff back there?"

Gebinsky waived his hand negatively at the younger men and continued his work as he muttered aloud under his breath about the situation.

"She shouldn't be here. Ted warned her not to be anywhere around here tonight. I told her to get back to Lauderdale, but she wants to earn her share. I wouldn't mind at all except that she has a way of screwing things up." Gebinsky slowly looked up at his two charges.

"Do me a favor for once. It's easier for you to talk to her. Tell her not to mess with the hardware or move anything around without asking us first. Actually, without asking me first!

"I'm the one who's responsible for this end of the operation. And I'd rather not end up dead or in the slammer because she was tidying up. Get it?"

Johnny agreed. "I'll talk to her about this. It won't happen again. She must have thought she was helping us get set up and just forgot to tell us."

"Well, no more forgetting! I'm making you responsible for her." Gebinsky slammed the suitcase down on the floor of the garage to emphasize his point.

Johnny nodded vigorously. "I'll take care of her. The three of us can do the loading. We do need someone here at the house just in case something goes wrong. We don't want to walk into a trap, do we?"

"Well, it's her father's house, isn't it! Then, again, I'm sure he doesn't know we're using it. And Ted, that fearless leader of ours, thinks we're going to some public storage facility out in the county. But we all know that that plan just wouldn't work. Someone would spot us unloading those vans for sure. We just have to hope that she keeps her mouth shut about this whole thing." Gebinsky had calmed down considerably and after a pause to light a cigarette, he continued.

"I'll admit it, boys, I like the idea of using this house as the holding area. We have a little more protection if we're careful, and it was her idea to use the place. I just don't want this part of the deal messed up because Harry will blame me for it even if it's not my fault. And he's a far bigger pain in the ass than she is. It just runs in the family, I guess."

Johnny was also worried about Kathy's father, and he parroted Gebinsky's thoughts.

"If Frank or Harry or Ted find out about the house, it's her idea all the way. She's the one who brought us over here. We're just following orders and doing the best we can."

Johnny patted the van on the fender as if it was a reliable farm animal and looked back at Gebinsky. "What about the other truck. Where is it?"

Gebinsky shook his head. He was sure that he had explained all of this several times already, and he couldn't understand why his associates didn't get it the first time.

"First of all, in this neighborhood, anything more than one vehicle at five o'clock in the morning is going to look real funny. These people are asleep by ten. If one of them gets up to take a crap and sees us, they'll call the cops thinking we're burglars. These old farts are so goddamn nosey, it's unbelievable!

With just one van coming in, everything should be okay. We'll be in this garage before anyone spots us and gets curious. And once we're in here, we work quickly, but quietly. No talking, no noise at all! Just concentration on the job!

"In the second place, Ted and Harry want the load split. I'm not even sure who's in charge of the other vehicle. Hopefully, they don't know who's on this one. The fewer people we know, the better for us. As far as I'm concerned, I don't know either of you. Never saw you before. And you've never seen me. Remember that!"

"The masks!" exclaimed Johnny as he reached into a shopping bag in the front seat of the van and pulled out several winter stretch caps with holes cut in them.

"Juan, here's your mask. When we get to the subdivision, put it on and keep it on. And don't talk unless absolutely necessary. Most of these guys would roll over on their mother."

Juan had been standing quietly, listening to the conversation for the past several minutes. He smiled as the others realized that they were making all of the noise while Juan was perfectly silent. Juan responded to Johnny even though it was no longer necessary.

"I won't say a word. I can work, and I can run. I don't like a lot of talking anyway. Say, what do you mean by roll over? It's probably a stupid question, but I haven't done this type of gig before."

Johnny answered his friend. "It's when someone gets caught but then tries to use his friends or people he was with to get out of jail. Say you get arrested and the rest of us get away. The cops pressure you. *Give us the names of your friends and we'll cut you a deal.* If you cave in, then they catch everyone."

Gebinsky shook his head. "That's usually the only way they catch anyone. Without rollovers they'd be out of business. The best part is that the squealer usually gets off and his friends do the time."

"The squealer's friends can't be too happy about that," Juan responded. "What happens when they get out? If it was my butt, I'd be looking for the guy who put me away."

"I'll leave that to your imagination," Gebinsky barked as he continued to pack his gear.

Johnny turned to Juan to continue the definition. "Hey, Juan, Harry told me about the Canary Brothers. Two guys from Detroit. They got caught and tried to help themselves by testifying against their partners and customers. They appeared in court twelve times, each time providing evidence for the State of Michigan or the Feds.

"Guess what! When it came time to reduce their sentences, the judge said no! They squealed all over the place for nothing. Can you imagine that? Now, they're doing time, and everyone knows about them, inside and outside of the joint. If they live long enough to get out, they'll wish they were back inside. Just one of the dangers of trying to save your ass by hanging someone else!"

Gebinsky closed his suitcase and pushed it into the rear of the van. "Let's hope we won't need any of that. Remember! Harry is rolling over right now. I know he's doing a deal with the Feds. If Ted wasn't in on this and this wasn't Frank's house and Kathy wasn't here, I'd be outta here. But I know he's frying some bigger fish. They should be looking somewhere else tonight. As long as the cops are busy catching someone else, we should be safe. I think we've got a clear track for once."

Gebinsky looked up at his two partners. He decided that it was time to go over the details of the plan. There was nothing complicated about it, but he just felt better making sure that the boys were focussed on the job at hand. And in spite of the assurances he had received from Harry and Ted Michaels, he wanted to go over every simple step to make sure that there were no simple mistakes.

"We'll be ready to go at two. From here to Denny's in fifteen minutes. Breakfast until three. While we are in the restaurant all we do is talk about fishing. Fishing, fishing, fishing! That's all we talk about. So don't start asking me anything in there about the operation. Got it?" Gebinsky didn't wait for a response.

"Then, on to the subdivision by three-thirty. Then, we wait. About four-thirty is touch down. If there's a problem, I've got the radio, and we abort. While we're waiting, we'll hide by the water with our fishing equipment. Remember, we are fishing, that's all."

The younger men nodded and waited for Gebinsky to continue.

"After loading, I'll drive the van here. The two of you take these bicycles. If all is clear, just ride home. Once there, you go to sleep. No screwing around!

"Then, both of you ride over to Frank Michaels's house by eight tomorrow night. Again, ride your bicycles! Don't drive over here. When you get here, put the bicycles in the storage shed.

"From here, we get to the farm by ten in the van. At that point we transfer and get paid. I'll drop you at the bus station at eleven, and you're on your own. I'll call you in a month or so. Don't call me and stay away from each other. And no bragging to your friends!"

"What about the masks and our clothes?" asked Johnny.

"That's what these plastic trash bags are for. If the coast is clear, we change clothes. You can drop them in a dumpster on the way home. Be careful. Make sure no one sees you. Just don't leave the clothes in the subdivision. We want to use it again. If they start finding garbage there, the contractor might start watching it.

"And one more thing, boys. Try not to spend the money all at once. Just be cool and live the way you've been living. No new cars, No new girlfriends! If I find out that you've become a big spender, you're out of the next gig. No second chances!

"Go to the bank and put the money in a safe deposit box. Take five hundred bucks with you and leave the rest there for at least three months. Then you can remove it about a thousand dollars at a time, and only once a month. That way no one will notice your newfound wealth, and you'll have some money for a while.

Remember! You may not see me, but I'll be watching you like a hawk. If I see you acting like a big spender, you're out. And Harry will be pissed because I'll tell him you're becoming a problem. Don't make that mistake!"

Juan nodded his understanding but Johnny had more questions.

"What if we get caught in there? What if we get caught in the subdivision?"

"The place has some beautiful small palms which are worth some money. If for some reason you get caught lurking around the subdivision, just tell whomever that you were fishing, and you were just looking at the palm trees. Or tell them you were there with your girlfriend. Kathy can back up one of you on that story.

"Try not to look too guilty. It might not be a bad idea to try and catch a few fish, too."

The boys snickered when they realized that their best alibi might be a few fish out of the canal. Gebinsky kept going.

"Just keep your cool. Once out of the subdivision, ride slowly. If you're stopped, just say you always ride at night. It's safer and you have to work during the daytime.

"Turn on your lights after you reach the main road, not inside the subdivision, for God's sake! If you get stopped with your lights out, just tell them you were fishing and forgot to turn them on. Can you handle that?"

Juan nodded again, but Johnny cast an unusually serious look at Gebinsky.

"You might not believe it because I know you think I'm an idiot, but I already thought about the fishing alibi. I even brought my fishing stuff to use as cover. I've got a valid license, too. I'll give Juan this old rod and reel to carry. That should do it."

"Okay," relented Gebinsky, "finish up, and we're on our way."

26

Change of Plans

That old shit-ass Raven has
gotten all of my things.

—**Mythical Indian Chief**

Over the Florida Keys

The lone twin-engine aircraft hummed like a bumblebee as it neared Marathon, Florida. The pilot studied the horizon looking for familiar landmarks while the co-pilot munched on a roast beef sandwich and washed it down with a cup of coffee taken from a large thermos bottle.

The pilot nudged the co-pilot and pointed toward the string of glowing lights clearly visible through the front windshield of the Beech 18.

"It always looks like an arrow to me, Charlie, like the ones you see moving on a big neon sign, pointing northeast and then north toward Miami and Fort Lauderdale. Every time I fly up this way, I want to put the old plane down right here on the highway and find a nice friendly bar near the beach."

Ron Hernandez was searching for a series of landmarks that would pinpoint his current location. Several large resorts, an old lighthouse and a cluster of shopping centers served his purposes.

Slowly, he began a descent to about four thousand feet as Charlie leafed through a small notebook of maps. After a few minutes of surveillance, the pilot motioned to his left.

"Those clouds are a little low, but if we can see the signal, we won't need the radio for confirmation. I'd like to stay off the air, if possible. It's after midnight so our signal should be visible. I'd hate to have to circle around on a night like this and run into Customs or wake up the Coast Guard."

Both men continued to scan the string of islands.

"There's the bridge and Pigeon Key!" exclaimed Ron. "Let's get down a little lower. We have to be careful here. I don't want to lose the load after all this work. Hey, C.B., we did bring the binoculars, didn't we?"

"I've got them right here, Ron."

The co-pilot continued to study the maps. He smiled as he closed the book.

"Let's hope Harry and his new friends go for it tonight. I like airdrops! They're much cleaner and a lot more fun, especially at night. And with multiple drop points we can pick the best one and not get messed up by bad local weather."

The pilot concurred. "There are some real advantages including the fact that we won't get caught on the ground. And with all the games that are being played these days, I like getting in and out fast.

"I think we're okay as far as weather goes, Charlie. Just some showers in the west, but farther up the coast. Ted Michaels will probably run into them on his way to Sarasota. If we're lucky, we'll just have some clouds but no rain. It's good cover. I wouldn't even mind some rain as long as the surface winds stay down."

"Ron, after this delivery, we should head back to Missouri. I could use a little peace and quiet for a while. I miss my woman and my hounds, and I sure would like to do a little hunting. Too bad we need fuel for this thing."

Ron was still studying the string of lights below. "We can't go straight north from here. They'll be looking for us on that trajectory. Half of the Customs fleet is probably circling over Naples or Fort Myers by now. If we do an airdrop down south, we can cut over toward Lauderdale and try the East Coast. Fort Pierce or Melbourne should be good places to land. We'll have to drop these clothes and clean up good. If guess we'll know where we're going soon enough."

"Ron, should we take another look for Ted Michaels?" asked Charlie as he motioned over his shoulder. "I hate to think that he has figured out that we've given him the slip. He could be sitting right on our tail. He could expose our strategy pretty easily."

"Nah, Charlie, he was coming in right behind the drone. Now, that was a great idea. Carlos is always thinking! What a military commander he'd have made. A brilliant but subtle strategy! He's got Ted Michaels following a decoy. I don't even know who's flying the drone, but I owe him a few beers."

"Excellent! If they stop him, the plane's full of used airplane parts direct from Frank Michaels's Honduras operation. Ernesto has some genius in him, too. Even Frank can't be pissed. Ted just followed the wrong plane. An easy mistake for anyone to make in the crowded skies over Honduras!"

"You'll never make a standup comedian, Charlie. Just stick to intelligence, okay!"

"They weren't looking for a switch, and I guess there was no reason for them to suspect anything unusual." Charlie paused. "Still, I'd like to make a loop to check it out before we run to the drop, if there's a drop."

"You've got it. First we'll get the signal, then we'll check on Ted."

The plane slowed as the occupants searched the shoreline for a special signal. Soon they saw what they were looking for. It was on the shore at Boot key, one of the many small keys in this chain of islands. Ron scanned a number of small houses set back off of the beach. Much to his satisfaction, he could see a dull glow on two of the rooftops.

"Chemiluminescence is a wonderful thing, Charlie."

The co-pilot thought for a while and responded. "Isn't it phosphorescence? I guess it doesn't matter, just so it glows in the dark."

"I think she's using a mixture of chemicals to make those markers. She turns them off with chemicals too."

"It's the binary part that I like, Ron. Who would guess that those three houses let us pick from eight different landing sites? An illuminated roof is a one and a dark roof is a zero. That signal is 101 which is binary for the number five."

The pilot shook his head. "With one number it's easier to get confused and easier to get caught. Just slide template number five over that map and let me know where we're going. I'll bet it's the Everglades."

"Ponce de Leon Bay!" Charlie pointed to the western edge of the Everglades.

"That's a nice spot for an airdrop. It's far enough from here, and it's far enough from Naples. There's very little population in the area with those mangrove swamps spread all along the shore, and the park will be closed. It should be quiet, but we'll have to slow down a little so that Ted doesn't run across us.

"Charlie, maybe we should look up the alternate site in case they aren't ready at the Bay or they have unwanted company in the water."

"Nah, that's bad luck, Ron. If we can't drop at the primary, it'll only take me a few seconds to check the alternate site template. I guess I'm just superstitious, but the last time we looked ahead, we had to go to the secondary, and I don't feel like it tonight!"

Ron nodded. "God! It's so good to see South Florida again. It's just like home. I love Missouri, but I must admit something. I could live down here, no problem. A margarita in one hand, a fishing pole in the other. And a good looking woman in the other. Well, you know what I mean. A little Jimmy Buffet here, some good rum there. That's the way life is supposed to be lived.

Charlie concurred, but it was back to business.

"You realize that the signal means that Harry Michaels has actually set the trap for us in Sarasota. He really is trying to nail us just to get himself off the hook. What a scumbag!"

"Good, he's taken the bait. Now we know for sure that we can't trust him. Or trust his brother, either. And that asshole Frank Michaels falls right in there, too.

"But Carlos knew that a long time ago. He's got something else working here, Charlie. Something connected to the Michaels family. In the future we'll have to steer clear of SETCOMP. I don't want us messing things up for Ernesto."

Ron turned the plane to the north as the co-pilot made his way to the side door. "Make sure you strap yourself in, Charlie. I almost lost you last time, remember?"

"How could I forget. Well, maybe I can learn to fly that way. I'm putting the mini-chute on just in case." Charlie struggled to strap on the small parachute that had been hanging on the side of the fuselage.

"I've practiced with this thing a thousand times. Even in the dark! It's still a pain in the ass. Well, better safe than sorry as they say."

"Just hang on Charlie, I'm going to loop around to make sure that we're alone up here. I'm going to take it down to two thousand feet and turn back for a few miles. Keep your eyes open!"

Ron took the plane down and around rather quickly in an attempt to surprise anyone who might be following them. After several altitude changes and small circles, he was convinced that the other Beech was on its own course and not tagging along behind them.

"Okay, rest for a while, Charlie. I'm heading for the drop zone. Then it's margaritas all around!"

After about thirty minutes the plane slowed again as the pilot searched for another signal.

"There they are! And in an almost perfect triangle, too. I have to hand it to those boys. Always on time and on station! And, they probably caught some dolphin while they were at it."

The co-pilot couldn't see the three boats in the water below from his position near the door.

"I'll bet they're just lucky. Let's hope it's them. It would be a big surprise for somebody if it wasn't."

"Well, all they get are two passes. The rest go into the 'glades. Just drop the boxes on the first run. Then the bales the second. Try not to hit anything. It makes a big mess in the boat."

The plane turned to the east and then did a smooth one hundred and eighty-degree turn. It slowed and dropped to about five hundred feet. No other boats were apparent on the water other than the three speedboats. They were about a hundred yards apart.

"Go ahead, Charlie. Drop!"

The co-pilot had already opened the side door and secured it. He began pushing small pallets encased in plastic wrap out of the opening. Eight pallets in all fell seaward.

"That's it, Ron. Give me thirty seconds, and I'm ready for the rest."

The plane turned slowly to the south and then to the east. Once again it glided over the triangle of boats and the drop started. By this time debris was swirling all over the inside of the aircraft. One by one, the cargo was dropped in a line near the waiting powerboats.

As the last large bale was pushed out of the door, Charlie indicated that the drop was complete.

"I'll leave this door open for a few seconds to clean out this crap."

The wind currents swirling inside the cabin were enough to pull much of the waste material and debris out of the door.

Charlie then began throwing the string and plastic and product that remained in the plane out of the door. "Hope I don't hit any gators with this stuff."

"Close her up, Charlie. Then we'll change clothes and head for Ft. Pierce. I don't see anyone around, but that won't last for long."

The plane climbed over the edge of the coastline until the outline of Highway 41 could be seen passing below them. Ahead loomed the darkness of the grasses and swampland of the Everglades. Soon they could see the glow of the lights from the east coast of Florida on the horizon.

Ron planned to stay between the Tamiami Trail and Alligator Alley until he reached the outer edge of the developed part of Broward County. Then he would turn north along Highway 27. Ron checked the fuel gauge again.

"I think we've got enough fuel to make it to Fort Pierce. But I do think it would be a kick if we dropped in on Frank Michaels tonight. I'm not sure he knows exactly what's going on."

Charlie shook his head.

"We'd never get the plane back. Besides, DEA and Customs would be all over this baby looking for fingerprints and buds.

"Remember, we have to take the decals off the side as soon as we can. Someone will be real confused if they see two N503E's in the air at the same time. If we were spotted, they'll get five oh-three instead of five oh-eight and think they were looking at Ted Michaels. That's what I like. I never would have thought of it."

"Carlos doesn't miss a trick. Here, take over for five, Charlie. Let me change. Then we can give the gators some new shoes."

27

Follow the Leader

*The role played by Cuba and Nicaragua
in drug smuggling is minuscule compared
to the role played by the countries that are
friends and allies of the United States.*

—Lee, *White Labyrinth*

Over the Gulf of Mexico

"Hey, Ted, I think we lost Hernandez in that last weather system. We were right behind him when we turned around Cuba, but I haven't had a visual since."

"Don't sweat it, Al. I'm surprised we stayed with them this long. Don't forget, this guy's a former Air Force pilot with plenty of experience. He's probably been worried about the Coast Guard and Customs ever since we took off from Honduras. So I'll bet he's not even the least bit concerned about being followed."

"Do you think he knows we're here?"

"How the hell would I know?" Ted replied in a sharp voice, obviously tired to the constant line of questions posed by his co-pilot. What does it matter? I'm more concerned with the reasons why Ernesto prevented Bill from coming with us. It's no reflection on you, but I just don't like the way he insisted on it. It makes me wonder whether he knows something."

"Who else is on that plane? I couldn't get a good look back at the field."

"I'm not sure about that either. There were several people in and out just before it took off. I didn't even see Hernandez."

"Ted, wouldn't it be a bitch if he wasn't on that plane?"

Ted disregarded that possibility.

"I think Hernandez has a friend who flies with him, but Harry isn't sure who it is. For all I know, he could be by himself or not be on the plane at all. We're just following that particular plane according to Harry's plan. And that's what really bothers me! It's Harry's plan! If any can go wrong, it will go wrong if Harry is involved!"

"Well, they could have turned northwest over the Gulf of Mexico, or they could just be a few miles ahead of us."

"I don't think they headed over the Yucatan or straight north over the Gulf. Don't forget, their destination is Sarasota, and they'll be landing just a few miles from the subdivision. Customs would have a much better shot at picking them up if they came in from the west straight off the water. They're ahead of us somewhere whoever they are."

"Should I keep looking for 'em?" asked Al.

"Nah. Don't waste your energy. It's not necessary to follow them all the way north. But it was a good idea to make sure that their flight was on schedule. From our point of view, it's the cover that they're giving us which counts. I like this much more than going in naked. Right about the time they're landing at Sarasota Municipal with so many uninvited guests to greet them, we'll be stopping in that subdivision and except for Gebinsky and his pals, we should be alone."

"They're sure in for a bit of a surprise when they get to Sarasota. It's not that I'm wishing anyone bad luck, but it's better them than us. That's a fact!"

"Yeah, but who really cares. I don't know what's worse, their apparent confidence or the fact that my brother is involved in this thing. If Harry can screw this up, he probably will. So I wouldn't count any chickens yet."

"Ted, no one other than Gebinsky and your brother know about our final destination. Right?"

"Don't worry about it. I wouldn't land this thing if I thought it was a setup."

"I don't know about you, Ted, but I got the clear impression that everyone was watching us get ready for this trip. I saw a lot of faces I didn't recognize. I had the feeling that those people knew we weren't stopping in Nicaragua for spare parts. Does FDLE and DEA know about us?"

"Don't start getting paranoid on me! I know this is your first trip, but, believe me, I don't trust anything Harry says or promises. He's absolutely the biggest liar I've ever had to deal with. And worse yet, he still believes he can con and charm anyone. I don't know a person who has worked with him who would loan that asshole a nickel."

Al shook his head. "But what about our landing site tonight. Could we be set up, too, the same way Hernandez is in Sarasota? Does Harry know where we're landing?"

"I don't think so. I didn't tell him. He just knows that we're coming but he doesn't know where. Come to think of it, he never really asked me about our destination. Anyway, I picked the landing site on this one myself. And I've worked with Gebinsky before so I have to trust his judgment as far as his people are concerned. Obviously, this whole project is not foolproof. But you're right, our main risks are Gebinsky and his people."

"Do you want one of these Cuban cigars, Ted? I got them in Honduras. Ernesto knows all the cool spots down there. And they we're expensive, too. We'd probably make more money if we smuggled cigars!"

"No, thanks, but pass me a beer from the cooler, would you."

Al reached over into the cooler behind his seat and opened a beer for Ted. Al was new at this game. He had lived most of his life in New York State not too far from Woodstock. He still had his long hair although it wasn't as thick as it once was, and a scruffy mustache and thin beard.

"You know, Ted, I thought I would feel guilty when I got up here, but I really don't."

"Guilty about what?"

"You know! Committing a crime and all that."

"A crime? Al, any prosecutor worth his salt could come up with five or ten different counts against us, not just one."

"Well, I guess it's just my upbringing. Catholic school and then, all of that Bible stuff. It makes a strong impact on you when you're a kid. But when the sixties came, I was smoking grass and drinking beer with the rest of them. And I liked it."

"Does the Bible say it's wrong to smoke pot and drink beer?"

"Well, not in so many words. I really don't know. Next time we go on one of these, I'll have to bring a book or two to read."

"Al, doesn't the Bible say that man is imperfect."

"That's what I got out of it, and I'm a good example of imperfection. Just ask my ex-wife."

"And men make the laws we're breaking, isn't that true?"

"You mean the legislature, right? They make more laws and break more laws than any other group I can think of. I guess that's because they're mostly lawyers."

"So, the way I see it, Al, we are imperfect people breaking imperfect laws made by imperfect people. Are you confused yet?"

"Hey, I'm just your average guy trying to get along in the world. And the more I think about it, the more confused I get about who is the final authority on what is right and what is wrong. Who do I ask about that?"

"It's easy! You have to ask yourself, Al. You're the only one who knows for sure. Do you think that your pet dog knows the difference between good and bad?"

"If he craps in the kitchen, he knows!"

"No, I mean good and evil. That's a better way to put it. Does your dog know what evil is?"

"Ted, I haven't asked him lately, but I would guess he doesn't have the concept of the devil hanging over him."

"That's the way I feel, probably just like your dog. We invented the concept of evil, primarily to control the behavior of people. To personify it, we invented Satan. If we didn't attach the concept to a person, the average human would have difficulty dealing with the abstraction of evil."

"So, where does that leave me, Ted?"

"You should be asking yourself the obvious question. *If evil is a construction of man, what does that say about good?*"

"Good is an abstraction, too? God is a construction of humans, too? I guess I never actually reasoned it out like this."

"You should read some Thomas Paine. It will make you think."

"So, Thomas Paine, huh. I'll remember that."

"Speaking of good and evil, there's Key West, Al." Ted pointed toward the cluster of lights coming into view.

"Wow, you're right! It's amazing how close to Cuba we are. Remember the missile crisis in the early sixties. The Russians were sitting right over there and aiming those things at us."

"1962!" laughed Ted. "It's a good thing that Kennedy had some backbone otherwise everyone in Key West might be drinking radioactive vodka instead of margaritas!"

Al got the joke, but quickly returned to his questions.

"When do we turn north again?"

"In a few minutes, then it's right up the coast to Sarasota."

After a pause in the conversation, Al wondered about his final destination.

"Ted, should I get off at the subdivision or go back to Lauderdale with you? I'd feel a lot better staying on the plane. I'd rather not deal with Gebinsky firsthand unless you want me to be there. If I stay on this baby, you'll get me home safe and sound. I can drive over to Sarasota tomorrow night if I'm needed there."

Ted didn't answer immediately. He was continuing to watch the emerging Florida coastline.

"Al, let's go up the middle, over the Everglades and along Highway 27, and then swing west above Fort Myers. I know that Customs has scout planes up along the coast. They'll be looking for Ron, but I wouldn't put it past them to miss him and zero in on us. It's in our flight plan, anyway. We'll be where we're supposed to be. If we stay east and come in from there or a little to the northeast, then we should be in the clear."

"Sounds good to me, Ted. Whatever's the safest."

Ted came back to the original question.

"As far as I'm concerned, you can stay on all the way back to Fort Lauderdale. Harry wanted you to keep tabs on the product, but they should have enough people there already. It's completely up to you. And, besides, you could help me clean out the plane on the way back."

"Good, I'd rather stay with you if you don't mind."

Ted Michaels agreed as he brought the plane over Florida Bay and took up a flight path which directed the plane across the Everglades and then along highway 27 to the area of Sebring. At that juncture he slowly turned west for Sarasota. To that point the flight was uneventful.

It was about four o'clock when Ted and Al sited the abandoned subdivision where the landing was to take place. The incomplete housing area looked the same as it had on the night three weeks ago when Ted had over-flown the landing site and conducted a mock approach and landing. Normally, he never flew near the actual location of the landing zone, but in this case he wanted to see what the streets looked like from the sky. He was actually pleasantly surprised at how closely the main street of the subdivision approximated a runway.

"Looks clear from here, Ted."

"Maybe we should take a closer look just to be sure." Ted squinted to try to resolve the objects scattered over the landscape inside the subdivision.

"One good thing about this place is the buffer around it. No houses or gas stations very close by. And you can see the Municipal Airport way over there."

As they took an initial pass over the grid of roads and canals in the subdivision, Ted could see several vehicles parked along the edges of the main road. "There they are. Can you see the trucks?"

"Yeah, no problem at all. At least they didn't oversleep. I think they see us." Al was pointing to the location where he saw activity by several vehicles.

"Good, we won't need to use the radio."

As Ted guided the plane to the south, he could see faint markers that were placed on the main road to help guide him in.

"There's the road we'll land on. It's not the widest runway, but I shouldn't have any problems. No surface winds to speak of. The tree line is off the road ten or twelve yards on each side for most of the length we'll need. Let's get down, dump this stuff, and get out of here quickly."

The co-pilot moved to the cargo area and prepared for unloading. He knew he would have plenty of help on the ground. Ted would keep the engines running. Once the product was removed, the plane would leave and head back to Ft. Lauderdale.

Ted made the final turn to the north and began his approach. The area was dark, so the faint temporary landing lights were easy to see. He turned back to his co-pilot.

"We're going in! Hang on."

28

Watching and Waiting

The slithy toves
Did gyre and gimbal in the wabe

—Lewis Carroll, *Jaberwocky*

Sarasota County, Florida

"I just don't understand it. I've been to Florida at least twenty times and you know what! I've never seen the beach! I've never gone fishing! I've never been on a airboat ride in the Everglades! And, I've never been to the Keys! Where did I go wrong?"

Agent Phil Costello stared out of one of the long, low restaurant windows at several small puddles that were growing in the middle of the parking lot. It was late, and he was tired. Even though he had looked forward to this trip and had slept late the morning before, he wasn't nearly awake enough. Several cups of coffee had not yet taken effect, and he began to wish that he could get a shower and a change clothes. It was going to be a long, muggy night. Even the air-conditioned area where he sat didn't seem to relieve the heaviness of the air. And, much to his dismay, his two companions were wide-awake.

"This may not be much consolation," Arthur said, "but, I've never seen the beach either, Boss. I missed those spring break trips in college.

Maybe we can take a few days of vacation after this is over and check out Fort Lauderdale and Key West. That might be fun."

This was Arthur's first encounter with Harry Michaels, and it was obvious that he was enjoying it. The two had been talking almost continuously for the last thirty minutes. Arthur seemed to be seeking information about drug operations from Harry, and Harry was trying his best to make points with Arthur just in case he might prove useful in the future.

"Tell me, Mr. Michaels, can you fly all these old propeller aircraft that the smugglers use?"

"Arthur, I'm not really a pilot. I'm a businessman. My father can hardly fly anything anymore, but he owns several large air terminals. You don't have to be a pilot to be in this business. Besides, it takes too much time to keep up with all this stuff. When I die, it's going to be with two feet on the ground!"

Despite his overworked state of mind, Costello had been monitoring the conversation between Arthur and Michaels for new scraps of data that might help him understand the situation or at least understand Michaels. But, so far, nothing new had surfaced. At least Costello didn't have to think. This sifting of data came naturally. He could listen to three separate conversations at the same time and still understand most of all three. It was one of his talents and an absolute must in a bureaucracy.

"Harry, don't encourage the kid. Give it a rest. Arthur is going to be a desk jockey if I get my way. No flying around in rat infested, bug infested, airframes for him. I'm going to make a gentleman out of him."

The three men sat in a small booth near the front of the restaurant. This gave each of them a clear view of anyone who might be coming or going. Costello felt it was important to keep an eye on the approaches to the airport. His primary concern was local law enforcement. Every time he dealt with problems in this part of the country, the same message trickled through his thoughts. *There is a big information leak down here. One or more officers are dirty. Maybe the whole system is dirty. We can never trust them.* As close as they were on this one, he didn't want one of the local boys spotting him now. They would know something was up. And they always seemed to recognize him. He would set just one foot in Florida, and every state law enforcement officer knew he was here.

They had all eaten breakfast, and were on their fourth round of coffee when Michaels noticed a single man walking on the sidewalk leading up to the restaurant.

"Here comes your agent, Costello. Is this the guy that lied to me?"

"Harry, how could you tell the difference? I've never met anyone who lied more than you. You make everyone else look perfect." Costello had spoken with an obvious smirk on his face.

Costello followed the lone figure as he emerged from the shadows and walked purposefully to the front door. It was definitely Josef. Casually dressed, as usual, and always looking like he belonged. Very low profile. *No wonder that even a habitual liar like Michaels would trust him at face value. What innocence! He doesn't look like a threat to anyone. It's a good thing he's on our side!*

Harry Michaels was still curious. He wondered who had rolled over on him and how they had obtained the information about his flight into Central Florida. He still kicked himself for going with the product instead of staying with his brother Ted on the Lear Star. *He would've gotten away with it, and no one would have dared to finger him. Instead, because he didn't trust his ground crew, he got nailed.*

Michaels kept thinking about the situation. *One of those idiots forgot the cut the telephone wires!* He was thinking about the telephone wires that serviced the houses near the airfield on the Governor's diary farm. *The landing went fine. The unloading was flawless. The plane lifted off without incident. They loaded the trucks quickly, quietly and efficiently. Then, as they drove off the farm, they were met by eight police cars!* One of the resident workers had seen the plane land on the airstrip.

Michaels was told that this employee had called the cops. *What were the chances of that happening?* Granted, the phone lines had not been cut as planned. This omission was critical, but there was something else about the situation that he couldn't put his finger on just yet. *These rural people are so nosey! Why couldn't they just mind their own business?*

But since when were the cops so efficient? Something just seemed out of place. This Josef Gerona was more than he seemed. What was it about him? Michaels searched for an answer, but came up blank.

Josef wasn't in a hurry as he opened the front door of the restaurant. It was probably because he didn't believe this operation would bear any fruit. Josef looked down the row of booths and spotted Costello. His eyes scanned across Michaels, but he showed no signs of familiarity. He walked up and sat down, introducing himself to Arthur and Michaels as he did so. He didn't defer to Michaels as a prisoner or informant. His eyes fixed themselves on Costello. It was obvious that the two knew each other quite well.

Costello appeared pleased that Josef had appeared. It didn't appear that he necessarily liked Josef, but he seemed to gain some comfort from his presence.

"Any news from the chase planes yet?" Josef's question surprised Costello.

"They're between Naples and Fort Myers, but no contact with Hernandez has been reported."

Josef turned his attention to Michaels.

"Has it ever occurred to you that Carlos is already here? And he's watching you while you wait for his plane?"

Michaels coughed. He tried to answer.

"How…he doesn't know we're here. Anyway, he'd be at the airport, wouldn't he?"

Josef shook his head as he sat down. He pointed out the window.

"Take a look at the parking lot. Full of cars at three in the morning! Looks suspicious to me. He knows you're here! The airport is where you're supposed to be to unload the plane. But look at the rest of these guys. If I were Carlos, I'd be watching you to see who tagged along. Especially just before and after an operation. They've probably fingered us already. I'm going home!"

Josef faked getting up from the table, but sat back down. His sarcasm had the desired effect.

Michaels looked at Costello who just shrugged his shoulders.

"Ten of our agents are already staked out at the field. We have three chase vehicles and the two chase planes in the air. I thought it best not to apprise the locals of our plan."

Josef nodded. "I try to avoid them, but on the other hand when they do show up, we can't run away. The leak has to think he's safe and undiscovered. We can always come back later and flush him out. But now, he's actually an asset. It's a good place to insert strategic information. Knowing he's here, we can use him, and we will use him when the time's right."

Michaels chose this lull in the conversation to ask Josef the question that really bothered him.

"How did you know we were landing at the dairy farm?" He waited while Josef measured his answer.

"I wasn't responsible for that. It was your own fault. One of the supervisors spotted your plane as it was landing." Josef spoke with the confidence acquired from a thorough knowledge of the case file.

"But the fuzz was there almost instantly. They couldn't have responded that quickly."

Michaels paused and then continued. "Rumor has it that you had the place staked well before we landed."

Michael's words had an element of truth, but Josef could tell that Michaels wasn't absolutely sure of his statement. *He's still searching for the real reason why he got caught. And Costello must have pointed the finger to me. That figures. Always passing the buck. He'll never really know the truth. This is no time to add any security to his position.*

"It wasn't me, Harry! I was in Colombia on the day they nailed you. Someone must have rolled over on you! One of your ground crew or someone on the plane or at your father's terminal in Lauderdale. You have a much better idea of the timeframe involved in that operation. It could have been Costello for that matter. He's starting to look a little guilty to me."

A smile appeared on Josef's face as he turned to stare out the window.

"I'll bet Costello knew about your dairy gig, but he doesn't know about the load your brother is bringing in tonight!"

Michaels swallowed hard. He didn't speak, and he looked away. Costello jumped up from his seat and grabbed Michaels's shirt with both hands.

"Are you and your brother up to no good again? If you mess this thing up, our deal is off, and he's going away with you! I thought we agreed that retirement was in the cards for you."

Michaels swallowed several times again. He tried to speak but then thought better of it. As the pressure on Michaels started to build, Josef came to his rescue.

"But we don't have Carlos yet, do we? Harry has to proceed with business as usual, Phil. Otherwise, Carlos will get suspicious and then he might pull in his feelers and disappear. That wouldn't do us any good, now would it? We've got to let Harry be Harry."

Costello sat back down and stared at Josef with some resentment, but it seemed to fade as he pondered the situation.

"You're right again! I guess it can't hurt if they play their little games. He mentioned a second flight to me earlier, but I thought he was bluffing. Shows you what I know!"

Costello now seemed resigned to the situation. Michaels looked at Costello, then at Josef and ventured a question.

"How did you know about the flight?"

"I didn't know anything, Harry," said Josef. "But you look so worried, so distraught and nervous, that I figured it was worth a try. I thought I would just rattle your cage a little. Try being a little more subtle next time, would you. Your brother seems to be a much calmer fellow. Let's hope he doesn't have the same bad luck you've had."

"Have you met Ted? My younger brother, Ted?"

Josef smiled. "I've met him, but I don't believe that he knows that he's met me."

29

Don't Look Down

Day destroys the night
Night divides the day
Tried to run, tried to hide
Break on through to the other side

—The Doors, *Break on Through*

Sarasota, Florida

"I know that goddamn shotgun is here somewhere! So are the shells. One of these days I'm going to clean this place out so I can find my shit!"

Chris continued the search while Josh stood watching with a smirk on his face.

"Ah! Finally! Here it is. And, the shells, too. They're a little old, but should be okay."

"If you would clean the place up once in a while," Josh retorted as he restrain the dog with a tight grip on the leash, "maybe you would be able to find what you're looking for."

Chris turned and pointed toward the kitchen as he inspected the weapon.

"Get us a couple of cups of coffee. And, look in the refrigerator. There should be a few donuts in there. I'm starving. And, put Harvey in the spare room. Give him some water. He should be okay until we return."

Having retrieved the shotgun, the boys jumped back into the truck and headed for Wild Acres.

The subdivision consisted of several square miles of paved streets interlaced with canals and rows of palm trees. The lots were platted and a display section of homes had been started, but exploding interest rates in the late seventies had doomed the project. Builders quickly ran out of cash.

The subdivision was usually deserted except for an occasional fisherman. There were no streetlights, and the main entrance was chained and barricaded with a large sign that prohibited trespassing. But the isolation of the subdivision and its extensive canal system made it a prime target for developers who wished to dispose of their trash without taking the inconvenient trip to the County Sanitation Dump. About once a month the County would get a tip on illegal dumping activities. Unhappy employees were usually the source of this information; however, it was occasionally just another builder doing his civic duty.

In this case the Sarasota Sheriff's Office had declined the assignment. Fred was all too familiar with the jokes about Fish and Game. Besides, this was an environmental matter, one better suited to Fred's troops. But, the fact that this was the only time anyone could remember that the Sheriff was actually concerned about the environment was not lost on Fred.

But there were unusual aspects to this tip. It came hours before the dumping was to occur. Usually the information pointed to an illegal dumping action that had already occurred. And, to make it even more unusual, the phone call was directed to Fish and Game by the informant, not to the Sheriff. That was really unusual.

Even more foreboding was the fact that they were ordered to take their weapons. Contractors dumping construction materials were hardly known as gunslingers. They were usually borderline contractors who where trying to squeeze out a living while they waited for construction work to pick up. Most of the time they were dumping for someone else. And it was usually just the remains of a building or repair job. Gypsum from drywall, concrete, wood scraps, and miscellaneous junk were almost always present along with an occasional old refrigerator. Most trash dumpers were even smart enough to remove the refrigerator doors so that children wouldn't get trapped inside if they were foolish enough to play with the old appliances.

If they were successful in their dumping operation, the trash would be overgrown in six weeks and no one would care much about it. But Fred had referred to a shooting that had occurred some time ago. As Chris remembered, that wasn't actually a contractor situation. It was a distraught husband who was destroying all of the family furniture in retaliation against his wife. He happened to have a gun and had the misfortune of firing it.

"Let's try the radio just in case," Josh suggested as he approached the truck. "We may need some help at the subdivision."

Chris reached for the jury-rigged police radio he had installed in the truck.

"We haven't used this thing in a long time so maybe it's rested and ready to go." After some work on the dials they heard the whistling and static which usually indicated that radio was working.

"Chris, this is your baby. If we run into any problems, you crank it up and make the call. I can never get this thing to work right, and we won't have immediate access to a telephone."

"Ah, it's not that bad. You could do it if you practiced a little. This radio could save your life one of these days! We even have an instruction manual somewhere. I just have to find it."

Josh clapped his hands together and jumped into the truck. "That's good enough for me. You can have it until you find the instructions. Then we'll talk about me dealing with it. I'm sure I won't have to worry about it for quite a while."

It took about fifteen minutes to reach the subdivision. The boys pulled into the entryway and removed the chain that was draped across the road near the half-finished guard station. The lights on their truck were already out. After looking over the area for a few minutes and listening for activity, they entered the subdivision and parked their truck under several large palms that had been planted near a main intersection. Josh hustled back to the entry and replaced the chain blocking the road. The moon was up, and the sky was clearing although some drizzle could still be felt in the air. It was 12:35 AM.

"Any gators in these canals this time of year?" asked Josh, knowing what the answer would be.

"You bet! But they're not too big. The big guys head for better cover to the east. The main varmints are raccoons. They'll sneak up on you. Just curious little guys, but they're partially tame, so they aren't afraid of humans. The last time I was out this way a couple of the critters just scared the crap out of me. I jumped and yelled, and they froze in their tracks. Then all of us ran away. It wasn't a pretty sight, and it looks bad on your resume."

"Well, a least they were scared, too", laughed Josh.

Chris handed Josh the flashlight and adjusted the back of his seat. "I'm going to take a little nap. Wake me up when you get tired, and I'll watch out for the bad guys for a while." Chris pulled a blanket out from behind the seat and fashioned it into a pillow.

From this observation point, Josh could see the entrance to the subdivision and also the large boat ramp that provided access to one of the wider canals. This area looked like the best place for a would-be trash dumper to operate.

Once inside the entry, they would have to drive right past him to get to the ramp. After that, it would be easy to block their escape and write them a ticket. Or place them under arrest if that was necessary. That decision could be made on the fly. If it were a minor operation, there would be no point arresting anyone.

Several hours passed without event, and Josh was starting to get tired of sitting. He quietly got out of the truck and walked to the back where he boosted himself up on the edge of the panel. It was after three o'clock, and the sky was relatively clear. With no ground light, the stars were exceptionally bright as he scanned the heavens looking for his favorite constellations.

Suddenly, he spotted two large vans as they turned into the subdivision and headed right for him. The vans turned off their lights and turned onto a street that ran parallel to the main street. Josh felt relieved because now they probably wouldn't spot his vehicle. Chris wasn't moving so Josh assumed he was still asleep.

As Josh watched, the two vehicles slowly drove past a corresponding boat ramp on the side street and came to a stop about a block and a half farther into the subdivision. The vehicles pulled off the paved part of the road and sat quietly. Josh waited for several minutes, but there was no activity.

Then, he moved slowly around the side of the truck to awaken Chris, but found that he was already awake and watching with some interest. Without speaking, they both stared at the vehicles waiting for some sign of movement. All was quiet.

"Since when do you dump from a van unless you have hazardous chemicals to deposit" whispered Chris.

"Should we grab them now?"

"Not yet." indicated Josh. "They might hear our radio and run for it. I have the binoculars on them, but they don't seem to be doing anything. "I hope we don't have a bunch of teenagers here".

Chris chuckled quietly as he carefully stashed his pillow behind the seat. "What if it's Sarasota County? The Sheriff's Office wouldn't normally use a van, would they? And they must know that we're here somewhere. It can't be them. We'll just have to wait these guys out."

The waiting lasted for almost an hour. All of a sudden several figures sprang from the vans and ran toward the main road about two blocks up from where the agents were parked. Josh could see dull specks of light being spread along the road over a distance of about a hundred yards. Luckily for the agents, the activity seemed to be moving away from them.

"What's this" whispered Chris. "Are we hunting night crawlers?"

Josh didn't respond. They continued to watch the activity until the three men who had left the vans had returned to them. It was quiet again. Because their eyes were well adjusted to the darkness, they could easily see the glow issuing from the main road. It was as if the men where marking a path on the road.

"Chris, it almost looks like they're illuminating a runway, doesn't it."

Both felt their curiosity increasing while they were wondering what was up. Another five minutes passed when Chris turned to Josh and indicated that it might be time to close in.

"Not yet, I've got to know what's cooking, and we may interrupt them. Look down this road. What does it remind you of?"

Chris thought for a while and he had to agree.

"Landing lights! They're landing lights! These guys are waiting for a plane. A plane is going to land here. A goddamn plane! What would they want with a plane? Whoa! It's got to be drugs."

Josh concurred. "It sure as hell isn't some amateur pilot practicing touchdowns. We've got ourselves a drug bust. That's why we have the shotgun! Oh, shit. Where are the shells?"

"Right here." Chris pointed down to the floor of the right front seat. "Don't worry. I didn't forget the ammo."

Just then a gentle humming noise could be heard in the distance, in the direction of the dim lights. The noise slowly became louder until Chris jumped up from his seat and turned to Josh with a wild look of excitement on his face.

"It's a plane, all right! I'll be damned. This is a drug operation! We're going to do a drug bust! What a rush! Eleven O'clock News, here we come!"

Chris' voice cracked as he pointed with child-like enthusiasm toward the plane which was descending onto the makeshift landing strip.

"Load the gun! Take the shells. Here, I'll crank up the old radio and get some help!"

Josh ran to the other side of the truck and secured the shotgun from behind the driver's seat. He pulled a box of shells from the truck and stuffed them into his pockets. He clipped a flashlight to his belt, tugged on his cap, and returned to where Chris was battling the radio.

"That thing is so loud no one will hear us. I'm going up the road to watch this. Get up there as soon as you can. We're probably outnumbered three to one." Josh crouched and ran carefully toward the action while Chris concentrated on the radio.

By this time the plane had touched down and was coming to a stop no less than a block from the truck. Josh hid in the palms while the plane executed an awkward turn. It came to a stop facing the direction from which it came. Obviously, the pilot intended to take off again on the same road. The two engines were creating an extreme amount of noise. They were also throwing a considerable amount of debris into the air.

The men from the vans were shouting at each other and at a solitary figure in the doorway of the aircraft. After some conversation the men boarded the plane using ladders and began throwing what at first appeared to be large cardboard boxes onto the ground.

Josh could also see what appeared to be plastic bags as they were being thrown out of the plane. The men on the ground were frantically loading the cargo into the two vans that had been driven up to the side of the plane.

Josh wondered if he should make his move now. Without Chris it might be dangerous. What if the men were armed? He could see markings on the side of the plane but he couldn't read them. The men were making fast work of the cargo when Chris came up behind Josh.

"They're coming. It will be three to five minutes. Should we try to stall them? Oh, shit, let's go for it. No guts, no glory!"

"Okay, let's go!" Josh yelled. "Make it look like you're armed! They won't be able to tell in this mess, and I'll put my flashlight on them as soon as we get there."

Just as the boys popped out from their cover and began sprinting the seventy-five yards to their target, the plane revved its engines. It started to roll down the street away from them, slowly at first, then more rapidly as the door on the side of the plane closed. The blast from the engines spread debris all around them. It quickly became apparent to them that part of the cargo was marijuana. Josh and Chris had both been to enough parties to detect it from a mile away.

As the plane roared down the makeshift runway, Josh threw the beam of his flashlight on the four men who remained on the ground. At first his presence didn't seem to have much impact on them. They seemed to consider him one of the crew.

"Shut off the fuckin' light, asshole. You're gonna mess us up."

The voice came from the person standing nearest to him. Then Josh could see another individual under one of the palm trees. This man must have known that something was wrong. He started running away from Josh and then seemed to jump on a bicycle. He sped off down the side road as fast as he could pedal as the others watched. It was too late to do anything about him.

The others didn't move. When Josh identified himself, he could see the looks of despair on their faces as they watched their only other avenue of escape climb into the sky. Josh could see a second bicycle leaning up against a tree. He moved over next to it to prevent another escape.

"Down on the pavement!" shouted Chris with surprising authority as he came up behind Josh.

"Stay right where you are, we're armed, and we will shoot if you make a run for it. There's no where to go out here. You can see that we have help coming!"

In the distance cars from the Sheriff's Department could be seen streaming into the subdivision. The cars appeared just in time to cause the remaining members of the group to freeze.

In a matter of seconds several Sarasota County Sheriff's Department vehicles were on the scene. The officers handcuffed the suspects and read them their rights. Several officers came over and shook the hands of the Fish and Game Officers.

"Nice going, guys. We were over at the Municipal Airport waiting for these guys and they landed here instead. We were lucky you were here. What was it, a lost dog?"

"No," said Josh. "We thought we had some trash dumping going on. I guess you never know about these things. Thanks for getting here fast. We just had this shotgun."

"You did good! Go get some coffee. The chief will undoubtedly send a commendation over to Fish and Game for you two. Thanks, again!"

After the excitement died down and the officers took over, Chris and Josh walked back to the truck. Chris was ecstatic.

"Hey, we're ready for prime time now! Maybe it's The Untouchables for us! The evening news for sure. How about a big raise for both of us! Better hours would work! And, maybe a real rank. Say General or Colonel. I like Colonel better. More vacation time to work on our basic skills. And, of course, product sponsorship and royalties."

"Oh, shit." Josh was angry. "I forgot about the guy on the bike!"

"What guy on the bike? Did someone get away? I really didn't count them when they first came in. I thought there were five or six at least." Chris's words expressed his disbelief.

"Yeah. One of them ran for it. Grabbed a bike and headed that way." Josh pointed to the east. " He might not be too far away. Maybe we should hit the truck and run him down?"

"Ah, so what! Let him go. This was a marijuana thing. I really don't understand why it's such a big deal. We'll save the kid some time and the County some money. Everybody will be happier. Just let it go. The only way he'll get caught is if his friends turn on him. It's happened before. Let's go and get some breakfast. We've earned it!"

Josh and Chris jumped into their truck and slowly drove past the Sheriff's Department vehicles at the entrance to the subdivision. Chris turned to Josh and smiled. "Guess what. I'd have let them all go except for one thing."

"What was that?" Josh wondered what Chris had in mind.

Chris laughed. "They did do some dumping you know. All that crap flying out of the plane and being blown into the water by the engines and those plastic lights on the road. It's an environmental hazard if I ever saw one."

Chris stopped and winked at his partner.

"And that's illegal around here!"

30

Flies in the Vaseline

*If one is at rest
relative to a gravitating body,
then the nearer one is to the body,
the more slowly one's time must flow.*

—Albert Einstein

Sarasota Municipal Airport

The airport was dark. Costello's watch read 0330. The DEA agents from Washington had taken up positions near two old unmarked vans. These vehicles were dark in color and parked well off the pavement. The agents were casually dressed in jeans and dark T-shirts, trying to simulate the profile of the unloading crew that Harry Michaels was supposed to provide.

They had an advantage. Because of the desire for anonymity, the crew of the incoming flight was not acquainted with the members of the ground crew. It was a safeguard as well as a risk.

Costello's plan was simple. Small lights would be placed at the sides of the main runway when the plane over-flew the airport. Then, after the approach and landing, the agents would converge on the plane with Michaels and begin unloading the contraband as if everything was normal. Harry would try to get the crew off the plane temporarily, and at that point they would be arrested.

Despite the fact that the crew was known to be unarmed, the agents all carried weapons. Michaels had argued against this approach, but Costello was having none of it. This operation would be conducted by the book! He didn't want any of his men getting hurt because he had violated operational procedures.

The remaining agents took positions in an old hangar that was empty except for two automobiles. The vehicles belonged to the DEA office in Tampa and were to be used for transport and communications. One of the Tampa-based agents sat in the vehicle nearest the front door. He was monitoring the aircraft frequencies waiting for contact with the chase aircraft even though contact wasn't expected for at least thirty minutes. Nevertheless, the planes had been airborne for over an hour, and there was always the chance that the incoming flight was ahead of schedule.

At about 0340 excitement began to spread among the waiting agents. It was an aircraft. Slowly and carefully the plane circled the field. With his binoculars trained on the craft, Costello could not help but note how surprisingly small the plane looked out in all that open space.

From the runway Harry Michaels took one look and motioned to the federal agents to return to the hangar. It was a Piper, definitely not the plane involved in his operation. It was much too small to carry significant cargo, and it definitely couldn't travel the distance from Honduras with a significant load.

After a rather shaky landing the plane taxied right up to the hangar. The two Sarasota businessmen on board were somewhat surprised when were unceremoniously greeted by the federal authorities.

They had been delayed in Tallahassee by some severe weather. After a few questions and identification checks, the pair was released.

At 0355 a vehicle was sited driving along the frontage road on the western side of the airport. It moved slowly and had its headlights turned off. In a few moments, a second vehicle was detected moving slowly along the frontage road, which bordered the western edge of the field. It also had its light off. Costello cautiously signaled his crew to keep their cover. There was nothing to do but wait.

"Gerona, what's up?" whispered Costello as he quietly made his way to the position where Josef and Arthur were standing.

"If we see two of them, there must be more. Or are we just lucky? Have any ideas?"

Josef smiled and shook his head.

"It can only be one thing. Can't you guess? Who drives to the airport in the middle of the night? This particular airport on this particular night! Not to a regular airport where scheduled flights take place, but this one!"

"Goddammit, Josef! How could this happen after all the preparation and security. There must be a leak in our office or in Tampa or Orlando. If I ever get my hands on..."

Costello's head dropped down after he had carefully scanned one of the cars with his binoculars. He was mumbling under his breath.

"It's those bastards from Sarasota County. How did they know? And don't tell me that they were just driving by. They have five or six cars here. I'll bet they let us see a couple of them just to piss us off right in the middle of our operation."

"Did you track Harry all day?" Josef asked as he turned his head to look out at the runway where Michaels was standing.

Costello gave a negative response.

"We couldn't do much about it. Because of our problems down here, we didn't contact agent Johnstone until Harry said they were coming. He's been on alert here for over a week so they should have been ready when we called. You think the leak is in our office, too, don't you!"

"No. Not necessarily! I'm just considering all the possibilities. It still could be just a coincidence. There are enough clandestine flights coming in from the south these days that they might stake this place out every night just in case."

Costello's expression stiffened to anger as he looked at Josef.

"Did you just insult me or am I losing it. What did you just say? Coincidence?"

Josef laughed and patted his boss on the back.

"Phil, I'm just amazed that you are able to keep your sanity. It was actually a compliment! Any rational government agency would have given up by now. They would have asked the Congress to legalize this stuff. Then just taxed it to make some money. Ah, that's probably too easy and logical. Anyway, I like these operations. You never know what's gonna happen with all of this money in play."

Before Costello could answer one of the two vehicles they were watching quickly turned on its lights and drove off at high speed. In the distance several other patrol cars could be seen racing east, lights flashing.

Finally, Costello threw his binoculars to the pavement in disgust.

"Did they lose interest in watching us or are the lights just for effect? Why not just light up the entire fucking county so that Carlos will know we're here waiting for him? Ah, screw it! I quit! I couldn't catch a cold down here if it walked up and bit me on the ass!"

As Costello was calming down, Josef walked out to the position where Harry Michaels was standing.

"How are you holding up, Harry?"

Hall seemed very disconcerted and did not answer immediately. He seemed to be doing some serious thinking.

Josef just patted Michaels on the back as he turned to walk back inside the hangar.

"These unexpected developments do make things more interesting, don't they, Harry?

As Josef approached Costello, he noticed that his boss was feeling better.

"We'll just sit tight and wait for something to happen, Josef. Not that enough hasn't happened already! I can't believe those assholes are on to us."

Just then, the officer who had been monitoring the radio in the DEA vehicle rushed up.

"Sir! Local police band is reporting a bust about ten miles from here at an abandoned subdivision. Maybe our target landed in the wrong place? Should I inquire? Florida Fish and Game officers are reporting this one."

"Yes, immediately!" shouted Costello as he grabbed Josef with both arms.

"It's too good to be true! Unless they had engine trouble, or they spotted us. I can't believe this. Stay here and keep your eyes open. Let's make sure before we expose our positions. With my luck, the plane we're looking for will land five minutes after we leave."

Costello moved over to the car and conversed with the local DEA officer and then on the radio with Sarasota County officers at the subdivision. As he came back, he was shaking his head.

"The plane got away…they let the fucking plane get away! All we got was the ground crew."

"Anyone we know?" Josef spoke softly and waited for Costello's response.

"Shit! I don't know. No identifications yet. Two vehicles were captured. At least one member of the ground crew got away on a bicycle. They're looking for him now. That's where our little friends in the cars were running to a few minutes ago. I can't believe it! All this work and those assholes get the bust. And, it was an accident, too. I've never been so pissed! How could this happen?"

"Probably independents, Phil. It couldn't be Carlos' plane. The pilot would be looking for Michaels. They wouldn't unload without Michaels. Unless…"

"Josef, unless what?"

"Unless they had an alternate plan. What if they spotted us? Or were warned!"

Josef looked up at Costello.

"Or Harry is pulling our collective legs!"

Costello began pacing.

"Hey, Harry is too scared to turn on us. This bust was going to be his meal ticket."

"Then either the leak that pointed the Sarasota Sheriff to us also warned the plane, or it's a different plane, and the original is still on the way. I'll bet that the plane that landed at the subdivision was piloted by Ted Michaels. Harry looks real nervous! We have to hold our ground, Phil. Wait for the real thing. If it doesn't happen, we haven't lost much."

Costello agreed.

"I have to get one of those search planes back in position. I just ordered both of them to look for the one from the subdivision."

Costello began to realize that all wasn't lost yet. He shook his head and mumbled as he ran back to the radio.

"I'll keep an eye on the radio traffic. Hold everyone in place. If necessary, we'll stay 'till 0800."

As he returned to the radio car, the agent monitoring the chase plane transmissions didn't seem happy.

"Agent Costello. The chase planes have reported in. They're flanking Naples. No positive sightings so far! Visibility is good, and they're working with ground radar. Nothing heading this way. Do you want to speak with the pilots? They wanted confirmation of your order to track the escaping flight here in Sarasota."

"No. Let's just sit tight," Costello replied with a sense of resignation in his voice. "We need more information. Tell them both to stay on station as long as they can. Have them report every fifteen minutes. We just have to be patient. We'll get Ted Michaels later."

"Yes, Sir. I'll report each contact."

As Costello sat down on the ground near Josef, he noticed Arthur who was attempting to nap near the hangar wall.

"And wake Junior up will you! I don't want him to miss anything exciting. He's going to have to file all of the written reports on this fiasco when we get back to Washington."

31

Talk to Me

You shall sleep in the desert,
You shall stand in the shadow of the wall,
The thorn and the bramble shall wound your feet,
The drunken and the thirsty shall smite your cheek.

—Enkidu in the Epic of Gilgamesh

Sarasota, Florida

The Sarasota County Sheriff's van slowly backed into the secured loading dock at the back of the County Jail Annex. It was almost 6 AM. The five prisoners were individually handcuffed and each wore leg weights that prevented them from running. They were escorted from the van into a receiving area and then to a holding cell, which already contained three other persons. Two of the original occupants were being held on DUI charges while the third was a burglary suspect.

After the first hour of confinement, the men were fed a breakfast of eggs and fried potatoes with black coffee. After breakfast, each man was fingerprinted and moved into a separate six-man cell on the third floor of the building.

During the first few hours after their arrest, the three men had been very quiet. Now that they were in the cell, Gebinsky was nervous and seemed to be talking to himself. His comments were loud enough for his fellow prisoners to overhear.

"Harry better not hang us out to dry. For all we know, this was his fault. What were those officers doing out there? I didn't see them when we came in. They were hiding! They were waiting for us! We were set up on this thing. Someone set us up, that's for sure."

Johnny was leaning against the cell door, tears forming in his eyes. He turned away from his friends for fear they would see him cry.

"Edward, how did this happen? You said we would be okay. Nothing bad was supposed to come down. Was it really Harry that did this to us. What will Kathy think? She'll wonder where we are, and why we didn't come back to the house."

Juan was his usual stoic self. He sat down on the padded bench and leaned against the wall. He was tired. His eyes closed, and he appeared to be wishing he were somewhere else.

"Johnny! It was an accident. Those were rangers that arrested us, the ones who check on fishing and hunting and all that. No one set us up. It was a terrible coincidence. You have to have some courage. We'll get out of this okay. Just be calm."

The other two men had arrived at the subdivision in a second van. They were very quiet as they sat at the other end of the cell. Gebinsky turned toward them.

"I thought there were three of you. Did someone get out?"

The two men looked at each other. The older one shook his head negatively. He spoke very quietly.

"We were by ourselves. Actually, we were going fishing and ran into the three of you. Then the plane landed. Then the cops appeared. This is all a big mistake."

Gebinsky's face held a look of disbelief. "And I suppose you don't know Harry!"

"Harry? I have an Uncle Harry. But he lives in Connecticut. And he's there right now! Maybe I should call him." A smile spread over the man's face.

"Uncle Harry would be pissed if he saw me here. Not for doing anything wrong, but for getting caught in this situation with you. He's a cop. He'd be pissed if he caught me jaywalking. But actually, they'll figure it out and let us go. Especially when they find the fishing gear."

"Fishing gear? We've got fishing gear, too!" shouted Gebinsky before he caught himself and lowered the tone of his voice. "If anyone was fishing, it was us. How many fish did you catch? If you were fishing, you must have caught some fish. And you should have some bait in that van somewhere. Right?" Gebinsky was feeling better.

"I don't know who the fuck you are, so Edward, or whatever your name is, let's leave the questioning to the police. I don't know who you are or what you were doing there, and I don't give a rat's ass about it either. Just don't try to hang this thing you were doing around our necks. That's not a nice thing to do to someone you don't even know!"

"Whose plane was that anyway?" Gebinsky shrugged and turned toward Johnny and suddenly the situation seemed humorous.

"Johnny, that's what you get for going fishing with us. Usually we don't catch anything. Did you bring the bait?"

Johnny, usually a happy-go-lucky guy, couldn't see anything funny in the situation. He turned to Juan who still had his eyes closed.

"Juan, I'm in trouble, man, in deep shit. I can't help it. I never thought we'd get caught…"

At that moment Juan opened his eyes and turned to look at Johnny. He slowly put his hand on Johnny's head.

"Johnny. Look at me. You're gonna be okay. Okay! Now look at me. You just be quiet. Don't say anything. If they ask you if you want a lawyer, say yes. If they ask you if you can afford a lawyer, say no. That's it. You let your lawyer do the talking, and you will be fine."

Johnny closed his eyes and covered his face with his hands.

"I won't let anything happen to you, Johnny. Your lawyer won't let anything happen to you. Understand me? You're going to have to grow up a little now. You have to look yourself in the eyes and see a man. A man standing on his own two feet. No moaning, no sniveling, no crying, no begging! Get me? You're a man, act like one!"

"How can you be so calm, Juan," Johnny replied. "You're in trouble, too. Maybe more than me. At least I have my parents and family here. Yours are in South America, aren't they? Can you afford a lawyer?"

"It doesn't matter. Find your courage and face this situation head on. Be a man!"

Gebinsky was listening intently to the conversation. He realized that Juan was mature beyond his years.

"Juan's right. Just be calm and don't say anything. Our lawyers will be here soon enough. And we can prove we were fishing. That will get us a fine. That's it."

Gebinsky looked at Juan, and they both knew that his words described a situation that was very improbable. Juan smiled. "What bait were you using, Ed?"

That comment caused Gebinsky to begin pacing the cell again. He began assessing his options.

Should I call Harry? No, he'll know because Ted knows. And Ted will get us some help. They'd better! I'm not going down on this alone. The way Harry's been acting, he must be working with the feds. He's a much bigger fish, and he's out there, and I'm in here. That can't be right. Besides, I'm as valuable to them as he is. I know where the stuff goes, and who brings it in. That must be worth something. I wish someone would get here!

Gebinsky continued to pace nervously while Johnny, Juan and the other two men sat quietly contemplating their fates.

32

Meeting in Maracaibo

When [the Medellin cartel] have a problem
with someone who hasn't paid,
then they turn them over to the DEA.

—Jose Blandon, *political advisor*
for Manuel Noriega

Maracaibo, Venezuela

"Eulalio, please forgive me for detaining you so unceremoniously. But speaking in public would not serve our purposes. These are very unusual and dangerous times, my friend."

Despite his blindfold, the prisoner managed a smile and responded sarcastically to his captors.

"Your apology is not accepted, Gilberto! I have always come to Venezuela anticipating its comforts and its generosities. And, as I take my respite, I am snatched off the street like a common thief!"

"So, you know my name, Eulalio Francisco!" came the surprised response. "I hoped to avoid the embarrassment, but it is not important. You have the reputation of an understanding man."

"Save your compliments for when we drink together. I would have preferred that we had met on more friendly and equal terms."

"Then, how do you know me so well, Francisco?"

"Your handiwork has been well noted outside of Cali! Gilberto Rodriguez Orejuela."

"So, your intelligence at CORU must be at a high level. I had assumed that my fame outside of Cali was minimal. This is disturbing to me, my friend."

"Let's cut the bullshit, Gilberto! Just call me Frank, okay. I'm just your ordinary Cuban-American. I drink beer, not wine! You Cali boys have delusions of grandeur. You think you are royalty. Something special! Well, just try coming out in the open some time and see how special the Americans think you are."

Gilberto ignored the insults for the most part. What he wanted was information and cooperation.

"Frank! Yes! How American of you! It must suit you when you wander the streets of Miami. I wonder what they would call me up there?"

"Cut the crap! Why am I here? I am not an enemy of the Cali cartel, Gilberto. Why am I treated this way? If the situation were reversed, you would be sipping our finest wine, if we had any."

"On the contrary, Eulalio." The captor hesitated as he realized his mistake.

"Please forgive me, Frank. On the contrary, you and your Cuban brotherhood are our allies and friends. The blindfold is merely a precaution for your own safety. I ask for your understanding and patience. Our friends here in Maracaibo would be at risk if you come to know too much. Notice that I will not ask you about CORU during this conversation. So, as I am sure you now understand, the unfortunate circumstances of our meeting are only the means of safety and security for both of us, CORU and my Cali brethren."

"Please proceed with your presentation," the prisoner said to his captor. "My degree of discomfort is rising."

"Frank, I will summarize the situation for both of us. Please stop me when you feel that my words do not match the facts as we see them around us."

"Don't worry, I will!"

"You are Cuban, and we are Colombian. We are both opposed to the socialist and communist diseases that have spread across our countries. You have Fidel Castro, and I have M-19. They are almost a common enemy. If we work together, we can help each other destroy those who threaten us."

"Gilberto, you speak of the Cali cartel and CORU as partners?"

"Yes, in a measure. You cannot deny that we both prosper from the same core business. You are more devious as to your reputation with the Americans, but the business is the same, nevertheless."

"We currently do not interfere in each other's business, but the same cannot be said for our brothers in Medellin. Lehder and Escobar are joined at the hip supporting these vermin and scum of the earth."

"And, who would that be again, my friend."

"Of course, you leave the honor of naming them to me. For you, they are the Cubans on the island. For me, they are the slime that calls itself M-19. And for us, there are the Sandinistas."

"But these have long been our mutual enemies. To kidnap me now is to react a little slowly. I am not sure about Cali, but we at CORU are fighting at least two of these enemies each day the sun comes up."

"And for that I thank you again, Frank. But, we have new players, and they not endearing themselves to either of us."

"And, who would that be, Gilberto?"

"The Medellin capos have introduced two malignancies. First, they are beginning to support our enemies in M-19. And second, they are attacking both of us from behind in the United States. In Miami they are removing your Cuban brothers and in New York they are trying to take our franchise."

"Gilberto, I am aware of the war which raged and continues to rage in Miami. I have lost some of my expatriate brethren to the Medellin. But I was unaware of your differences in New York. I was always under the impression that you had a working agreement with Medellin. I always assumed that you split your territories in a peaceful manner."

"Lehder and Escobar and the others seem to have forgotten our understanding."

"But as to your second point, Lehder is not the type I would name as support for M-19. If anything, he is not a communist. A facist, yes. But not a communist! The political party he is forming in Colombia is a carbon copy of the German National Socialist movement in the 1930s. The boy is a first class nazi!"

"My information says otherwise, Frank. I know it is unreliable, but the Americans tell me that Carlos Lehder is the hand behind M-19. But, that is our problem, my friend, not yours. We can take care of that business ourselves. The problem I bring to you is one of mutual interest and related strongly to what we have discussed so far."

"The Sandinistas?"

"No! No, I assume that your efforts with the Americans through CORU will succeed and relieve us of these criminals. We will help you in that matter where we can. The problem I want to focus on today involves the other man who calls himself Carlos."

"The other Carlos? The young Carlos? The old Carlos! The Carlos with no name! You will have to give me some help for I know many men named Carlos."

"The Cuban Carlos. The one who has, to our knowledge, intercepted two major shipments of yours headed for Miami! The Carlos who has directed the government to our Villavicencio laboratory! The invisible Carlos who moves through the night like a ghost! The one who has cost the lives of several of your best operatives! The Carlos who has alerted the Americans to several of our major shipments routed through Mexico! Enough clues? That fucking Carlos!"

"You say he is Cuban?" said Campa coyly. "Tell me more about this man."

"You know as well as I do that his father is being held near Havana by Castro for crimes against the revolution. You were the one who left him at the Bay of Pigs! You shouldn't have forgotten that already."

Campa decided to continue his tactic of playing dumb in order to determine how much his captor actually knew of the situation.

"Is this man Raymond Chacon? Captain Raymond Chacon. I didn't leave him in Cienfuegos. He went to Havana and was captured by the revolutionaries."

"You are a quick study, Frank! But, for the record please understand that I do not believe you."

"Of course, I know this man! Are you telling me that the Carlos we are speaking of is the son of Raymond Chacon?"

"None other! I would not have brought you this far from your home if I did not have information which is of grave importance to you and your associates."

"It's becoming more clear to me, Gilberto! All this time I was led to believe that Lehder was attacking us. I even sent a mission to him, and he denied intercepting our commerce. I didn't believe him. Now you tell me that the Carlos we are all seeking is a Cuban and that Raymond Chacon is his father!"

"That is the conclusion we have drawn. There can be no mistake."

"Indeed, Gilberto, it seems that we are natural allies. Tell me what you want of me."

"We have failed over the last two years to find this man, this Carlos. We have concluded that you must convince the Americans that they would benefit significantly from his demise. You must find a way to get your friends at CIA to help us remove this disease. We know that you have their confidence and support and that they have the means we may lack to accomplish this task. In return we will help you with your enemies in Medellin and Nicaragua."

"Gilberto, I find it hard to refuse your hospitality. We will form an alliance that will help both of us. You can count on me! And, I am sure that the Americans will find reason enough to help us."

"And, Frank, when we have had our way with this man, Carlos, we will drink that wine you spoke of!"

33

Look into My Eyes

> *Strike, smite them, spare them not,*
> *for many reasons,*
> *But most because they have*
> *blasphemed the Gods!*

> —**B.B.Rogers, translation of**
> ***Birds* by Aristophanes**

Sarasota, Florida

As Josef Girona and Phil Costello entered the interview room of the Sarasota Jail Annex, a sheriff's deputy was clearing some old newspapers from the lone table in the center of the otherwise unfurnished room. Both men were tired and each took a seat on the folding chairs that lined the wall. A stenographer came to the door and indicated that she would wait outside should statements be required from any of the witnesses.

Costello usually enjoyed these post-capture interviews. Often he could save himself a lot of work with some well-placed questions. And, usually the nervous prisoner would start talking and say too much. He approved of the good cop-bad cop style, as long as he could be the bad cop.

"Who should we do first, Josef? Of all the mules, this kid Johnny seems to be the shakiest. He looks like he's ready to cry!"

"You're probably right," said Josef after some consideration. "The two taller guys seem to be avoiding the rest, separating themselves from the group. I can't tell whether they know each other. We might have to squeeze Michaels to find out.

"The one I want to save for last is the older guy, Gebinsky. He's try-ing to look cool, but I bet if he gets the idea that the kids are spilling their guts and making a deal, he'll crack. I'm a bit surprised that they all agreed to speak with us without their attorneys being present."

The deputy shook his head.

"Well, that's not exactly true, Sir. They've asked for a public defender. One of them should be here in a few minutes. But with the docket calls they have, it may be a few hours. You might as well get some coffee while we wait for one or more of them to show up. The prisoners may change their minds after they talk with an attorney."

Costello yawned as he poured himself a cup of coffee.

"I thought they might reconsider," Josef replied as he leafed through the preliminary arrest reports. "If they do come in, this guy Gebinsky interests me, too. He was wearing a trench in the cell floor this morn-ing. I hope he's as tired as I am."

The stenographer who had been waiting outside of the interview room politely tapped on the door and opened it slightly. She motioned to Costello to come outside into the hallway.

"Mr. Costello, you have a phone call. One of the attorneys asked me to tell you to go to room 302. You have a call holding there for you."

"Thanks, Mrs. Cartwright. Would you do me a favor and tell my friends in there that I'll be back in five minutes and to wait for me before they begin."

Mrs. Cartwright nodded and walked toward the interview room as Costello headed to the elevator and punched up the third floor. The old, rickety elevator groaned as its doors opened and the agent stepped in. He took the trip to the third floor and after exiting the ele-vator, he scanned the walls for room identifications. Room 302 was at the north end of the building, and he entered without knocking. This office housed several of the States' Attorneys for Sarasota County. Costello stepped up to the receptionist and asked for the location of his phone call.

"You may take the call in the conference room over there." The receptionist pointed to a small room that was unoccupied. The multi-line telephone on the table had one flashing line. Costello closed the door and sat down near the phone. He picked up the line and introduced himself to the caller.

"This is Frank Campa," came the response. "I've been referred to you by CIA Station Chief Joseph Fernandez."

"Well, my old buddy, Joseph. Tell me, Mr. Campa, how can I help you?"

"I've been following your work with Harry Michaels with some interest. They tell me that you made an unexpected catch this morning."

"We went after a sailfish and caught a few catfish. Well, actually, Sarasota County caught the catfish. Are you CIA?"

"A Special Agent. When they want something from me, the CIA pays me. We have some overlapping interests with this fellow Michaels."

"In what way?" asked Costello.

"We have some interest in a Colombian smuggler called Carlos. We believe that he is the same one you are pursuing. There is a possibility that he is Cuban. He has given our organization quite a bit of trouble lately. We've lost some agents, lost some busts, and worst of all, several special ops misfired or had to be cancelled. We think we can trace most of it to this man."

"It's so nice to know that you have friends in your time of need, isn't it. It couldn't be that the CIA is actually asking for help, could it? Even though we missed this time, we think we're getting close." Costello really enjoyed having the upper hand for once.

"What is the current situation?"

"We have five of Michaels' people in custody. They won't be much help on Carlos, but they might be the tools we need to set him up."

"Interesting! Michaels has a reputation for screwing up. We have some people near SETCOMP in Honduras. It's a terminal owned primarily by his father, Frank Michaels. Our agents down there tell us that he comes to them with all kinds of information that we would have to chase other people for. He'd shit if he knew how many of our people he's talked to in the last year without knowing it. I hate the thought of taking him off the street; one of our best sources of information would be gone."

"Well, Mr. Campa. What can I do for you?"

"I believe I can do something for you. Our sources in Havana tell us that Fidel Castro is considering the release of Raymond Chacon. You know who he is, don't you?"

Costello shook his head in disbelief.

"There's no way Chacon would be released. He was at the invasion, and he's thought to be a Batista man. A high level Batista man who participated in the Bay of Pigs! He got life. Don't they usually execute their lifers once they get tired of them?"

"That may be so, but Raymond Chacon is thought to be the father of this fellow Carlos. With the money he has managed to accumulate, the son may have arranged for the father's release."

"And, you think he will lead us to his son?"

"Not willingly, I agree. But, Carlos will contact his father once he's released. That's our opportunity. I will contact you when I have more information."

Costello hung up the phone and headed back to the interview room. As he entered the room, he was surprised to see Josef speaking with a public defender. His name was Larry Morse, and he had been summoned to the jail to represent Juan Rodriquez. The other four prisoners had declined to be interviewed and had decided to be represented by private counsel. Morse turned to Costello and began a proposal.

"My client and I have had a short discussion of the situation, and he insists on being co-operative with the State and Federal

Governments in this matter. He would like some consideration in return for this cooperation."

"Larry, we always try to help witnesses who help us, especially in cases like this. Our main concern here is the identity of those on the aircraft."

At this point Juan interrupted the conversation.

"If you don't mind, I would like to speak to you alone. My lawyer will help me negotiate an agreement with you, but I want to speak to only one of you about this matter."

Josef rose from his chair and started for the door.

"This is your baby, Phil. I'm going to get something to eat and head back for Fort Myers if you don't mind."

Costello was puzzled by Josef's quick withdrawal, but nodded as he shook hands with the attorney who was headed out of the door with Josef.

"Would one of you ask Anne to get us some coffee and a few donuts. I'm sure that Juan is as hungry as I am." Josef nodded to Costello as he left the room.

Slowly, Costello turned his attention back to Juan, and asked how he believed his testimony or information would help.

"Agent, I have just two parameters here. First, I don't want to testify against my fellow prisoners. You already have them nailed, and someone else can point the finger at them. I have to be firm about that. I don't want to hurt them."

"Okay, that's one. What else do you want?"

34

The Bait

Our business is not unknown to the senate;
they have had inkling this fortnight
what we intend to do,
which now we'll show 'em in deeds.
They say poor suitors have strong breaths;
they shall know we have strong arms too.

—Shakespeare, *Coriolanus*

Saint Joseph, Missouri

The Bull was a small neighborhood bar located in the west-end of St. Joseph, Missouri. It was a popular gathering place for Ron and Charlie and their friends. The service was good and the owner knew how to make Tex-Mex and Cajun snacks to perfection.

Linda had inherited this business from her husband about two years ago when he had the unfortunate fate of being killed in an automobile accident in Kansas. Eric had just finished dropping off his daughter at his ex-wife's house when a drunken bricklayer ran a stop sign and ended his life.

Eric had put his soul into the bar, and Linda found it impossible to give it up. So she quit her job with a local insurance company and took over the operation herself. After about six months it became obvious to everyone that she was born to run a small business like this. She was friendly, organized and efficient, and her customers were hard pressed to find a place they would have liked better; some even liked it better than their own home.

Ron had started coming to *The Bull* for happy hours during the time when he was working as a flight engineer for TWA. His boyhood friend, Eric, had grown up in Plainview, Texas and they both attended Louisiana State University in Baton Rouge.

The Bull had a Texas décor and a touch of Louisiana that made Ron feel right at home. All that was missing was some Cajun music that Ron always threatened to bring with him the next time he came to St. Joe. After Eric died, Ron didn't want anything to change in the bar, so he never brought the music with him.

On this particular evening Ron was accompanied by his friend Charlie, his girlfriend Lottie, Charlie's wife, Charlene, and his friend Pat. Pat lived in St. Joe and worked for the Missouri Highway Department as an engineer. Pat had just become engaged and the group was celebrating the event although his bride-to-be was in Chicago visiting her parents. Charlie was working hard trying to get Pat to give him a clue about what he and Charlene should buy as a wedding present.

"Ah, com'on, Pat! Give me an idea. If Christine were here, she would tell me. You must have some ideas! A brand new set of tools? Season Tickets to the Chief's games? I know she's a football fan!"

Pat shook his head vigorously as he swirled the beer in his glass.

"Look, Charlie, how the hell do I know what we need? I'm just the groom! But, she did tell me that she has registered us at Sears and J.C. Penney. Christine listed all the stuff we need to set up housekeeping. Actually, you're right about the tickets. She'd probably love season tickets, but not in the end zone. She'd want to be right between the tackles or on the bench helping coach the team. And then I'd have to start being a full time fan. Then she'd be calling Charlene every week to drive to Kansas City for a game, and we'd never get anything done. So, forget the tickets! Okay?"

"Okay, I'll get Charlene to go to J.C. tomorrow and find something nice. But don't be surprised if it's a set of tools or twenty cases of beer!"

Ron and Lottie had just finished some chicken wings covered in Linda's special hot sauce and ordered another pitcher of beer. They had been discussing the same subject with Charlene who had given them some good ideas for wedding presents. Ron picked up his beer and headed for the jukebox that stood in the corner of the bar. Charlie followed him and the two began looking down the list of available songs. Charlie took the opportunity to discuss some private business.

"Have you heard anything from Carlos?"

Ron shook his head negatively. "Nothing yet, Charlie. You can never tell what a turkey like Michaels would do to save himself. We just have to wait and let it play out."

"Yeah, you're right. The kid knows what he's doing."

Lottie strolled up to the jukebox to help her friends with the music. "We're not doing the shit-kicking stuff, are we? After all, its Pat's gig, and he likes rock'n'roll. How about a little *Jimi Hendrix or Grateful Dead.*"

Charlie looked at Lottie and smiled. "I love the *Grateful Dead*, Lottie. Jerry Garcia is the best! Ron, give the little lady what she wants."

Without speaking, Ron punched up three Dead numbers that were on the box. He had to admit that he liked them a lot himself. If there was no Cajun music on the box, the *Grateful Dead* would do fine.

The trio walked back to the bar in cadence with the melody of the first song. Ron walked over to Pat and slapped him gently on the back.

"Enjoy yourself while you can, my boy."

They toasted each other with glasses of beer and ordered more wings. As they hummed the music and drank sips of beer, Ron finished his glass and casually looked at Pat.

"Say, Pat. Hypothetically, speaking, let's say you had several metal or plastic containers full of tools. Pretty heavy stuff. And, let's say that you wanted to get them across a river. How would you do it?"

Pat scratched his head. "Sounds like a problem for the Seabees to me. Or I would just use the bridge!"

"Nice try, Pat. Say there was no bridge."

"I suppose that you, hypothetically, are in the middle of nowhere with almost nothing to work with. Right?

"You're getting warm."

"You would want to float them somehow. Do you have a boat?"

"Okay. I'll give you a small raft with a hundred horsepower outboard."

"Are you in a hurry?"

"You might assume that. A big hurry would be appropriate. And some silence would be beneficial."

"I know that you're going to tell me that I can't put the containers in the boat. So, we need to float them. Foam might work. Or something you could inflate and attach to the containers?"

"I'll give you some help. You'll be in salt water. That should help."

"Ron, you're so generous. But, that'll help a lot. At the risk of repeating myself, you'll be in the middle of nowhere. Am I right?"

"Absolutely! In the middle of fuckin' nowhere."

"Try cutting down some light trees and strapping them to the containers. You'll need heavy-duty tape or construction strapping. We use some heavy shit to hold the steel rods together when we ship them out to a bridge or highway job. Do you need something like that?"

"That would work. Charlie and I may need your help. Don't worry about the cost. We've got funds to cover it. Take a look and see what you can come up with."

"What's my time frame?"

"Two weeks okay?"

"Piece of cake! Give me the number of containers and their rough dimensions and I'll have what you need by the weekend."

As Ron and Pat talked, Linda brought another plate of chicken wings and topped off their beers.

Charlie strolled over to the front window of the bar and scanned the street. He could see his car and Ron's Mercedes parked directly across the street. But he wasn't really interested in those vehicles. It was a blue Buick that was parked about half a block down the street that drew his attention. He motioned to Ron and as Ron approached the window, Charlie stepped back and pointed toward the Buick.

"They're still watching us! I wonder what's keeping them. They know we're in here."

"That's easy, Charlie. They're waiting for me to go to the storage area. I'm sure they think that we'll lead them to something illegal. And I mentioned St. Joe to Michaels when I talked with him. They've concluded that something's here.

"Well, I shouldn't disappoint them, should I? I need to borrow one of Pat's wrenches so he and I can slide out to North Kansas City and get it out of his storage area. He knows what's going on and the locker is clean. Hopefully, they'll go for the bait. Make sure that you follow us in about five minutes. When they get their surprise and find nothing, they may try to plant something to strengthen their case."

"Sounds good to me, Ron. Charlene and I will take Lottie with us. I'll be able to answer any questions she might have. We'll take care of her until they let you out. Give me a few minutes to put on my disguise. I don't want them to be able to recognize me later."

Charlie and Ron turned away from the window and walked back to the bar. Ron stood next to Lottie, who was talking with Charlene, and put his arm around her waist.

"Pat and I have to run a little errand. It's possible that I may not be back for a week or so."

"Does it have something to do with those people who followed me over here?"

Ron and Charlie looked at each other in surprise. Ron took Lottie's hand and walked her over to the window. "Was it that car over there?"

Lottie nodded. "They aren't very good, are they? I spotted them immediately. They must know that I know about them because I drove around the plaza three times before I came over here. I remembered what you told me last month about this type of thing so I let them follow me over here."

"Honey, you did good! I wanted them to find me. You saved me some time."

"Ron, everything's okay, isn't it?" Lottie asked, her voice reflecting her concern.

"Everything is great. This thing's a little tricky. If I get hung up, make sure you stay in touch with C.B. and Charlene."

"I will. Charlene has been hinting at something. She wants me to come and visit for a few days. I think I'll do it. Give me a kiss. Let us know where you are as soon as you can. Are you going to need an attorney for this escapade?"

"That's being arranged. We have help."

"Oh, those mysterious friends of yours. As I remember, the last time you set out to play spy versus spy, you crashed your plane and had to swim home. Let's hope that this one is a little less tricky!"

"Honey, I can't sneak anything past you, can I? Ah, did you really go around the block three times?"

"No, but I wanted to see what you would say. You didn't even pass out! I just wanted to show you that I can do cloak and dagger stuff too!"

Ron kissed Lottie and followed Pat out of the front door of the restaurant. They crossed the street and got into Pat's car without looking around. Pat pulled out of the parking spot slowly and headed south toward North Kansas City.

"Ron, what kind of wrench was that you were talking about? It sounds more like you need something bigger. Something that will get you out of a bear trap!"

35

Mexico City

And we are here as on a darkling plain, Swept
with confused alarms of struggle and flight,
Where ignorant armies clash by night.

—Matthew Arnold, Dover Beach

Mexico City, Mexico

The Mexicana Boeing 707 groaned as it dropped slowly through the thin air above Mexico City. The passengers had been instructed to straighten their seat backs and stow their tray tables. The seatbelt and no smoking signs were illuminated. The man in seat 4A continued to stare out at the hilly and mountainous terrain as the plane came closer to the International Airport that served the City.

He was a distinguished man with a generous crop of gray hair that was carefully combed. He was dressed in a fine Italian suit and could easily have been mistaken for a business traveler. He had only one piece of carry-on luggage, a black briefcase that was full of folders and papers.

As the plane was making its final approach, the traveler quickly reviewed several documents before he returned them to his briefcase. He checked the inside pocket of his suit coat for his passport, ticket and drivers license. Then he scanned the customs form that he had filled out about an hour ago. He had identified himself as an American businessman whose business was with Amermex, a Mexican oil services company.

When one of the stewardesses inquired about his comfort, he responded in Spanish with a gentle voice that brought a smile to her face. He had been to Mexico City on several previous occasions so he was familiar with the customs and baggage procedures. The flight finally rolled to a halt at the gate, and the passengers prepared to disembark. The man picked up his briefcase and walked slowly out of the plane and through the exit tunnel into the international section of the airport.

After passing through the duty free shopping section, he arrived at the custom's processing area. Several minutes later he had displayed his passport and identification papers to a customs official and made his way to the baggage area to collect his luggage. He had checked one bag. It contained a few articles of clothing but nothing of importance in it's interior. It was the exterior of the bag that had significance. As instructed, he had placed two strands of white adhesive tape on each side in the form of an X.

As he stood near the baggage carrousel, he scanned the other passengers who were waiting for their luggage to arrive. They were mostly American tourists who were bound for Acapulco and other popular resort areas. Most of them were dressed informally. He was looking for one or more men dressed in business suits somewhat like his. Several men fit the description, but none seemed particularly interested in him.

Soon his luggage could be seen coming down a ramp on the carrousel and around a curve toward him. He stepped forward to pick up the suitcase and as his hand touched the handle, he was surprised to feel the presence of another hand, that of a female. He turned and to his surprise he saw a very beautiful Hispanic woman in business attire smiling at him.

"Let me help you with your luggage, Mr. Chacon. As you might remember, my name is Maria." She spoke perfect English.

"Maria! How could I forget? But what are you doing here in Mexico. I would have expected to see you in Havana or Santiago."

"Raul has asked me to come to Mexico City to talk with you. He still thinks as highly of you as I do. It has been a long time since you left Cuba, and the years have been kind to you. I have always had a crush on you, you know."

"Maria, if I had known it was you…" Oscar just stopped and stared into her sparkling eyes.

"I could never have left Cuba and my family, Oscar. No matter how much I loved you. And I know you understood that. We each did what we had to do at the time."

"Maria, I have often wondered whether we made a mistake. But we have other problems now."

"I know. Come, get your luggage, and we can move to a more comfortable location. The Mexicans do not waste air conditioning on their tourists. I will guide you to the embassy. I have a cab waiting outside."

Oscar was somewhat surprised, but he recovered enough to speak. "Thank you, Maria. Please forgive my surprise, but I expected a male guide. Seeing you has brought back so many memories."

"I hope you are not disappointed." Maria's voice was smooth and reassuring.

"I could never be disappointed with you, Maria. I guess I was busy trying to decide what I would say to my escort, and you surprised me. All of my preparation is gone so you will have to put up with whatever comes to my mind."

"That's always better. I am now acting as Special Assistant to the Ambassador. He would have greeted you himself; however, he is in Argentina this week. He asked me to assure your comfort and safety. As I said, you are still highly thought of in Havana. There are few Cubans in the United States who are as highly respected as you are. But I am sure that you are aware of this."

"I love Cuba, and I love America. There are some Cubans and some Americans I do not particularly enjoy. But most people in each country are decent and respectable. I often find myself caught between the two camps. In this case my interest is very personal as you know."

"I have been briefed on your mission, but it is better that we do not discuss it here in public. Raul Castro himself has been lobbying hard for you and your brother. There has been much misunderstanding and considerable bad luck. Even Raul does not always have great influence with his brother."

"He and I have been friends for a long time. It is unlikely that I will see him so I would appreciate it if you would tell him that I am very grateful for his help."

"When I return to Havana, I will deliver your best wishes. As his official representative, I bring his wishes for good luck, and I am here to help you if I can."

As the couple came around a corner and exited the airport building, Maria pointed to a taxi that stood near the sidewalk.

"Please excuse the rather small taxi. Most people here travel in Volkswagen cabs, and I was unable to find a larger vehicle with a reliable driver. All of our embassy vehicles are in use at a conference."

Oscar and Maria entered the VW taxi and after a drive through the busy part of the City, they entered the driveway of a building that served as the Cuban Embassy. The guard waived Maria and her guest into the courtyard where they left the taxi and entered the building through a side door. They found themselves in a hallway with doors leading to relatively small offices. After they had passed seven or eight doors, they came to a reception area that held a secretarial desk and several sets of sofas and easy chairs.

Maria became much more formal.

"Mr. Chacon, please take a seat. I will see if the men you are to meet with are present."

Maria turned left into a hallway and disappeared into an elevator. Oscar was alone except for two security cameras that scanned the room. He took a seat and picked up a magazine from the rack that rested next to his chair. To his surprise it was Time Magazine. Several months old, but nevertheless, it was Time. It seemed odd to him that an American publication would grace the Cuban embassy visiting room. Then again, maybe it was just the natural bias he had against the current Cuban government. A bias which he tried hard to understand and control. The success of his mission and the fate of his brother rested with these elements of cooperation and understanding.

36

The Lineup

If any man hopes,
in anything he does,
to escape the notice of
the gods, he is mistaken.

—Pindar, Greek myth

Federal Courthouse, Saint Louis, Missouri

The prisoner was being detained in the holding area on the first floor of the Federal Courthouse. He was patiently waiting for the arrival of his accusers and his defenders. Even though he had never been in jail before, he was unusually confident and maintained his calm demeanor. After all, he knew that he was innocent of this particular crime, and that as soon as the witness or witnesses saw him, they would confirm that fact.

Besides, he had an alibi and alibi witnesses. Unfortunately, he might have to modify his story slightly. When the arrests were made at the subdivision in Sarasota County, was he fishing off the Everglades? Or maybe he was just having a drink with Charlie in Marathon or Key West. As he thought about the situation, it would be easier just to have the witnesses confirm that he wasn't present at the scene, whoever those witnesses were.

As he was pondering his strategy, a U.S. Marshall walked into the holding area and connected a telephone to the wall outlet at a desk near the cell door. The Marshall opened a small sliding door on the cell, one usually used to serve food to the detainees, and passed the telephone in to the prisoner.

"It's your attorney, Mr. Hernandez. We have to wait a minute for them to transfer the call. The phone will ring when the transfer is completed. Just pick it up. Apparently, the U. S. Attorney has invited him to the lineup he's holding for you. At least that's what they told me. It's very unusual for them to invite attorneys. You must have some pull upstairs."

The prisoner shook his head. "If I had some pull upstairs, I wouldn't be here right now, would I!"

The Marshall smiled. "You've got a good point there. When I worked for the State, we had lineups all the time. And for the most part they were pretty ridiculous. We used to bet that we could pick the prisoner out of the lineup without even knowing the crime. He was always the most nervous, the one whose eyes were blinking the most. Hopefully, this will be a little different. Most of the time, those poor bastards did-n't have an attorney. The public defenders were so overloaded, most of them didn't have a fighting chance."

"I'll keep that in mind," Ron replied as he sat down next to the phone.

"Let me know when you're done. And, don't make any outside calls on this phone. I'll take you to the phone room for those. Okay?"

"No problem." At that moment the phone rang meekly and the prisoner picked up the receiver. He announced his presence to the caller. "Hello?"

"Ron?" The voice was one that Hernandez was unfamiliar with.

"Yeah, this is Ron Hernandez. I understand that you're my attorney."

"That's right. Your friend came to my office and explained your problem. Well, part of it anyway. He asked me not to identify him over the phone."

"He's a good friend of mine, always taking care of me."

"How did you get my name? My main practice is not criminal law. I explained that to…, ah, your friend, but he didn't seem to care."

"I have no idea. But he must have had a good reason for picking you. You must have gotten his attention somehow."

"Well, it's not that important. It's just a bit unusual. You know about the lineup, right?"

"Yes. They told me this morning. Is it good or bad?"

"Actually, it's good. We can get a look at their main witness or witnesses. I called the U.S. Attorney, and he's going to let me in on it. I'll talk with you afterwards. From what your friend says, we have plenty of witnesses as to your whereabouts. So this should all shake out positively after they get their informant or informants to look at you. We can go over this later, but I presently don't know who they're bringing in to look at you."

"Sounds good to me. I do have one problem with a lineup. I have a…maybe I shouldn't say it over the phone. I need to clean up before the lineup."

"Ron, do whatever you believe is in your best interests. I'll be down there in thirty to forty minutes. The lineup is set for two o'clock so you have three hours to get ready."

"Great. They told me I could shower and shave so I'll see you after the lineup, and they'll see me at two on my best behavior!"

"Okay. Oh, your friend said to tell you that Lottie is coming over from St. Joseph to see you tomorrow afternoon. It's something to look forward to, but we may have you out of there today."

Ron expressed his appreciation for the help and after hanging up the phone, he called the U.S. Marshall to the holding cell.

"Say, thanks for the phone. My attorney said I should shower and shave before my interview at two o'clock. Can I do that now?"

The Marshall nodded. "It's okay. We have limited facilities, but we do have a shower with warm water, and I guess I can trust you with the razor. You'll have to use soap instead of shaving cream. We're out of that stuff. I use an electric myself otherwise I could get some for you out of my locker."

"Thanks, I appreciate it. This is much better than the jail in St. Joe where I stayed several nights ago. I can see that Missouri doesn't spend any of its tax money on their jails. That place was worse than a dog kennel. I have to remember that if I ever decide to become a criminal! Always commit a federal crime! If you get caught, the facilities and treatment are much better. Especially the food!"

"You're right about that in most places, but here we send people over to Belleville. Now that's a hole! Here's your towel and soap. The shower is located through that door." The Marshall pointed toward the back of the room. "I'll lock this front door. Just knock on it when you're done."

"Thanks, my girlfriend is coming to visit me, and I'd rather not look like shit."

Ron spent the next hour cleaning up while his attorney made some last minute calls from his office. It was about 12:30 PM when Jim arrived at the Federal Courthouse in St. Louis. Parking was at a premium so he had to walk several blocks through the drizzle that had been falling since early in the morning. He had very little information on the case, but it sounded interesting. His client gave a favorable impression over the phone so Jim looked forward to meeting him. He had represented several other pilots, but those were all cases before the Tax Court.

Jim entered the U.S. Attorney's Office on the fifth floor and took a seat in the waiting room. After a few minutes, Richard Froehling entered and introduced himself.

"I'll be handling the lineup. I'm not too familiar with the case, and I'm sure that under the circumstances you are in the same boat. Have you talked with your client yet?"

Jim shook his head. "No, I thought I would wait until after you look at him. I've got a lot of questions, and I need some time."

"This is an unusual situation. We haven't had a Grand Jury, and your client was not arrested on the scene. The DEA just grabbed him over in St. Joseph, and they've been holding him under questionable circumstances. If the lineup doesn't produce a positive result, I'm going to release Hernandez."

"How many witnesses do you have?"

"To tell you the truth, Jim, I'm not sure. All I can say is that the DEA has at least one."

"I don't know if he's said anything yet, but I believe we have several alibi witnesses. This should be interesting!"

"Well, let's go downstairs, and we can get this over with."

Froehling led the way as they walked out into the hallway to an elevator that took them down to the first floor. As they entered the witness room, Jim saw several men talking to a relatively young lad. They turned and Froehling introduced Jim to Phil Costello and Arthur White.

"Phil and Arthur are with the DEA, Washington, D.C. Office."

Costello pointed to the witness.

"That's the witness. His name is Juan."

"Is he the only one?"

Costello nodded.

"Juan was on the ground crew which was arrested in Sarasota. We're trying to find the pilot of the aircraft. That's where your client comes in."

Jim looked at Juan as he sat in the far corner of the room.

"He seems very calm, considering the circumstances. How old is he?"

"I'm not sure," replied Costello as he picked up a phone and talked for about thirty seconds before hanging it up again. "Let's get started."

Froehling shut off the lights, and the parties took their seats. To Jim it seemed like a small movie theatre. The viewing room was suddenly lit and five males ranging from forty to fifty years of age entered the room. Jim scanned the group trying to determine which man was his client.

Costello whispered some instructions to Arthur and then turned to Juan who was seated next to him.

"Take your time, Juan", Costello whispered. The men can't see you. Look at each one and tell us if you see the pilot of the Beech 18."

Juan slowly looked across their faces, first from right to left and then from left to right. Each man was wearing a large tag that displayed a number from one to five. The second man from the right seemed interesting. Juan stared at him for a few seconds and then his attention was drawn to the man on the far left.

Costello waived his hand at Arthur who picked up the phone and simultaneously threw a switch on the wall.

"Starting with the man on the left, number one, please read the sentence which appears on the wall in front of you." One by one the men read a standard phrase while Juan listened. After they had finished Costello turned his attention back to Juan.

"What do you think, Juan? Take your time."

Juan slowly lifted his hand and pointed at the second man from the right, the one wearing number four. "That looks like him right there, number four. Yeah, I believe that's him even though he's changed."

Costello did a double take as everyone listened for an explanation. "He's shaved off his handlebar mustache. Yes, the mustache is gone. In the picture you showed me, he had a handlebar mustache!"

Froehling immediately stood up and waived to Arthur that the lineup was over. "Get those people out of there. I've seen enough!"

Once the men were clear of the viewing room, Froehling stepped up to the witness and asked the question which was on everyone's mind.

"What picture, Juan? Are you trying to tell me that these men showed you a photo of one of the men?"

"Well, Mr. Froehling, they showed me a picture of this man who was supposed to be the pilot. And in the picture he had a big mustache. Here was the same man without the mustache. It's pretty definitely him!"

"Juan, did you see this man in the aircraft when it landed in Sarasota?"

Juan hesitated. "Ah, not exactly. Someone said something about a mustache, and this man had a mustache in the picture. I figured that the agents knew who the pilot was. I just don't want to go to jail!"

"Juan, how many people on the ground crew at Sarasota have mustaches? How many of the people you worked with on the ground wear them?"

"Ah, I guess most of them do. I don't, but Gebinsky…I mean just about everyone does. They are very popular."

"And didn't you say in your statement that you were wearing a black pull-over ski cap with holes in it so that you wouldn't be recognized?"

"Yes, I did! I was wearing the hat so no one would be able to recognize me."

"Was the pilot wearing a mask, too"

"Mr. Froehling, I'm not sure."

Costello looked down at the floor and knew he was in trouble. The attorney motioned to Froehling.

"Rich, we have to talk, somewhere private. This witness is tainted. I would like to see you release my man if you haven't anything else. Let's talk."

As the men left the witness room, a strange combination of depression and happiness spread over the group. Only Arthur, who was busy coordinating the lineup, was in the dark about what had just happened.

37

The Devil's Helpers

*Any man who has the brains to
think and the nerve to act
for the benefit of the people
of the country is considered
a radical by those who are
content with stagnation and
willing to endure disaster.*

—William Randolph Hearst

Broward County, Florida

The black Jaguar pulled up to the visitor's parking area in front of Captain Mike's Marina. The marina was located at the Hillsboro Inlet in Pompano Beach, Florida. A sign across the dock entrance read *For the Ultimate in Sport Fishing and Pleasure.*

Ted and Harry Michaels stepped out of the vehicle and walked along the wooden dock past various supply buildings and storage facilities until they came to a mooring which held the sailboat *Aquarius.*

This sixty-foot ferro-cement ketch was easy to spot among the smaller powerboats and sailboats that were docked here. The two large masts were bare of sails and the aft section of the deck was piled high with cardboard boxes. Harry and Ted could hear activity below decks so Harry announced their arrival as they stepped onboard.

"Captain Gebinsky," shouted Harry Michaels as he looked around the deck. "What the hell are you doing? Not leaving town on us are you?" Harry pounded his fist on the sliding roof that covered the companionway to emphasize his point. "We'll find you wherever you go! The Bahamas, Bermuda, Haiti, anywhere!"

After a few seconds, Edward Gebinsky scrambled up the main stairway into the cockpit of the ship and sized up his two visitors.

"It's about time you showed up!" gasped Gebinsky as he steadied himself. It was obvious to his visitors that they had interrupted him in the middle of a project. "Maybe you can do something useful for a change and help me with my spring cleaning. After all, you drink all my beer and eat all my food. The least you could do is help clean up after yourself."

Gebinsky looked at Ted Michaels and continued. "Not you, Ted. It's your brother here. If he wasn't so ugly, he could get a girl, and she could keep him busy and out of my refrigerator!"

Ted looked from Gebinsky to his brother. "Not much chance of that happening. I'd put a lock on it if I were you. Every time he visits me he eats me out of house and home. We're starting to refer to him as Porky. The newspaper's got it wrong. He's not Harry, *The Fox Michaels*! He's *Porky* Michaels!

Gebinsky's eyes lit up. "Where did you get *Harry, the Fox*?"

"It's those stupid bastards in Ft. Lauderdale," Harry replied. "They did a profile on my dad's terminal, and they referred to me as Harry *The Fox*. Just what I need is more publicity.

"And Dad is madder than hell! He's blaming it all on me, too. The FAA and the City of Fort Lauderdale are coming down on him for minor shit, and he thinks it's all my fault."

Ted patted his older brother on the back. "Harry is a star. Any way you look at it, he's in the public eye. Lookout Hollywood, here he comes!"

Gebinsky shook his head and laughed as he pointed toward Harry. "Hollywood, Florida, maybe?"

Harry was not in the mood for small talk. He motioned for the group to retire below. After they entered the main cabin, Gebinsky extended a folding table that was built into the interior of the ship. He then went to the refrigerator and returned with three bottles of beer.

"Look, Ed, this bastard Juan has put us between a rock and a hard place!"

"Us!" yelled Gebinsky excitedly. "What do you mean, us? I'm the one who is fucked here! Or maybe you haven't noticed."

"I suppose I was the one who picked him?" laughed Harry.

"Maybe not! But I sure as hell didn't show him the photograph. Who's brilliant idea was that? One of your government-fuck up buddies?"

"How the hell else was he supposed to identify Hernandez? I didn't hear any great ideas coming from you! And, I didn't see you volunteering to do the deed yourself, did I?"

"Well, maybe I got my scorecard wrong, but wasn't you who was supposed to arrange the whole thing. Wasn't *The Fox* supposed to have his buddies at Drug Enforcement set up and control the whole thing? Wasn't I just supposed to keep my fucking mouth shut? That's a quote isn't it? *And remember Ed, keep your fucking mouth shut!* Ring any bells?"

"A lotta fuckin' good that does me now, Ed old buddy! Your man chopped up my meal ticket. He ate my *Get Out of Jail Free* card, didn't he!"

Ted had remained silent, letting the antagonists run out of material before intervening.

"Harry, we wouldn't be here if that little bastard that works for DEA hadn't snagged you. You were sure as shit positive about him. You must have looked like a big ole catfish when he planted that hook into your big mouth. Ed didn't do anything worse. Or any better for that matter. He trusted Juan, and Juan isn't even a government agent. So he screwed up! The two of you will just have to get over it."

"Who's side are you on anyway, Ted?" Harry slammed his fist on the table and stood up. He picked up his beer and took a long drink. Then he looked at his brother.

"It's easy for you to talk. We're both in the frying pan, and you aren't. Dad doesn't shit all over you when he sees you, but he would if he knew what was up."

"Get over it, Harry! Dad gets all that money for what? He knows what's up. He knows I'm flying those loads in. He knows you're running the show. He knows that most of the SETCOMP money is dirty. He's just smart enough not to open his mouth. He knows that there's a tap on his phone, but he does his legal business and there's nothing they can do to him. The only thing he doesn't know is that Kathy is involved with it. He'd kill us if he found out about that!"

Harry took another drink and slowly sat down at the table. He looked at Ted and then at Gebinsky.

"Okay, I just went off the track a bit there. Let's try to solve the problems we have. I'll try not to criticize either of you. But I'm not in the mood for any more mistakes!"

Gebinsky took a drink and began to try to formulate a strategy.

"We have to do something about Juan, you know. If his attorney calls him as a witness, we're probably dead on your deal with the DEA. Who does he have for an attorney anyway? A public defender?"

"You should be so lucky, Ed," mumbled Harry. "Why don't you take a guess."

"Hey! I wasn't there. I have no idea. Clarence Darrow?"

"Try Jim Johnson!"

"Oh, fuck! Not again," gasped Gebinsky in disbelief.

"Yep! It's just like your divorce all over again."

"I hate that bastard. He found all the assets I hid from Dipstick."

Harry was laughing so hard that he almost couldn't speak.

"By Dipstick, I presume you mean your lovely ex-wife, Darlene? Am I right?"

"How the hell did Hernandez find him?" Gebinsky murmured out loud.

"You tell us, Eddie! How do you think they found him?"

Gebinsky didn't reply, but it was a question that would continue to bother him.

"Let's get on to the real problem," Ted interjected. "You two can figure out something later. Right now we need to replace Juan's testimony. And, Ed, you are the only one left who can do it."

Gebinsky looked a little stunned even though he had already come to the same conclusion. Ted and Harry waited for a response. It was slow in coming.

"Well, I know what he looks like. I guess I can pick him out of a lineup. I can convince myself that he was flying the plane. That's all fine. But what if this guy Carlos finds me before they find him. What then?"

Ted had some reassuring words for Gebinsky.

"Hey, nothing happened to Juan. This character doesn't do hits in the U.S. As long as you're here, you're safe, and they'll catch him sooner or later.

"Look, we need to hide Juan, and we can do the same thing with you until the trial, or whatever, is over. Then the government should be able to hide you. Actually, you, Juan and Johnny can all lay low until the deed is done. Then you'll be okay because these guys aren't going anywhere when the feds catch them. After this thing goes down, we'll all have to hide for a while. We're all in the same boat, and I'm not talking about this bucket of concrete!"

Gebinsky knew that his fate was sealed.

"Costello told me that these guys are not violent types. They don't pack weapons, but what about those CIA agents you were talking about. Didn't you tell me that the reason they were after Carlos was the fact that a bunch of their contacts in the Caribbean were turning up dead. That doesn't sound nonviolent to me!"

Harry took another drink and thought for a second.

"Look, I can't explain everything. Maybe Carlos is just pointing out these people to his friends, and they're eliminating them. He's probably tight with the Cali and Medellin cartels. How the hell would I know? If we just stay out of Colombia, we'll probably be okay. Anyway, we haven't got many other options. We need you to testify. It's the only answer to our collective problems. You have to agree with that."

Gebinsky nodded as he walked to the refrigerator for another beer. After getting the beer he reached behind one of the seat cushions and retrieved a letter-sized manila folder. He opened it and placed the contents on the table.

"I guess your CIA buddy had the same idea about this. He was here a few hours ago and gave me these."

Harry picked up the documents and photographs.

"Photos of Hernandez in…Honduras? Did he tell you where he got these?"

"No, I didn't ask him about the location. The relevant point here is identification. Notice he also gave me photos from the first lineup. He wasn't wearing the handlebars at that one. So unless he changes into a werewolf, I should be able to identify him in the dark if I have to!"

Harry clapped his hands together. "Those sneaky bastards. Always thinking of the next step. Always ready to put our necks in the noose. Well, at least this shows that we probably have the right idea."

Ted concurred. "Look, Ed, the path out of this is laid out for us. Once you identify this guy Hernandez, he may crack and start cooperating. If he does that, you won't even have to appear in court. Costello and this CIA turkey will take it from there. The future doesn't look as bad as it did a few minutes ago, does it?"

Gebinsky raised his bottle of beer and proposed a toast.

"Here's to all the government agents we know and love and lie for. May they burn in hell!"

38

Plan B

Many a law, Many
a commandment,
Have I broken,
But, my word
Never!

—Sir Walter Scott, *Ivanhoe*

Orlando, Florida

Phil Costello never did like the city of Orlando. He would tell his fellow Washingtonians that it was just too Mickey Mouse for him. The line got him some laughs the first few times he used it, but the anecdote soon began wearing thin on even the most loyal northerner.

It wasn't so much the fact that he actually didn't like the city or its tourist attractions as it was his dislike for Carl Adams, the Orlando DEA Station Chief. Carl was easy going and not the kind of person to become easily upset under pressure. During emergencies Carl tended to keep his cool and maintain a sense of order even while those around him were, as he would say, *losing their heads.*

So Costello was not a most happy person when he was called to a meeting in Orlando at the DEA Regional Office. The subject? Confidential! It could only mean the Chacon matter. Adams was pulling the cloak and dagger stuff again!

So it was with renewed apprehension that Costello drove into the parking lot across from the Orlando DEA Field Office. He stepped from his rental car and entered the front door. The receptionist recognized Costello immediately.

"Second door on the left, Mr. Costello. Mr. Adams is on the telephone, but he is anxious to see you."

Costello went straight to the meeting room without saying a word. As he opened the door, his eyes fell on an unwelcome sight. The man sitting at the table was facing away from him, but his identity was unmistakable even though Costello had not met him before.

"Frank Campa, Special Agent for the Caribbean. I'm working with Central Intelligence. We spoke several months back."

At first, Costello was at a loss for words. The men shook hands after which Costello circled to the other side of the table.

"You are interested in the Sarasota case?" The words came slowly from Costello who was still standing.

"That's correct," was the reply.

"We have had a few problems." There was no point hiding the obvious thought Costello as he took his seat. "You just can't find a good informant these days."

Before Campa could respond, Carl Adams entered the room. He didn't speak, but took a seat at the head of the table. Campa glanced at Adams before speaking to Costello.

"I understand that your witness did not do well at the lineup."

"He wasn't my witness!" was Costello's immediate response. As he listened to his words fly across the room, he decided to take the offensive.

"If this meeting was called to place blame, this meeting is over!" Costello abruptly stood up from his chair as he spoke.

"Phil! Sit down!" were Adam's first words. "We are not blaming you. We need some cooperation from you. We're all on the same side."

"We are, are we?" said Costello as he slowly reclaimed his seat.

Campa waited until the silence became uncomfortable before speaking again.

"We are going to help you with the case, Phil." Campa's words were now almost too friendly for Costello's liking.

"I didn't think we needed help, Frank! Is this the CIA helping or is it your pet project, Commando of United Revolutionary Organizations?"

"Your attitude in this case has to change, Phil. I have men in Central America whose lives may depend on your cooperation. I am sure that they would not take kindly to any resistance."

"Well, I wouldn't want to mess up your bombings, assassinations and kidnappings, would I? And, how's your old buddy, Orlando Bosch? Now, there is a piece of work! My contacts tell me that every other load of shit that comes into the States belongs to CORU."

Campa had reached his boiling point, but he restrained himself because he did need Costello's cooperation.

"You still didn't answer my question, Frank! CIA or CORU?"

"I thought we already covered that ground. Definitely CIA! And, I'm not asking for your support, Phil. It's required!"

Costello could see that he had no way out of the situation. Any serious complaints would have to wait until he returned to Washington. He could only marvel at the cleverness of Campa having this meeting at one of his field offices. Costello was trapped!

"I'm listening," was his response.

"Your witness is going to take a vacation."

"You can't mean…" muttered Costello before he was interrupted.

"He will be leaving very shortly. We are making all of the arrangements."

"But, he's under subpoena and an indictment! I can't approve anything like that without the U.S. Attorney's cooperation," countered Costello.

"It's not your problem. Everything will be taken care of."

Costello was shaking his head as he interjected his disapproval.

"Why are you telling me, Frank? Are you just looking to cover your ass in case you get caught?"

"Whose side are you on anyway. We are going to catch this fucking Carlos, and we'll take him any way I can get him. If you have a better idea…"

"No! Not me! It's your show Frank. I just want to watch from a distance."

"Relax! You will be getting another witness in his place. This one will do a whole lot better."

"Don't tell me any more, Frank! I'm getting a headache."

"Just one or two more things, Phil. And, this is where you come in."

"I knew there was a catch. There always is!"

"First, We want you to put pressure on the pilot. He's your prisoner. Do whatever you have to, to scare him!"

"What else?"

"Most important. Don't let your agents screw this up! Understand?"

Costello didn't respond and looked away in disgust.

"I understand that you have a special agent on this case. The one who brought in Harry Michaels. Put him on the pilot. But, keep him away from the rest."

"I suppose you mean Gerona?"

"Yes! I have heard a lot about this man in Central America, but I have never had the pleasure of meeting him. Make sure that he doesn't do any freelance work on this one! And, if you can arrange it, I would like to meet this man."

"Josef is a low-profile type, Frank. He doesn't like publicity. But, this was his case. What can I tell him about your newfound interest in it?"

Campa didn't like the question, but he answered anyway.

"We have certain arrangements with various centers of power in Central and South America. Suffice it to say that two major Cali contacts are having problems. And, their problems often become our problems."

"Ah, Frank, that's what Gerona has been telling me. This Carlos fellow has his good points. He has been messing up the cartels' businesses."

"Listen, Costello. This may be a joke to you, but it is important to us. Keep Gerona on a short leash. If he has something going in Columbia, tell him to stop until this operation is over. Once we have Carlos, your man can do whatever he wants, within reason. Got it!"

"Fine!" acknowledged Costello. "Just let us know what's coming a few seconds before it happens."

39

The Visitor

Yeah, here comes the rooster,
Yeah, you know, he ain't gonna die

—Alice in Chains, *Rooster*

Belleville, Illinois

"I hate this fucking holding cell! No food! No television! And, the place is filthy," complained the first prisoner as he paced slowly back and forth. "What are you in here for? We don't get too many white guys down here?"

"I'm a federal prisoner," responded the second man quietly. "They brought me over here from Kansas City. I guess I go to court in St. Louis tomorrow."

"Kansas City? How are the Chiefs gonna do next year?"

"Well, I'm not much of a football fan. You'd have to ask my girlfriend about that. My name is Hernandez. Ron Hernandez."

"Hernandez! You don't look Hispanic to me. Where are you from?"

"Houston. My grandfather was from Cuba."

"Ah, well, that explains it. My name is Robert Smith. It's a pleasure to meet you despite the circumstances."

"Robert, this is a county jail, right? I was so tired when they drove me over here that I have no idea where I am."

"You are on the east-side, my man! You're in the beautiful State of Illinois. This is Belleville, and that shit hole you drove through was East St. Louis. I used to live in East St. Louis, but it was too much like a war zone."

"Do you have family here in Illinois?"

"If you call an ex-wife and two juvenile delinquents a family! They're the reason I'm in here. The judge found me in contempt for not paying child support. Hell, child support, I haven't even been able to feed myself lately.

"The county trash hauling service laid me off a few months ago and my unemployment ran out. And all they can say is that we have no job for you, Mr. Smith. At least after they transfer me somewhere more permanent, I'll get some reasonable food."

"I'm not a lawyer, but I thought contempt sentences where usually short."

"You obviously didn't hear of the *Chicago Seven* or was it the *Chicago Eight*. Just piss off his highness, the judge, and you can go for years. They think they're fucking gods, but I'll bet that if I met one of them in the alley, we'd sure as hell find out who was god!"

"I can't disagree with you, Robert. I have the same problem, but with the federal government. They want me to be someone I'm not, and they'll do anything to make me be that person."

"Sounds tricky, Hernandez."

"It is, I think! Say, why did they lay you off if they knew you had to pay child support?"

"Well, you obviously don't have children, and you've never worked for a bureaucracy. It was simple. They picked up some guy off the streets who was a little off the main line. You know, he was a few bricks short of a full load. And when he wouldn't cooperate, the cops in East St. Louis beat him up. They hurt him real bad! Guess what?"

"Got me. It sounds bad," Ron replied sympathetically.

"So the poor bastard sues the City of East St. Louis and wins. He wins the title to the City Hall, and he now owns the trash business."

"Wow! That's the way to strike back!"

"For him it was okay. But they laid me off in the middle of the whole thing when they were trying to cut costs and fight the lawsuit. Now the City is bankrupt, and I don't have a job. But, I shouldn't be unloading all this shit on you. I'm really a fairly cheerful guy."

"Hey, Robert, I've got plenty of time. Go ahead. I'm a good listener."

At that moment one of the officers approached the holdover cell.

"Hernandez, your lawyer is here from St. Louis. I'm going to put you in that interview room over there. He'll be with you in a few minutes."

Ron was removed from the cell and was placed in a small room with light green walls and an observation window in the far wall. After about five minutes, the attorney walked in the door carrying a briefcase and a cup of coffee.

"I'm Jim Johnson. We talked on the phone. Your friends must have told you that I was coming over to talk with you."

"I hate to break you away from your fun and games at the courthouse, Mr. Johnson," joked Hernandez. "Actually, it's good of you to come and see me so quickly."

Ron shook Jim's hand, and they sat down at the lone table in the small room.

"I would have talked with you sooner, but after the lineup they whisked you out so fast that I had to wait until you got over here to see you."

The attorney opened his briefcase and shuffled through several files. Finally, he pulled out the one marked Hernandez and laid it on the table. "Generally speaking, I'd say they're in trouble."

"They're in trouble?" laughed Ron. "I thought the whole idea was that I was in trouble! But it's a great concept."

"You'll just have to ride it out until I can get a hearing, maybe as soon as this afternoon if the federal magistrate is in. At least the magistrates over there aren't like the rednecks most of the judges imitate."

"It sounds like you've run into them before."

"You bet I have. Not often but enough to know what it's like. It's pretty sad when a judge is more interested in the decorum of the courtroom and the control he has over the attorneys than the defendant's right to a fair trial."

"That doesn't sound good to me. Maybe I should start worrying?"

"I mean things like how far the defense attorney stands from the podium, how loud or soft he speaks, or the latitude he's given in cross examination. Things like that.

"And they take it real hard when the government loses. The last case I had ended in a hung jury, and I thought the judge was going to have a heart attack. It was almost as if he had money on the outcome!"

"It sounds like I have the right guy defending me!"

"Well, I'll do my best. What I lack in skill, I'll make up for in enthusiasm. I just want to get you out of here quickly."

"Don't worry about me, Jim. I'm okay. There are some interesting guys in here. It's quite an experience for me. Not too different from basic training except we don't go anywhere, and we don't do anything.

"I've already picked up the finer points of arson using model airplanes to carry the payload, blowing up cars without using any separate explosives, and pulling off a residential burglary. These county jails are like a university. They're just tooling these guys up for when they get released. And under the circumstances I can't blame them too much. I guess the States of Illinois and Missouri can't spell the word *rehabilitation*."

"You're right, Ron. But they, or should I say we, end up paying for it many times over. The people who run these county governments are basically religious nuts who are still in the eye-for-an-eye generation."

"In any case, I'm getting along fine in here. Actually, I might come up with a few new clients for you if you need any more business. Some of these guys need an attorney real bad."

"We can look at that later. First, I've got to take care of you. You shouldn't be here in the first place. It's pretty clear that they have their eyes on someone, and it certainly isn't you. You're just the means they plan on using to get there."

Ron smiled and clapped his hands together. "That's an understatement if I ever heard one! I certainly wouldn't be flying a plane for Harry Michaels. Their basis for holding me is the fact that I spoke with him once. Only once, mind you, and he doesn't even remember me or what I look like."

"That's good. How long ago did you meet him?"

"It was two months ago at his father's air terminal in Honduras. He was drunk, and I was a little bit under the weather myself. But I remember him and his brother Ted."

"Still, they couldn't exactly identify you as the pilot of the plane that landed in Sarasota because they were both supposed to be somewhere else. Am I right? Wait, don't let me get ahead of myself. Let's start at the beginning.

"I know about your military record and your work in Cuba for the CIA. Is there any chance that the two events are related?"

"I'm not sure, but my past is not supposed to be common knowledge."

"Ron, let's just say that a friend of yours filled me in. He wanted to be sure that I had the proper perspective on this case."

"It's all a matter of what we've done for them lately. They forget very quickly. But, I learned my lesson. No more volunteer work for me. No more excess patriotism either. As someone once said, *no good deed goes unpunished!*" Ron sat back in his chair and pulled out a cigarette.

"I thought you were quitting?" Jim referred to a comment Charlie Bill made when he had hired Jim.

Ron smiled and put the cigarette back into the pack. "Charlie's right. I am quitting. It's just more difficult when there's nothing much to do."

Jim leafed through the file he had brought into the interview room.

"By the way, is anyone watching your farm in Missouri? The way these guys are acting I wouldn't put it past them to plant some shit over there and blame you."

"Charlie is staying there for the time being. A good friend of mine, Pat, and his girlfriend will move into the farmhouse if I'm not back when Charlie leaves. Nothing to worry about. They'll take care of me. I'm just going to sit back while this plays out."

"Sometime, you should tell me about your witnesses. We can stay mum about them for the time being."

"I agree," replied Ron as he took a sip from the coffee cup.

"They really seem hot for this guy Carlos. Do you know him very well?"

Ron paused. Then he looked his attorney right in the eyes. "Never seen or heard of the fellow!" A smile crept across his face as he spoke the words.

"Well, it's irrelevant anyway. We'll worry about Carlos and Michaels and the rest of these people after you're out of here.

"Next, I'm going to take a statement from this kid Juan so he doesn't change his mind or lose it for that matter. I don't know if you were told about his identification, but he was given a picture of you prior to the lineup so that he could recognize you. He admitted it to me in front of the U.S. Attorney. That was a lucky break if I ever saw one."

"He won't change his mind. I have a real good feeling about him."

Jim stared at his client as he digested his words and thought about the consequences. *He knows more than he's letting on. Does he know the kid? That's dangerous ground for us. I'll let it go for now, but that could hurt us.*

"Jim, you look worried all of a sudden," said Ron as he noticed the concerned look on his attorney's face.

Ron paused but then decided to explain his comments.

"I don't think I've met this fellow Juan. I don't know how he can know me, but you meet a lot of people down south. So, let's just let this play itself out. I have a good feeling about him."

Ron shrugged his shoulders as his attorney continued to stare at him. "Anyway, it's a warm and fuzzy feeling!"

40

Protective Custody

When the truth is known to be lies,
And all the joy within you dies

—Jefferson Airplane

Fort Lauderdale, Florida

"Juan, I just can't understand how you could have screwed things up so badly."

"It was an accident! I didn't try to mess it up. It just happened. I'm sorry!"

"I could understand it if Johnny had pulled this. If he had done what you did, I would have taken it right in stride. I might have even expected it. But I couldn't expect this from you! And what gets me is the fact that you normally keep your mouth shut. All you had to do was pick Hernandez out of the lineup and not say a word."

Juan sat quietly and listened to Gebinsky as he paced up and back in the living room of Harry Michaels's condominium. He listened for more complaints from Gebinsky, but did not respond beyond his initial apology. He had learned that it was better to let Gebinsky vent his anger before arguing an opposing position. Besides, it sounded like he had already made a decision on a course of action.

"Fortunately for all of us, Juan, there is a way to rectify this situation. But, it will take your cooperation."

Juan decided that it was time to show that he wanted to help.

"I'll help any way I can. What do you want me to do?"

"What we want you to do is...absolutely nothing. We don't want you to testify about Hernandez. When the trial comes down, we don't want you to be available to the defense. Without you to help him, Hernandez will have to cooperate or do some major time."

"So the idea is to hide me so I can't testify about the lineup, is that it?"

"They just want you to lay low, stay out of sight so the defense can't find you."

"Who's they? You or Harry? Or the DEA?"

"That's not important, Juan. What's important is that both you and I can get out of this if you get lost for a while."

"Whatever you say, Ed," Juan responded with obvious resignation. "Johnny and I will get lost together. No use leaving him sitting around."

"That's a good idea. Keep him out of this, too. I'm going to testify against Hernandez. Johnny is the only other person who could do it, and I just don't trust him. He'd probably do the same thing you did, except worse."

"Do you want to know where we are during this whole thing?"

"I have a place near the Lake of the Ozarks. It's rather isolated. I want you to take Johnny, and go to the Lake and stay there until Harry and I get there. Don't go anywhere! Don't do anything! Just relax and watch TV or fish off the dock. Here are the keys."

Gebinsky reached inside his pocket and took out a key ring that held four keys. "This key is for the front door. Take it."

As Juan looked at the key ring, Gebinsky took a sheet of paper out of his wallet along with some money and handed both to Juan.

"Here's a map that shows you how to get there. It's real easy to find. And, here's three hundred dollars. Get some food on your way out of here. There's a big refrigerator and a freezer that have plenty of food in them right now so you shouldn't have to make any trips into town.

Harry and I will be there in two or three weeks. Just keep an eye on Johnny. And remember, no phone calls!"

Juan nodded. "What about checking in on our bail bond? We're supposed to check in every once in a while."

"I've taken care of that. Frank Campa convinced the Probation and Parole Office to waive your reporting requirements. Here's a letter from Probation and Parole confirming your status. If the cops stop you or anything like that, just show them this letter. Don't lose it!"

"When should we leave?" asked Juan as he read the letter and placed it in his wallet.

"This afternoon. Go get Johnny. He already knows he's going to the Lake. He should be packed and ready when you get there."

Juan started for the door, but stopped and turned back toward Gebinsky. "Which car should I take?"

"Don't take Johnny's beater. You'll never make it." Gebinsky reached in his pocket again and handed another set of keys to Juan.

"Here, take Harry's Jaguar. But be careful with it! If you mess it up, it's your neck!"

Juan smiled with expectation as he took the keys and headed out the door.

41

The Grand Jury

I pull in resolution, and begin
To doubt th'equivocation of
the fiend That lies like truth.

—Shakespeare, *Macbeth*

Saint Louis, Missouri

Edward Gebinsky walked into the large classroom-like chamber on the first floor of the Federal Courthouse. On this day some twenty-odd people sat in the seats and watched as U.S. Attorney Richard Froehling pointed to the witness chair. The witness was sworn in and took his seat.

"Please tell the Jury your full name."

"Edward Jason Gebinsky."

"Mr. Gebinsky, where do you currently reside."

"In Missouri part of the time and in Florida during the winter."

"Where is your residence in Missouri?"

"I live on a small farm at the Lake of the Ozarks. It's Rural Route 42."

"Is it true that you were arrested several months ago while unloading controlled substances from an airplane in Sarasota County, Florida."

"What do you mean by controlled substances? I was just fishing and these forest rangers arrested me!"

"Never mind! Let me put it another way. Where you arrested in Florida."

"Yes, Sir."

"And was there an airplane at the scene on or about the time you were arrested?"

"I believe so. An airplane landed and then it took off again."

"Exactly where did it land?"

"On one of the streets of the subdivision."

"And this subdivision is incomplete, that is to say, no one lives there."

"Yes. It was started and never completed."

"Now, Mr. Gebinsky, I want to explain your rights to you. This is a Federal Grand Jury which has been given the task of investigating certain illegal drug trafficking activities which may be originating in the States of Missouri and Florida."

"I understand. I'm not sure about the drug trafficking!"

"Mr. Gebinsky, I want you to understand that this Grand Jury is not a trial court. It is an investigative arm of the U.S. Attorney's Office. It has the power to bring charges against violators of federal law. These people are not a jury like the one you would see in a trial. They are investigators. You will be telling this group of investigators what you saw on that night in Florida. Do you understand what I have just explained to you?"

"Yes, I do. Could I have a glass of water? I guess that I'm a little nervous."

"Of course. There's some water in that pitcher on the table. Just take one of those glasses over there. I think I'll join you."

Gebinsky retrieved the water and after drinking a glass he returned to his seat.

"Now, Mr. Gebinsky do you understand that this Grand Jury is not here to bring an indictment against you."

"I hope so. I just want to help you with your case!"

"Do you understand that the Grand Jury is here looking for your help. It is here to investigate a crime, and you are here to help it do its investigation. Is that correct?"

"That's my understanding. I do want to help with this case!"

"Now, has anyone told you that cooperation with the Grand Jury will lessen or do away with the charges pending against you? Go ahead, you can tell them about any discussions you have had with me or anyone in my office."

"It is my understanding that if I help you and this Grand Jury, you will recommend to the Federal Judge that the charges against me be reduced or eliminated."

"That's close to being correct. Actually, if you cooperate fully, it is possible that this Grand Jury will not indict you for any crimes. These are the people you must convince of your full cooperation. They have the power to indict you or not indict you. Is that clear?"

"Yes."

Gebinsky stared at the jury members just like a puppy begging for a dog biscuit. He looked ready to do whatever it took to get favorable treatment.

"What about the State of Florida?" mumbled Gebinsky.

"We are working with them. I would expect them to allow us to do all of the work in this case. It is unlikely that they would intervene and indict you after we have reached a working agreement."

Froehling continued his questioning.

"Today we are studying the involvement of one Ronald Hernandez in the illegal drug trafficking operation of which you were a part. Let me phrase that again. In the illegal drug trafficking operation which you observed in Sarasota. Do you know Mr. Hernandez?"

"Yes, I have met him on several occasions. He is a pilot. I believe that he was once in the Air Force."

"Would you be able to recognize Mr. Hernandez if you saw him today?"

"Yes. I could recognize him if he walked into this room."

"Thanks. Could you tell the Jury whether or not Mr. Hernandez was in any way involved with the incident in Sarasota County?"

"Yes, I can do that. Mr. Hernandez was part of the smuggling operation. He was hired by….by the leader of the operation."

"That would be Mr. Harry Michaels, wouldn't it."

"Ah, I believe so, but I…"

"It's okay, Mr. Gebinsky. Mr. Michaels has already testified before this Jury. Let's go on."

"Okay, what would you like to know?"

"Please tell us the full extent of Mr. Hernandez's involvement."

"Well, he was the pilot of the plane that landed on the street that night. He flew it from Honduras or Nicaragua, I believe. I'm not sure of the exact point of departure. He flew the plane to Sarasota and landed it in the subdivision."

"Was that the abandoned subdivision in which you were arrested?"

"Yes. That was the subdivision that I mentioned before. He flew the plane that we unloaded. I mean he was flying the plane that I saw being unloaded. I didn't…"

"That's okay, just go on with your description."

"He then took off in the plane before we were arrested."

"Did he have anyone with him?"

"Yes, but I couldn't identify anyone else. We were wearing ski masks to keep our identities secret. Mr. Hernandez did not have a mask on."

"Was there anything unusual or characteristic about his appearance on that date?"

"Yes, he had a mustache."

"Was there anything unusual about the mustache?"

"Oh, yes. It was what I would call a handlebar mustache. It bent down at the ends. Or it bent up at the ends. I can't remember which way, but it was very unique and unusual. It made him very easy to identify."

"Do you know anyone else with a handlebar mustache?"

"No, Mr. Hernandez is the only one I know with a mustache like that."

"Please look at this picture. Is this Mr. Hernandez?"

Gebinsky studied the photo for a few seconds.

"Yes, it is. He doesn't have the mustache, but it's definitely him. You could draw the mustache on the picture and it would look just like he did on that night."

"And you're absolutely sure that Mr. Hernandez was the pilot of the plane?"

"Yes, absolutely!"

"And would you be willing to testify to that fact before a judge and jury upstairs?"

"Yes, I would."

"Thank you for your cooperation, Mr. Gebinsky. The Grand Jury will analyze your testimony, and we will let you know when you should appear next. You may leave now. Don't forget to go to the probation office and tell them that you have completed your testimony."

Gebinsky nodded and slowly got up from his chair and walked out into the hallway of the courthouse. There he saw Harry Michaels sitting on one of the benches.

"Well, it's done, Harry. I told them what I saw. Ron Hernandez is their man. I guess we can relax for a while."

42

Capitulation

Every successful revolt
Is termed a revolution,
Every unsuccessful one,
A rebellion.

—Joseph Priestley

Isle of Pines, Cuba

The mud-covered jeep sped along the dirt road leading to the island prison. As the vehicle approached the first set of security fences, the passenger slowly removed the contents from the brown envelope inside his jacket pocket. He once again scanned the documents, double-checking that the actions they were about to undertake were in accordance with the official written directives. There could be no misinterpretation!

As the vehicle reached the first guard-post, the driver greeted the armed sentry with a smile and displayed a large military badge. The sentry waived the men through to a second set of fences and guards. The concertina wire on top of the interwoven obstacles immediately suggested the presence of a high degree of security.

The jeep finally came to a stop in a small parking lot surrounded by high stone walls, and the men dismounted and entered a secure area where they were searched and debriefed as to their mission and authorization. The head security officer placed a brief call into the prison, and after·a wait of several minutes, the men were directed to enter a small administration building where the acting warden was waiting.

After a short but animated conversation with the warden, the two soldiers were led into the heart of the prison by the warden's military assistant. They walked quickly down a dim hallway to a staircase, which led to the third floor of the building. Once on the third floor they were joined by the watch commander of the prison guard who preceded them as they made their way down a grim corridor past small barred cells, each containing one or more prisoners. All that the visitors could see in the small cells they passed were the consequences of years of extensive malnutrition and poor hygiene. The odors caused even the watch commander to cover his nose and shorten the depth of his breathing.

The commander stopped suddenly near the far end of the corridor and reached for a metal ring hooked to his belt. He slowly searched the keys in the dim light, and, after selecting one, made an effort to open a rusted cell door. His first attempt failed, but upon reconsideration, he chose the correct key and with a quick turn of the wrist followed by some serious pounding with his fists, he opened the massive metal door.

The barrier swung open with a low, grinding groan, and a fine mist of dust rose throughout the small, musty room. There were no windows in the cell, and only the dim reflected light from the corridor provided illumination. The guard snapped on an old military flashlight, which flickered unpredictably in the darkness, and pointed it toward the far end of the cell.

In a corner of the room, a single figure slowly and awkwardly struggled to his feet, shielding his eyes from the unaccustomed light. With a shuffling motion he turned to face his visitors.

Even in the near darkness, the men could see that the prisoner had suffered these many long years. His clothing was ragged and torn and his face was covered with what seemed to be a permanent coat of dirt and grime. In spite of his weakened condition, the man struggled to attention, his many years of military training still evident in his posture and bearing.

"Inmate Chacon, we have visitors for you," came the sharp voice of the watch commander. "Step forward! Don't make me drag you out of here!"

The eyes of the prisoner, still sensitive to the light of the flashlight, resolutely fixed on the watch commander with an unmistakably clear animosity, but he did not speak. Then, after surveying what he could see of his visitors in the hallway, he carefully stepped through the debris on the floor of his cell, past the commander and into the corridor.

"Inmate Chacon, I am Sergeant Ruiz of the Revolutionary Guard," stated one of the visitors in a monotone voice devoid of all emotion. "General Castro has determined that you have troubled the revolution for far too long. But he also believes that you have been taught the evil of your ways over the last twenty odd years." The element of sarcasm was not lost on the prisoner, nor was the danger in the meaning of the individual words.

"He has decided to pardon you," continued the Sergeant with a vengeful look on his face.

"Permanently!"

The prisoner's mind reeled with the impact of these words. He had heard this same speech once before. Were they not the words spoken to a former cellmate over five years ago by this very same messenger of death? The man had been dragged from the cell into the central yard of the prison. The prisoner had been forced, along with the rest of the prison population, to watch, as the capital punishment was carried out by firing squad.

His heart sunk as he realized that a similar fate awaited him. The hopes that had kept him alive all of these years, the hope of seeing his children and his wife, and the hope of reaching America again, crumbled. A blistering pain ripped through his body like a raging fire, and he lost consciousness as his body collapsed to the cold concrete floor.

43

Dog Town

Fifteen men on The Dead Man's Chest-
Yo-ho-ho, and a bottle of rum!
Drink and the devil had done for the rest-
Yo-ho-ho, and a bottle of rum!

—Robert Louis Stevenson, *Treasure Island*

Saint Louis, Missouri

The only man sitting at the bar was a regular customer. He had been stopping at O'Learys in west St. Louis on most weekday evenings for over ten years. On this particular night he had pulled up a barstool at the center of the front bar and requested his usual drink from the lone bartender.

"Is practicing bartending anything like practicing law?"

"Not the same thing at all, Steve. I always thought that a bartender would have to know how to make fancy drinks like a *Long Island Ice Tea* or *a Pina Colada*. Not so around here! It's either a shot or a bottle of beer. In two weeks no one has even asked for a Margarita. I haven't had to open the book or call for help once."

"Say, Jim, how is Billy doing anyway. I know he had an appendectomy, but I haven't heard an update on his health. He's coming back, isn't he?"

"Absolutely! Billy will be back next week or the week after at the latest. I don't mind subbing for him, but it makes for long days, and I'm already falling behind at the office. My paralegal is working ten hours a day just to cover for me."

"It sounds like business is good. You should be happy."

"Well, business and paying business are sometimes two different things, but somehow they both require a lot of work."

As the two men were talking, one of the waitresses who worked the back bar came up front to get some mustard and ketchup from the storage room and waived to Jim.

"How're doing, sweetie. Are you hungry? I'm making some burgers, and I could add a couple to the pile."

"That would be great, Diane. I didn't get to eat anything at the courthouse. We ran over again. Sorry I was late."

"Hey, don't worry about it. We could always press Steve into emergency duty behind the bar."

"If you have a Coke back there, Diane, I could use a couple. We're all out up here."

"No problem, Sweetie. By the way, someone called for you about four o'clock. He said he was sort of a client of yours. I told him you'd be here about five, and he said he would call back."

"Sort of a client?" Steve interjected sarcastically. "What kind of client is that? Now I know why lawyers become bartenders!"

"How the hell am I supposed to know? I've got paying clients, non-paying clients, and now, apparently, sort-of clients."

Several other people from the neighborhood eventually joined the conversation and began their celebration of happy hour. Two were plumbers and one was a real estate agent. They were soon accompanied by a number of friends, and the happy hour party at O'Learys was in full swing. After two weeks Jim had come to recognize almost every face which frequented the bar. He didn't always know the name that went with the face, but he was learning fast, and he was enjoying himself.

At about six-thirty a moderately built well-dressed Cuban man with sprinkles of gray hair entered the bar and took a seat at the far end. He was obviously a stranger Jim had not seen before, so he greeted the man and asked him what he would like to drink.

"A rum and coke will do. May I inquire as to your name?"

It was an unusual question, especially coming from a stranger, but Jim saw no reason to suppress his identity.

"My name is Jim Johnson. Mr. and Mrs. Green are good friends of mine and their son, who normally runs this place, is in the hospital, so I was drafted to help him."

"Ah, I can see why they chose you!"

"Well, they didn't choose me for my bartending skills, that's for sure. A rum and coke is about as complicated a drink as I can make for anyone."

"No, I do not mean for this bartending job. Maybe I should explain. I am an acquaintance of Mister Charlie Bill. Does the name ring a bell?"

Jim thought about the phone call which came to the bar earlier that day.

"Did you happen to phone me earlier today, here at the bar."

"Yes, I did call. I hope it wasn't an inconvenience. I wanted to speak with you in person. I hope you don't mind. Coming to your office would have been inconvenient."

"May I ask who you are?"

"Of course! My name is Oscar. I am actually the one who hired you to defend Mr. Hernandez. I was unable to talk with you prior to today so I asked Charlie to make the arrangements. If you don't mind, I would like to stay out of the picture, if possible. If anyone inquires about the money paid for his bond or his attorneys fees, please mention Charlie."

"Absolutely! No one has the right to know who is paying for Mr. Hernandez's defense. I won't ask your last name if you don't mind."

"An excellent choice, Jim. Let me tell you why I am here. I am somewhat familiar with the case of Mr. Hernandez, and I have learned that your main witness has or will disappear."

"Juan is a key witness for us," Jim replied. "He can establish that the government was trying to make him commit perjury by lying about Hernandez."

"With a little luck and help from my friends, I should be able to determine the approximate location of his hiding place. But once I do that, I will not be able to do much more. Mr. Hernandez must depend on you to find the boy. Charlie Bill will contact you as soon as he learns of the location. I want to assure you that you will be paid very well for your work and that you should find yourself in no danger as a result of your search."

The man reached into his pocket and handed the attorney an envelope.

"Please, don't open this until you get home. I must be leaving now. You are doing a good thing for many people. They all thank you very much."

"Well, I haven't done much yet, Oscar. There's still a long way to go."

"And, there will be some surprises. Don't be worried if your client does not do what you expect him to do. Just be assured that Mr. Hernandez is doing the right thing."

"Ah, I'm not sure I understand."

"You will understand. I must leave. Thank you for your time. The best of luck!"

After paying his tab, the man stood up from the bar and walked out of the front door. Jim looked at the envelope and then at the disappearing silhouette of his visitor. He squeezed the thick envelope and could imagine that it contained only one thing. As he squeezed it again and again, a smile began to spread over his face.

As he turned to walk back down the bar, Jim noticed that Steve had been watching him during his discussion with Oscar. Steve raised his glass to toast the bartender.

"Jim, here's to more clients in the sort of category!"

44

Hide and Seek

Fair is foul, and foul is fair,
Hover through the fog and filthy air.

—Shakespeare-*Macbeth*

Washington, D.C.

"You're in a tough spot, Asshole! Look at me when I'm talking to you!"

The man sitting in the chair didn't respond. His eyes were trained on the floor in front of him.

"And, it's all your own fucking fault!" whispered the tall man angrily as he paced up and back puffing on his cigarette.

Again, the man sitting in the chair did not respond as he watched his interrogator walk back and forth in front of him.

"How in the hell are you gonna get out of this? I'm right! Admit it! You're a complete idiot!"

The man asking the questions stopped pacing to listen for an answer, but still there was no response.

"Costello and Gerona have been pretty easy on you, Harry. Too goddamn easy! You're lucky I'm not in charge of this case. If I were, you'd be pounding rocks right now. Then, you'd be on your fucking knees begging me for help! Not sitting there with that shit-ass grin on your face."

A slight smile could almost be seen forming on Harry Michaels' face, but he resisted the urge to speak.

It was very obvious that the two men in the interview room did not like each other. The DEA agent had a deal to offer Michaels, but he would have to soften him up first. The deal would have to appear to be the only way out.

"Harry! It looks pretty straightforward to me. Interrupt me any time you think I am wrong, will you?"

Agent Dubinski looked at Michaels again, a snarl splashed across his face. Somehow *I've got to break this bastard*! Dubinski thought to himself.

"You're the hot shot, the mover and shaker here, aren't you? First, you get yourself involved with those annoying Colombians. Not bad, you think to yourself. I'll make some big bucks. I'll be the man!"

The interrogator stopped abruptly and snapped his fingers in mock disgust before continuing.

"Ah, tough luck! You get caught. Gerona nails you. How were you to know who he was? You walked right into it. It was a bad break. It could have happened to anyone, right?

"No, Harry! I think you're just a stupid fuck! A goddamn idiot! A fat, stupid flop! Don't you agree?"

The prisoner took the full brunt of the sarcasm, but he remained motionless and the expression on his face didn't change. He solemnly waited for more.

Dubinski lit another cigarette. After a few puffs, he walked over in front of Michaels and knelt down on one knee, so he could look up into Michaels' face.

"Then, Harry, you finally get smart! You're thinking straight again. You'll cooperate with the government. It's pure genius. You set up the deal. Things are starting to look better."

Again, the agent snapped his fingers sarcastically.

"Ah, but then the plane doesn't show up when it's supposed to. What bad luck! What a bummer for you! This could have happened to anyone in this situation, you tell yourself!"

The agent stopped and scanned his prey for any sign of a comment. Michaels remained stone-faced. Dubinski stood back up and began pacing again.

"So, I'll try again, you say. There'll be other flights, other attempts. We can get this guy. Trust me you say! Trust me!"

Again, the prisoner took the insults and sarcasm without moving or responding. He just kept his eyes on the agent as the latter waived his arms in the air with every sentence as if he were acting the part of the prisoner on a stage.

"But, I forgot, Harry, you had to be cute," whispered the agent as he pointed toward Harry. "It's your style. Why not make a little money on the side? You can feather your nest. What could be easier you think? I'll just send my brother with a load of shit parallel to the other Carlos' load. Why not! What can go wrong? And, you wouldn't be risking your brother's safety, would you? He's doing this gig for you, and you're doing your duty for your country! He takes off right behind the other plane in Honduras. No problem!"

At this point the prisoner unfolded his arms and shifted his weight in the chair. *I'm beginning to have an impact*, thought Dubinski. *Just a few more minutes and he'll open up like a clam shell.*

"Ah, Harry, what a bad break. Your brother Ted gets caught! Well, not exactly caught, you sigh with some relief. Ted gets away, but his ground crew gets caught. That's brilliant! Lucky, but brilliant."

"Lucky, my ass!" shouted the prisoner with a suddenness that caused Dubinski to drop his cigarette.

After pausing to be sure that his prey was not going to speak again, the agent bent over and pick up the half-smoked cigarette.

"Harry! Then, you began to think of how to play this new problem. Ah, it comes to you like a bolt out of the blue. You can use the ground crew to your advantage. They must have seen the pilot! Not the actual pilot. The pilot you were trying to give up to us. Ah, this kid Juan saw the pilot! He can remember his face! He can get you and your brother off the hook in one fell swoop. You lost the load, but you can all go home happy."

The agent paused to see if Harry would respond. When he remain silent, the agent continued again.

"Why not give Juan a little help? Refresh his recollection. Brilliant! Show him a photograph. Notice that handlebar mustache on the pilot? It should be easy to find him in any kind of lineup. Easy to identify him! Anyone could do it. It's a sure thing, you think to yourself. I'm home free at last, you say to yourself."

After taking a deep breath, the prisoner looked away from the agent in apparent disinterest.

"But, much to your dismay, Juan isn't the sharpest pencil in the desk, is he? He steps up to the defense attorney, and politely tells him that Mr. Hernandez is the guy in the picture we showed to him. He knows Hernandez is the guy because he looks like the guy in the picture we showed him. The picture the government showed him! A simple mistake, huh?"

The agent paused again and stared at the prisoner who just kept staring at the floor. Dubinski slowly walked up to Michaels and put his hands on Michaels' shoulders.

"Harry! That would have been no problem," whispered the agent before pausing to take a deep breath. Then he shouted at the top of his lungs.

"Provided the pilot and his attorney *are complete idiots* and the courts have suspended the rules of criminal procedure!"

Michaels jumped up from the chair, bumping his forehead on the agent's chin.

"You wouldn't have done any better, you asshole!" Harry shouted as he pushed the agent away to arms' length.

Dubinski stepped back from the table rubbing his chin. His face was flushed, and he was shaking visibly as he glared at Harry. It seemed to Harry that the agent had stopped just short of throwing a punch at his prisoner.

Michaels stood motionless waiting for the other shoe to drop. Dubinski must need something otherwise what was the point of this encounter. Just creating more alienation could not help their case. Something new must be on its way! *I have to wait, let him come to me!*

The agent composed himself and continued with his original description of the situation.

"And, on we go, Harry. Now, this guy Gebinsky, your pal, is ready to identify the pilot. Things are going from bad to worse. How deep in this shit can you go, Harry? How deep?"

Michaels continued his silence and waited.

"I'd like to see this guy Gebinsky on the witness stand, too, but only if I was the defendant! Gebinsky hasn't done an hour's honest work his whole life. Even his ex-wife didn't ask for anything from him when they got divorced. She just wanted to get as far away as possible. One look at him and one look at this kid Juan…and the pilot will walk!

"I'd say that you've probably run out of material at this point. You've been walking the plank, and now you're at the end!"

Michaels maintained his silence. He sat back down and stretched his arms, but he didn't speak.

"But, Harry, you are such a lucky guy! Once again the fates have intervened. Is it in your favor this time? Well, only time will tell!"

Here it comes! Harry thought to himself.

"Harry, you asshole, don't you want to know how fucking lucky you are?"

Michaels just shrugged his shoulders.

"Well, our sources tell us that Raymond Chacon is being released from his sentence in Cuba. Does that name ring any bells in that empty head of yours?"

Harry shrugged his shoulders, but did not speak.

"Harry, unlike other people we know who have the same last name, this guy Chacon is clean. He's also a hero with the Cuban expatriates down in Miami. And the best part is that we believe that he's Carlos' father!"

The agent paused again and slowly lit another cigarette as he gained time for the information to settle into Harry's thought patterns.

"Can you believe this? Now we should be able to stand back and wait for Carlos to go for the bait. Just watch his father, and Carlos will come. What do you think of that?"

Harry decided that it was time to reply, but he would have to be careful. The possibilities created by this new information were interesting.

"It matters nothing to me, chief."

"What?" roared the agent as he threw his cigarette down on the floor and stomped on it to vent his anger.

"I don't know either of them. There's nothing I can do about Fidel or Carlos except try to give you the pilot. And I'm doing my best!"

"Haven't you been listening? If this is your best, I'd hate to think of what would happen if you tried to screw things up!"

"I had nothing to do with that other flight," yelled Harry in a high-pitched voice. "I doubt that my brother was involved either! But, of course, I wasn't there, so I couldn't know anything for sure. I was with your pals at Sarasota Municipal."

The agent shook his head in disgust as he walked away from him.

"Harry, I know you haven't done your best," Dubinski muttered in a tone of voice that indicated capitulation. "Costello tells me nothing but bad things about you."

The agent took another cigarette out of the pack he held in his left hand and lit it after several misfires with his lighter. He turned back toward Harry and smiled sarcastically at his prisoner.

"I think that there probably is something you can do to redeem yourself! That's why we're here today. To try and help you out of this mess."

The agent had obviously tried to switch from his bad cop mode to his good cop mode.

Hall sat straight up in his chair and pointed at the agent.

"Hey! Costello and I already have a deal!"

"Come on, Harry. What are you talking about?"

"Costello and I have a deal! Have you suddenly gone deaf? I'm doing what I was supposed to do."

"But, Harry, where are the results. We need results! We need positive results! We need to make progress. I don't see any progress that you are responsible for."

"If you want me to help you with something else, you've got to help me a little too, you know! Otherwise, just give me a badge, and I'll go out and get them for you myself! I don't see you making any great progress on this case!"

The agent grimaced and turned away for Michaels. He puffed on the cigarette and then spoke in a very mild voice.

"That's not quite what I had in mind, Harry."

He faced away from Michaels for a few seconds, then turned and looked directly at him.

"I can't tell you what to do," the agent whispered, "and I won't, either. But if the kid Juan can be made to see the light, or, at least get lost for a while to think about it, well, then your future would be looking brighter. And, if Gebinsky doesn't blow it when he testifies, your future would look a lot brighter, indeed!"

45

Rumors of Freedom

As a follower of Marti,
I believe the hour has come to
take rights and not beg for them,
to fight instead of pleading for them.

—**Fidel Castro**

Orlando, Florida

The secure facsimile line hummed and buzzed. Soon the printer roared into action and the first of two pages slid slowly into the catch tray. The cover sheet was standard with the exception of the word *FLASH* stamped in large letters near the top of the page.

The duty officer ambled across the empty communications room and glanced casually at the top sheet. As soon as he saw that it wasn't the usual employee payroll confirmation traffic, he grabbed the telephone and buzzed the Station Chief.

"Chief Adams is still out on a luncheon appointment, John," answered the familiar voice of the receptionist.

"Okay. Just tell him we have some flash traffic from D.C."

DEA agent John Phillips was the duty officer on this shift. It had been a quiet day at the field office. He had given a briefing to several new interns who would be handling the mundane activities associated with budget projections, and he had requisitioned special medical supplies for several agents attached to the Panama Canal unit. But after reading the status of the fax, John knew that the level of activity in the office was about to increase significantly.

After another few moments the second sheet of information rolled out of the machine. It contained a plain text message for the Orlando Office Chief of Operations. The duty officer scanned the message, copied it, and placed the copy in an envelope. The original found its way into the main filing cabinet in the secure document storage room. The envelope with its copy was placed in the Chief's incoming mail slot.

Just as the duty officer had completed and logged the message, the current Station Chief appeared in the doorway carrying a briefcase and raincoat.

"John, how's it going? It's pouring out there again. If the landlord doesn't fix the goddamn parking lot soon, I'll have to swim back to my car. Maybe I'll just buy a boat instead. How's our petty cash looking?"

"I'm parked over near the low end, too, Carl," responded agent Phillips as he pointed toward the north end of the building. "They were working over the drain when I came in."

Phillips waited for Carl Adams to hang up his coat before he mentioned the fax.

"You just received a flash from Washington. Apparently, Castro must be releasing someone of interest. It's been too quiet down there lately. I guess Fidel hasn't seen his name in the Miami Herald for a few days, and he craves some attention."

Chief Adams walked back toward his desk while trying to comb his thinning hair.

"Where is the message, John?" asked the Chief as he looked around. Before Phillips could answer, the Chief found what he was looking for.

"Sorry, John, here it is right where it's supposed to be. You're just too efficient for me. I don't know what we'll do without you when you're elected governor or whatever it is you're running for."

"Don't get excited," laughed John in a somewhat embarrassed voice. "It's just the presidency of the PTA. And, you'll have to keep me even if I get elected. Besides, there's no assurance that I'll win unless we stuff the ballot box. I have a couple of opponents, but unfortunately, they're very conservative. They'd have our kids studying in trailers out in the swamp just to save money. I've tried to point out how low our taxes are down here, but they are deaf as a stone."

"Well, they just figure that they got a good grade school education, so why should anyone else get one. Especially these retirees over in the suburbs! Their children are out of school so why should they pay for anyone else's education. Just wait until we have another war or space race. Just you watch them piss and moan at how dumb these kids are down here. And they'll be sure that they didn't have anything to do with it. Ah, but that's going to be your problem, John!"

The Station Chief's eyes widened as he scanned the message. Agent Phillips noticed his boss read it over several times.

"This has to be one for Josef Gerona," commented Chief Adams as he folded the copy and placed it in his jacket pocket.

"Do you want me to contact him?" answered John as he sat down on his desk.

"No, let me go over the protocol list first. Washington wants us to bring in the CIA on this. Something big must be cooking down there. The last time we had to deal with Frank Campa, it was a disaster!"

"I remember the incident. He had more contraband on that boat than any ten people we bust. What makes him immune?"

"I don't know, but keep this to yourself. Word has it that he's partnering with the Cali cartel. As a matter of fact, John, I'd forget it altogether. People have died for knowing less! These characters are terrorists. Killing and kidnapping is their main talent. Just play dumb and don't ask any interesting questions."

"That'll be easy, Chief!"

"John, this is very interesting," wondered Adams as he looked through the Cuba file, which contained information on Cuban political prisoners. "I wonder how they got this information? I didn't think that we had a reliable source in Havana. Someone else must be eavesdropping on Fidel. Amnesty International usually beats us on these releases, but they say the announcement won't occur until next Wednesday or Thursday."

John was curious about the named prisoners. "Are any of those guys on our pickup list? Maybe Fidel is planning a mini-Mariel for us."

"No, apparently they have been cleared by the INS. They're all real political prisoners. All three of these guys have life sentences from the Bay of Pigs fiasco. They were pretty young when they were captured, which would put them in their mid to late forties if my calculations are correct. Fidel must just be getting old or his conscience is bothering him. Maybe the Pope is threatening to visit the Island? Who knows?"

John looked at Carl and shook his head. "It's the Company on this one, for sure. They probably have Fidel's toilet bugged. Maybe they're playing subliminal tapes to him when he's asleep. I just wouldn't put it past them."

"You know, Carl, for the few years I've been in this agency, I could swear that they've been bugging us and that they have moles in our organization."

"You're right! Little furry people who go through our files at night to see if we know anything they don't know. They gobble up data about everything. Actually, most of it is useless."

"They always seem to know what we're doing before we do it. I really don't trust them at all."

"Now, John, you know that The Company is our best buddy. Take a look at your paycheck before you complain. They fund some of our best operations. It's indirect, I must admit, but we usually don't have money problems with Congress. And they do give us some support in the field once in a while."

Carl paused after listening to himself defend the CIA and wondering why he did it. Maybe it was because he too always assumed that someone was always listening.

"Nevertheless, John, I don't trust them as far as I can throw them. You're right! I hope you win that P.T.A. election. At least they might not be able to infiltrate that while you're in there!"

"Don't laugh too hard, Carl. I'll bet the Company is financing ninety percent of the drug smuggling activity we're trying to shut down. They do it to keep their jobs. Put up the strawman and knock it down."

"It beats having to work for a living, John. I just saw some statistics from the Bureau, and it turns out that eighty percent of all state and federal prisoners are there because of drug or alcohol related charges. We'd have a lot of empty jails without them! In case they're listening, I didn't say that!"

Both men continued to scan the information in the hard file. The Chief came across a short article from the Miami Herald, which mentioned Raymond Chacon's sentencing.

"This guy appears to be the father of one of our Colombian targets," Carl whispered as he pointed to the article. "His name came up in a meeting we had here with Costello. But this is the first thing I've heard about a release. The other two people mentioned here don't ring a bell. They could be associates of Chacon. As I remember, he was arrested alone so the other two must not be part of anything he might have been involved in. I think Chacon has other family members in Cuba, too. I wonder if they'll try to make a run for it now that he will be in the U.S.?"

"How can you be sure that he'll come to the States?"

"He has a brother here somewhere. But, it's the son that Costello is interested in."

"So, you think they want to use this poor guy as bait? He's been eating cardboard for twenty years so he can't be in great shape. Carl, I believe that Hell sounds good to me compared to a Cuban jail. Hell? I'd rather go to Tijuana!"

"They think he's currently being held at the Isle of Pines Prison and is being transferred to Havana in a few days. The whereabouts of the other two are unknown. Also, we have no information on the location of his wife and daughter. So far, John, we're batting close to zero!

"You know, Carl, for all the time I've been here, I really know little or nothing about this guy Gerona. I hear a lot, but it's always third hand."

"Gerona! He has a reputation, John. Most of our CA and SA kills and captures are credited to him. They say his family was liquidated by Castro when he took over from Batista. If Fidel gets taken out, we'll probably know who did it."

"It's a small world. Drop a stone into the water, and it comes back twenty years later as a tidal wave. I'm glad I'm just a goddamn accountant and babysitter, John! Everywhere you look there's intrigue. If you're a field agent, how can you tell who the good guys are?"

"Good guys? There aren't any, except maybe you and me! And every once in a while…"

Carl smiled jokingly. "You're right as usual. Without us, America couldn't survive. See you later, I've got a bunch of reports to generate for the bureaucracy."

Carl waived his hands in the air slowly and turned to get back to his office and the more mundane work of managing his district.

John picked up the original fax and headed for the secure room. As he walked down the hallway, he wondered why he bothered to be secure when the original message was sent to him in the open. He knew that this happened all the time and secure communications were always the subject for ridicule in the service. The last thing a smuggler would want to do was waste his time listening to DEA traffic.

46

Staying Alive

The typical tyrant dislikes
serious and liberal-minded people.
He regards himself as the only authority;
if anyone sets himself up in rivalry
and claims the right to speak his mind,
he is felt to be detracting from the supremacy
and absolute mastery of the tyrant.

—Aristotle, *The Politics*, tr. T. A. Sinclair

Saint Louis, Missouri

Ron Hernandez sat quietly in the holding cell on the second floor of the federal courthouse. He had just attended a hearing before the U.S. Magistrate where his bond was set at fifty thousand dollars. Considering the relative magnitude of the charges levied against him, it was a reasonable amount which could be satisfied with a ten percent cash deposit.

Charlie Bill made the trip to a local bank and, after some phone calls, was able to procure the five thousand dollars he needed. With a cashier's check in hand, Charlie returned to the Clerk's Office and deposited the funds as required by the Magistrate. Now it would only be a few minutes before Ron would be released.

At the same time that Charlie was setting up the bond, Ron's attorney was busy in the outside hall talking with one of the prosecuting attorneys and a DEA agent. As Charlie walked by the three men, he noticed that the conversation was very animated. Something was up!

Ever since he had discovered the tainted lineup and knew that he had a witness who could testify about government misconduct, Jim was sure that Ron would walk and the charges against him would be dismissed. He knew he had a solid case for misconduct, which would strongly supplement the testimony of the alibi witnesses.

A female bartender, Charlie Bill, and Ron's cousin had all placed Ron in a seafood restaurant in Fort Lauderdale, Florida as late as two o'clock on the morning of the flight. If he was present in that restaurant at that time, it was inconceivable that he could have been onboard the Beech which landed in the Sarasota subdivision.

So it was easy to understand why Jim was somewhat dismayed when his client announced that he was going to cooperate with the government. Ron had called Jim late the night before and indicated that he wanted to change his tactics without admitting guilt. So this morning Jim had arrived at the Federal Courthouse and extended the offer to U. S. Attorney Richard Froehling, but only after a two-hour discussion with his client during which he tried to change his client's mind. In the end he remembered what Oscar had said about what Ron might do.

Ron was firm in his conviction that his action was appropriate. He reassured his attorney that there was no physical danger to himself or Charlie. Jim argued the alternatives, but in the end had to go with his client's decision. It wasn't his neck that was being placed in the noose!

All of Jim's information about Carlos was indirect and circumstantial. Yet one thing seemed certain. This man must have many loyal friends. He didn't seem like the kind of person one would want to antagonize. And another thing was sure. It would be difficult to hide from this man. And Ron said he was going back to his farm after this was over. If Carlos were apprehended, his friends wouldn't have to look too far to find the man who had betrayed him.

What was most perplexing was the fact that Ron and Carlos were supposedly very good friends. Even the government seemed to know that. Jim had more trouble with the concept of giving up a friend, even a friend who smuggled drugs, than, say, representing a criminal client who he knew was guilty. It also bothered Jim that his client didn't seem like the kind of person to voluntarily turn on his friends. He was sure that something funny was going on here.

It was also possible that Ron didn't have a lot of faith in Jim's ability to get his acquittal. After all, Jim was not an experienced criminal attorney. Criminal law was not his main thing. But he had offered to find a more experienced attorney to represent his client, and Ron had turned him down. Ron's response was to the effect that Jim was as good an attorney for his case as he could hope to find. The whole situation seemed a little crazy.

So, it was with some negative feelings that Jim listened, as the DEA agent stated the conditions of this new agreement. Jim's inherent mistrust of government employees must have been visible on his face. The agent would pause after just about every sentence and ask if the attorney understood what he was talking about. Jim would just nod slightly with a nasty smirk painted on his face.

"We're just trying to help each other. Your client wants to help his country and secure his future." The agent was looking for some sympathy.

"I never thought that attempting to give up Colombian smugglers was a way to secure your future!" Jim directed his words to Froehling. "Especially, when the Government has no case. You know that I have evidence of misconduct. If this is another element of that same theme, I won't rest until I see all of you swinging from the Arch."

The prosecutor seemed understanding, but he was also a pragmatist. "Jim, it won't do any good to chase us around here. Just look at the situation. Your client wants to help. Guilty or innocent, he wants to help.

We didn't force him into this. No one talked with him. No one coerced him. This is his idea!"

"The apparent release of the father of this Carlos character…whoever he is, is the break the DEA has been looking for. He's the bait. No one has to know that Ron is cooperating. We will arrest Ron with the rest, and you can represent him. The judge will grant a motion for a separate trial, and we can use government misconduct as the basis for his release and dismissal of all charges. Only you and your client and our office know of this arrangement. And we will keep our promises.

"Ron walks away clean in three months, and he can go back to his farm. No ID change! No running and hiding! You get everything you want, and we get everything we want. But we need your cooperation. Rather, Ron needs your cooperation. You'll feel good when he walks away. The DEA plan covers all of the bases. If you wish, you can withdraw from the case and we'll get someone else. But it won't look as good. You should do it. Your client is counting on you."

"I need this in writing." Jim pointed out this requirement to Froehling.

"No problem. We'll seal the case file and enter an agreement. Your client will be protected. Come to my office on Monday, and we'll sign and enter the agreement."

Jim turned completely around as he stared at the ground. "Your right! It's Ron's play. I'm here to help him. Okay. I gather that there's not much for me to do. Just wait for your call or his call and show up on Monday."

"That's right. I know you are aware of this, but I must say it. Avoid talking about the case to anyone. Not only your client's life is in danger, but the lives of several of our agents are also involved here. I want your promise!" The DEA agent extended his hand.

"Okay, it's a deal. Just don't let my client get hurt."

"Jim, we will do our best. He should never be in any danger, trust us."

47

Hound Dog

Freedom hath been hunted round the Globe.
Asia and Africa have long expelled her.
Europe regards her like a stranger,
and England hath given her warning
to depart. O! receive the fugitive, and
prepare in time an asylum for mankind.

—**Thomas Paine**

Saint Louis County, Missouri

The Plaza was an office and entertainment complex located in west St. Louis County and positioned conveniently alongside Interstate 244. It contained office buildings, parking garages, movie theatres, major hotels and entertainment facilities and high-end shopping enterprises. Mexican, Thai and Chinese restaurants were mixed among art galleries, bookstores and game arcades. A twelve-story office building covered with gold-reflective glass was the focal point of the development.

The law office was on the second floor of a four-story office building on the western edge of the Plaza. The upper three floors of the building were primarily occupied by a major insurance company while the bottom floor held several restaurants and brokerage offices. Besides the law office, the north wing of the second floor housed employees of the insurance company. The center section of the second floor held a public restroom and a staircase and elevators that led to the first floor. The other wing housed an answering service, the accounting services for a restaurant chain and a small independent engineering company.

Jim Johnson's office was typical for a sole practitioner. It was small, consisting only of a reception area, a storage room, and the main office. He employed a full-time paralegal assistant at this office. Sheila proved to be very skilled at composing wills and trusts and setting up corporations as well as doing individual tax returns and accounting for his clients. But her main skill from Jim's perspective was her ability to tell his clients that he was busy somewhere else and that he would contact them later.

The storage room contained a small refrigerator and several filing cabinets. A wooden ¾ inch dowel that extended across the gap between two cabinets served as a support for clothes hangers. It seemed as if every square inch of this room was in use. Law books and related documents were piled on top of the files and a small microwave oven could be found in the rear of the room.

The main office held a large desk and credenza suitable for an attorney. Bookcases lined one wall and a sturdy couch and end table sat under the windows that ran the length of one side. A stereo and TV were conveniently stacked near the sofa and several chairs were placed near the front of the desk. These were obviously for the use of clients during their visits to the office.

It was 8:20 PM and Jim was still at work. He had several Domestic Relations cases on the St. Louis County docket the following morning morning, and he was reviewing his schedule. One motion was directed against the son of one of his tax clients. It was a contempt motion for failure to pay child support. Jim's best guess was two weeks in the slammer. He scribbled a note to himself, a reminder to tell his client to keep quiet and do the time.

The other hearing was a petition for dissolution of marriage. Uncontested divorces were easy, and his client and soon-to-be ex-spouse were on good terms. This probably meant lunch with both of them; Jim viewed the opposing attorney as anally retentive and not about to fraternize with his client and the former opposition. Jim knew he had prevented a war in this case, which also meant that the other firm's fee was much smaller than they had hoped.

He recalled that another lawyer in the same opposing firm had once called him a liar. He could still remember chasing that bastard through the courtroom, into the hallway and down the escalator out onto the roof of the County Building next door while a lunchtime crowd of litigants watched in amazement. Even in a simple case like this, he had to be careful and double-check his work because they would jump at any chance to get him back.

As he was studying the files, the phone on his desk rang, and he punched the flashing button before lifting the receiver. He assumed it was one of the two domestic relations clients.

"Law Offices!"

The voice on the other end of the line surprised him. It was Charlie Bill.

"What are you doing in the office at this hour? You should be out drinking!"

"I'm not that lucky, Charlie! What's up?"

C.B. lowered the tone of his voice to a near whisper.

"I hope they haven't tapped your phone."

Jim paused before answering.

"Do you think the government would stoop to that? It's too dangerous. If I caught them, it would be all over."

"I know where your witness is!" came Charlie's reply.

"But, I thought Ron was cooperating with the Feds. We really don't need him now."

"That's not necessarily the case. I can't tell you why, but Ron may need him."

"Where is he? Can you get him to call me?"

"Gebinsky and Michaels are taking care of him. It should be easy to find them. I would do it, but I'm going to be busy with another matter. Can you help us out?"

"I've got two cases tomorrow morning. After that I can get free for a couple of days. Sheila can cover for me. What do you want me to do?"

"I'm in O'Fallon right now. I just left an envelope in your mail box. The one at your O'Fallon office. I've never met a sole practitioner who had two offices!"

"How did you know that I had an office in O'Fallon?"

"Easy! It's on your business card."

"Got me on that one! What's in the envelope?"

"Directions to the place where Juan is being kept."

"Charlie, you're talking as though he's a prisoner!"

"Not exactly. But, he has a lot of pressure on him. Michaels and Gebinsky don't want him to testify. We just need to know where he is and keep a subtle eye on him. Ron and I will be there to help in about a week. We have some other business to conduct."

"Okay. I've got some appeals work I can do while I'm waiting. But, I can only last for a week or so. Then, I've got to get back here."

"Don't worry! I've included an emergency contact you can use if something happens and you can't stay at the site. There's some travel money, too."

"Where am I going?"

"Like I said, Jim. Your phone may be bugged. Let's keep it our little secret. Later!"

With that, Jim hung up the phone and set about gathering his court-room materials and packing some clothes. He left a brief note for Sheila. She had grown to expect unpredictable changes, so this would not be a big surprise. The note contained the usual request to tell everyone that he was in trial and not to expect him back for a week.

48

Break-in

*Behavior is criminal only
because society says so.
There cannot be psychological
tendencies to engage in
behavior defined so arbitrarily.*

—Herrnstein and Murray, *The Bell Curve*

O'Fallon, Missouri

The white pickup truck pulled into the parking lot of the small converted office building, which housed a law office and a real estate company. The words *Douglas Construction* were written in large black letters on the side panels of the vehicle. Richard Douglas, a lifetime resident of O'Fallon and owner of the building, hopped from the truck and headed through the front door of the law office.

"Richard, what brings you to see us today? Jim probably won't be here until one."

The greeting came from Brenda Jackson who served as a part-time secretary and paralegal assistant.

"That's okay, Brenda. I just dropped by to see if everything was all right."

"Well, the office in a mess, but otherwise the place seems shipshape. Is something wrong?"

"To tell you the truth, I'm not absolutely sure. I was coming home down the Interstate at about two in the morning with my wife and kids and passed this place, I noticed several cars in the parking lot. Someone was standing on the porch, but I didn't see any lights in the office. And, I didn't see your car or Jim's car."

"Come to think of it, the front door was open when I got here this morning. I just assumed that Jim was here and forgot to lock it when he left for St. Louis County. And, the phone on my desk had been moved over to the other side. Sometimes he works here at this desk so I didn't think anything of it."

"Well, Brenda, I took the wife and kids home and drove back over here, but no one was around when I drove past the place. I didn't try the door."

"When Jim gets here, I'll tell him. He has a few strange cases going on these days so you never know what might happen."

"Give Jim my best, and tell him about his late night visitors." Richard waived goodbye and returned to his truck.

Under the circumstances, Brenda thought it best to wait for Jim to arrive instead of leaving for her usual lunch break. She sat back down at her desk and opened the file drawer where she kept her working files. As she scanned the files carefully, she noticed that they were no longer in alphabetical order. Once again, it could have been Jim, but with the other information in mind, she now was becoming somewhat more skeptical.

About ten minutes later, Jim walked through the front door. He seemed to be in a good mood.

"Hi, Brenda. Have you looked at the mail?"

"No. It usually doesn't get here until two. Why? Are you looking for something in particular?

"Yes. You remember that smuggling case I have downtown, don't you? I should have received some information from them in the mail slot."

Brenda reached into the inside mail box, which was next to her desk and retrieved an envelope.

"Do you know that we had visitors last night?"

"Visitors? At this office? Who was it?"

"I don't know. The door was left open and someone went through the file drawer. Richard was here earlier. He saw someone here, but when he checked they were gone. It was 2 AM!"

"Maybe I just left the door open yesterday afternoon? But I wasn't in the file drawer. That's strange. Oh, well, as long as nothing is missing."

"I don't think anything is missing. There is something here in the mailbox. No stamps on it! It must be what you are looking for."

Brenda used a letter opener to open the envelope and then handed it to Jim. He looked carefully at the three pieces of paper and looked at Brenda with a smile.

"Florida, here I come!"

After a few more seconds, Jim's smile faded from his face.

"It's not like them at all. Charlie told me that he would include some traveling money, among other things. Well, the Cuban guy paid me quite a bit at the bar the other night. I guess I can eat the expenses on this one."

As he began to put the papers back into the envelope, Brenda cleared her throat several times to get his attention.

"What?" mumbled the attorney. "Did I forget something?"

"No! But you did say you were going to let me go on one of these Florida trips. Did you forget?"

"Hey, this one is a little tricky. This isn't a court case. It's more like detective work. Next time, I promise. Go get some lunch. I'll man the fort until you get back."

"Okay," Brenda replied reluctantly, "but next time for sure or you have to double my salary."

"No problem. Hey, bring me back a sub sandwich or something, will you. Take it out of our petty cash."

"What petty cash? You took it all to the video game place last week. Remember? Don't worry, I'll cover for you this time."

With that, Brenda picked up her purse and strolled out the door. Jim took the envelope over to the copying machine and made several copies of the map and instructions just to be on the safe side. Then he went into his office and sat down at his desk to study the map more closely. Slowly his thoughts wandered to visions of the beach as he wondered how much free time he would have. As he looked up from his work, he was startled to see that someone else had entered the room. Charlie Bill was standing in the doorway to his office quietly watching him.

"How long have you been standing there? And, where did you learn to be so quiet, Charlie? You scared the crap out of me!"

"It was all those years in the military."

"Anyway, I got your instuctions. So he's down in Florida. I always like going down there."

"Nope!"

The expression on Jim's face turned to surprise.

"What do you mean by that? Has he moved already?"

"What I mean is that those are bogus instructions. The feds left them here last night. They replaced the envelope I left for you with their own set of directions. They want you out of the way for a few days. I told you that your phone was tapped!"

"No shit!" Jim muttered as he looked around his office.

"They probably didn't take anything. But it was a sloppy job. All they really had to do was remove my letter from your mailbox and insert theirs. Very sloppy!"

"What should we do now, Charlie? It probably won't do any good to report a forcible entry. And, I can't be sure who it was."

"That's not a problem, Jim. We would rather have them believe that you haven't noticed anything unusual. Here are the instructions I told you I was going to leave last night. If it was the Feds who stopped by, all they got was the information they tried to feed me. I instructed you to go to Florida, but I put a few errors on the map so you would never have ended up where they wanted you to go. You'll notice that those instructions you pulled out of the mailbox probably direct you to Everglades City. Am I right?"

"That's correct. How did you know?"

"Oh, they gave us some clues in hopes that we would get you to follow them. Your witness will be on a farm near the Lake of the Ozarks. I don't know the location of the farm, but you can pick up Gebinsky's trail from the Harley shop. He'll have to go there to pick up his bike and you can follow him."

"How did you figure all this out?" replied Jim in amazement.

"Hey, military intelligence! It just gets to be a habit. Besides, these guys are not very good at covering their tracks."

"What's in this smaller envelope, Charlie?"

"Some mad money for the trip. If you don't stay at your condo on Horseshoe Bend, you can get a room at Four Seasons or Arrowhead."

"Did I tell you about my condo? Never mind! It may be rented anyway. I'll have to call the rental agent and tell him I want to do some repairs if the place is vacant. I can do that when I get there."

"Well, Jim, sorry to mess up your Florida vacation. But, the Lake is nice. Don't forget, it could have been Detroit or Pittsburg!"

As Jim was studying the map included in the new set of instructions, Charlie disappeared as quickly and quietly as he had appeared.

49

Strategem

Deathless hand in land where devils roam,
Who with a switchblade cut the head of hope,
It's time to exchange the evil, blow by blow,
Without a star the water turns to stone.

—Big Head Todd and the Monsters

Bogota, Colombia

A black limousine pulled into the secured parking area next to a three story government building in downtown Bogota. The building was enclosed by a concrete wall approximately twelve feet in height. Security cameras were mounted on the corners of the wall, and a concrete guardhouse and wrought iron gate completed the barriers to admission.

Three men left the vehicle and walked to an internal security checkpoint. Two of them were Americans. The third was Cuban. After a thorough search of their persons and verification of their identities by uniformed guards, the men made their way to a first floor elevator.

When they reached the third floor, a military police officer joined the group. He spoke very fluent English. He directed them to a small conference room that presented a dazzling view of the City of Bogota. Almost immediately, several uniformed Colombian military personnel entered the room along with the Colombian Ambassador to the United States.

The well-dressed Cuban man stepped forward to shake hands with the Ambassador and then with the others.

"Mr. Ambassador, it is a pleasure to see you again. I understand that you were fully briefed on our project just before you left Washington."

"You are correct Mr. Campa. We had several lengthy meetings at the Pentagon just before I left. This man you seek is apparently very elusive and very destructive. Everyone agrees that he is a clever fellow, and I am not convinced that this plan has a high probability of success. In addition to that fact, I am not convinced that this man is Colombian. Our intelligence officers believe strongly that he is from Central America or Cuba."

"Mr. Ambassador, we realize that the strategy we are offering is not perfect," replied Frank Campa. "However, it appears to be the best approach to the problem under the current circumstances. We would like to believe that the plan does meet with your government's approval? Of course, we are receptive to any suggestions that you or your military personnel may have. What is important here is the capture and neutralization of this man and his organization."

"Actually, Mr. Campa, we are also at a point where we might try anything. Our intelligence sources seem to match yours in that this man does not appear to be violent. But he seems to know about our activities even before we think of them. If you know about the release of his father, he must also know. And if this man is really his father, there can be no question that he is not Colombian."

"Mr. Ambassador, I would not necessarily agree that he is not a violent adversary. We believe…or actually, I believe, that he is responsible for the deaths of seven of our highly placed agents in Honduras, Nicaragua, and Guatemala."

"I believe that you have lost a few people here in Colombia, also."

"That's true. The men who were lost were allied with your government. Those agents have been actively working against Cuban agents and sympathizers. And I think we all agree that Carlos and his associates have been active in the drug trade with the United States. I find it hard to believe that this man isn't responsible, in large part, for those deaths. And, it is reasonable to assume that this man is actively supporting our mutual enemies."

"I can understand your concern, and I do not claim to have clear information which decides the issue one way or the other. We want to cooperate with your effort, but we do find weaknesses in your plan. But, I might add that we do not have a better plan to offer to you at the present time. It is a difficult situation. We cannot negotiate with an invisible enemy."

"That's an important consideration, Sir, and we are aware of the weaknesses, but this is one of the few real opportunities we've had on this one. The Swiss have confirmed that Raymond Chacon and two others will be released next week. They will apparently be placed on a plane in Havana. It's a commercial flight, which is supposed to stop in Bogota on its way to Argentina. Our opportunity seems to be the hour the flight will spend on the ground here in Bogota."

"Your plan involves the removal of this newly freed prisoner and the substitution of an agent for him on the flight. Am I correct?"

"Yes, we have an informant who is a close friend of the target. This man will lead us to Carlos by using his father as bait."

The ambassador nodded. "We have a special customs team ready to go. We'll use the Main International Terminal. You will be able to place agents in the airport and work with our people in there. We can isolate the flight from other international traffic which should make it easier to get him off the plane."

"At least one thing is in our favor," commented Campa. "The time! According to our sources the flight should arrive after dark. Actually, well after dark. It should be easier to make the switch and send the flight on its way."

"Mr. Campa, we are trying to get some additional help for you. We should know how the passengers are dressed about two hours before they leave. The information you gave us on height and weight may not be correct so we will have some time to make adjustments."

"Mr. Ambassador, you do know that all three will have to come off. We have another two agents who will go on the Argentina just in case Carlos is watching. His fellow travelers would be too suspicious if Chacon didn't continue on with them. Their confusion could mess things up once they got to Argentina. You can hold the other two men temporarily and send them on in forty-eight hours. By that time it should be done."

"So you've arranged for this American to appear at the terminal?"

"The pilot.... Yes. He's the key. Carlos will know that his father has connected with his friends. It was his idea to make the substitution. That way we will have the father to bargain with if the main plan fails. We can hold him as a material witness. He's our insurance policy both against the pilot and Carlos."

"But the trip to the airfield...what if they decide to take him before this pilot gets him to the field?"

"It's a risk, but we have backup, and, besides, removing Raymond Chacon before he and the pilot get to the jungle field is not in the plan. The agent will be substituted for Chacon at the airport, so if Carlos tries to take action before they get to the cargo plane, the agent has orders to kill the pilot. He will also be in radio communication with two chase vehicles that will be less than a mile behind. We'll also have two additional agents on the cargo plane that is carrying the drugs. This will give us three agents when the plane sets down in the United States. Those two will be in place six hours in advance, and I will be one of them."

"But there is still something I don't understand. Why wouldn't Carlos just let his father complete the trip to Argentina and then to the United States just like the others Castro has released. Once in the U.S. he could easily contact his father. Raymond Chacon has no reason to hide. According to our information, he has hero status among those who where involved in the Bay of Pigs thing. Why take the chance?"

"I really couldn't tell you. I didn't formulate the plan. You should ask DEA Special Agent Gerona. He is as close to this as anyone. I wouldn't be surprised if he isn't in the trunk of the car when it leaves the airport. I've stopped trying to keep up with him."

"Ah, Josef. He has the knack, as you Americans would say. He has helped us many times. He is a man of few words but many actions. If I were a betting man, I would bet many dollars that Josef will get his man."

"We hope you're correct. He's putting his neck on the line. If he's not careful, Josef may get his wish and come face-to-face with Carlos. Nonviolent or not, Carlos just seems to have a lot of friends who might appear at the wrong time. And I'm sure that Carlos would like to eliminate the man who is pursuing him."

The ambassador stopped to check some notes he had listed in his personal notebook. "Ah, let's see. We will make sure that none of the flight activity is interrupted on that day. We will also cancel all helicopter flights to the region. It's time for a safety inspection in any case. We are bringing in some new X-ray equipment to look at the rotors. This is perfect cover for the patrol interruption. The grounding will be announced two days in advance. I think that should cover it. All I can do is wish you the best of luck."

"Thanks, Mr. Ambassador. We were worried that your interdiction might be too efficient. This bird needs to get away!"

50

Dog Patch

Beneath the pressure of torments such as these, the
feeble remnant of the good within me succumbed.
Evil thoughts became my sole intimates-the
darkest and most evil of thoughts.

—Edgar Allan Poe, *The Black Cat*

Lake Ozark, Missouri

The drive west from St. Louis over Interstate 70 to Missouri Highway 54 was uneventful. Jim turned south through the State Capitol of Jefferson City and on to Bagnell Dam. The Dam was constructed during the depression, and by containing the waters of the Osage River, it created the Lake of the Ozarks, one of the largest recreational areas in the country.

Jim was very familiar with this drive, but he drove more slowly than usual as he passed over the dam. Just ahead was the main business area that was better known to local residents as *Dog Patch*. It was a popular gathering point on weekend evenings during the summer tourist season, but at most other times the road was sparsely traveled. Jim rarely paid much attention to the individual small businesses that lived on the roadside, but this time was different. He was searching for the location of a particular business that might lead him to his missing witness.

After passing through *Dog Patch*, Jim turned west on State Road HH and then onto Duckhead Road. His condo was located on the top floor of a three-story building that was situated on the shore of a small cove at the four mile marker.

He unloaded his suitcases and took a quick look around his unit. It was relatively clean for a rental unit. But, there was good news and bad news. The fireplace hadn't been used in a while so it wouldn't have to be cleaned; however, the refrigerator was empty so a trip to the grocery store was in order. First, Jim took a much-needed shower and then settled down in the living room with the local phonebook and the notes Charlie had given him.

Buddy's Bike Shop. On Business 54 across from Linda's Restaurant! It's located between HH and the dam. I must have driven past it on the way in, but I didn't see it. He laid the note on the coffee table and glanced at his watch. There was plenty of time to scout the place for tomorrow's adventure.

Armed with the address and phone number, Jim jumped back into his car and headed back for *Dog Patch*. The bike shop was located on the corner of an old concrete block building. The other end of the building housed a small real estate office and a shop that sold local arts and crafts. The rear of the building butted up against an oak tree forest on a steep ravine. The only entrances to the shop were a customer door in the front and a garage door on the side.

Jim parked his car down the road about half a block closer to the dam and walked to shop. He entered the small customer reception area that was sparsely furnished with two old chairs and a coffee pot on a small table. Behind the counter was an old typewriter on a bench-like desk and two four-drawer metal filing cabinets. No customers were in this area.

Jim stepped to the open door that led to the garage, and saw two men working near the back wall. It was a rather large garage area with tools and tires hanging from the wall. After walking past several cycles in various states of disrepair, he caught the attention of the taller man.

"Is Mike here? I have a message from a good friend of his in Marcelene."

The two men looked at each other before the shorter man responded.

"He's probably across the street at Linda's. It's the coffee shop across the street." He gestured toward the front of the building. "Can we help you with anything?"

"No, we have a mutual friend, and I want to give Mike his phone number. I've never met Mike before; how will I recognize him?"

"He's wearing coveralls similar to the ones we have on and probably a St. Louis Cardinal hat. This is a slow season for us so we spend a lot of time drinking coffee over there. Do you want one of us to go with you?"

"No, thanks. If I can't find him, I'll come back and wait. There can't be that many people in the shop. Thanks, again."

As Jim crossed Business 54, he surveyed Linda's Restaurant and the group of cars parked in front. It struck him that the coffee shop might provide a good place to roost while waiting for Gebinsky to return for his cycle. The front of the restaurant gave a clear view of the cycle shop and its parking lot. It was also difficult to see into the building because of the reflective coating that the owner had applied to the windows. He carefully scrutinized the several customers seated nearest to the front window, but was unable to resolve any defining characteristics among them. He would be able to occupy a position near the front window and not be easily identified from the bike shop.

Upon entering the door he was greeted by a friendly waitress who had obviously worked at this restaurant for quite a while.

"Just sit anywhere you'd like. Coffee?" She hesitated and waited for her customer to answer.

"Yes, with milk. I'll just sit at the counter."

Jim walked to the center of the counter and sat down. He had glanced at the three other customers already seated at the counter and decided that none of them were the person he was looking for. Then he studied the two other customers who were sitting in booths near the rear wall. One was an older gentleman who looked more the part of a tourist while the other fit the profile of a mechanic. He appeared to be wearing a shirt that matched the description he was given.

"Miss, could you tell me if that's Mike from the cycle shop sitting over there in the end booth?"

The waitress nodded affirmatively as she poured his coffee. Jim stood up and went to the booth where he introduced himself.

"Charlie Bill referred me to you, Mike. Here's my card. I'm the attorney representing a friend of his in a rather serious criminal matter. Charlie said you might be able to help me with a little problem we have."

The man was in his thirties. He shook hands with the lawyer, and asked him to sit down. Jim retrieved his coffee and settled into the booth.

"Mind if I ask for your driver's license. Charlie told me to be careful. I hope you don't mind."

Jim pulled out his wallet and showed Mike his license and his Missouri Bar registration card. Mike smiled when he was satisfied with the identification of his visitor.

"I'm glad you're here. This guy Wilcox brought in his bike…carburetor problems. But his name isn't really Wilcox. Charlie knew the serial and license numbers on the bike, and it's registered to an Edward Gebinsky. He gave us a St. Louis address so that probably won't help much. But he appears to be the guy Charlie was looking for."

"When is he supposed to pick up the cycle? I gather he didn't give you a phone number either."

"It's a St. Louis number. He told me that he was staying with friends. He's supposed to check in tomorrow. You may have to stick around and wait for him to show up."

"Mike, have you ever seen this guy before?"

"Yes, several times spread over a couple of years. Our records show that he's had his cycle in here for service three or four times, but I never paid any attention to him and he never left a local address. Somehow, Charlie knew that he would bring the bike in for service and that it would be a carburetor problem. He also knew that he wouldn't give his correct name. How did he do that?"

"Interesting! I haven't got a clue. Either Charlie knew where the bike was stored or he knows someone who has access to the bike. What other possibilities are there?"

"I've known Charlie Bill for a long time, and I've stopped trying to figure out how he does it."

Jim thought and responded. "What time do you open in the morning"?

"Nine o'clock. No one's here before that, and the cycles are locked up. If he shows up before nine, he'll have to wait anyway."

"If Linda doesn't mind, I'll just drink coffee all day and watch for the guy. With the beer belly he's carrying, I'll be able to pick him out from here with no problems."

"He had a young kid with him when he brought the bike in. The kid was driving a fairly new Jaguar."

"In case of any problems, Mike, the best way to get me is through this real estate company." Jim handed a business card to Mike.

"The phone at my condo is shut off. The unit is rented most of the time, and clever tenants were calling Mozambique on my phone. So I killed it."

"It's no problem, Jim. Charlie Bill has always been a good friend of mine. He helped me get this shop going and was a good customer when he was living here. I hope he and Charlene are doing well."

"Oh, yes. C. B. is a resourceful guy, and although I don't know Charlene at all, everyone says she's a great girl. I'll give Charlie your best when and if I see him."

With that, Jim shook hands with Mike and headed out the door toward the grocery store.

51

The Starting Line

*The Reagan-Bush bluster against Nicaragua
was, in short, a classic example of the Big Lie.*

—Peter Scott and Jonathan Marshall,
Cocaine Politics

Barranquilla, Colombia

"Well, there it is! The Magdelena. It's not the Missouri, but it has some good fishing now and then, Charlie. Maybe some of those lures you built will work down here."

"You never can tell. Sometimes they work and other times they don't. I really can never tell when I've done it right or not. With those things you have to do the experiment and let the fish tell you."

"Charlie, hand me that chart of the Barranquilla area. I've got the field marked with a red circle. See if you can spot it from here. I've landed here before, but it was a long time ago."

The third man in the plane was scanning the horizon. "You're right. We should be able to see the field from here."

"There it is!" shouted Charlie as he pointed to the south. "See those brown patches along the tree line? They mark the near end of the runway."

The airstrip was just west of the shores of the Magdelena, which ran to the Sea from deep inside the heart of the country. After the plane completed its bumpy but successful landing and taxied to a temporary hangar area, Josef Gerona got the attention of his two charges.

"Okay, this is where the plane will stay until we hear from Frank Campa. Do you see that kid running across the field toward us?"

Both Ron and C.B. looked toward the figure galloping toward them. Charlie laughed as the running man stumbled and fell into a small ditch that had been created by recent rains.

"I wish I had all that energy. Who is he? He looks like an American. No one else would fall in the hole that easily."

"He's an intern just out of college," Josef explained. Works for my boss, Phil Costello. They want to give him some field experience. Frank Campa made it a point to get him out here. I think it's because the kid is so impressed with Campa. You know what I mean, ranger training and paratrooper stuff. Arthur is at an impressionable age. Don't be surprised it Campa puts a chute on Arthur and makes him jump. We should have brought a camera for that!"

Ron turned to Josef. "Do you think that's a good idea. He's just a kid. From now on things could get a little dangerous especially for a kid who doesn't realize what the score is."

"Don't worry, Ron. If we get into trouble, I'll make certain that he gets out with us. I agree that he really doesn't know what's going on out here, but he's a quick learner, and the sooner he gets his feet wet, the better."

Arthur continued his trek across the field toward the aircraft and greeted the group as they stepped from the door of the plane.

"Hi! Mr. Campa sent me ahead to make sure everything is ready. You are ahead of schedule. We didn't expect you to arrive until tonight."

"We were lucky, Arthur. No headwinds and an early start. The weather was perfect. It sure beats flying commercial."

"Well, I think I'll get my chance to find out on the way back. Mr. Campa wants me to go along with the three of you. I sure hope I can!"

"Arthur, have you met our crew for the flight? This is Mr. Ronald Hernandez, the pilot, and his co-pilot is Charlie Bill. Come to think of it, Charlie, I don't even know your last name. But that's not important. Arthur, they will be helping us capture Carlos. Are you staying here with the plane?"

"No, as soon as the three of you are settled in, I have to go back to Bogota. Frank Campa indicated that the three of you are to stay here until things look like they're ready to go. Then Mr. Hernandez will have to come to Bogota to pick up Mr. Chacon."

"So Frank's running the show," laughed Josef. "I guess that's to be expected. What's the word on Raymond Chacon. Are the Cubans releasing him?"

"I don't have any more information on that than you do. They don't tell me much of what's going on. I guess they don't trust me enough yet."

"Don't worry Arthur, the three of us don't have a clue either. Do you know about the switch?"

Arthur hesitated. "I know something is happening with the man, but I don't know if I'm supposed to know."

"Don't concern yourself, Arthur. I'm sure Frank will fill you in on the details when you get to Bogota. He's going to need your help at that point. I'm sure he doesn't want Chacon to see him."

"Why is that, Josef? Does Chacon know him?"

"You might say that he does. But, don't mention it to Frank because he'll just get nervous. When you get to Bogota, just do what he tells you."

"I will, Josef. Right now I have to call Costello and tell him the status of the operation. He's anxious to get to the landing site in the States."

"He might be disappointed. Apparently, even Mr. Hernandez doesn't know the final location. Tell Costello that his best bet is to get to Orlando and stand by at the office. We can notify him when we're over the Keys. At that point we should know our final destination."

"Is there anything else you want to tell him? He made a point to me that I was to ask you if you needed anything else."

"No, tell Costello that all is well. We'll see him, probably in Florida. Tell him that I'll keep an eye on you!"

"Oh, thanks. That's all I need. He doesn't trust me in the first place."

"I was just kidding, Arthur. Just tell him that we are fine. Actually, the way this thing plays out may require all of us to keep an eye on each other. It could get a little tricky out there."

Arthur pointed toward the aircraft as he posed another question.

"Should we place a guard on the plane?"

Josef nodded.

"That's a good idea. By the way, how did you get here from Bogota?"

"The Colombians flew me over yesterday. They left right after they dropped me off. I have to call them for a ride back. Apparently they don't like coming in and out of here."

"Maybe I'll just drive you and Mr. Hernandez to Bogota when the time comes. We need to check the road because he'll have to drive back from there. We can also see how long it takes us. Do we have a vehicle?"

"Well, there's the station wagon that's parked behind that building over there. I think it belongs to us because it has a U.S. Consul marking on it."

"Arthur, have you seen any weapons around here. We might need some insurance if we drive."

"Weapons! Have we got weapons. I don't think we have any problems there."

"That's about all we need for now. You're doing a good job. Tell Costello that I said so!"

"Okay. Let's go to that building over there and get something to eat. After that I'll show you the quarters they've prepared for you. This place looks like it could be fun for a few days. You can go fishing and swimming in the river if you're courageous enough."

The men started the walk across the field toward dinner and their new accommodations. They would need all of the rest they could get.

52

Tracking the Enemy

*There once was a
lady named Bright,
who traveled much
faster than light.
She departed one day
in a relative way,
and came home
the previous night.*

—popular limerick

Lake Ozark, Missouri

It was almost 10 AM, and the attorney had been lounging in a booth at Linda's Restaurant for almost two hours. He had finished a Farmer's Breakfast, which featured eggs, fried potatoes, pancakes and grits. The waitress had just poured his fifth cup of coffee. He was watching and waiting. Would Gebinsky appear?

At 10:15 his question was answered. A late model Jaguar pull into the parking lot across the road. Jim recognized the car instantly. It belonged to Harry Michaels. And, the Florida license plates confirmed that fact. Two men emerged from the vehicle; one was Michaels and the other was Edward Gebinsky. The two men carried on a short conversation before entering the front door of the shop.

Jim waived to the waitress as he placed a twenty-dollar bill on the table. His immediate destination was his car, which was parked in front of a hardware store some fifty yards up the road.

From the front seat he could see the building and the Jaguar. After recording the license number, Jim reached below his seat and pulled out a Polaroid camera and took a photograph of the Michaels' car.

Now he waited. He was beginning to enjoy his work as a detective. The fact that the cycle needed repairs at this opportune time continued to intrigue him. The more he thought about it, the more likely it was that someone working with Michaels or Gebinsky was leaking information to Charlie Bill. That person also could have conveniently messed up the carburetor on the bike. *Juan must be the one!* Jim thought. *Juan has been in on this all along!*

In a few minutes Harry Michaels exited the front door of the motorcycle shop and walked to his car. He paused by the left front fender and appeared to be watching the rear of the shop. In a few seconds, Gebinsky rolled out of the garage on a motorcycle and made his way toward Michaels. The two men then began an animated conversation.

"Okay, Ed, I'm going up the road to get some alcohol and a few steaks. You'd better get back to the farm before those two punks do something stupid! I get nervous every time we leave them alone."

Gebinsky revved the engine of his cycle several times before replying.

"No problem. I'll baby sit them until you get back. But, this afternoon I need to check out the acceleration on this baby. The mechanic said one of the cylinders wasn't performing up to specs. He seems like he knows what he's doing. And, I want to talk with Juan about this thing. He seems to know a lot about motorcycles."

"Well, I'm glad to hear that he's good for something! I'll never understand how he could have screwed things up for us so completely. Especially since he seems to have his shit together most of the time. Just keep a close eye on him."

Michaels climbed back into his Jaguar and started the engine.

"I'll be back in about an hour. After all this babysitting, we deserve some kind of a reward. Maybe we can find a spot for happy hour around here. Between those children, all those fuckin' agents, and Carlos or whoever, I'm beginning to wonder whether I'm coming or going."

"I've got the perfect place, Harry. It's a local hangout and nobody messes with you. It's called Captain Hooks. When you go past HH up there, look on your right. Stop in and check it out!"

Michaels didn't respond as he pulled out of the parking lot and turned south on Business 54. Jim watched him drive over a nearby hill as he focussed his attention on Gebinsky who was still revving the engine of his Harley and listening for irregularities.

Finally, satisfied that the engine was running properly, Gebinsky pulled out of the parking lot and also headed south with Jim following at some distance. After about a mile Gebinsky turned east on State Road 42, a two-lane road full of twists and turns. He rolled through the small town of Kaiser and continued for another half mile. There Gebinsky turned north on a spur road off of 42 and then entered a dirt road that led to a small farmhouse.

Jim drove past the dirt road and continued on for a few hundred yards. He found a grove of trees with room enough to park his car, and he began to walk back along the road. When he could see the farmhouse from the road, he took a path that wound through a cluster of oak trees to a point about fifty yards from the building.

Gebinsky was still looking over his parked motorcycle, and Jim could see Johnny watching him tinker with the machine. There was still no sign of Juan. Jim managed to take several pictures of the house before he saw Juan emerge from a nearby barn with several shotguns. *They're going hunting! This is not the time to get caught out here!* Jim crawled back to the path and made his way quickly back to the highway and his car.

He threw the developed pictures into the glove compartment and started his car. Jim didn't want to take the chance of driving past the farm again so he continued on the spur road for several miles until it lead him back to Highway 54.

Just as he was about to turn off spur road onto Highway 54, a dark colored Jaguar shot in front of him causing Jim to slam on his brakes. *It was Michaels! He had almost had a collision with Michaels' Jaguar!* Luckily, the Jaguar kept going, and Michaels gave no indication that he had recognized his adversary.

53

Plans within Plans

Till they stand beside him upon the field,
To the death together their arms to wield.
Ah, timeless succor, and all in vain!
Too long they tarried, too late they strain.

—The Song of Roland

Cartagena, Colombia

The black Porsche pulled into the paved circular drive of a large house on the outskirts of Cartagena. A young Cuban man stepped out of the car and made his way up the entry stairs to a high wrought iron gate. He searched the wall for an intercom speaker and pressed the entry button twice. After a few seconds a woman's voice softly asked the visitor's identity.

"Diaz. It's Chico Diaz. Klaus should be expecting me."

"Ah, Diaz! It is good of you to come. Just one second, and I will open the gate. It has been a long time. Please come in."

With that the lock on the gate clicked, and Chico Diaz entered the courtyard. The main house sat in one corner of the spacious garden that also held a small swimming pool and hot tub. Two children were in the pool laughing and splashing each other. Diaz passed through the rear entrance of the house and into a large modern kitchen.

Klaus was a German telecommunications engineer who had found the mountains and warmth of Colombia to his liking. He had traveled to South America on business in the winter of 1969 and had fallen in love with the climate and the people. His wife had grown up in Argentina. Currently, she worked for the Colombian airline as a service supervisor.

His job involved maintenance of several large telephone switching networks installed by his employer, a major German company. Klaus had received his engineering education in America. He prided himself on being on the front edge of technology and his prize possession was an Osborne Executive Computer, which was one of the first personal computers to reach the market. If he wasn't watching football matches, he could be found attempting to program his computer.

Diaz saw Angelina working near the refrigerator as he walked in.

"Ah, Angelina, it is good to see you again. Is that lazy husband of yours awake yet?"

Angelina smiled and pointed toward the living room.

"He's waiting for you. You may have some problem getting his attention because he's into one of those football matches he loves so much."

"Well, not everyone gets to play in the World Cup! He's just reliving his glory days."

"You men are all alike. Always defending each other."

Angelina reached into the refrigerator and handed a bottle to Diaz.

"Here's a beer for starters. Let me know if you two footballers get hungry."

"Thanks, I'm a little thirsty. You may want to come in and join us. Your advice might come in handy."

Diaz accepted the bottle of beer and walked through a central alcove into the large living room. Klaus was seated on a couch that faced the television set.

"What, Klaus, are the Germans losing again?" Chico knew he could get Klaus' attention.

"Say, Diaz, my boy! How are you? Ah, no such luck. It's Brazil again. I have money on those goats from Argentina. They are running like chickens and kicking like wild horses. No plan! No control!"

Klaus got up from the couch and extended his hand.

"What's up, Chico. You're call was interesting, but not revealing?"

"I just got back from a business trip to Honduras."

"Did you get a chance to see Ernesto?"

"Yes, my brother is fine. His warning is the reason I went up there. He's been keeping an eye on the Americans and CORU as well as the cartels. The volcano is active! We've got some work to do."

"Great, I have been getting a little bored with my job. My part time work is always much more fun!"

"It's getting interesting for our friend. The Americans are plotting against him. Remember your recent trip to Florida?"

"That was fun, and it worked out well."

"True! But they have not learned their lesson. They are trying to catch Carlos with a different bait."

"That would make Orejuela and Carasquel very happy. It's like a three way gunfight between Cali, Medellin and the Cubans in Miami. I'm sure that the Cali boys are the ones we're looking for."

Klaus' interest turned from the game to Diaz.

"If we could only be sure. I have suspected them from the beginning, but I have little information on which to base a sound judgment. The people in Medellin are also getting a little nervous. I was there last week working on the central switch, and I was able to listen in for a while. Unfortunately, I did not have a means for recording the conversations, but they were very interesting. After the last two failures they suffered, they are looking for a scapegoat. That kind of behavior can be danger- ous for all of us!"

"Ah, Klaus, we may get our chance to find out. This American, Harry Michaels, has had several meetings with cartel members at SETCOMP. They are aware that Carlos has been messing up the cartels and mess-

ing up the American CIA too much for their liking. They are too close
to figuring out the fact that Carlos is beginning to create a war between
the cartels. We can't let that happen."

"So, tell me, was Ernesto successful? He has the missing piece to
the puzzle."

At that point Angelina walked into the room. Diaz turned to include
her in the conversation.

"Ernesto had good news. The negotiations are complete. Apparently,
the Cubans are going to release Raymond Chacon and maybe a few others. It has been twenty-one years."

Angelina smiled at the unexpected news.

"Maybe that man Castro has a heart after all!"

Klaus looked at his wife with an expression of mock joy.

"And I'll bet he'll hand 'em boxes of Cuban cigars on their way out!
It wasn't an act of conscience or an act of mercy or forgiveness. We are
already sure of that."

"There's more!" said Diaz. "The plane is to land here in Bogota on its
way to Argentina. The Americans want to pull Raymond Chacon off the
plane in Bogota and use him as bait to trap Carlos."

Klaus looked over at this wife.

"Can we pull it off?"

"Everything's arranged. No one will stop the Americans at the airport. Ernesto wants photographs at every stage. He doesn't trust our
Cuban friends. Chico, do you have the flight schedule?"

"Not yet, but you will have it at least a few hours before the flight
leaves Havana."

Diaz flashed a confident smile, and headed for the door.

"Get back to your game, Klaus. It may be a while before we can
relax again."

54

The Cargo Handlers

No crime so bold, but would be understood,
A real, or at least a seeming good,
Who fears not to do ill, yet fears the name;
And, free from conscience, is a slave to fame.

—Sir John Denham, *Cooper's Hill*

The Northeastern Coast of Colombia

"Get the last few bales in here now! And get the rake and clean up all of this debris and burn it. I want to get out of here in one piece with no traces that we've ever been here. After it's loaded, pull the truck up on the trail and get rid of these tire markings."

The voice was that of Raphael, the foreman of the loading crew. He and his men had built a cottage industry out of packaging, transporting, and loading various smuggled products aboard planes all across coastal Colombia.

He looked into the humid air at the billowy cumulus clouds and scratched his head.

"I can usually smell those government choppers even before they take off. But somehow today is different. I haven't heard anything or seen anything all day. No aircraft in the sky at all! It is very disconcerting. I'd much rather know where my enemies are rather than to sit out here with the sky like this!

"Either they've given up on us, or they've stopped for a purpose," replied Victor as he loaded a bale of marijuana.

"I don't really go for that rumor on inspections, Victor. Usually, when we hear a rumor like that, the number of surveillance aircraft doubles. Are they trying to get us to relax? Remember, we have a couple of trips scheduled for tomorrow. I don't feel good about this!"

"It has been unusually quiet, Boss. You're right about today and about yesterday. The rumor among the men is that the military has grounded its patrols. They said there have been too many losses in recent raids up north. Pablo told me of three crashes in the last month, all pursuing prop-driven aircraft. He believes that they are rearming the helicopters for air to air combat. He thinks they're going to shoot the planes down with missiles. But then, he's prone to exaggeration. Don't we pay them enough just to keep them away?"

"Ah, Victor, it's the Americans. They are in Bogota every day talking with the Government. They want to stop our little sideline business and roll the country back into complete poverty. The last time I was in Miami all I heard on the radio and TV was drugs, drugs, drugs! And then I heard Colombia, Colombia, Colombia! All this talk really does is raise the street price, which raises our profits, which raises our payoffs. I'm not an accountant, but I know that our net per kilo stays constant. It is as if our military is taking dollars directly from the American people. They are too busy watching television to see it, but it's pretty obvious to anyone who looks."

"You can see it because you do not use the product. Am I right? I have never seen you take as much as a puff or a pill. And now you are sending your son to college in England and soon your daughter will want to go. You are a wise man, Raphael! You will be able to do for your family what every man would want to do for his. And you are a good influence. I haven't touched anything in two months. It's been tough, but I'm sure it will be worth it."

"There's an old street proverb that tells me what to do here," Raphael replied with a smile. "Don't shit where you eat, Victor! Don't shit where you eat! This is my job, my livelihood, my profession! I would rather be teaching physics or practicing medicine, but the fates have not led me there. They have put me here, and this is my job. I would be a fool to become a customer, too, wouldn't you say?"

"Your logic is unassailable, Raphael. By the way, I'd rather be playing football or reading Hamlet! Well, back to work. We must have a drink when we are finished. I have seen you drink rum and beer quite regularly so I can safely say that you are not involved in smuggling those commodities!"

Victor patted his boss on the back and turned to complete his tasks.

"Okay, just keep an eye on everyone. I'm going to check the lookouts and make sure they are not asleep." Raphael started a quick tour of his security positions. His men obeyed Raphael without reservation. He saw that they were well paid, and he protected them and their families. In consideration, they worked hard and fast whenever a load of contraband was being processed.

On this occasion the men rushed the remaining bags of Quaaludes and bales of marijuana into the cargo bay of the Beech 18. One thing Raphael did notice about this particular flight was the minimal size of the payload and the presence of extensive emergency food and flotation gear. *These guys must be amateurs or just very conservative. They're not even here to check the load. And that's always a good sign*! Although he often loaded planes with clandestine cargo, he still was glad not to see the personnel who were manning the flight. He enjoyed anonymity and the large cash payments that went with it.

Normally, as planes arrived they would be tracked by radar. The Government response was usually about ninety minutes. He guessed that that was paid for also. So a plane would have to be refueled, loaded, and in the air in an hour to be safe. Obviously, it was then unwise to leave within an hour of the last flight. Several presumptuous pilots had met their doom by ignoring this hard and fast rule. They would run into the teeth of the government patrol and several were forced down into the hilly terrain or into the ocean just off the coast.

Still, this flight seemed somewhat unusual. The plane had been here at the field hidden in the brush for over a week. Usually pilots flew their planes in, took a break in the shade while the planes were loaded, and took off again with some urgency. The Colombian government flew frequent patrols in this area, but the large payoffs his employers made to the military prevented this field and the land routes to it from being raided. Yet, once the planes were into the air and cleared the coast, they became fair game. The absence of helicopters and the presence of this particular plane were not coincidences. Something unusual was going on, and it made Raphael nervous.

And then there were his employers. He rarely dealt with them directly. He'd even gone to the trouble to disguise himself and carry false identification wherever a meeting was planned. But of all his employers, Raphael was the least familiar with Carlos and his organization but the most familiar with his reputation. He had never seen the man yet he had loaded many old aircraft for him, and he had been paid handsomely for his time and risk. He had heard that this was one of Carlos's deals, but with the cargo and the timing, his intuition told him that something was different or wrong with this one. *I can't believe this thing is correct. But, then again, I am not paid to think, just to transport and load and beat it.* His wondering was interrupted when one of his men signaled completion of the job.

"Very good. Pick up your water bottles and keep your gloves on until we hit the road. Bring in the lookouts, and let's get going. Is everyone accounted for?"

Victor confirmed that all of the men were present, and as they turned the truck around, two men came running in from the tree line. Both men were heavily armed and were wearing fatigues. They jumped on the back of the truck as it headed out on a narrow trail through the heavy brush and trees.

"Did we get a full fee for that one?" asked one of his men.

They all must have noticed the difference in the payload thought Raphael as he nodded his head.

"Yes, your belly will be full of wine within the hour. Just keep your mouth shut and your eyes open, as usual. Don't question the goose that lays the golden eggs for us. There is probably a simple explanation for the size of that load. Maybe it's going to a State where the penalties are based on quantity. Our employers are not stupid. They are usually very careful to do thing the right way. After all, they did hire us to do the transportation, and we are the best!"

The truck sped through the trees and heavy brush along the trail. It slowed near a small hill where the driver issued a hand signal to several sentries who guarded this entrance to the field.

I would like to see the fellows who are flying this one. The more I think about it the more I know something funny is going on. Raphael caught himself as he almost wondered aloud.

Raphael found it hard to relax even though they seemed to be out of danger. As he looked around the truck, he noticed that his men were a little more thoughtful than usual. Their thoughts mirrored his.

If we could just make it out of the valley, we would be safe.

Victor was riding in the right cab seat; he was armed with a rifle and handgun and carried several grenades. As the truck turned each corner his grip tighten on one of the grenades; he was ready to launch it at the slightest irregularity. He had the same misgivings as Raphael.

But, as the truck made the last turn and its tires came in contact with the main highway, a smile slowly crept across Raphael's face and a collective sigh of relief seemed to come from all of the men at once. Soon they cleared the summit and entered a well-traveled trail which led to the small town where they lived.

If it were a bust, it would have happened by now. Raphael sat down with his men and enjoyed the remainder of their trip back home. It was time for beer all around!

55

The Switch

You are a prisoner with two guards,
each guarding one door to your cell.
One guard always lies,
and one is always truthful,
but you do not know which is which.
You may leave your cell
by one of the two doors.
One door leads to the
execution block and death.
The other leads to freedom.
You may ask only one question,
which you may address to either
of the guards but not both.
What do you do?

—**Yuri B. Chernyak and Robert M Rose,**
The Chicken from Minsk

The Isle of Pines, Cuba

"Bring them over here!"

The speaker wore a Cuban Militia uniform and spoke in an aggressive voice. He pointed to the two men on the left and waived toward a small bench next to a rectangular table.

"You two, sit down here and be quiet! Chacon! Move over there and sit down. Remain in those positions until we tell you to move."

In response to the commands the three men parted without speaking. All three were clearly prisoners and their poor physical condition and shabby clothing indicated that they had been in captivity for some time. All three men wore handcuffs and where shackled with leg weights.

The military man walked over to the two men he had addressed first and reached into his jacket. He pulled out a ring of keys, which he searched with his hands. Finally, he found the keys he was looking for and he began removing the leg shackles and handcuffs from the men. As these devices were removed, each man rubbed his wrists and ankles. It was easy to see that they were happy for the physical freedom.

The Cuban soldier put the keys in his pocket and motioned for the men to stand up.

"The two of you are going to board the Swiss Airliner when it arrives. I want no talking before you get on the plane or after you get on the plane. Not to the other passengers, and not to the crew. Do you understand?" The two men nodded meekly.

"Speak to the hostess only if she speaks to you. We have men aboard the plane. They will be watching you during the entire flight. Just sit in the seats, which are assigned to you. You will sit here quietly and wait until your, ah, your companion arrives."

The two prisoners again nodded their compliance. Soon another man arrived. He appeared very agitated as he leafed through several documents he had been carrying in a briefcase. He walked up to the empty table that was located near the prisoners and dumped a bunch of documents out of a file folder.

"Your passports! Your release papers! Everything is here." He looked up from the documents that were spread on a small table and pointed to the two men sitting in front of him.

"Now, your clothes! Change quickly into these!" He pointed to two small stacks of clothing that had been placed on the floor by the military man.

"We mustn't have our Cuban-Americans looking sloppy in public. That wouldn't do now, would it!" The speaker didn't expect a reply from his prisoners.

The two men rose from the bench and retrieved their clothing. They removed their shirts and pants and obediently dressed in the new clothing. After they were finished, they sat back down on the bench. A look of anticipation and excitement began to become obvious on their faces, but they knew they were still not out of the woods. They were still held tightly by their jealous captors.

"Chacon!" snapped the civilian.

"Se, what is your pleasure?" Raymonds's voice was somewhat sarcastic.

"Do you mock me, Chacon? Do you think this is a joke? Haven't you learned anything from your experience?" The speaker paused, but the prisoner did not respond.

"You are not getting on this plane with your friends! You are very special. Very, very special."

The prisoner looked up at the civilian. "If I am not leaving, then why am I here?"

"I didn't say that you were not leaving. You don't listen too well, do you? You jump to conclusions!"

This time the prisoner did not respond but instead stared at his captor. After a few seconds the civilian broke his intense expression and relaxed his mood.

"I cannot tell you where you are going, Raymond Chacon, because I do not know. You must wait here for your escort. Someone has much bigger plans for you. Your friends will be safe, and I am sure that you will be safe also. If harm is done to you, it will not come at the hands of the Cuban Government. Ah, here they come. It's about time!"

An old Jeep pulled up in front of the hangar where the men were standing. Two men got out of the vehicle and walked toward the prisoners and their escort. After looking at the men, one of the two spoke to the member of the Militia.

"Sir, place these two on the Swiss aircraft as soon as it arrives. It will be here within the hour. They will be joined by another man. Please make sure this man gets Mr. Chacon's passport and documentation." The speaker pointed to the papers on the table."

"We are taking Mr. Chacon with us. Here are the transfer papers. We have his new passport and clothing in the Jeep. Would you please remove his handcuffs and shackles. Senor Raul Castro thanks you for your service to the Revolution."

As soon as Raymond Chacon was freed, he was ushered to the Jeep and placed in the back seat. No words were spoken until the vehicle began to move across the airfield.

"Raymond Chacon, we are here to take you to Nueva Gerona. From there you will be transferred to the Cayman Islands. From there you will be flown to the United States." The man who spoke wore a Cuban military uniform but no indication of rank.

"Have we met?" Chacon searched his memory for the identity of the owner of this voice. "Your voice is familiar to me. But it has been a long time." Chacon leaned forward and looked at the man, studying his face in the darkness.

"We have, Raymond. And it has been a long time!"

The voice was more relaxed than when Raymond had first heard it. "On that night when you were aiding the escape of your friends from Cienfuegos, do you remember the children Chico and Ernesto?"

"I remember two boys who sacrificed for the others. The raft was too full, and they came back to shore. As I remember, their parents and their sister were killed by the bomb in the other raft."

"Yes, and I didn't believe what the boys told me. I assumed that you were the cause for my brother's death. I was overpowered by grief. I wanted to kill you!"

"I am sorry about your loss. I was the leader of the patrol, and the two men who killed the parents of the two boys were under my command. They were trying to kill us with that bomb, but they got the civilians instead. I am so sorry!"

"I am not proud of what I have done to you, Raymond. And, had I known you were looking for your wife, I would not…." The man turned his head away and stared across the field.

"The past is just that, the past! We must all look to the future and spend our energies making a better future for all of our people." Chacon listened to his words reflect across his memory. It seemed so long ago. He stared at the man he had not seen for over twenty years weighing his response.

"But if I had just thought for a moment, if I had just listened to the boys, then this would not have happened, and they would probably be living happily in the States much sooner. Your brother did send for them and they have grown up to be fine lads."

"Do not be angry with yourself, Colonel Diaz. It was your duty. You could not have known my situation. And the invasion was a foolish thing. You did what you had to do. And remember, if I can walk out of Cuba, they should be able to do the same thing if it is their wish. And I would do everything I could to help them."

"We would not have captured you except for the behavior of the American agents. The woman you contacted in Havana was a CIA contact for the Americans, but we had easily turned her. She fed you to us. You didn't have a chance."

"When I contacted her, it was not to conduct a military activity. I was trying to find my daughter and my wife. I told her that and took the risk. She didn't even blink. My family was of no concern to her."

"And now they have chosen me to give you your freedom. For both of us, the last twenty years have not been profitable. You have lost your family. I have lost the revolution. The dreams we had have become nightmares."

The Jeep made its way across the field past the main hangars. The driver brought it to a stop near a relatively new Cessna.

"Raymond, your clothes are in the plane. Here in this envelope are your new passport and medical papers. We will wait here for the pilot. Then we will fly to Nueva Gerona. I will be coming with you at least that far. I have sworn to see you safely off Cuban soil. I still obey my orders!"

"If I might ask…", Chacon looked directly at his escort.

"Please, I will try my best to answer any question you have."

"Why am I not leaving with my comrades? Should I fear for their safety? Or for my safety?"

"No. You're safety is the reason we are here. I do believe your comrades are safe. However, did you see the man who came to the hangar with me?"

"I did. He came to me and asked my name. Then he inquired as to my health and my family. He did not identify himself."

"He is taking your place today, with your comrades. It is his life, which might be in danger. I do not know this as certain. After so many years…I feel these things even when they are not spoken."

"He mentioned my son, Carlos. He said that my son and I had many friends in many places. These words were strange, and I could not trust myself to ask why he said them."

"I have heard it. But I believe that it is your brother and your son; they are the reason you are being freed. Your brother has been seeking your freedom for a long time. But Fidel Castro does not easily cooperate on anything associated with the Americans. He is convinced you were with the expatriates on the Zapata. Even when I told the inspectors of your wife, they turned away from me. It was Fidel's brother who has made your freedom possible. I have never met your son or your brother, but they have softened some hard hearts."

"Carlos! I have not seen Carlos since he was five. Now, he is a man. I asked for a picture of my son. But they denied me everything. They would not even let me write to him. And, my brother, Oscar! It may be that I will see him again."

"You will see them soon. But I ask a favor of you, Raymond."

"Please, ask the favor."

"Do not tell them I was responsible for your capture. To make more enemies at my age is not a good thing. And I have suffered for my deed more than you can know or understand."

"They will not know, Colonel Diaz, unless you tell them!"

Soon the pilot of the Cessna appeared. With its two passengers safely onboard, the plane rolled down the runway on its way to Nueva Gerona.

56

Another Suspect

No wonder that jails are crowded,
and taxes and poor-rates increased.
Under such systems,
nothing is to be looked for
but what has already happened;
and as to reformation,
whenever it comes,
it must be from the nation,
and not from the government.

—Thomas Paine, *The Rights of Man*

Orlando, Florida

It was a busy day at the Orlando office, particularly for a Saturday. Carl Adams, John Phillips and Phil Costello of the DEA waited for their special representative from the CIA to arrive. The importance of today's activities was clear to everyone. It was time to plan the final details of Carlos's capture.

The Beech 18 with its cargo of drugs and agents and a cooperating witness would be coming in over the Keys to look for the coded signal. From there, it would be routed to a landing site or a drop zone. If it were a drop zone, the plane would proceed to a final coded landing site after the drop. From the landing site, the apparent Raymond Chacon would be taken to a safe house, there to be visited by his son. At that point the agencies would pounce on the man they had been trying to capture for five years. Point! Set! Match! It was easy, at least in theory.

It was difficult to find a weak point in the plan. The plane would have a cooperating witness at the controls. And, he was going to be watched by armed agents. The two CIA field officers had vast experience in clandestine activities in the Caribbean so it would be tough to fool them. The key DEA agent was saddled with an inexperienced DEA intern, but that shouldn't be a problem.

Once in the jaws of the trap, it was difficult to see how Carlos could escape even if he had a small army at his disposal. There was strong feeling of pressure to get this job done correctly, but there was also a reasonable amount of confidence in the room.

Costello was on a conference call with agents in Washington and Fort Lauderdale. During the call he referred to a list of possible landing locations in Florida and a situation map which had been faxed to him from CIA headquarters in Virginia. After he was satisfied with the results of the call, he signed off and studied the map one final time. One of the secretaries came into the room and handed Costello another set of faxed material, which had just arrived from Washington. Costello looked at his watch.

"When is Dubinski supposed to get here?"

Carl Adams, the Station Chief, glanced up at the clock on the wall. "In about five minutes. If nothing else, these guys are punctual."

"I guess I can understand why Frank Campa would want a CIA agent on the ground for this exercise, but I also hope that they know we're not holding up the show for them. The way things are going I wouldn't be surprised if the FBI didn't send some representatives so they could get a piece of the pie, too! And you watch, those guys will want all the credit. But if things go badly, they'll disappear, and we'll take the rap for screwing up. That's always the way it is."

Just as Costello completed his complaint, Adams pointed toward the door.

"And speak of the devil, here he is." Adams got up from his chair and extended a hand to the CIA Special Agent.

"Brian, let me introduce you to the rest of our team. You already know John Phillips, I believe. You've worked with John before as I remember. Next to him is Phil Costello from Washington. Phil is leading the project from our side of the fence. Most of the progress on this case so far has been the result of Phil's work and that of his team."

Dubinski extended a hand to Phillips and Costello and then took a seat next to Adams. He placed his briefcase on the floor as Costello called the meeting to order.

"The flight is in the air as we speak. I'm going to run down the preparations just to make sure we're okay. The Lear is on call at the airport. We'll be in the air as the flight nears the Keys so that we can respond to the final destination quickly."

"What about our backup, Frank. Where are they?", asked Dubinski.

"We have ten agents from Louisiana and Texas on standby in Fort Lauderdale. They will go up when we do. We'll call them in when we have a fix on the location. We have worked out operational details for all of the reasonable possibilities and locations. I have the playbook here, and they have a copy in Lauderdale."

"That should do it, Phil. FAA is on alert for this so we shouldn't run into any traffic delays. Customs has a plane ready in Miami just in case.

Now that Costello had a single CIA agent alone in a DEA environment, he came forward with a question that had been bothering him for a while.

"Brian, you've worked with Frank Campa before, haven't you?"

"Yes, on occasion. As far as I know, he isn't with the agency. We just support some of his activities in Central America."

"So, I gather that he has something going on the side."

"Well, rumor has it that Frank came into a lot of money when Batista left Cuba. He has used it to finance a counter-revolutionary movement against Fidel Castro and his supporters. Frank is not someone you should ignore. He isn't a politician or a talker. The man is a doer if I ever saw one. He has the equivalent of ranger training and is an explosives expert. There are a few sugar mills and department stores in Cuba that have his name on them, after they were blown up, I mean! This CORU group should not be taken lightly. They control a good part of Venezuela's security forces, and he has informants all through Central and South America."

Costello pressed his question. "For such a powerful guy, he seems very interested in Carlos. I know that he has complained of losses that he has ascribed to this smuggler, but if anything, Carlos is an enemy of Fidel and the Cuban revolution. Why would Carlos attack Frank's efforts with such enthusiasm?"

"I've never thought of that angle. It's a good question. One that I'm not sure I can answer, but you are right when you say that he seems to have a thing for this character Carlos."

Costello glanced around the room to see if anyone had any more questions. Dubinski sorted through his papers and then looked at Costello.

"I've only got one minor but nagging problem, Phil. It might not be anything serious, but I'd better bring it up just in case."

"What's that, Brian. We need to make sure everything is in place. Now is the time to put everything on the table."

"Well, it's this guy's brother, Oscar Chacon. You know, the brother of Raymond Chacon."

"I thought we had surveillance working on him for the last two weeks!"

"We did, Phil. But he's disappeared. He was working in Hialeah just like normal until a few days ago. He went fishing on Saturday and did-n't return with the boat. He must have known something about us watching him."

Costello looked at Adams before he responded.

"We've been careful to keep local law enforcement out of the loop on this one. Hernandez swears that they don't have a mole in the Sarasota County Sheriff's Department or anywhere else in Florida, but I don't believe it. Too many coincidences have occurred for me to believe that all of our bad luck has been based on random events. Where was he when he was fishing?"

"He gave us the slip off Key Largo. It was probably another boat. Who knows! All I can say is that we've lost him for the time being."

"Well, that's probably nothing serious. There's not a lot he can do alone."

"But that's not all, Phil. There are a few other things we've discovered about him. Several months ago he went to Mexico."

"That's not such a big deal. Maybe he wanted to buy a Volkswagen." Costello was his usual sarcastic self.

"But he didn't go to Pueblo," Adams replied. He went to the Cuban Embassy in Mexico City. We have a bug there, but we didn't get anything from him on it. Whatever happened at the embassy didn't occur in the main conference areas. What we do know is that he was contacted by a female Cuban agent at the airport."

"Why didn't we find out about this sooner? What could he be doing with the Cubans?"

Agent Phillips chimed in. "Well, he's Cuban isn't he? Maybe he was lobbying for the release of his brother."

Phil sat back in his chair and looked up at the ceiling. *From the mouths of babes*...Phillips had hit on something so obvious. Yet it was something none of them had followed up on in preparation for this operation.

Oscar Chacon has obtained the release of his brother! He's the one who started this whole thing! "Say, Carl, you looked over Oscar's vitae, didn't you?" asked Costello. "Who are his main contacts in Cuba?"

"They go pretty high, chief. Raul Castro, no less! For an expatriate, he has a lot of friends near the top."

Costello shook his head. "Well, he couldn't have that many friends. Otherwise, his brother wouldn't have spent twenty in the slammer down there. That sounds like a reasonable analysis doesn't it?"

Carl continued. "Hey, Fidel is pretty autocratic. Maybe even Raul couldn't get him out right away. But now Oscar seems to have pierced the veil."

"And who was this female agent he met in Mexico City. Was she a player or just his escort to the embassy?"

"Maria Valdez is her name although she goes by several different aliases."

Dubinski snapped his fingers as he listened.

"Valdez! I've run across her name before! Frank Campa was warned about her by our contacts in Havana. But, there was nothing about being attached to the Cuban Embassy.

"She's known to have the ear of Raul Castro, and she's been spotted in places like Czechoslovakia and East Germany. She was educated in the United States, graduated from Agnes Scott College in Atlanta and did graduate work at Yale. This woman obviously knows her shit. I can't believe that with all the tracks she's made in North America, we don't even have a good photo of her."

"Hey, we have a hard enough time keeping track of the heads of state!", Carl replied. "Valdez has not been a major problem for us so we have pretty much ignored her. She was probably trying to find out what CORU was doing in Nicaragua and how much Frank was doing to aid the Contras. Frank's not a ladies man so she might have given up and returned to the diplomatic corps."

Costello thought more on the subject. *I'm missing something obvious here. Something in plain sight! These people are all related in some way to our project and some dealing is going on. We see it, but we don't understand it.*

"Why would Fidel deal now and not deal before? Has he changed his mind about Chacon? No! He is only using him to trade for something.

What would he want to trade Chacon for? What do we have that he would want to trade for Chacon?

"Is it monetary or military or political? He wouldn't get any money unless Carlos was buying his father's freedom. Nah! Fidel wouldn't lower himself to deal with a drug smuggler."

"Military is out of the question. He has the Soviets in his pocket. As Sherlock Holmes would say, eliminate the things which don't make sense, and you should be left with the answer.

"So it's got to be political! What kind of political advantage could he possibly extract from the situation? What political advantage would involve the Chacon family?"

Costello paused to let his comments be absorbed by his listeners.

"Back to beginning again! Why would Fidel deal now for political advantage and not deal before?"

"Before what?" asked Phillips.

Costello looked at Phillips and replied without thinking.

"Before this flight!"

Costello's words hung in the air as the group began to see the implications of his statement. All of a sudden, Costello jumped up and pounded his fist on the table. The unthinkable thought raced through his mind.

The Cubans are going to intercept the flight!

57

Who's on First

*What do Americans know about
...a tyrant's atrocities,
except in novels and movies.*

—Fidel Castro

Bogota, Colombia

Frank Campa watched as the Swiss Air 727 rolled slowly toward the International Terminal. He had taken a position on the second floor of the terminal, overlooking the passenger area.

It was an unnerving moment for a man who prided himself on toughness and fearlessness. His memories from the Bay of Pigs fiasco were still vivid. Could this be the confrontation he had hoped would never come? A confrontation with a man whose friends he had assassinated and whose life he had destroyed.

Campa realized that there was a way out. He could leave the airport before the passengers exited the aircraft. He could turn over the process of identification to the DEA agent assigned to him. But, it wasn't that easy.

Agent Arthur White was inexperienced and too young to be counted on. And, after all these years and the debilitating effects of imprisonment, would even Frank Campa be capable of recognizing Raymond

Chacon? There were no photographs available of the man he had stranded in Cienfuegos.

Campa decided to take the middle ground. He would view his adversary from a distance. Once identification was confirmed, he would turn the rest of the process over to White. After all, he also had the assistance of three Colombian customs officers, men directly assigned by the ambassador to the United States. Finally, he was comfortable with the situation.

"Hey, kid! Where the fuck is Hernandez? Is he in position to pick up our man after we detain Chacon?"

"Yes, sir! After Chacon goes through customs! We'll switch them in the security area."

Campa was still worried about the switch of passengers.

"I wonder whether the Cubans placed any agents on the plane? From the passenger manifest it appears that only seven passengers boarded in Havana. That leaves four possibilities. Do we have anyone watching those passengers?"

"We discussed it in Washington, but the consensus was to ignore them."

"That figures! If Costello had half a brain, he would be dangerous!"

"Don't worry about the switch, Mr. Campa. The three customs people here will be the only ones to talk with the Cubans in public. Everything will look normal. I'll interview Chacon in the security area. Only the passengers will see me, and I'll be wearing this uniform. I think we're covered."

As Campa watched the passengers from the Swiss plane enter the terminal, he saw three men with bewildered looks on their faces, take a seat on a bench near the check-in desk.

"Well, there are our passengers. They certainly look like they haven't out in the sunlight for a long time. Notice their eyes, still squinting! Let's get the show moving, kid. We can't let them get picked off here in the terminal by some leftist maniac!"

Before Arthur could signal the custom's agents, Campa grabbed him by the shoulder, stopping him. He had noticed several tourists passing close to the Cubans. A rather good looking woman, who appeared to be the mother of the two small children in the group, stopped and pulled out her camera. The group posed as she took several photographs. It was a common occurrence. Tourists taking pictures, even inside the air terminal.

But to Frank Campa it seemed to be more than that. *Why did they stop right in front of the Cubans? From this angle it appears as though all three of them were in the pictures. Coincidence?*

As he pondered the situation, the tourists walked toward the desk in front of Gate 5 and began talking to one of the airline personnel. *These people don't fit the profile of typical Cuban agents*, thought Campa. *They must be tourists.* After a few more seconds, Frank's attention swung back to the Cubans only to find that Arthur had some questions.

"Mr. Campa, which one is Raymond Chacon?"

"You'll find out when you interview them!"

"Sorry, Mr. Campa. What I meant was that I had a feeling about him from our discussions. As I look at those three over there, none of them fits the picture which all of this has created in my head."

"I met Chacon some twenty years ago, Arthur. Prison has taken a toll on him, but he looks to be the one on our left. He's the most important, but we are taking all three off the plane just to be sure."

"You actually met him at the Bay of Pigs?" said Arthur White in obvious awe of Campa's experience. "Maybe you should do the interview!"

"No! Definitely not! He and I would not get along very well. Remember, you are not to mention my name. He is not to know that I am here. If he learns that I am here, it will jeopardize our plan. Understand?"

"Yes, sir! Agent Costello stressed that point when he briefed me in Washington."

Just as Frank Campa finished speaking, one of the Cubans got up and stretched. He stood in front of the other two and pointed down the corridor toward the rest room area. After some discussion, all three of them were up and walking.

"Go ahead!" whispered Campa. "They're heading for the men's room. Now is your chance. And, keep your distance so no one connects you with the passengers."

"No problem! I'm going to watch from the other side." Arthur started walking away from the group.

With a signal from Campa, the customs officials fell in behind the Cuban passengers as they walked down the corridor. Quickly, the customs officers converged on the Cubans, and, one by one, escorted them to airport security where each man was placed in a separate interview room.

After entering the room holding Raymond Chacon, Arthur carefully scanned his passport.

"Mr. Chacon, do you speak English?"

"I do. But, it has been a long time."

"My name is Arthur White. I'm with the Drug Enforcement Agency of the United States."

"You are American! Why would the Drug Enforcement Agency have any interest in me? I only have the clothes on my back."

"Sir, I am only here because we are short personnel, and I was available to talk with you. Colombian customs and embassy personnel will talk with you later."

"I was told that I was going to Argentina."

"I was told that you would be going straight to the United States. However, it will be several days before you can leave Bogota. It's all red tape. We will place you in a good hotel and provide for your security."

"I appreciate your concern for my safety."

"Here are some immigration forms, Mr. Chacon. Please fill them out so that Colombian and American authorities may begin processing you. In particular, please identify any relatives you might have who are living in the United States. We will try to contact them for you. Also, you will receive a complete physical examination. How old is this photograph on your passport?"

"It was taken today, in Havana. It was all very strange. I don't even remember being photographed when I was arrested or while I was in jail."

"Could you tell me the nature of the charges against you?"

"I'm sorry. I was never formally charged by the Revolutionary Council. They just issued a general order of imprisonment, which is usually a death sentence. Then, for some reason, they commuted my sentence to life without parole. They described it as an act of compassion, say that I had been brainwashed by Batista and the Americans and that I couldn't help myself."

"Commuted? That doesn't sound like a commuted sentence to me."

"I thought much the same. When they told me that my sentence was commuted, I assumed that I would be freed shortly and that I would be going home. So for a few hours I felt like I had been given my life back. I cried with happiness! But, then they moved me back to the Isle of Pines."

"And, you had no lawyer, no representation."

"No! As I said, I didn't have a trial so why would I need a lawyer? Well, all I know is that the firing squad was ready for me when he did it, when he commuted my sentence. It was a last minute change. I had given up all hope of living. I had given up all hope of seeing my children and my wife and my brother."

58

Tree Top Flyers

Mary Jane, Mary Jane,
Please don't leave me baby,
I just found you again.

—Spin Doctors

Barranquilla, Colombia

The airstrip in the dense vegetation near Barranquilla was alive with activity. The Beech had been loaded and fueled, and the crew began to assemble for the flight to Florida.

Frank Campa had a lot on his mind. As he walked toward the aircraft with his backpack, weapons and ammunition, he noticed two men standing near the cargo door engaged in an animated conversation. The American didn't interest him. It was the other man.

"Good morning, gentlemen! Has the pilot arrived?"

"Not yet!" answered Charlie Bill.

"And, you must be Josef Gerona. Am I correct?"

The other man nodded in the affirmative.

"I have heard quite a bit about you, Mr. Gerona. You are so young to have such a big reputation."

"I have been fortunate, Mr. Campa."

"You look very familiar to me. Have we met before?"

"Not that I know of. I have spent considerable time in Central America, so it is possible, I guess."

"You are Cuban, correct?"

"I was born in America so I would say that that makes me an American. But, my family is from Cuba."

"I know of several Geronas in Cuba. They could be relatives of yours."

"My grandparents lived in Havana their whole lives."

"Havana? No, one family makes Santiago their home. The other is from Cienfuegos. Do you know them?"

"Sorry. I rarely get to Cuba, as you might understand. And, all of my surviving family members are in the United States."

"There is just something about you that reminds me of someone. It will come to me. How long should it take them to get here? The pilot and the substitute for Chacon."

"We assumed that it would take them twelve hours," Charlie Bill replied. "I have a contact in Aquachica where they were supposed to stop for food and gas. We received confirmation from them about five hours ago. So, they should be here within the hour."

"Do you know the replacement?" asked Campa nervously. "He's supposed to be regular CIA."

When no reply came to his question, Campa continued.

"Apparently, he's got a lot of experience in Central America. I haven't met him, but my sources say that he's been sick. So, he should be able to pass for a prisoner. But, I hope he's well enough to do his job!"

"I know he's well enough to do his job," said Gerona. "I was the one who recommended him!"

Campa looked carefully at Gerona again.

"So, he's your man! I should have guessed."

"He might have been sick," Gerona replied, "but he's a brutal sort. He doesn't take a lot of shit from anyone. He hates all of these people in the Caribbean and Central America. I never understood why he chose to work this area. But, one thing is for sure, I do believe that he hates me the most. Yet, he's definitely the man for the job. Brutal!"

"The boys in Washington pretty much give you everything you want, don't they, Gerona. I have the reverse problem. They don't trust me!"

Campa decided to change the subject as they waited.

"What's this plane like? And, what about the pilot?"

"No problems there!" said Charlie with some pride. Hernandez is good. You won't feel a bump."

"I just don't feel like jumping today."

As Campa turned to load his equipment, another man approached the plane. He was special agent Steiner. Steiner didn't speak, but nodded to the three men and jumped aboard.

"Is he the guy who's taking Chacon's place?" asked Campa. "He looks like he's been through this before."

"Everyone knows him, and no one knows him," said Charlie.

Steiner was followed in a few seconds by Ron Hernandez.

"What a trip! Next time I'm flying over here. I don't know how many times we were stopped on those nasty dirt roads! If you can call them roads! Using a beat-up car was an excellent idea, otherwise the military or the banditos would have wanted it. Luckily, we looked so poor and so out of it that they let us pass."

Gerona patted the pilot on the back.

"I told you it would work. Never go through some of those areas with a new vehicle unless you're armed to the teeth and ready to fight! Are you rested enough to fly or do you need some sleep?"

"Ah, I'm okay. Steiner actually drove most of the way. I got a few hours sleep in the back seat. He's probably pretty tired, though. And a little irritated. I don't think he likes his role in this thing very much."

"Don't worry about him. He'll get over it. And, as far as some rest for you goes, if you get tired, Charlie can take the controls for an hour or so. You can nap on the plane. Let's get this tin can off the ground!"

With the men and payload aboard, Ron and C.B. began the pre-flight checks. Steiner looked around the inside of the aircraft and muttered some obscenities under his breath.

"This place stinks like shit!" He paused as he surveyed the cargo and then added, "It must be near the end of our fiscal year. We don't even have a full load. What have you been doing over here, smoking all the grass while we were driving through that hell hole?"

No one bothered to answer him.

As Hernandez brought the engines up to speed, he noticed someone running across the field.

"Hey, Charlie! It's that kid from DEA. Open the door."

Once Arthur White was aboard, the plane bumped along the crude runway and groaned as it lifted off the ground into the wind. As soon as it was up over the treetops, Gerona scanned the horizon and breathed as sign of relief.

"At least they got it right this time. Not a single government aircraft up in front of us! A good sign, indeed. Usually, you can count on them to screw these things up. Maybe it's our lucky day!"

The crew watched the ground pull away from the aircraft, and then they settled in for the long flight. Campa spent some time bringing Steiner up to date on the plan. Steiner knew that he was supposed to be the bait, and he had dressed according to plan. Campa looked him over as he sat belted into one of the temporary passenger seats.

"Steiner, at least you have a scruffy beard and don't have a suntan. I'm sure that's why you were chosen. And…you're an old fart too."

Steiner wasn't amused.

"Campa, I've heard about you and your expatriate pals. Twenty years and you haven't accomplished shit. This kid Carlos has been kicking your ass all over Central America. Everyone knows it."

"You just do your job, Steiner. I'll take care of Carlos."

"Big talk from the one who's being gutted. How many of your gigs has he disrupted? I'll bet he has a fix on every one of your operatives in

Central America. I know he knows your people in Venezuela. Hell, even I know all of them. You might think I'm old fashioned, but a little training would go a long way. Remember the Bay of Pigs? Since when do you dig in on the beach and wait for the enemy to engage you? That was sheer stupidity, you must agree."

"I won't argue with history. But don't blame me! I was on a special op, and it went fine. The main force just had bad leadership and bad advice. What can I say? The Americans thought that we could bluff just like in Guatemala. Che wasn't the sharpest knife in the drawer, but he wasn't an idiot either. You and your CIA buddies were the ones who guaranteed the slaughter and led with other people's lives. I think there's some shame in that!"

"Well, it just goes to show that when we want something done, we have to do it ourselves. Your little CORU organization isn't exactly setting Cuba on fire now, is it? And, don't blame it all on this guy Carlos. I was under the impression that he hates Fidel Castro and those lunatics in Havana more than you do. You should team up with him, not exterminate him. But, shit, that would leave me unemployed this week so forget what I just said."

Gerona listened to the combative conversation over the roar of the engines. The two Caribbean veterans were just jabbing at each other searching for a weakness that might be exploited if they met again. Gerona turned to Campa as a sarcastic smile crept over his face and made an observation while he pointed to Steiner.

"He doesn't look much like Carlos' father to me!"

59

Trouble in Paradise

Runnin' on empty, runnin' wild,
Runnin' into the sun,
But, I'm runnin' behind.

—Jackson Browne, *Running on Empty*

Over the Caribbean Sea

The Beech groaned its way northward over the Caribbean Sea toward the Florida Keys with its illicit cargo and cadre of law enforcement officials. Of these men, Felix Steiner was the oldest and most experienced. He was also the most verbose.

His experience led him to more questions than answers. Questions that didn't always make sense, but questions which he often asked anyway just to see what his companions' responses would be. He wouldn't necessarily direct the questions to anyone in particular; he would just complain and mumble and hope to stir up some action.

"Why didn't you boys just wait at the landing site? All of us don't need to be on this plane, do we? We wouldn't have had to endure this noisy, uncomfortable trip."

When no one answered his hypotheticals, he kept going.

"You know what? We could be doing this whole goddamn thing for nothing! That would just about make my day.

"Here we are, flying through nowhere in this piece-of-shit airplane. Didn't we invent jet planes a while back? If these smugglers make so much money, why not use modern planes? What the hell's wrong with those bastards? As dumb as they are, if we can't catch them, how smart does that make us look? Ah, fuck me! I never should have agreed to this mission."

"That would your error, wouldn't it?" whispered Campa with some satisfaction.

Steiner responded by giving Campa the finger.

"Hey, Gerona," said Steiner as he directed his question to Josef, "what do you know about the op?"

"About as much as you do," Josef replied.

"Com'on, cut the shit! Give me some details to work with. I'm flying blind here."

"Carlos doesn't set the landing site before the flight lifts off. We know that he uses several alternate fields in Florida, Texas and Mexico."

"That's good, Gerona! Keep going."

"Our pilot, Mr. Hernandez, has a course and a time. In this case once he reaches the Marathon area, he is signaled from the ground. Only then does he know where and when to land or do an air drop. Because of you, or maybe I should say, because of Raymond Chacon, we are assuming that this will be a landing and then a drive to a safe house. For all I know he may want you to parachute out of this tub into the Everglades. Have you ever wrestled an alligator?"

Ron turned his head away from the conversation to try to keep from laughing. He also wanted to indicate his general disinterest in their discussions. He had no intention of disclosing some of the finer secrets of his trade. His military training had taught him the 'need to know' criteria. He might be helping them try to capture Carlos, but he sure as hell didn't have to disclose his techniques, and he didn't want to endanger all of those other tree-top flyers who used similar stealth techniques to avoid detection. In his judgment he had no legal or moral obligation to give them up. That's what the government agents were paid for.

Gerona looked at the pilot and continued.

"He won't give us the signal codes or signal site location. He tells us that his girlfriend is making the connection, but we don't know who she is or where she is."

The pilot smiled but didn't speak. Steiner thought for a few moments, then tried to contribute.

"Okay, if this guy Carlos is so slippery, what gives you the impression that he will show up at the landing site? Or, at the safe house! And, if he doesn't, what do I do?"

Campa didn't like the tone of Steiner's comments.

"I thought you were briefed on this mission, Steiner. Don't tell me you accepted this without knowing what was coming. If he doesn't show, you wait. If he finds you and has the advantage, just tell him you were in prison with his father and that they made a switch at the airport. You should know all of this stuff!"

"Don't worry about it, Frank," Steiner replied sarcastically. "I was just checking to see if you boys knew what we are supposed to be doing. I'll get the little bastard. I can walk like his father, talk like his father, look like his father. He'll be there! If not, the ground crew will take me to him. I've got enough microchips in these clothes to light up New York City. Just to be sure, I may have to kill everyone who is near his age, height, and build. Don't worry, I'll get him."

The rest of the passengers were quiet for a while. Steiner didn't look like the type who would back off when it came to hardball. Frank Campa sat back in his seat. He mused about the landing possibilities.

"Steiner, what the hell do you need us for. I guess we'll just sit back and watch the master at work!"

"Don't get slimy on me, Francisco! You'll probably get your chance. Try to get there before I kill him!"

The definiteness of Steiner's voice indicated that this conversation was over. About fifteen minutes passed without anything else being said. The passengers settled back for some rest as the Beech plowed northward through the Caribbean air.

The plane reached a set of thunderheads in an otherwise clear sky so the pilot swung around the ominous clouds and dropped his altitude slightly. The ride was getting progressively more bumpy. As the plane began to bump and lurch slightly, Arthur came forward and looked over the control panel.

"The storm must be making the air rough. You've got to have a good stomach to fly one these babies on a regular basis."

"I wish you were correct. Actually, I think we're having a mild problem in the port engine. It's been bumping and grinding for the last ten minutes, and it seems to be getting worse rather than better. Can you swim?"

The pilot looked over his shoulder to see the impact of his words on Arthur's face.

"I can fly better than I can swim, Mr. Hernandez. I'm not kidding! This thing will stay up, won't it?"

Suddenly, there was a loud crash and bang as if something had exploded. The plane buffeted wildly and turned into one of the large cumulus clouds that were hanging nearby. As the plane gyrated and shook, Ron noticed that the controls were spinning randomly.

"Hang on! We're upside down!"

Ron slowly but firmly applied pressure to the stick as the plane rolled over and churned through the clouds. After a few terrifying moments, it came out into the clear sky and stabilized.

Campa caught his breath.

"What in the world was that? Is the plane intact?"

Charlie Bill was busy checking the superstructure and the engines.

"Everything looks okay! We've still got power and two wings. I assume the vertical stabilizer is still with us!"

Ron made a wide sweeping turn with the Beech as he looked up and down for an explanation.

"That was a sonic pop, Charlie. Help me find him. I'll stay near the clouds just in case."

In seconds there was another high-pitched squealing noise followed by a lesser bang and then a low-frequency groan. Ron pointed frantically out of the front of the plane.

"It's...it's a MIG! A Cuban MIG fighter! He just buzzed our ass. Charlie, check out our position. We can't be that close!"

Charlie carefully pulled out the Caribbean map and after a few calculations pointed to a spot fairly far south of Cuba. "He's outside his area. We'd better hide for a while."

"Yeah, let's get in the clouds! He probably isn't crazy enough to try that inside." Slowly the Beech groaned as Ron took her up in altitude and into a cloud formation of unknown depth.

"Let's hope this is big enough to hold us for a few minutes until he gives up."

Charlie almost immediately had bad news.

"It's pretty thin! We're losing our cover!"

As the plane emerged from the other side of the clouds, everyone was scanning the sky for the location of the MIG. Ron didn't want to chance another encounter with the MIG, so he circled the Beech back into the clouds for another minute or so before emerging again.

"I don't see him, Charlie! We have to go on. We're too far out to hang here too long. Keep yourselves strapped in for the duration. I don't know what to expect."

Quickly, the passengers tightened their seat belts. Ron turned to Charlie with a request.

"After a few minutes, Charlie, go back and check the survival gear. If we have to ditch, we want to get out of here as fast as possible!"

"Got it! Let me check our position again, and then I'll get the gear ready."

Ron continued to survey the horizon as they continued. He wondered about the amazing experience they had just endured. *Why did he buzz us and then leave? Did the Cubans call him off? Are there American planes in the area?* His thoughts raced to each extreme, but then he realized that it really didn't matter. There wasn't anything he could do about it!

As the plane roared on, one of the engines started to run rough again. Even Steiner and Campa noticed it. Steiner was particularly worried.

"There it goes again. Something's wrong! Something's definitely wrong with the engine!"

Ron tried to calm him down.

"We're okay, but we may have to stop along the way. I think I know what's wrong."

"Stop where?" yelled Campa in disbelief.

"Don't panic!" said Ron calmly as he looked straight at Steiner and Campa. "We have a half-way strip with service capabilities. We aren't too far from it now. I'm going to turn east and land there. We have a stash of parts and the means to contact Florida and apprise them of our situation. You'll be able to get some sleep. It shouldn't take more than eight hours if I'm right about the problem."

Gerona looked at Ron and spoke with great purpose.

"This better be on the up and up. We're not in the mood for a scam. You're not going to walk if you're leading us into a dead end!"

Campa jumped forward and put his hands on the shoulders of the pilot.

"Hernandez! We've got a deal. Don't screw it up!"

The pilot looked at Campa and then around the cabin.

"Hey, it's your call. We can go on, but don't come down on me if we end up in the Florida Straits in that raft back there. I'm just the pilot on this thing. You make the call and live with it!"

Steiner finally broke his silence.

"Take it down. I hate the water! You're in this with us so be gentle."

The others quietly agreed. Hernandez turned the plane to the east and began a slow descent. After about fifteen minutes everyone could see the shape of an island and after several more minutes the crude outline of a landing strip became visible through the scattered clouds.

Hernandez made the appropriate adjustments to the aircraft, and it settled in for what was hoped would be an uneventful landing.

60

The Stranger

The fates lead the willing man,
They drag the unwilling one.

—Voltaire, *The Ignorant Philosopher*

Lake Ozark, Missouri

Johnny and Juan jumped out of their car and jogged out onto the dock to the spot where Gebinsky's sailboat was docked. It was a thirty-five footer and was unusual only because the Lake of the Ozarks was dominated by power boats. Johnny jumped on the deck with the bag of groceries he was carrying and immediately went below decks to put the food into the ship's refrigerator. Juan looked over the boat with some admiration.

"Johnny, this guy has a sailboat down in Florida, doesn't he?"

Johnny was still battling the food, but he attempted an answer. "Yeah, Gebinsky has at least three boats. He's been making some money from this business."

"What's the other one?"

Johnny finally emerged on deck and pointed down the dock at a powerboat that was tied near the far end. "It's that power boat over there. He a boating freak! And he has a Harley! He must be doing something right."

"Well, things have taken a turn for the worse. Will he be able to keep all this stuff if he goes to jail? The farm, the bike, the boats, and whatever else he has?"

"I have no idea. Do you want to take this baby for a spin. I can sail it. The only problem is the wind. It's pretty calm out there."

As Juan was contemplating the question, he noticed a man walking slowly down the dock toward him. He wasn't too tall, and he looked Hispanic. He was wearing a baseball cap and a light jacket. The man was glancing at the boats, but it seemed to Juan that he was the main object of this pedestrian's attention. Johnny didn't notice the man at first as he turned to Juan.

"Say, I'm going to run down to the power boat and see if she has fuel. Gebinsky said we could use it as long as we replaced the gas we burn. Let me take a look, and we can go out on that one. Johnny stepped onto the dock and began walking out toward the powerboat.

The older man quickened his pace when he saw Johnny walk away. As he approached, his eyes met Juan's. His face somehow seemed familiar.

"How are you, Juan. This is a nice boat."

Juan was surprised. "Could it be…? How did you find me?"

"A mutual friend of ours told me. I think you know him or at least you know of him."

"Who would that be? Is it the man who owns this sailboat?"

"Oh, no! His name is…Carlos."

Juan glanced nervously from side to side. "I don't know anyone named Carlos, do I? You must be mistaken."

"That's okay, Juan. It doesn't matter. I am Carlos' uncle. They call me Oscar. We met briefly a long time ago."

"How did you know who I was?"

"Carlos gave me a photo of you and Johnny. He's the boy who went up to the boat, wasn't he?"

"Yes, he is a good friend of mine."

"Well, it would be better if he didn't know that we talked."

"I have heard many good things about you, Oscar, if you are really Oscar Chacon."

"Have you seen this medallion before?"

Juan's heart jumped when he saw the piece of eight hanging from a chain around the man's neck. "I might have. I'm really not positive. I believe it's a symbol."

"Yes, a symbol of good luck and a symbol of hope for those who are not as fortunate as we are. You probably understand what I mean, but I don't expect an answer."

"I know of the symbol. I have the same medallion. It hangs on the door of my home in Mexico City. It was given to me by a very good friend. Has your medallion brought you luck?"

"Exceedingly so. I have not been locked in a cell on the Isle of Pines! I am here on this glorious day talking to a fine young man like you. A young man who has risked much to help my nephew and my brother. My nephew sends his best although he cannot be here just yet."

"My luck has not been as good."

"Don't look down so hard on your fate. You will find that the gods will favor you in the future. I can tell just by looking at you that you are a fine and true lad. And the day of your redemption is at hand."

"You sound so serious. What is it that you require of me?"

"I do need a favor, Juan. I am the brother of the man who sat in the cell on the Isle of Pines." As the man spoke those words, he pulled a package out of a bag he was carrying and handed it to the boy.

"Please put this on that power boat over there. Just stick it in the refrigerator. Try not to let your friend see you. If he does, just tell him it's something for Mr. Gebinsky."

"I can do that. Is there anything else you require?"

"Yes, here is my phone number and a list of instructions from Carlos. Please read this, save the phone number and destroy the message. It is important to Carlos that you follow these instructions to the letter. I must leave now. It has been a pleasure to talk with you, Juan. Now I know why Carlos holds you in such high esteem."

With that, the man turned and walked away. Juan watched him as he disappeared off the dock. He glanced at the package. It was about the size of a half loaf of bread. He put the package under his arm and started walking toward the powerboat.

61

Spare Parts

Give me your tired, your poor,
Your huddled masses, yearning to breathe free,
The wretched refuse of your teeming shore,
Send these, the homeless, tempest-tossed to me:
I lift my lamp beside the golden door.

—Emma Lazarus

A small island near Cuba

The Beech landed without incident and taxied to the end of the simple dirt runway. This landing strip was much shorter and narrower than the one near Barranquilla. The passengers could see several small shacks along the left side of the strip and the essential elements of a hangar built into the tree line on the right. The field was dry, and the pilot didn't hesitate to pull the aircraft into the hangar area.

Campa and Steiner hit the ground with their weapons drawn.

"Get those engines shut off," yelled Campa over the noise. "Steiner, you check the field. I'm going around the back."

Josef Gerona stepped out of the plane, but did not draw his weapon.

"Gentlemen! This field is already secure. Search, if it makes you feel better, but don't shoot at anyone!"

Steiner surveyed the field and turned back to Gerona.

"What happens next, agent Gerona?"

"Mr. Hernandez tells me that help will be coming. He is going to assess the damage and determine what hardware he needs to repair the plane. Then we leave."

Campa returned to the hangar and approached Gerona cautiously. He had his revolver in his hand.

"I've been all over Cuba and you haven't. How is it that you know so much about this island and I was unaware of its existence?"

"That's easy to explain. I have been here before. When one infiltrates a cartel, one learns many of its secrets. This is a freelance operation. The Cubans look the other way. The cartels pay the operators of this field. The operators pay the militia. Everyone is happy!"

"Where are these operators?" asked Steiner.

"They will be here within the hour. Allow the pilot to deal with them. They might get nervous if they don't recognize you. Understand?"

Meanwhile, Hernandez pulled a small ladder out of the cargo area. After waiting a few minutes for the engines to cool down, he climbed onto the wing to check the fuel lines. Gerona offered his assistance, but the pilot indicated that it wasn't necessary.

"I think we've got what we need, gentlemen. When our friends get here, we can retrieve the hardware, replace this fuel line and be on our way."

Gerona turned when he heard the sound of a motor vehicle. He could see a Jeep approaching along a trail, which paralleled the landing field.

"Here comes the cavalry!" shouted Hernandez as he jumped down off the ladder and watched the vehicle make its way over the bumpy road. There were two men in the Jeep. One of them waived at the group as the vehicle approached causing Steiner and Campa to relax considerably. Both holstered their weapons.

The men jumped out of the jeep after pulling to a stop near the tree line. They both approached the pilot with a familiarity, which indicated that they knew him and were glad to see him on their island. After shaking hands and exchanging some greetings, Ron turned and introduced the two men to his passengers as "my Cuban friends".

The three men made a cursory inspection of the Beech. After several minutes of discussion and inspection, they seemed to agree on just what repairs would be necessary. As they were still working on the plane, Ron came over to his passengers and described the situation.

"I'll have to get some parts. Several of you should remain here and guard the plane. We have never had any problems, but since this is our way home, don't take any chances. We have to travel to a nearby island and these two guys won't be going with me. One of you will have to come along. I'm not armed, and it's best to have some protection. Besides, I'll need some help removing what we need from the other plane."

"You mean these are used parts?" mumbled Steiner in disgust. "How do you know they'll work?"

Hernandez explained the situation calmly.

"We have another Beech on the next island. We rotate these two planes. We could take the other one, but then we'd have to move the cargo, too. It's easier to make this repair. We'll have to bring some equipment along, too, so it will take a while. Don't worry! This will cost us some bucks, but my credit is good here so that's a bridge we'll have to cross later."

"If you can't repair this one, can we fly the other one out?" asked Campa anxiously.

"Yes, but we'd have to do the same thing. Take parts from this one and run them over there. I don't recall what the problem is with the other aircraft. I'll find out, and we can make the switch if this repair can't be made."

"How's our security here?" asked Steiner of Hernandez as he glanced around the field. "Are we in Cuban waters? Do we need to set up a perimeter?"

"Relax! You'll be able to stay in that hut over there. The boys will bring some food and bedding for you. It now looks like twelve to eighteen hours before we'll get back. Do I have a volunteer for this trip? Don't be bashful!"

Arthur, who had been absolutely silent up to this point, jumped forward immediately; however, Ron waived his hand negatively.

"You don't look Spanish, Arthur, and I'll bet you don't speak it either. I could use someone who looks the part." He pointed to Josef. "How about you, Gerona?"

"I'll go with you," replied Gerona who then turned to Arthur. "You might get your chance later. If we need some help, I'll send someone for you. In the meantime help Frank protect the plane. We need it to get this job done."

"What about the delay?" asked Campa. "The entire timing of this operation is screwed up now!"

Ron pointed to a radio tower that stuck out of the trees at the end of the runway. "This happens all the time. Our delay will be signaled to Marathon as soon as I get to the transmitter. We'll signal again when we leave, and everything will be on schedule. There are many things on this island that you cannot see. Carlos is one of the investors in this island. So, it shouldn't come as a surprise to learn that he probably already knows we'll be late."

Campa frowned. "You are enjoying this problem too much for my liking, Mr. Hernandez. "Remember, I wouldn't hesitate to waste you if I thought you were running a game on me."

"I confess that I am enjoying this, very much, Mr. Campa," Ron replied with the trace of a grin on his face. "I love the look of amazement on your face when you realize how organized we are."

Arthur walked up to the group after watching the men inspect the plane.

"Hey, those guys are wearing the same jewelry around their necks that you have, Mr. Hernandez."

Ron glanced over toward the plane and then looked at Arthur.

"Oh, this piece of eight. It's a good luck charm. You'll see a lot of them around here. I got mine from Carlos' father a long time ago."

Ron turned quickly toward Steiner and pointed to emphasize his point.

"If you were really his father, you would have known that!"

Steiner backed up a half-step and acknowledged the new information.

"Shouldn't I be wearing one of those?", he said when the symbolism of the medallion began to sink in.

"Steiner, I'm taking care of you, don't worry. I'll give you mine when we reach the States. I need it just now and Josef needs his."

"Do you have one, too?", Steiner asked of Josef with some surprise.

"I've had this medallion for quite a while. I got mine in Colombia from a friend of mine. Unfortunately, he is no longer with us."

"It's strange that I've never seen this before," said Campa as he inspected Ron's medallion. And, I've been all over the Caribbean for twenty-five years. It must be a small club that believes that this brings luck. It didn't do much for the Cubans or the Spanish, did it!"

"It's usually given as a gift. It is passed from father to son, or from mother to daughter. Raymond Chacon saved my life a long time ago. I treasure this medallion. It has a lot of meaning for me."

"And Josef, how did he get his?" muttered Campa suspiciously.

"I don't know. Why don't you ask him?"

Campa turned to talk to Gerona, but found that he was already on his way to the Jeep. It was a question he would have to remember to ask on the flight back to the U.S.

As the pilot walked toward the Jeep, he turned and tendered some advice.

"Stay out of sight. We don't want anyone spotting us from the air. Cover the plane with underbrush and make yourself at home. You'll get some food and supplies within the hour. If you're hungry, use some of the rations on the plane. We'll replace them before we leave.

"And, most important, don't get trigger-happy when those lads come with the food. If you shoot any of them, they will just get irritated, and you won't get anything to eat!"

62

Treasure Island

> *It is by will alone*
> *I set my mind in motion.*
> *It is by the juice of Safu*
> *that thoughts acquire speed.*
> *The lips acquire stains.*
> *The stains become a warning.*
> *It is by will alone*
> *I set my mind in motion.*

> —**Frank Herbert,** *Dune*

Cuba

The small plane had landed on the island of Nueva Gerona. The prisoner now began to sense that his freedom was not as far from realization as he had thought earlier. When he stepped from the Cessna, the pilot and his guide did not get out. His guide pointed to a small building near the end of the runway and waived as the plane turned and made its way into position for a takeoff. Raymond's mind raced with memories and questions. *Why have they left me here alone? Am I exiled here? Is this my new prison?*

As he staggered toward the building, he could see a man leaving the front door and walking straight for him. Something deep in his memory remembered that walk. It was so familiar even after all of these years of isolation. It was the walk of a friend.

Alberto!

Raymond's eyes strained to see the details of the man's face in the darkness. Then the man opened his arms as he approached and threw them around Raymond. Even without words there was no question. *It was Alberto!*

The two men embraced as tears were pouring out of Alberto's eyes.

"Amigo! It's been so long! My soul has been locked with you in that cell. I cannot forgive myself for leaving you behind."

Alberto's heart sunk as he held the weakened body of the man he hadn't seen in twenty years.

"My brother! You did not leave me behind. You executed my orders as I would have executed yours. My memories of my family and my wonderful friends such as you have kept me alive these many years. I knew deep down inside that I would not die a prisoner. And now, my heart leaps for joy that you are here, and I am free. We have much time to make up for, my friend!"

Alberto held Raymond's shoulders at arms length and looked at him. Tears were still running down his face as he pointed toward the building.

"I have more good news for you. I can only thank God that I can be here to witness this moment. Come with me."

Alberto grabbed Raymond's hand and led him toward the building. Raymond stumbled several times, and Alberto stopped to hold him up. The malnutrition that had been imposed on him for so many years had weakened a once proud and strong man, and the excitement of this day was almost too much for Raymond to bear.

"Rest for a moment, Raymond."

As the two men stood before the building, first one, then a second figure emerged from the building. In the darkness Raymond was still able to see their long hair and slight bodies. They were both females, and when the younger one cried out, he knew his dreams had been fulfilled. His daughter rushed forward and the enthusiasm of her greeting caused both Raymond and Alicia to fall to the ground. She kissed and hugged her father only the way a daughter could. As he was lying on the ground, Raymond could see Ana's face as she knelt down by him.

"The years have been kind to you, Ana, my darling." Raymond reached up slowly and touched her face. It was moist with the tears of joy.

"Do you cry for me, too, my love? I always knew that I would see my beautiful daughter and my lovely wife again. Forgive my weakness, but the food in Havana is nothing to brag about. I much prefer your home cooking."

"Raymond, we are so happy to see and hold you again. I was so wrong to leave you. I was young and..." Raymond interrupted her by placing his hand over her mouth.

"My darling, we will more than make up for the lost time. This moment is worth a hundred lifetimes without you. The promise of your smile kept me alive these many terrible years."

Alberto leaned over and helped Raymond and his daughter to their feet.

"My friends, it is a joyous moment, but we have much to do and little time. Another plane is arriving soon. And we should look through the cargo and choose what we will take and what we will leave behind."

Raymond looked at Alberto with the question written all over his face. He was almost too weak to speak. Alberto touched his arm and pointed to the building. "Batista's containers. They are in here!"

Raymond tried to collect his thoughts. "How?"

"Rest, my friend. When we heard that you would be freed, we came back and went to the church. Fernando and Rene helped along with Chico and Ernesto. Do you remember the boys?"

"Were they the boys who jumped out of the raft?"

"Yes! Oscar managed to get them out shortly after you were captured. Their uncle was the one who caused you to be arrested. Oscar brought them to Miami and took care of them. You will meet them again soon."

"I'm glad they are okay. I know their uncle. He was on the plane that brought me here."

"Oscar has told me that he has tried, without success, these many years to obtain your release. He even petitioned Fidel Castro for your release, but his pleas were not heard. He was devastated when he learned of the mistake he had made."

"It was a mistake, Alberto. The man has shown great courage to tell me. His brother was killed by Frank Campa so I can imagine his grief and sorrow. The boys were so young that they probably couldn't explain what happened clearly to their uncle. It's all in the past. We must forget these lost years and live for the future. Tell me about the containers."

"I will soon enough, Raymond. But first I must speak about Frank Campa. He is currently on another island just a short distance from here. Your son Carlos has a little surprise waiting for Mr. Campa. With any luck, he will pay for what he has done to you and the others."

"As much as I could hate the man, I am too overjoyed to think of revenge. He will get what the fates have in store for him."

"Our little adventure to retrieve the containers turned into a harrowing experience. We were trapped on shore for almost a week, but with some luck we were able to get all of the containers here without being detected. The old church was still there the way we left it although it was overgrown many times over. It took us several trips but we eventually got them over here without being detected.

"The Cubans do not know what we have here. But your son and your brother have made a deal with them so that they will leave us alone on this island until our transport comes. I didn't feel right opening the containers without you being present so we left them sealed just as they were when Batista sent us to the chemical complex.

"But we must leave tonight. Ernesto and Chico are bringing a plane to take us to the Cayman Islands. We must look through the containers and take what is of value and leave or destroy the rest."

Slowly the group made its way through the front of the building and back out the rear door. Alberto grabbed several flashlights and they walked about fifty meters through some thick brush to an area that held several temporary sheds. There, to Raymond's amazement, sat eight large containers. He remembered that day at the church as if it were yesterday.

Alberto quickly opened the first and then the second and so on until they were all accessible. He glanced inside each one as he opened it, and when he reached the fourth container, he stopped and pointed inside. "I suggest you start here, Raymond."

Raymond stumbled over to the container and slowly grasped the top package. It was heavy and the wrapping had survived the many years in good shape. Alberto reached to his belt and pulled out a rather large knife. "Let me cut that for you."

With a slash the covering gave way and slowly the contents poured onto the ground. Each person watched in wonder as the contents fell almost as if in slow motion. The light of the flashlights reflected off of the multiple surfaces as the objects fell to the ground and cast an almost heavenly glow over the group.

Gold Coins!

63

The Patron Returns

All that glitters is not gold,
Often have you heard that told;
Many a man his life hath sold,
But my outside to behold;
Gilded tombs do worms infold.
Had you been as wise as bold,
Young in limbs, in judgment old,
Your answer had not been inscroll'd;
Fare you well; your suit is cold.

—**William Shakespeare,**
The Merchant of Venice

Horseshoe Bend, Lake Ozark, Missouri

The attorney had just finished cleaning off the third-floor deck at his condominium when he decided it was a good time to go to the hardware store for some wood sealer. The deck was exposed to the late afternoon sun because it was on the western side of the building, and it had been some time since he had done any meaningful maintenance.

At the same time he thought about stopping at the real estate broker's office to check on rental prospects for the coming season. The Lake Realty Company had always done a good job for him. It was also a good excuse to drop in on an acquaintance of his. Shirley Barnes always carried on an interesting conversation, and he might be able to talk her into a drink after work.

When he arrived at the office building, which housed Lake Realty, he climbed the stairs to the third floor and walked into the main reception area, which featured a spectacular view of the Lake. He had always thought that his view from the condo deck was good, but this view defied description. After he entered the reception area he asked the receptionist to page Shirley.

"I'm sorry. Shirley is in court today. She's had a couple of speeding tickets lately, and they wouldn't let her out of it. She was certainly upset when she left here this morning."

"Did she go to Camdenton? Maybe I ought to go down there and see if I can give her some moral support."

"That's right, I forgot! You're an attorney from St. Louis. I would think that she'd appreciate any help you could give her. And, by the way, she left a message for you in case you arrived while she was out. Actually, it's a message from someone else. Here, let me get the envelope for you. The man was here yesterday and asked Shirley to give this to you."

As the receptionist passed the brown envelope to Jim, he couldn't help but wonder who would have left him a message here at the Lake. Charlie Bill was a possibility because he knew about the realtor. It must be Charlie!

Jim opened the envelope and inside found a note from Shirley and another note from someone named Oscar. *Oscar! Was that the guy who gave me the cash at O'Learys?*

Jim quickly read the note from Shirley. She described the man in some detail. It sure wasn't Charlie, and it did sound a lot like the bar patron. With a P.S. Shirley noted that she would be at happy hour down at the Four Season's Lodge by five o'clock if she wasn't in jail. It was clearly an invitation he had been looking for.

Next, he carefully read the other message. The writer didn't identify himself except to say that he hoped Jim was getting better as a bartender. *It was Oscar for sure*! He wanted a meeting with Jim, the sooner the better. He was staying at the Arrowhead Lodge on Business 54, which was only a short distance down the road.

Jim scribbled a short note for Shirley and thanked the receptionist. His first encounter with this man had been very rewarding. He wondered whether the second meeting would be as fruitful.

After arriving at the Lodge, Jim went to the check-in counter and asked to call Oscar's room.

"Sir, I believe that you will find Mr. Chacon over there by the fireplace."

"Did you say his last name was Chacon?"

The man behind the desk double-checked his listing. "Yes, sir."

The name Chacon immediately conjured up questions in Jim's mind. There was Raymond Chacon, the prisoner in Cuba. He had also heard the name Carlos Chacon, the invisible smuggler from Colombia. Then there was Oscar Chacon, the kind benefactor. As he walked to the fireplace his eyes focussed on the gray-haired man who was reading the local newspaper. It was the man he had met at O'Learys.

"Oscar, it's a pleasure to see you again. I'm trying my best to earn the generous fee you have advanced to me."

Oscar was obviously pleased to see the attorney. He stood and shook hands with Jim and asked him to sit down. They were seated to one side of the large fireplace which graced the lobby of the motel and between the crackling of the fire and the television set which droned on in the far corner, they were able to converse in some privacy.

"Were you able to find the place where they are holding the witness?" asked Oscar.

"Yes. I followed Gebinsky when he picked up his Harley. I didn't actually see Juan, but it doesn't look like he's being held prisoner. They're moving around too freely for that to be the case."

"Excellent! We are almost done with this matter. There are just two things I would like you to do for Ron. The first one is to give me a map so that I can locate the place where Juan is being kept. I'll be responsible for Juan and the other boy who is with him. No harm will come to them."

"Here, I can show you how to get there on this map. Be careful because the last road is a narrow county spur, and it will be easy for them to see you approaching." Jim picked up a map from a local advertising stand and traced out the path to the farm.

"Don't worry. Gebinsky and Michaels won't be there when I go to see them. That's where you come in."

"Do you want me to call them? We can find the number."

"No, they will come to you. Or, you will come to them. They'll be meeting a CIA agent at Captain Hook's Restaurant this afternoon between three and four. If I hadn't been able to reach you, I would've had to go instead and that would have made the conclusion of all of this difficult to achieve."

"What do you want me to do?"

"Just go over about three-thirty and sit down with them. Try to get them to release Juan to you voluntarily. It just might work. If it doesn't, just engage them in conversation until the CIA agent shows up. He'll identify himself. If they won't give you Juan, just drag the witness tampering and kidnapping past them. Argue with them as long as you can and then you can leave. Don't endanger yourself. There will be someone in the restaurant watching out for you the whole time. Nothing bad will happen. Just be relaxed and play lawyer to the hilt. If they want to talk a lot, let them go. The longer you keep them all busy, the easier it will be for us."

"If you don't mind, who is us?"

"That will become clearer with time. Just be relaxed and argue your best. If they give up Juan voluntarily, it will be the best for all concerned. If you fail to gain his release, it will be their loss."

64

Island Girl

I saw society cut into two:
Those who possessed nothing,
united in common greed;
Those who possessed something,
in a common fear.

—Alexis de Tocqueville

A small island near Cuba

"What time is it, kid?" Steiner was up and crouched near the door of the hut in which the three men were sleeping.

Arthur rolled over and groaned.

"Don't you have a watch? Let's see…it's 6:20. That's Florida time."

Steiner looked down at the sleepy novice curled up with his small stack of hay.

"I do have a watch, dummy. Fidel Castro gave me one on the way out so I could remember how long I'd been in the slammer!"

With that Arthur slowly sat up and looked around.

"Is anything wrong?"

"With the exception of the fact that we are on some godforsaken island somewhere in the goddamn Caribbean with an airplane that won't fly and a pilot we can't trust and…" Steiner was pacing up and back as he surveyed his environment.

419

"And that this island probably is much too close to mainland Cuba. And that we are guarding a plane loaded with fucking contraband Mary Jane and Quaaludes. Oh, and that the three of us are alone. The only guy who knows anything about this is Gerona, and he's running around out there looking for engine parts or so we're supposed to believe. Other than that, it's a goddamn paradise!"

The conversation had awakened Frank Campa. He listened to Steiner because he had some of the same misgivings.

"Something strange is going on here. We haven't seen Gerona or Hernandez for much too long. I smell a trap! And, I'm beginning to feel like the bait. A little voice is telling me to get the fuck out of here and fast! Airplane parts or no airplane parts!"

Arthur was slowly waking up, and he didn't like what he heard from the two older agents.

"How would we get out of here? I can't swim that far!"

Steiner seemed to be trying to remember his Caribbean geography as he drew a crude map in the sandy soil just outside the hut.

"We must be somewhere just south of Cuba. I'll have to get the maps out of the plane. If we head east from this island we could hit Jamaica or the Hispanola. The rafts and food are still in the plane. We also have the portable transmitter. Once we get far enough out to sea we can run up the S.O.S.

"But if everything is okay, and Gerona gets back here and we're gone, we will have a lot of explaining to do. They will rag our asses all the way back to Washington. I guess the best thing for us to do is to guard this goddamn plane, but at a safe distance. Campa, you and I can take up a position fifty yards each side of this hut. Arthur can check out whoever shows up before we commit ourselves."

Arthur looked confused. "But, Mr. Steiner, what will I tell them when they get here?"

"If it's anyone except Gerona or the pilot, just tell them we left yesterday. We'll take the survival gear out of the plane and stash it in the jungle. You're going to have to trust us to get you out if the wrong people show up. Whatever happens, just act like you're supposed to be here and don't give up our positions. You've got to trust us!"

"Well, if worse comes to worse," said Arthur, "I can swim. I spent two years on the college team, mostly freestyle relays. We weren't that good. Anyway, salt water makes things easier, doesn't it?"

After giving Arthur a reproachful look, Steiner set out with Campa to scout the positions they would use and also to find a place to locate the survival gear. Arthur went back to his makeshift bed.

"I'm going back to sleep for a while. Let me know when you find a place for the raft and supplies. I'll help you move the stuff."

As Steiner stepped out of the hut and looked across the field, he froze in position. It was just before the sun began to light up the sky as he noticed a single figure walking straight across the field toward the hut. He quietly warned the others, and they quickly drew their weapons and remained motionless.

As the figure approached within about twenty-five yards, Campa whispered to the others.

"It's a woman! It looks like she is alone."

"Mr. Campa? Are you there?" The voice was definitely female and probably Spanish.

"Please raise your hands in the air. Who are you?"

The woman slowly raised her hands.

"Mr. Gerona asked me to come. He needs some help. He wants me to bring the boy, Arthur. The machinery is heavy. Gerona needs help to carry the equipment."

"How far from here? How far is the...machinery?" Campa kept is voice low.

"It is five kilometers to the sea, then we must take the boat across the bay, another three kilometers. Gerona asked me to give you this paper."

The girl handed Campa a small piece of paper, a page torn from the notebook Josef carried with him. The message contained good news.

The needed parts had been removed from the other plane. Josef wanted Arthur to accompany the girl.

"Maybe we should all go with you." Steiner's words hung in the air as he waited for a response.

"No, we can't!" Campa replied.

Campa knew that he had little choice in this situation. And, he knew that he needed to stay with the survival gear just in case something went wrong.

"The plane must be kept intact! How long…how long before you return?" Campa waived the note in the air. Steiner took it out of his hand and read the balance of the message.

"By an hour after sundown." The woman spoke with an air of confidence.

Steiner seemed convinced.

"We just have to lay low until sundown. He's estimating two hours for the repairs and takeoff at dawn. I can live with that. Kid, get your ass out of bed and follow this young lady. Try not to show her what lousy shape you're in. Okay?"

Arthur nodded as he scrambled to get dressed. He was happy to go. More adventure ahead. Sitting around in this hut with these two old farts for another day wouldn't be fun. Their paranoia was starting to get to him.

"What's your name, young lady." Campa smiled at the woman as Arthur got ready.

"Maria. You may call me Maria. We must hurry. Mr. Gerona is very anxious to move the machinery to this place."

Arthur was soon fully dressed and ready to go. He was already eating some of the rations from the plane as he walked out of the hut and began moving across the field with Maria.

"I feel better now," said Steiner to Campa. "This should be over soon."

Campa watched the two people until they were out of sight. As he sat on the ground, he seemed to be deep in thought.

"You know, Steiner, I could swear that I've seen that woman before. Her hair is somehow different and she's dressed differently, but I could swear that I've talked with her before. I just can't place her. Where was it? What were we doing?"

"She didn't seem to know you from the way she acted. Quite a few women are named Maria in this part of the world, and she might just resemble someone you knew."

"I don't know. I'll have to ask her more about where she's been and what she does the next time I see her."

65

Confrontation

*A public force being necessary
to give security to the rights of
men and of citizens, that force
is instituted for the benefit of
the community, and not for the
particular benefit of the persons
with whom it is entrusted.*

**—National Assembly of France,
*Declaration of the Rights of Man and of Citizens***

Lake Ozark, Missouri

"Harry, get me a gin and tonic. I'm going to phone Johnny and tell him where we are."

"Ed, tell the little bastards to stay put. They looked a little restless this morning. I don't want them wandering around. Tell them that we'll bring back some wine and cheese. They'll like that."

Gebinsky turned and walked away toward the public telephone as the bartender came up to Harry for the order.

"How about a gin and tonic and a rum and coke."

"You've got it. Anything to munch on?"

"That sounds good. What do you have?"

"We've got a happy hour spread around the corner and the chicken wings are good."

"Okay, let me have an order of wings and make them hot."

"No problem. My name's Nino if you need anything."

Harry waited for the drinks and took them over to a booth that had a nice view of the Lake. Captain Hook's was relatively empty at three-thirty in the afternoon. Most of the locals arrived for happy hour between four-thirty and five.

Gebinsky picked up the phone and dialed the farm. He let the phone ring about ten times before hanging up. *The little fuckers are already out somewhere*, Gebinsky thought. *Let's hope that they've just gone fishing!*

Next Gebinsky dialed a long distance number and waited for an answer.

"Hello. This is Edward Gebinsky. I'm calling from Missouri. Could you get Mr. Frank Campa for me?"

There was a pause before the answering party responded.

"Would you hold the line for a few seconds. I don't believe Mr. Campa will be in this afternoon. I'll connect you with Mr. Hansen. He might be able to assist you."

The telephone line buzzed as the connection was attempted.

"I'm sorry, sir. Mr. Hansen doesn't seem to be available either. May I leave a message for either of them?"

"Have you seen Mr. Campa today? Is he in Washington?"

"I'm not certain, sir. I just arrived, and I haven't seen him yet this afternoon. Only Mr. Hansen would know where he is. I will make sure that he gets your message as soon as he comes in."

"Yes, please tell him that Edward Gebinsky called from Missouri. Tell Mr. Campa that I'll call back again tomorrow morning."

Gebinsky hung up the phone, and after visiting the men's room he returned to the booth and Harry Michaels.

"No luck, Harry. No answer at the farm! Then, I tried to get Frank Campa. I got the usual runaround. Couldn't tell whether he has returned, but it doesn't sound like it. From the song and dance I got I'll bet he's still in Colombia."

"Or floating around in the middle of the Caribbean on a raft surrounded by sharks!" said Michaels. "Hey, when are we going to take your boat for a ride. That thing's been in dry dock for over a week, hasn't it?"

"It's ready now. I put it in storage last fall and shit happens when you're not paying attention. We can take it out for a spin, but first I want Johnny to shake it down for me. He has a lot of experience with bigger boats."

"Juan is working on your bike and Johnny is working on your boat. Do you do anything yourself?"

"You should talk, asshole! I'm having a pretty good day, so far, so don't try to piss me off just for fun, okay?"

As they talked, Nino appeared with a plate full of chicken wings and some napkins. He noticed that the two men were looking out over the water.

"Pretty nice day for a little boating. This weekend there will be so many boats on the Lake that you should be able to walk from one side to the other without touching the water. If you want anything else, just yell."

Once again the sparkling waters of the Lake of the Ozarks drew the attention of both men. Power boats zigged and zagged randomly before them like little bugs on a warm spring day.

As Michaels and Gebinsky watched the activity on the Lake, the restaurant slowly began to fill up. What they didn't notice was the attorney who quietly took a place at the bar. He ordered a drink as he watched Gebinsky and Michaels converse. After several minutes, he got up from the bar and walked over to the telephone where he dialed a local number.

"Hello, Charlene. I'm at Captain Hook's. They're here!"

Jim listened for several moments and then hung up the phone. As he walked back to the bar, he motioned to Nino that he was going to join the men in the booth. He picked up his drink and walked toward Michaels and Gebinsky. He began speaking before they saw him approaching.

"Well, look who the cat dragged in. It's not every day that I get to see two out of the top ten from the most wanted list."

Michaels turned and did a double take. Gebinsky looked up at the attorney and tried to keep from appearing surprised.

"You're on dangerous ground, aren't you?" said Gebinsky. "Witness tampering is a serious crime especially with Washington."

The attorney chuckled and sat down without waiting to be invited.

"Kidnapping and witness tampering are even more serious! If you don't tell on me, I won't tell on you."

Gebinsky and Michaels exchanged glances before Michaels responded. They didn't see the humor in the situation.

"What do you want from us? Gebinsky here can identify your client as the pilot, and I'm the one who set up the deal. There's not much you can do about that!"

"Harry, you surprise me. Why right now I could be over at the farm with a few U.S. Marshals asking Juan how he got there. But, that would be too easy. Besides, there are more players in this game than you can count on your fingers and toes."

"Gebinsky, let's get out of here. This turkey isn't making any sense at all."

Hall stood up and reached for his wallet to pay the bill. Jim raised his hand gently and asked him to sit down.

"Harry, you may want to hear me out on this one."

Hall looked at Gebinsky and then sat down again. He reluctantly put his wallet back in his pocket.

"We have a private meeting, right here, in a few minutes with our own Federal Marshal or Agent, whatever he is. If he finds you here talking to us, he's probably going to arrest you."

"I take that chance, Harry. I'd like to talk to him about Juan anyway. When is he supposed to get here?"

"What time is it?" Michaels looked at Gebinsky for assistance. "I left my watch at the house."

Gebinsky glanced at his watch and responded. "Three-thirty five. He should be here."

"Well, boys, he's right on cue. Is that him walking in the front door?" Jim pointed to the door at a well-dressed man who was looking at the people seated at the bar searching for a friendly face.

Harry stood up and waived to the man.

"Over here, Dubinski. We've got company!"

The agent recognized Michaels and walked quickly over to the booth. He was carrying a briefcase in his left hand.

"Who's this guy, Harry?" The agent was staring at the attorney and seemed highly agitated.

"He's Hernandez's attorney. He seems to have lost a witness somewhere, and he seems to think that we have the boy."

Jim met the agent's stare with confident logic.

"Yes, and I know where he's being kept. So why don't you help your pals here stay out of jail and go with me to get him? We can pick him up, and I won't say a word about the whole incident. All I want is his testimony. Remember, he's not testifying against any of you, so why should you care about him?"

The agent was still standing at the table. He picked up his briefcase, opened it and withdrew a folded copy of the New York Times. He looked at the attorney with a fury in his eyes as he slammed the paper onto the table.

"Your clients are in trouble! You're in trouble! My advice to you is that you leave immediately before I…" The agent hesitated and unfolded the paper.

It was with some surprise that the three men at the table read the headline on the front page. No one spoke while they digested the information. The attorney looked up at the agent and pointed to a chair that was standing unoccupied near the booth.

"Sit down, Dubinski! This could complicate things a bit for all of us!"

66

San Juan Hill

*You can't take on an operation of this scope,
draw boundaries of policy around them,
and be absolutely sure that those boundaries
will not be overstepped.*

—**Richard Bissell, Central Intelligence Agency**

An island near Cuba

As the sun set over the western perimeter of the field, Agent Steiner kept his vigil from a strategic point about forty yards from the Beech. With the exception of the receipt of food supplies and the landing of another drug-laden plane, the day had been quiet. Early in the morning the two Cubans in the Jeep had returned with food and drinking water for the agents.

With the onset of darkness, Steiner was the first to detect the muffled roar of an automotive engine. Soon Campa heard it also, and they both focussed their attention on the far edge of the jungle. Soon both could see the outline of a Jeep and then a small truck.

As the Jeep approached the spot where the Beech was parked, Steiner recognized the presence of the Cuban woman who had visited them in the morning. Quickly, she beeped the horn on the Jeep several times. Steiner could see Campa walking out of the jungle and making his way down to the plane. Something made Steiner hesitate as he watched Maria and Campa talk.

"Mr. Campa, we are ready to leave. Mr. Gerona has decided along with Mr. Hernandez to take the other plane. I have brought several men with me to move the payload from this plane to the other. Would you get Mr. Steiner, and we will get going immediately."

"Will we be able to leave tonight?" Campa seemed very anxious to leave the island.

"Yes, but we must hurry. We have heard that there are Cuban Militia in the area."

Campa signaled, and in a moment Steiner could be seen emerging from the underbrush. As he approached, he noticed that Campa was visibly upset and seemed to be arguing with Maria.

"What do you mean you can't trust us! Our very lives are in your hands. What will blindfolding us accomplish? The other passengers weren't blindfolded when he left here."

"Mr. Campa, we know exactly who you are. We cannot allow agents of any country to know how we run our business. There are no exceptions! Mr. Gerona, Mr. Hernandez, and Mr. White were all blindfolded before they left the field. Please understand that your life depends upon you not knowing exactly where you are."

Steiner did not speak, but he slowly holstered his weapon as if to accept the requirement.

Campa stepped closer to the woman to continue his argument. Suddenly, he grabbed her around the throat and pulled out his .45 in one quick motion.

"No one is blindfolding or disarming me, honey!"

Everyone else froze, including the three workers who had accompanied the woman in the Jeep.

"Now, we're going to drive over to see Hernandez, you and me, by ourselves. Everyone else is going to stay here. Mr. Steiner will entertain your friends while we are gone. I'm going to get some answers, and they better be the right ones."

Campa looked over at Steiner as the latter drew his pistol and trained it upon the men in the Jeep.

Campa tightened his grip on the woman and began pushing her toward the vehicle. As he waived with his right hand for the men on the Jeep to lie down on the ground, it happened. In a flash Campa felt a sharp elbow punch into his stomach. The quickness of the blow caused him to bend over as the air came rushing out of his lungs. With a quick spin, the woman had taken the gun from his hand.

Before Steiner could react, she took a position behind Campa and trained the weapon on Steiner.

"You have three seconds to drop the weapon, otherwise I will kill you!"

Lacking a clear shot, Steiner hesitated, but then let his revolver drop to the ground. The woman motioned to the three men to take charge of Steiner and Campa, who was lying on the ground in the fetal position, gasping for air.

"Gentlemen, I hope that you will forgive my insistence upon your cooperation. It is my job to provide security for our visitors, whether they want that security or not!"

Soon both men were blindfolded and disarmed. They were helped into the vehicle and the convoy turned and entered the jungle.

After about ten minutes of bumping and swerving along the dirt road, which wound up and down over the steep hills of the island, the convoy arrived at another airstrip. This one was considerably smaller, and a single-engine plane was waiting. Maria helped both men from the truck and guided them to the door of the aircraft.

As the plane lifted into the air, Maria reached up and loosened the blindfolds on both agents. Through the darkness they could now see the aircraft lift up into the sky. Campa rubbed his eyes and turned to speak to his attacker.

"How far to the second plane?"

"Just a few minutes, Mr. Campa. Just relax and enjoy the flight. I apologize for your inconvenience."

Campa stared at the woman for a moment but did not speak.

At the same time, Steiner was scanning the interior of the aircraft. The pilot and co-pilot both wore military fatigues. Steiner noticed an insignia on the control panel above the co-pilot. It was one he had not seen before.

"Hey, Frank. Have you seen that logo before? I saw it on the side of the truck parked back at the field."

Frank analyzed the symbol, but he shook his head negatively.

"That insignia up there, on the panel, what is it?" Steiner directed his question the woman sitting behind Campa.

Maria smiled.

"Oh, Mr. Steiner, you haven't seen that before? That's the new insignia of the Revolutionary Air Force of Cuba!"

67

An Accidental Tourist

*Drug enforcement abroad has been compromised
because intelligence agencies care nothing
about drug enforcement, although they care
quite a lot about narcotics. They have used
it as common coin for the purposes of
espionage, paramilitary operations,
covert trade and counterintelligence.*

—Alan Block, criminologist

Orlando, Florida

"We're bringing in some portable cots, Phil. You've got to get some rest. If the signal comes, we need you awake and ready for some quick decisions." The speaker was agent John Phillips, and he did not look too well rested himself.

Phil Costello couldn't remember when he last had a full night's sleep. For that matter, he had not left the building, which housed the DEA office in Orlando, for over two days.

"John, I'm past the point of no return. Have the cots set up in the storage room in back, and I'll take a nap. But, only if you stay here and watch the phone. You have to keep Customs awake, too. They're ready to give up. Do you have any word on the search planes?"

"Yes, the Coast Guard and the Air Force are running search grids from the plane's last known position. As far as I know, they will keep going for at least another day."

"Good! Where's Carl?"

"He went home. I'll stay on duty until he returns to relieve me. He told me to remind you that you're welcome to rest at his place. He has a guest room with a separate bathroom and comfortable bed just waiting for you."

"I appreciate it, John, but I have to stay here. I'm going to test out the cot. Let me know if anything happens."

Just as Costello was leaving the room, the phone buzzed. Agent Phillips picked up the receiver.

"Agent, this is Betty Rhoman in Washington. We have a call to forward to agent Phil Costello. Do you know where he is?"

"He's right here, Betty. Who is the caller?"

"It's agent White, Arthur White."

Agent Phillips handed the receiver to Costello. "Phil, this is Arthur White!"

Costello grabbed the phone as newfound energy ran through his body.

"Arthur, where the hell are you?"

"Well, Boss, they tell me that I'm in Honduras. But, the sign outside reads *Holiday Inn*. And, everyone here speaks Spanish and English, so I guess I'm probably in Honduras."

"What the hell's going on? Where's Gerona? And where's Campa?"

"I don't know for sure! I'm not even certain how I got to Honduras. They tell me I'm near a town named La Ceiba, but I can't be sure. All I remember is that we were buzzed by a Cuban MIG and then we had engine trouble and then we landed on an island for repairs and…"

"Wait, Arthur, slow down a bit. You were on an island?"

"Yes! Agent Gerona, Mr. Charlie and Mr. Hernandez went for spare parts. Then, a woman came for me. She said she was taking me to agent Gerona. She brought me to a truck and then to an airplane. I was blindfolded and handcuffed. They gave me something to eat and drink, and then I got drowsy and fell asleep. The next thing I knew, I was waking up in bed in the Holiday Inn in Honduras or wherever the heck I am."

"And that's it?"

"No! There's the note from the woman. Her name is Maria. She is definitely a military officer of some type. She seemed to be in charge of the men who brought me here. Do you want me to read it to you?"

"Of course! Tell me what it says. Can you send a facsimile?"

"I will, but it just says something to the effect that I was not guilty of any crimes and that Carlos was releasing me. She even attached some money to the note for my hotel bill and airline ticket back to America. My head still hurts a little. Is this Carlos the same guy we are trying to capture?"

"I have no idea! You're the one that got kidnapped! Any word on Gerona?"

"I'm not sure. But, I thought I heard her say something about Josef. She was talking to one of the men. They were talking about searching for Josef and the other two men. The woman said that there wasn't time. That's all I remember. I was feeling very tired. I couldn't keep my eyes open."

"They must have drugged you. Who were these people, smugglers, Cubans?

"I don't know, Boss. They were wearing fatigues, and they were all heavily armed. My guess is that they were in the Cuban militia or whatever you call it. I have no idea where Mr. Campa and Mr. Steiner are. I left them back at the plane. They were guarding it and waiting for the parts. That's the last I know of them."

"Okay, Arthur. You did your best. When are you coming back?"

"A man named Ernesto called me about an hour ago, and he said he was coming to pick me up and take me to the airport. He said he was sending me back with an American from Fort Lauderdale."

"Who the hell is that?"

"All I know is that the man is a mechanic from Michaels Air in Fort Lauderdale."

"Shit, this must be the work of that worm Harry Michaels! But he's in…well, never mind. Just get back here as soon as you can. I've got a lot more questions for you. But, try not to get kidnapped between Honduras and Fort Lauderdale, okay?"

"No problem. Someone's knocking on the door. I'll see you in a while."

68

The Trade

What are the traditions of the navy?
Rum, sodomy and the lash!

—Winston Churchill

Lake Ozark, Missouri

The headline said it all. U.S. *Agents Caught with Drugs in Cuba.*

Steiner and Campa had been arrested by the Cuban Militia and charged with conspiracy to smuggle drugs into Cuba. In addition, Frank Campa had been charged with multiple counts of murder. Credit for the arrests was given to Cuban special agent Maria Gomez. A Beech 18 registered to an American was also recovered along with a large quantity of illegal drugs! Several Americans, including a government informant, were reported missing.

The attorney sitting at the end of the booth shook his head and smiled.

"Well, Dubinski, I guess we won't be seeing Frank Campa for a while. I understand that he was the one who wanted to keep Juan from testifying. Under the circumstances, why don't you just come with me to the farm? We'll pick up Juan and take him back to St. Louis. That way everyone here can walk away clean."

Dubinski seemed bewildered and angry at the same time. He looked at the attorney and angrily pointed his finger.

"If I didn't work for the Government, I'd…" He was interrupted by the attorney.

"You'd what? Punch me? Well, don't let your badge stop you. I won't tell anyone. Let's go, just you and me! Besides, I think you're chicken shit anyway. The badge and gun make you think you're tough. Let's find out right now. I could probably help you by straightening those two crooked front teeth!" Jim started to get up from the table.

Gebinsky and Michaels watched in shocked amazement. They had just discovered that their main government contact had been captured, and they were about to witness a fistfight between a CIA agent and an attorney. Michaels didn't give the agent one chance in five. He was amazed at how quickly the attorney had switched to the offensive. *I wish my attorney was that aggressive. Maybe I wouldn't be here now*!

The agent glanced at the two witnesses and then back at the attorney. He had decided on a safer strategy.

"You're under arrest!"

Jim looked at the agent with some surprise.

"You can't be serious! You are chicken-shit! But this is an even bigger mistake. You can kiss that badge goodbye."

"Get up!" Dubinski shouted. "Let's go. I'm taking you back to St. Louis. We'll see how tough you are when you're behind bars!"

"Are you going to slap the cuffs on me or did you forget them at home?" the attorney replied sarcastically.

"If you make any moves, I'll just blow you away. Now, let's get out to the car before I pull this gun. If I have to pull the weapon, I'm going to use it, and my witnesses here will back me up, won't you boys?"

Hall and Gebinsky just stared at the two combatants.

A smile spread across Jim's face as he got up from the table.

"And what are the charges, Dubinski, or is that too much to ask?"

"I'll think of something before we get there, don't worry. Now get going!"

Jim decided to cooperate. There was no reason to give the agent an excuse. Besides, his arrest would blow open the Government's case against Hernandez and give Jim a chance to disclose the misconduct regarding his witness. As he walked through the front door of the restaurant with Dubinski right behind him, Jim could see someone coming toward him. It was a familiar face. The man spoke quietly to the agent.

"Hands up, Dick Tracy! This is a real gun, and I'll use it if you even twitch."

The large-caliber weapon was hidden in a newspaper and was pointed at the agent. The agent began to reach for his weapon, but thought better of it.

"Ron! Don't worry about this! I can take care of this turkey. You shouldn't get involved."

"Jim, this guy is a fraud. He's hiding a federal witness."

"This isn't the way to do it," Jim replied. "Let him take me back to St. Louis. I'll break the whole misconduct thing over their heads."

"Oh, I don't know," Ron replied. "By the way he's shaking I'd say this might just be the way to do it!"

Hernandez quickly searched the agent. He took the agent's gun and his badge and gave them to the attorney. Then, he pointed back toward the table where Michaels and Gebinsky were sitting, frozen with fear.

"Now, Mr. Agent, why don't you turn around and quietly go back and sit down with your pals. I want to speak with my attorney for a few seconds. Don't try anything funny! I'm a very good shot!"

Dubinski muttered something and turned around and slowly made his way back to the table. All this activity was not lost on Gebinsky and Michaels. A glint of light off the barrel of the gun was enough to keep them in place. Michaels held up his hands and pointed at the agent.

"Dubinski! Don't come back here. This was your idea. I'm not getting myself shot for you or any agency. You're in way over your head!"

"Shut the fuck up, Michaels! Hernandez told me to sit down, and with that gun pointed at me, I'm sitting down. Now be quiet, or I swear I'll shoot you the moment I get my gun back."

The three men watched as Hernandez and his attorney carried on an animated discussion. Hernandez pointed to the parking lot and then pointed to Michaels and Gebinsky. After a few minutes, Ron patted the attorney on the back and turned back toward the front door. Jim watched Hernandez as he left through the front door. Then he walked slowly back to the booth.

"Well! Here we are again! And have I got a surprise for you!"

"I'm tired of your surprises," yelled Dubinski. "If you don't get my gun and badge back, you and your client are going away for a long time."

Dubinski was getting his courage back, slowly but surely. Nevertheless, Jim could still see his hands trembling from the incident he had just experienced.

Michaels looked at the attorney and asked the obvious question.

"What's the surprise? Ah, forget it. If you don't mind, I'd like to leave right now."

Michaels started to get up but the attorney put his hand up to stop him.

"That wouldn't be smart, Harry. You could get yourself shot!"

"Okay?" said Harry as he slowly slid back into his seat. "What's the deal? We give up Juan, and we get nothing?"

"Oh, no! It's a much better deal than that. I wouldn't want you to walk away from the table with nothing. Hernandez and his friends outside want to make a trade."

"We give you Juan," said Dubinski. "Who are you giving to us?"

"Agent Gerona!"

Dubinski almost leaped out of his seat.

"You have Josef Gerona? Impossible! He's in Cuba!"

"Hey, I don't have anyone!" the attorney said to Dubinski. "I'm just caught in the middle here just like you are. Hernandez has Gerona and Michaels and Gebinsky have Juan. Make the trade, or you don't go home in one piece! That's not me talking. It's what I was instructed to say to you. Make the trade and everyone walks away!"

Dubinski turned toward Michaels and Gebinsky.

"Enough of this shit. Get the kid! Gerona is a top agent. I can't give him up to these guys. Get the kid over here!"

Hall looked at Dubinski.

"How the fuck can we get them. Hernandez is in the parking lot. They're not going to let us out of here!"

Dubinski thought for a moment.

"Gebinsky, you have a boat, don't you?"

"Of course. But, it's not here! It's at the dock."

"That's just as well. Call the witness and tell him where the boat is and how to get here. Have him bring the boat over here and dock it at this restaurant. Then we can leave that way. We won't have to go through the parking lot."

"Good idea," whispered Gebinsky. "Once we get Gerona, we'll head out over the water. Saving his ass should be enough for him to remember us kindly when our cases come up. We don't need Frank Campa. I'll be right back!"

Gebinsky got up slowly from the table and headed for the phone booth. He placed a call to the farm and after several minutes of conversation he returned to the table.

"Luckily, they were there! They should be here in thirty to forty-five minutes."

Hall looked at the attorney and made a suggestion.

"Maybe you should go tell your client that Juan will be here shortly." As the attorney started to get up, Michaels stopped him. "Don't tell him about the boat! You could get us killed."

"Look, Harry, I want nothing more than for all of us, and I mean all of us, to get out of here alive. Even Dubinski here should get out alive. I'll kick his ass later, in court."

69

Come Together

*Will all great Neptune's
Ocean wash this blood
Clean from my hand? No;*

—Shakespeare, *Macbeth*

Lake Ozark, Missouri

The attorney stood by the rear window and watched as the blue and white powerboat was being tied to the dock below. Two men stepped along its length and up the rock stairway that curled toward the crest the hill and ended in a large outdoor patio.

Hall, Gebinsky and agent Dubinski remained at the table and maintained their watch on the parking lot, their main source of concern. When the two men who were climbing the stairs reached the patio, they hesitated.

Out in the parking lot, Ron Hernandez could be seen standing next to a car which held Charlie Bill and agent Gerona. All in all, nothing on the surface indicated the existence of a hostage situation to the patrons of the restaurant. Customers flowed into and out with a normal frequency.

As the parties to this strange interchange converged on the bar area of the restaurant, the attorney felt the role of arbitrator and referee fall to him by default. *Someone had to mediate the situation.* In spite of his vested interest in Juan as an important witness, he also felt a duty to assure the safety and freedom of agent Gerona.

Johnny and Juan finally left the patio and entered the bar. They stopped to survey the room. The bartender waived at Johnny and pointed toward the table where Michaels and his associates were seated. Jim walked over to the young men before they reached the table.

"Good to see you again, Juan. And, you're Johnny, aren't you. How do you like the Lake? It's not Florida, but it has some nice features." Johnny was surprised at the casual level of the conversation.

"It's a great place for a vacation", replied Johnny in a stuttering voice. "I'm coming back here for sure." Johnny paused and then continued in a lower tone of voice that revealed his concern.

"What's going on?"

Jim pointed to the table where the men were still sitting.

"Nothing much. Harry wants to talk to you. After that, we can talk again. At this point you'll have to take my word for it, but everything's okay. Whatever happens, just let it happen. It just may seem a little strange."

Hall had noticed the boys talking with the attorney, and he came over to join the conversation.

"Johnny! About time you got here. Now, let's all sit down for a second and talk about this thing."

Hall turned and led the way back to the table. After everyone was seated, Michaels continued.

"Mr. Johnson, you're going to have to get agent Gerona. I don't want Gerona to get hurt. He's our ticket out of this mess so don't screw it up."

"You're the one who should be worrying about screw ups," the attorney replied. "If you hadn't hidden Juan, we wouldn't be going through all of this."

Before Michaels could reply, Jim turned and walked toward the front door. Just before he reached it, he heard the bartender call him from behind the main bar. Jim turned and walked over to where Nino was standing.

"Jim, you do know Charlie Bill, don't you?"

Jim nodded. "Yeah. Charlie's outside."

"Well, his plumber called and said to tell him that the leak was fixed. It's pretty bad when you plumber knows where you go for happy hour! Would you tell him if you're going out there?"

"No problem, Nino. I'm going out to see him now. I could probably use a plumber myself. Thanks."

Nino grabbed his arm before Jim could leave.

"Oh, another thing. Do you know that guy over there at the back of the bar?"

Jim scanned the dark corner of the bar, which ran toward the service area.

It's Oscar!

"He told me to tell you that he was here, but he doesn't want you to talk to him. Just go on with your business. Does that make any sense?"

"Nino, right now nothing much makes sense. Buy him a beer and put it on my tab. He may be just the person I need."

Jim left the bar and walked out the front door into the parking lot. Ron was still standing outside of Charlie's car while C.B. and Josef remained inside the vehicle. When Ron saw Jim coming toward him, he gave the attorney a look of anticipation.

"Are those assholes ready to go?"

Jim nodded. "Juan just arrived. He didn't say much, but he seems okay. Let's get this over with."

"Why the hurry? The fun's just started." The voice was that of Charlie Bill from inside the car.

"Hey, we have no backup here except that I just saw Oscar Chacon inside. He shows up in the strangest places. We have to get Juan back to St. Louis and take his statement. I'm glad you're sure about this whole thing."

"Oscar's our ace in the hole," said Ron confidently. "Don't mention him to the boys inside. When Oscar's friend shows up, don't mention him either!"

"Hey, I'm so confused now, all I want is Juan, and I'm out of here!"

"Okay, let's get Gerona out of the car and make the trade. He's a reasonable sort so I don't expect any trouble from him."

Ron motioned to Charlie and in a few seconds the four men were headed back toward the restaurant. They walked through the front door and headed for the bar. At the entrance to the bar area, Ron stopped the group and turned to Jim.

"You go ahead with Josef. Charlie and I will stay here. It's better that way."

"Oh, I almost forgot," said Jim to Charlie. "You had a call. Something about your plumbing."

Charlie looked over toward the bar, but spoke to the attorney.

"Is it fixed?"

"The bartender said that your plumber called and that your problem was fixed."

Charlie looked at Ron and then at Josef.

"Nothing like a good plumber to bail you out when your toilet backs up. A flush sure beats a full house!" Ron laughed and even Josef had a smile cross his face for a moment.

"Okay. Josef, let's go. I'm sure that you want to get this over with as much as I do. Are you ready?"

Josef responded with a smile.

"I'm ready. I appreciate your patience and consideration." Josef stepped forward and walked into the bar. He was carrying a small briefcase and had a newspaper under his arm. As the two men approached the table, Michaels and Gebinsky stood up and Michaels greeted the agent.

"Well, agent Gerona, I see that you got yourself caught! I guess Gebinsky and I aren't the only dummies around here!"

"Thanks, Harry, I appreciate your words of encouragement. And, you, too, Edward. Agent Dubinski, how are these scumbags treating you?

Dubinski just shook his head, but did not respond.

"Send Juan to the front door!" Gerona pointed toward the parking lot. Michaels couldn't believe what he just heard.

"What? We don't have to send him now! You're safe, and I'm almost positive that only Hernandez and his pal out there are armed. Just arrest them!"

"So, Harry, you don't want to keep the deal, am I right? You want us to shoot up this place!"

"Absolutely! Gebinsky and I have guns, too. We'll help you. That should count for something."

Josef extended his hand toward Michaels. "Give me the guns, Harry. We made a deal, and we're sticking with it."

When neither Michaels nor Gebinsky immediately produced their weapons, Gerona took the paper from under his arm and threw it on the table. It was the St. Louis Post Dispatch.

"You must have read this by now. You're no longer the big game in town. We just want to get out of here alive! I'll forget to tell parole about your weapons."

Dubinski chimed in.

"Michaels, give it up. We have those guys on a bunch of charges. Hernandez pulled a gun on me! We'll nail them later. Right now, listen to Gerona."

Gerona repeated his request quietly.

"Give me the weapons. We can still win this thing but not by shooting up the place. Let's have them."

Gebinsky reached inside his jacket and pulled out a small handgun and handed it to Michaels. Shaking his head, Michaels wiped the fingerprints off of both guns and handed them to Gerona.

"Here they are! I hope you're happy. Now what?"

"Jim! Take Juan over to Charlie Bill and get him back to St. Louis. Your client has a different set of problems now, and Juan's testimony is no longer as important."

Jim motioned to Juan and the two walked out toward the front door of the restaurant.

"How did this happen, Gerona? You were there, weren't you?" Michaels was visibly disturbed.

"Carlos got lucky. We had engine trouble. Campa stayed with the plane, and they found him. Arthur and I were able to get out with the help of those two guys outside. You two are okay. I'll make sure you get the deal you made with the government. I'll do for you what Campa would have done. Okay?"

Michaels and Gebinsky looked relieved.

"That's a deal, Gerona. You caught us! You get us out! No complaints from us."

Michaels turned to Johnny who had been standing against the wall looking out the window.

"Johnny, take the boat back. We'll see you back…"

Gerona interrupted the conversation.

"No, Harry. You can't do that. Agent Dubinski here will take you and Gebinsky back in the boat. I'm still concerned about your safety. Those two guys are pissed."

Dubinski look puzzled.

"Why should I go with them?"

"Carlos is still a factor here. He nailed Frank Campa and somehow I have a feeling that these two guys are pretty high on his list. They need some protection. Take the boat. I'll keep an eye on Hernandez and his friends. As a matter of fact, I'll probably just escort them back to St. Louis to keep them out of trouble. They don't need me any more so I think I can talk some sense into them."

Gerona turned to Michaels and Gebinsky.

"And you two get out of here and don't let me see your faces again unless I call you. Stay with Dubinski and do as he says. If I hear anything bad from him, you deal is gone. Understand?"

Gebinsky put up his hand.

"What about our indictments?"

"Call in to St. Louis next Monday. Ask for Richard Froehling in the U.S. Attorney's Office. He will tell you if you are clear or need to do anything else to get rid of the indictment. I'll make sure that your obligations to the government are satisfied. The future is all yours."

Michaels waived at Johnny to follow him out onto the patio; however, Gerona intervened again.

"I need Johnny for this trip. He's going to be my backup. Don't worry, I'll get him back here by Friday. And I'll make sure that his expenses are covered for the trip back to Florida."

Michaels waived his hands in the air.

"You're becoming a real human there, Gerona. It's getting hard to hate you!"

Dubinski, Michaels, and Gebinsky exited the restaurant and made their way across the patio and down the staircase to the water. Gebinsky's power boat was still tied up at the dock. The men jumped into the boat and prepared to make their way out onto the lake. Gebinsky relaxed after he looked back up the stairs and scanned the patio area. No one appeared to be watching them.

Meanwhile, Gerona picked up the weapons off the table and motioned for Johnny to follow him. When Johnny passed through the front door, he was surprised to find Juan waiting for him.

"Let's go back to the bar, my friend. The others will soon follow us." Johnny noticed that Gerona was speaking with Ron and C.B. and their attorney. Eventually, they all turned and headed for the bar where Nino was busy preparing a round of Margaritas.

"Nino, you are short three drinks here. The voice was that of Gerona."

Nino looked around and was puzzled by the comment.

"And who will be drinking those other three Margaritas? Or will you be downing more than one at a time?"

"One is for you, my friend!"

"And the others?" Nino was busy preparing the three drinks in question.

"First, a toast. A long overdue toast!"

Jim picked up his drink.

"What or who are we toasting?"

Gerona smiled as he carried his drink over to the window, which provided a panoramic view of the lake. At the same time, Oscar Chacon was joined at the corner of the bar by another man whose presence was still unnoticed by the others. Oscar put his arm around the man and then quietly pulled a small transmitting device out of his coat pocket.

Josef lifted his glass.

"There are two toasts for you on this beautiful afternoon. The first is a toast to life, to Mother Nature, to those that we love and who love us. And to the removal and destruction of all that is evil! It's certainly good to see them go."

With those words Oscar Chacon carefully inserted a code into the device and pressed a small button on the transmitter. After a delay of what seemed like five seconds, there was a flash of light and the delayed report of a loud explosion.

Jim jumped up from his barstool and scanned the lake for the source of the fury. Then he saw it. Gebinsky's boat had erupted into flames and a ball of oily smoke rose slowly off the surface of the water.

"It's the boat! Gebinsky's boat just blew up!"

Everyone at the bar had a clear view of the burning wreckage, and there was silence for a few seconds. Customers in the restaurant section were streaming out onto the patio for a better view of the tragedy. Then, while the group at the bar was pondering the events that spread before them, Gerona lifted his glass again.

"And most and best of all, I raise a toast to a great man, a man who has suffered unjustly, and a man who is loved by his countrymen and his family. A man who has finally attained his freedom!"

Josef turned and raised his glass toward a man who had been sitting with Oscar in the corner of the room.

"My Father!"

70

Grim Justice

Isle of Pines, Cuba

The mud covered truck sped along the dirt road leading to the island prison. Two prisoners were secured in the rear of the vehicle.

After a brief processing session, the two men were pushed and shoved unceremoniously up the concrete staircase to the third floor corridor. The watch commander held a handkerchief over his nose as he directed the prisoners to their cells.

"You Americans should enjoy our accommodations! Prisoner Steiner, in here!"

Steiner was pushed into a small cell on the corridor. Quickly, the cell door was slammed behind him."

"Ah, Mr. Campa is it! We have a special home for you! It is just as Captain Chacon left it."

Campa was dragged down the corridor to the very end where an old iron door was opened by one of the guards. There were no windows. As he fell to the floor of the musty cell, he could hear the door slam behind him.

As he lay on the floor, his heart sank. This was the very cell Raymond Chacon had occupied for over twenty years.

Slowly, he crawled to his knees. The cell was cold and damp. There was no bed. The only fixture he could see in the near darkness was a rank latrine in the far corner. He could hear the methodical drips of water falling near the latrine from an overhead pipe.

As his eyes adjusted to the darkness, he noticed the solitary rays of light from the corridor, which beamed through a small hole in the iron door. The light fell upon a small section of the rear wall of the cell.

As Campa studied the rays of light, he thought he noticed a scrawled handwriting on the wall just where the beam illuminated it. Slowly he made his way over to the wall and rubbed his fingers over the word that had been carved in the old concrete. At first his eyes failed him. Then, slowly, as the letters came into focus, his voice gasped the two syllables just as they were written.

Carlos!